4/22

THE LAST COMANCHE
WARRIOR

THE LAST COMANCHE
WARRIOR

JAMES D. CROWNOVER

THORNDIKE PRESS
A part of Gale, a Cengage Company

LIBRARY OF CONGRESS CIP DATA ON FILE.
CATALOGUING IN PUBLICATION FOR THIS BOOK
IS AVAILABLE FROM THE LIBRARY OF CONGRESS.

ISBN-13: 978-1-4328-8598-4 (hardcover alk. paper)

Published in 2022 by arrangement with James D. Crownover

Printed in Mexico
Print Number: 01   Print Year: 2022

To Carol

PREFACE

Yet when two peoples come together that
one which is most efficient will survive,
and the other will absorb or vanish . . .
it is the way of life.

Sackett's Land

It became apparent to both sides early on
that the cultures of the white man and the
red man could not coexist. One culture was
based on and rooted in Judeo-Christian
principles, the other its antithesis.

The American Plains Indian measured his
wealth in horseflesh; the more livestock,
material, and humanity he could own, the
higher his standing in the tribe.

There were many reasons for the practice
of taking captives: replacement for lost
children or wives; the need for slaves;
augmentation of a shrinking tribal population, especially of warriors; or the esteem of
his fellow tribesmen. Approbation from the

7

warrior's fellow tribesmen was paramount.

It was a very harsh life the Plains Indian lived and the captive had to adjust quickly to it to survive. Ideally, the captured boys would become warriors and the girls the wife of a warrior. Those that showed strength and resolve were adopted into the families of the clan. The weaker captive might become a slave. The weakest didn't survive.

— James Crownover

CHAPTER 1
THE BOY WARRIOR

Fredericksburg, 1865

I could smell him before I could hear him, he was that close. A rustle no louder than a beetle burrowing through the leaves and I knew he stood above me on the bank.

Noah had seen them coming across the cornfield, bold as soldiers, with painted faces and horses and naked save for moccasins and breechcloth. "Run for the creek, Adam," he whispered, and was gone. He wouldn't say it a second time and there was no need of that on my part.

I lost my hoe at the brush line and dived over the bank at the creek right above the overhung hole we hid in. Noah wasn't there and there was no time to wonder about him. I crawdaded back into the hole as far as I could so he could get in if he came. Trying to stop my panting made me dizzy until I finally caught up my breath. It seemed forever before I heard that Injun above me.

9

You can bet my breathing almost stopped. He stood there a long time with me about to gag from smelling his sweat and smoke and bloody dirty body. I gripped my round beatin' rock I kept in the hole for defense and waited.

There was a rustle and a grunt of surprise above me. I heard a thump and the crack of wood. The head and broken shaft of a hoe spun into the creek and the Injun fell off the bank after it. Like a dummy, I sprang on him and swung my rock at his head. My blow landed with a satisfying thump and the man lay still — then I realized he might not have been alone. When I looked up at the bank, there stood Noah holding the remainder of his hoe handle.

"I broke my handle," Noah groaned, knowing the chewing he would get from Pa. There was shooting coming from the direction of the house and I knew the folks was fightin' off the rest of the raiders.

"Don't worry, Noah; I saw where the head fell. We got time to fix the handle afore Pa sees it." We were talking in American.

"Not now, we gotta go see if we can help Pa an' Ma." He hopped off the bank and started across the creek.

"What about this'n?" I asked.

"He ain't goin' nowhere," Noah muttered

over his shoulder, " 'less'n he's a fish."

Then I noticed the warrior had fallen facedown in the edge of the creek. If our blows didn't kill him, the water had. Noah was climbing the far bank before I got out of the water and as I scrambled up the bank, here he come back, jumping over my head and dragging me behind the root ball of a big sycamore fallen in the creek. We wasn't set before horses splashed across the ford, Sol, our mule, in th' lead and four Injuns driving him.

"There goes Injun supper," Noah growled.

"O-o-oh, they got Sol," I groaned.

"That ain't all, here comes that jughead o' your'n, tryin' t' catch up." Noah was almost grinning. He hated my pony.

I had to whistle three times before the little mustang mare heard me and skidded to a stop. She turned broadside in the path to see where I was, and Pa on King near-'bout run over her. He quirted her rump as he passed and Amigo jumped and trotted toward me. I grabbed the broken tether rope and jumped on her back. We ran across the ford after King and Pa, my bare heels beating a tune on Amigo's ribs.

When we broke out of the woods, Pa was a good quarter mile ahead of us and the Injuns was a quarter mile ahead of him. King

11

was closing the gap fast and I wondered what Pa thought he could do agin four Injuns and his gun most likely empty.

I heard a shout and shots being fired and a bunch of men appeared from the woods running straight at those Injuns, who veered sharply away from behind that old mule Sol and that mule kept running straight ahead. With the men pressing them close behind, Pa turned to head off the fleeing raiders. Sol slowed to a trot and then stopped, too winded to be interested in anything else. Amigo nuzzled up to the old reprobate and while they talked things over, I got his short halter rope in hand. It had been cut. The sound of shooting was coming from the direction of the chase and all I could see was wisps of black powder smoke above the grass and brush.

Noah was standing at the edge of the trees at the ford when I rode up. "What we gonna do about that dead Injun, Noah?"

"Hop down an' come help me," he said.

We went to the body and Noah turned him over. The water had washed the paint from his face and he stared with unseeing eyes. "Jee-hoshaphat, Noah, he ain't no older'n you!"

Noah looked a little pale and only grunted. We dragged the body to the ford and laid him in the path, facedown in the water, knees on dry land as if he had fallen there, and made sure there were enough tracks to cover any sign a runner might have left. Noah hopped on Sol and we rode to the house.

Eve, my twin sister, stood at the door with Mary and Martha peeking from behind her skirt. They were holding on so she couldn't leave the doorway. Ma was sitting on the stoop with the barrel of her long rifle propped on the hitching rail, the stock in her lap. When she saw us, she cocked the gun and sighted it at us.

"It is me and Adam, Mother," Noah called in German. She relaxed a little, but the gun remained cocked.

"Amigo is back, Amigo is back!" The little girls forgot their fear and danced across the porch, releasing Eve from her captivity.

"We heard you whistle for Amigo, did she stop then?" Eve asked.

"Stopped and near got run over by King," Noah said in disgust.

"Some men came up the road and headed off those Injuns, Mother, and they are helping Father chase them," I explained. Ma looked relieved.

"Not likely to catch them, but it may make

them think afore coming here again," Noah added.

"It is good you got the stock back; I suppose you watered them when you crossed the creek." Ma looked awful tired. She was still pale and her hand shook a little when she smoothed her dress. "Lock them in the barn and shuck out a little corn for the hens. I will have supper ready directly." She turned to the door, shooing the little girls before her.

Noah got down and carefully uncocked the rifle. It was an old-fashioned Kentucky rifle, near as tall as he was and at least half a foot taller than Ma. She couldn't lift it and aim, but if she could prop the barrel on something, her aim was sure. Pa said she was the fastest reloader he had ever seen.

Eve hopped down and grabbed Sol's halter rope and we walked the animals to the barn while Noah put the rifle up and got pounced by Mary and Martha.

"We near got caught for the third time," I whispered to Eve. We talked American when Ma might hear us, 'cause she didn't know it too well.

"Was it close as the last time?" she asked, her voice just above a whisper.

"Just as close — maybe closer. One of them chased me to th' creek, but he didn't

14

see me git in the hidey-hole. He was standing on the bank above me an' Noah knocked him in th' creek with his hoe. I finished him off with my beatin' rock." I didn't mention he landed with his face in six inches of water. "We laid him out at the ford where Pa or someone would find him."

After the first time the Injuns tried to steal us, the three of us made it up we wouldn't tell the folks about it, else they wouldn't let us be out of their sight and we would never get anything done. Now, Noah was getting his man size and most likely the Injuns would try to kill him instead of stealing him. Noah needed a gun. I guess he was trying to protect me instead of coming to the hidey-hole. It made me a little mad. I ain't no sissy needing protection.

"Did you boys see that dead Indian at the ford?" Pa asked when he returned from the chase. We were all sitting on the front stoop waiting for him.

"We did not see him —"

"— until we got out of the hole," Noah finished.

"Did you shoot him, Father?" Eve asked.

"No-o-o, he was not there when I first crossed." He eyed me with that look of suspicion when he thought we were lying. "There was a gash in his head and his face was under the water when I pulled him out. We'll have to bury him if he's still there in the morning."

The second time the Injuns got after us, me and Eve was picking up walnuts in the walnut grove when we saw 'em coming. It didn't look like they had seen us, and we ducked low in the brush and scooted for the creek and the hidey-hole. Eve scrambled in and I pushed her rump all the way to the back.

"Stop it," she hissed.

"Hush up." I grabbed my beatin' rock and waited. There was a low whistle and Noah backed into the hole, pulling a whole bush after him. "You want my rock, Noah?"

"Naw, I got th' corn knife." He settled himself and we scrunched around until we found a comfortable position. It sure was cramped and hot in there.

"Move your elbow, Ad, it's hurtin' my ribs," Eve whispered.

"I'll move it if you quit breathin' on my neck," I shot back. I moved my arm so my elbow didn't touch her.

"Now that danged rock is punchin' *my* back." Noah wriggled away and the bush almost rolled into the creek.

"Stop shakin' that bush, Noah, or they'll

find us," Eve demanded.

"Why do girls have to talk so much?" I asked. Saying something like that always worked to shut her up. She pinched my side until I grunted. We waited and waited.

There was a splash in the creek, not much more than a little wave hitting the rocky bank, and we all froze, straining to hear. Another soft splash and we knew someone was wading down the creek. I raised my head to peek over Noah's shoulder. After a moment or two, I could see movement beyond the leaves of the bush. A stick moved by my peephole, then a string; it was a bow. It was drawn back a little and I knew there was an arrow nocked up. Black hair came into view and the warrior stopped. Slowly, the man turned his head, searching the bank. I couldn't see the left half of his blackened face and when it seemed he was looking straight at me, all I could make out was the far half of his face painted yellow. It looked as if he only had half a face. I held my breath until it seemed I would pass out. Eve gripped my arm, but I couldn't let her know it was hurting. The Injun took another step and I couldn't see him anymore. My neck cramped and I laid my head down and squeezed my eyes tight. Red and white and green lights flashed behind my eyelids.

Eve's grip relaxed. She sighed and her body went limp. She had passed out and I half wished I could too. We only heard another little splash, then all was silent.

The cr-r-rack-boom of that Kentucky rifle made all three of us jump. Eve's grip on my arm came back and I squeezed her hand hard to keep her quiet. Girls.

Pa's rifle boomed and then we heard his pistol. He had one of those five shot Colts he got when he rangered and we heard two more shots from it, then Ma's Kaintuck. Pa fired the pistol twice more, then it was quiet a moment. I could picture Ma reloading while Pa watched and when he fired his rifle, I knew Ma had reloaded her gun. The pattern of their firing went on, it seemed, forever. Always one of them had a loaded gun and the Injuns was scared of that "Gun That Keeps Shooting." Some time in there, the Injun in the creek came splashing back by, probably headed for the battle. I got a glimpse of his yellow face in the gloom as he passed. Noah made to go after him, but I held him and hissed, "No!"

It was a good thing I did, for we heard someone running over our heads. There had been two of them searching the creek for us. We heard a long wolf howl and the In-juns suddenly began their yipping and yell-

18

ing. Pa's Colt fired five times in quick succession.

"O-o-o-oh, they got Ma an' Pa," Eve sobbed.

I shook my head so she could feel my movement.

"No, they ain't, Eve," Noah whispered.

We heard horses coming toward the ford at a gallop. They splashed across the creek and with a few more yips, the sound of their running faded. We stayed put until we heard another horse walking to the ford.

"Noah, Eve, Adam, are you there?" Pa called.

Noah kicked the bush out of the way and answered, "We are safe, Father."

It was hardly accurate to say we scrambled out of that hole. Noah straightened up real slow and I almost fell. Both feet were asleep to my knees and so was the arm I was lying on. Eve grunted and rubbed her hand, "It's cramped up."

"No wonder, you most squeezed my arm in two." I swung my forearm up and down to get the circulation back.

"I didn't squeeze you *that* hard," Eve vowed, but she wasn't so positive about it when my arm turned blue where her four fingers pressed, and a black spot showed up where her thumb was on my underarm.

I dropped to my knees and drank from the creek. It tasted a little muddy from where the horses had stirred it at the ford, but I didn't care. Noah was drinking and washing his face. I pictured Eve's face scrunched up in the gloaming when she grunted, "Drinking out of a horse's hoof-print. Ug-gh."

Pa rode toward us, "Did you see any Indians?" he asked, speaking German.

"Not after we saw them coming," Noah replied. "We scooted for the hidey-hole and never saw a thing."

"Well, come on to the house. They will not be back tonight. We will have to watch for them about sunrise." He turned Sol and rode back to the house.

"Did you see that half yellow face?" Eve asked in American and shuddered.

"He wasn't fishin' for perch, was he?" I leaned toward her so she could see my grin.

"Git outta my face, Ad, you was just as scairt as me."

"We all better be scairt when such as they are around," Noah said. "Don't take them light or you might be skinning buffalo with a flint knife and wearin' not much more than a bunch of stripes and bruises."

Pa spent that night in the barn with the stock and about sunrise shot an Indian creeping up to the door. Then he let loose one barrel of the shotgun and put a bunch of bird shot in the two Indians who carried off their dead companion.

"That will make them think twice about robbing us," I said.

"It will make us prime targets, I am afraid," Pa had replied.

CHAPTER 2
A HOME IN THE WILDERNESS

Panther Creek, 1866

The trunk leaned slightly and his next axe blow freed the tree to fall almost gently to the ground. Rogers Bain sighed, another rooster-comb stump. He sat on the fallen trunk and looked at his blade. It seemed sharp enough. *It may be that I'm too tired to make a good cut,* he thought, and he was more right than wrong. *This cabin building's going to be the death of me yet.*

It sometimes puzzled him why he would choose to come this far from Fredericksburg to build a farm. It could have been overweening parents and in-laws who criticized 'most everything he tried. It could have been the freeloaders in the community that always showed up at mealtime and didn't mind eating the food intended for his family. It could have been that all the good ground around Fredericksburg was taken up and he had to contend with a rocky sidehill patch for his potatoes and garden. To complain about neighbors being too close and nosy is too common an excuse for moving on. Rogers knew that all these reasons and more were what had convinced him it was time to seek a new start.

The Pinta Trail was old when the white man found it. No one knows its age, but it served as the road into the heart of the Texas hill country and beyond. The first written mention of the trail was from the pens of Nicolás de Lafora and the Marqués de Rubí when they traveled the trail from the Guadalupe River to San Antonio in 1767. In 1846, German settlers followed the Pinta Trail north to the Guadalupe to establish Fredericksburg a couple miles upstream from the Guadalupe Crossing. This was the trail Rogers Bain took when he left Fredericksburg looking for new land to settle. He had inquired about land for sale or open land for settling when someone mentioned that there might be suitable land around the Llano River. At the Beaver Creek Settlement (later to be renamed Hilda), he learned that Ludwig Martin had established a settlement he called Hedwig's Hill at the Llano River Crossing of the Pinta Trail. The land there was already settled, but there was still open land upstream from there.

So he had ridden old Sol, his mule, west to the head of Panther Creek. They rode the bluff on the east side of the creek down to the Llano — only to find that Panther fell over a bluff into the river. There was no way down the bluff, and he had to ride back the way he came until there was a place to get down to the creek bed. Riding west he was stopped on top of a bluff cut by another creek that flowed into the Llano just above the mouth of Panther Creek. Again, there was no way to get down to the river. The only way out was the way he had come in, and the sun was in its last moments above the horizon.

Sol was pleased to crop the brown grass within the reach of his tether, and it made a pleasant and comforting sound as Rogers watched his coffee coming to a boil.

"At least, old fellow, we know no Indian will come skulking over those bluffs on three sides of us. The only way is down the divide between the creeks and we could see them a long ways off." Rogers spoke in his native German tongue, as did the German immigrants he lived among. Sol had become bilingual since he had been bought from an American immigrant. Although Rogers and his wife, Fannie, only spoke the mother tongue, their children spoke English rather well.

Sol looked up from his harvest, chewing his latest bite, and seemed to nod agreement.

As if that thought, *Safe on three sides,* hit him for the first time, Rogers suddenly stood and stared all around him. Depending on where the bluff ended on that west drainage, there could be 1500 to 2000 acres here inaccessible on three sides — safe from prowling thieves and marauding Indians.

He strode down to the point over the river. Bare limestone across the Llano shone white in the gloom, while where he stood was red soil and the bare cliff faces were red sandstone. The grass grew tall and thick around him. This red soil would be fertile. He turned and looked up the divide. A thousand acres of grass would support four, maybe five hundred head of cattle in a good year. With a little hay, they would winter well without much need for shelter. They would be contained right here without straying and with almost no fencing required — no open range and mixing with someone else's cattle.

This is it! Rogers Bain punched his fist into his palm again and again. *My — no, our — farm, our ranch, our home.* He would have skipped a dance step or two if the sound of his coffee boiling over into the fire had not brought him back to reality. He was too excited to remember his glove and burned his hand rescuing the coffee. It mattered little, *I have found it! I have found our home, Fannie! You are going to love it.*

A thousand thoughts ran through his mind, all night long, it seemed, and by morning his enthusiasm had cooled to rational thought. With Sol tethered on fresh grass near a shaded spot, he determined to walk the boundary bluffs to assure himself there was no way down them and to see how far up the western stream they extended. No one had mentioned the name of the creek, possibly because it was most likely dry the bulk of the year.

"We will call it Bain's Creek," he said to Sol as he gave the tether stake one last blow. "Now, you stay here and see how fat you can get on this grass while I look around." With that, he picked up his rifle and crossed the neck of the little plateau to the newly named Bain's Bluffs.

They were nearly forty feet high at the river's edge, where any water in the channel below reaching that point would fall another twenty feet or so into the river. To his right as he faced the Llano and beyond the mouth of Panther Creek, the ground rose to be cut off by a vertical red sandstone cliff Rogers guessed would be more than a hundred feet high.

The land on top of Bain's Bluff was rolling, the streambed below it rising until the bluff was only twenty-five feet high on the average. He had walked more than four miles, he judged, before the bluffs were only ten or twelve feet above the arroyo bottom. From there, he paced due east a satisfying two and a half miles through scrub oak and cedar to Panther Creek. There were still pools of water where the stock could drink, though the stream was not flowing. Some pools were stagnant and green. *Probably could walk on it,* he surmised, then laughed at the idea of walking on water just as the Lord had. *Not the same, is it, Lord?*

Turning back west, he walked slowly, seeking a favorable spot for a house. A knoll about the middle of the distance between the bluffs promised a good view down the long divide to the Llano when enough trees were cleared.

After breaking camp, they rode back up the divide and Sol showed Rogers where a running spring and small pool was on Bain's Creek. It was a hurried trip back to Fredericksburg, much to the mule's annoyance. Sol's stubborn insistence on slow plodding only served to make his ribs sore. Rogers insisted on a faster pace. It wasn't until he recognized where he was that he voluntarily picked up his pace in anticipation of the corn in his manger when he got home.

Rogers nodded in satisfaction at the shocked cornstalks that dotted the fallow corn patch. The boys had done a good job. He grinned as he watched the porch fill with waving girls. Noah stood at the barn door and watched his approach. Adam trotted down the trail to meet him.

"Did you have a good trip, Father?" he asked as he trotted beside Sol.

"It was a good trip, Ad, I will tell all of you about it. Give Sol a little corn and rub him down before you turn him into the pasture. I will not say a word about the trip until you get to the house."

"All right, Father; come on, Sol." The mule needed no urging and hurried Adam to the barn.

Rogers had hardly finished greeting the three girls and Fannie when Ad trotted out of the barn door.

"That mule got more promise than rubbing down." Fannie smiled at her husband and stilled the rebuke he had formed.

"Sol was too impatient to wait for a rubdown, Pa; I will get him rubbed directly," Adam panted.

"Tell us about your trip," Eve coaxed.

"Yes, do, Father." Mary danced on her toes and clapped her hands.

"The land around Hedwig's Hill is pretty well taken up, but the men at Beaver Creek said the land upstream on the Llano River had not been settled, so I rode over to Panther Creek and down it to the river." He tried to hand Martha to her mother, but she clung to his neck and he had to kneel in the dirt with the little girl sitting on his knee. "The river comes down from the northwest and hits a red-rock bluff and turns like this." He drew in the dirt. "Then the Panther falls over the bluff into the river here, and a little ways up the river another creek runs over the bluff — here. This area in between the creeks," he waved at the long triangular piece of land, "has high bluffs on three sides of it. We could keep our stock in here and only have a little fencing to build across from Panther Creek to the bluffs here on this creek. It is the perfect place to keep horses and cattle and wild kids corraled, Fannie." He grinned up at her and stood up. "Now, how about some food for a starving man? That mule was in such a hurry to get home he would not let me eat."

"Bet he ran all the way," Noah said with a grin.

"Yeah, he was in quite a lather when I took the saddle off," Adam joked.

"Table's set and we are nearly ready," Eve assured her father. "I will put warm water in the wash pan."

Fannie kissed her husband's cheek and hurried off to serve supper while the rest of the family attended to pre-supper chores. Soon they were seated at the table and asking Rogers a hundred questions.

After everyone had eaten, Pa said, "It is getting late in the season and cold weather will be here sooner than we expect. We will take tomorrow to get ready and Noah will go back with me to help build us a cabin for the winter. When it is ready, we will come for you and move to the new land. Ad, you take care of the stock and have them close so we can gather them when we are ready to move. Fannie, there is a road to the Beaver Settlement. After that, we may have to pack everything in. You should pack the wagon so we can get to the essentials easy enough. Furniture and the bulky things will have to wait."

"Father, we are going to need more dogs than old Dan —"

"We will, Adam, use your judgment and get us some good hunters. Two or three will be more than enough." Pa's eyes said more than his words and you can be sure I understood.

The next day was a busy one and we didn't quite get everything done that needed doing. It was midday the day after before Noah and Pa were caught up enough to leave. They took Sol and Amigo and left me to gather cattle with King.

"I had rather hunt cows on foot than on King," I said to Ma.

"If you do not teach him, that horse will never learn to work cattle," she returned.

"I guess you are right, I will try." And "trying" was about the all of it. His attitude was as plain as if he said it aloud, "I'm good for parades and races and not for chasing cows through brush and dust." We fought all morning until I tied him to a tree and gathered the cattle on foot. It was easier.

Eve came down to bring me sausage and biscuits for lunch. "Ma's gonna be mad when she finds out you're not riding King," she warned.

"Tell you what, Evie Girl. Hop on ol' King there and go bring back that steer on th' hill while I finish lunch."

"You think I can't?"

31

"Show me."

Eve untied the horse and after a couple of circles managed to get on him — astraddle — and headed up the hill. When the steer ran, the horse was after him in an instant. The steer veered off to the right and King continued straight ahead like he was on a racetrack. Eve didn't do a bit of good trying to turn him. The steer had disappeared by the time King decided the race was over and he was the winner. He trotted back, bobbing his head to the imagined applause of the crowds.

"I'll take that thing back to the barn when I go back," Eve growled. Her hands were red from sawing on the reins.

"Help me move those cows closer to the house and I'll go with you."

"And we'll leave that devil horse tied to the tree." She was really mad at King.

"Now you know why I'm working afoot." I grinned at her.

"Why in the world does Pa keep that thing?"

I popped the last sausage into my mouth and wiped my hands on my pants legs. "Because he will outrun any Indian pony, Eve. That gets important — whether you're in front of or behind those Injuns."

"Hurry up and let's get these cows moving, Ma expects me right back." Eve dusted her hands together and headed for the right flank of the cows. I headed the other way and we had them moving without much trouble. I hung the bell on the bell cow and staked her near the barn. Grass was good there and since we were leaving, the cattle could graze and stay near the bell cow. That steer followed us from afar and when we left, he trotted down and joined his herd.

Adolph Zesch, our closest neighbor, had the best pack of hounds in the country. After I had checked on the cattle next morning, I trotted on over to his house. He was sitting on a stump in the yard sharpening his scythe.

"Hello there, Adam," he called in the mother tongue, "Pull up a stump and rest."

"How are you, Herr Zesch?"

" 'Finner'n frog hair,' as these Texians would say." It took me a moment to understand that American language through the heavy German accent and I grinned.

"Are you going to learn their language, Herr Zesch?"

"Only as much as I have to — and hope it does not pollute my tongue." He grinned at me. I enjoyed talking to Adolph Zesch because he treated me like an equal and not a kid to be seen more than heard. He used to insist on me calling him by his first name, but I didn't out of respect. He accepted that and we were good friends.

"I saw you trying to gather the cows with King yesterday. Did not look like he was doing much good."

"No, sir, he is not good at much more than racing," I answered. "I did more good on foot."

Adolph chuckled, "Good only for outrunning Indian ponies, I would say, and that for short distances. As the Texians say, the mustangs have more 'bottom' and would win a long race, even if they all were reduced to walking."

"Do you think in a long race Amigo would outdistance King?"

"I am sure of it, Ad. You should try it some time." Adolph studied his blade carefully. "See, I am down to the wire edge, now I will hone it off and have a blade to shave with." He chuckled and reached for his leather strop hooked to a nearby stump. Folks laughed that he had left tree stumps high in his yard, but he made good use of them. Of course, everyone had a hollowed-out stump by their door for pounding out grain and making hominy like the Mexicans.

"I am looking for a couple of hounds to

take with us to our new farm," I said. "Do you have any good hunters you would like to trade?"

"Rogers told me about your new place. It sounds like it could be a good farm. I will miss my good neighbors when they are gone."

"And welcome your new good neighbors when they come," I added. It would be unusual for Adolph *not* to get along with his neighbors.

"Your father mentioned that you would be looking for more hunters and I have been thinking about that. I do not have any dogs I could let go right now, but I do have a proposition for you to consider. I have a bitch I did not catch in time and she has been bred in the pack. She will most likely have pups from three or more sires and that would give you a good variety of hunters when they are grown. I'll give her to you for the pick of the litter."

"I am not sure Father would like that," I said. "It would be something I would have to think about."

"You would not have need of hunters until winter a year from now and the pups would be old enough to train by then. Your Dan will be adequate for this winter."

Dan was three years old and hitting his

stride as a good hunter, be it deer, coon, or possum. "What does the bitch look like?"

Adolph put his fingers to his teeth and whistled. In a moment, a hound came trotting around the corner of the cabin. She was a black and tan shorthair with long ears. She had one glass eye and the left one was brown. Her feet were big, her legs and shoulders were well muscled, and she had a deep chest. Already, her belly was swelling.

"It will be about six weeks before she whelps," Adolph said. "She had six pups the last time I bred her, and I imagine that will be what she has this time."

"I will have to think about it, we only wanted a couple of dogs," I said. I liked the dog and would take her in a minute, but Pa said only two. He wasn't likely to take kindly to seven or eight pups hanging around the place.

"You can let me know in the morning," Adolph said. "If you do not take her, I will look for someone else."

When I asked Eve what she thought about taking the bitch, she said, "Sounds good to me. It sure would be an easy way to move dogs, wouldn't it? Any pups we didn't want we could get rid of one way or another."

It was no use asking Ma. Pa would say women had no business putting in on a man's affairs. In the morning I went over and got the dog. Schnapps, Adolph called her, but with Mary and Martha, she became Snap. They took over care of the dog and we had no worries about her running back to Zesch's place. Ma was glad to have the girls out from underfoot while she and Eve packed. She even let the girls sleep downstairs by the fireplace with Snap between them.

It didn't take long for us to pack what little things we had and it all fit on the wagon except for the plow. Pa had been gone three weeks and I was getting worried that Snap would whelp before he came back. Eve and I talked it over and that night, we cornered Ma at the table.

"Mother, it is getting late in the season and Father has not come for us," Eve said. "We could save time if we left here and met him somewhere on the road or even got to the new place before he finished our house."

"Eve has a point, Mother, we had a pretty good frost the other morning and it is not going to be warm much longer. It would be awful hard moving in cold weather," I added.

Ma's attention was drawn to the girls. "Martha, do not eat with your hands, use your spoon." She spent several minutes teaching the girl how to eat, then turned to us, "Now what was that you were saying, Eve?"

"Mother, she was saying that it would be better to meet Father along the road than wait for him here and move in the dead of winter."

"I will not have you using that tone with me, young man. Show some respect for your elders or I will pound it in on your backside."

"Yes, ma'am, but you were not listening when we had something important to say."

"Well, say it."

"The wagon is almost packed, let us finish it in the morning and start for the new place. We can meet Father and Noah on the way and save several days and not be on the way in the cold."

"I have been thinking the same thing. Eve and I can have the loading finished by midmorning if you can gather the stock and yoke the oxen."

I'll swear she talked like it had been a settled thing and we were just hitchin' up to go visit folks down th' road.

"Yes, ma'am." I ducked my head and finished my meal. Eve nudged me with her knee. Mary dropped her spoon on the floor and swiped her fingers through her mashed potatoes. Ma sighed.

It might have been a little past midmorning before we were set to leave. Ma sent Mary to Zesch's with a note that we were leaving. When she got back and settled by Martha with Snap between them, Eve cracked the whip. The oxen set their shoulders to the task and we were on our way. King was tied to the tailgate next to the plow and Dan and I herded cattle afoot. It was a long day without nooning and we camped just shy of Cherry Mountain. Next morning, Dan and I were footsore so he took Snap's place and I saddled King. We were only shy one head in the herd but when we were strung out, I looked back to see that shy steer standing in the middle of the trail, head high.

We nooned early at Hilltop so Ma and the girls could visit. Dan whipped the dogs in the settlement and I had to hold Snap from lending a fang. Dan got by with a bloody ear and I near had to whip some kid that wanted to kill him. No dogs came out to send us off when we left. I thought Dan limped a little at first.

The campsite at Cherry Spring was nice. An extra long trek the day after that got us to Beaver Settlement. It was good to put the cattle in a pasture. Even Shy Steer let me hold the gate for him. We rested here a day while I repacked the wagon for the rough trail to the farm.

There was no trail to Panther Creek and it was so rough riding in the wagon that we all walked except Ma, who rode King and kept the cattle together. I walked ahead and rolled the biggest rocks out of the way and by noon, I was fagged out.

"If we ever do this again, I'm switching to packhorses at Beaver Creek," I said at noon. "If we make the pull to the top of the mountain this afternoon, we should camp there and get to the farm tomorrow, Mother."

"That will be fine, Son, we will all be ready to rest by then."

When we started again, Ma put the girls on the horse and she led him by the reins. I rolled rocks and Eve drove. We didn't get to the top of the hill soon enough for me. I got my chores done, ate a bite, and crawled under the wagon in my blankets and slept.

Someone kicked me hard in the ribs. "Wake up, Ad, th' Injuns're on us," Noah said in a hoarse whisper. I forgot where I was and banged my head on the wagon bed when I sat up. Noah laughed and I lay back down.

"What are you doin' here, Noah? Got th'

cabin built a'ready?" It felt like a knot was already growing where my head hit the wagon. I grabbed a boot and pulled it on.

"Timber's up. Needs chinkin' an' we left that to you kids."

"Kids my a—"

"Shhh, Ma knows that much American." He kicked my other boot out of reach and moved off to help Ma with the fire. I crawled over and shoved the other boot on.

"Adam, hurry up and gather your cattle," Pa directed.

Amigo was tied to the tailgate and nodded a greeting when I untied him. We made short work of rounding up the cattle. Pa was sitting on Sol when we got to camp and Eve handed me a sausage wrapped in a biscuit as we passed. Pa heeled Sol ahead, and Amigo and I got caught up on the latest news as we rode.

Noah had the oxen yoked and they were moving out when we topped the last little rise. Ma had Martha on King and Mary sat in the wagon, Snap lying on one side and Dan sitting on the other.

"I saw that glass-eyed bitch you picked up," Pa said after we turned the cattle into the land between the creeks. "Nearly bit me when I reached for the girls."

I could tell Pa wasn't too happy about my

choice. "It was all Zesch had that he would let me have."

"Looks like she's going to pup soon."

"Yes, sir. It seemed the easiest way to haul a bunch of dogs." I grinned and Pa snorted. "Zesch wants the pick of the litter as his payment."

"You can see to that. I do not know when we will ever get back there."

I hadn't seen the cabin when we turned the cattle out and when we got to it, I still hadn't seen much. It was the result of hasty construction. Some of the gaps between the logs were as wide as the logs.

"Gonna take a lot of mud, ain't it?" Noah growled under his breath.

"Adam, put Amigo and King on tethers close to the house where we can keep an eye on them," Pa directed. He handed Eve Sol's reins and nodded toward me. We took the three and staked them close.

"Pa wasn't very happy about Snap, Ad," Eve said as we headed for the wagon.

"I'm hopin' th' girls will convince him we need her to watch after them."

Eve bumped me with her shoulder, "You think she'll have a big litter?"

"I hope not. That'll make Pa even madder."

"Well, I hope she does so we will have a

lot of pups to play with."

"What makes you think we'll have time t' play while we're chinkin' those logs?" I asked.

"Oh, there'll be time enough."

A heavy gust of cold wind blew dust into our faces. "I think we're gonna be awful busy chinkin' in a cold cabin, Eve."

The cabin Pa had built was about fourteen feet square.

"Fourteen by sixteen," Noah asserted.

It had one door and there was a window high on each sidewall. "Gives ventilation, but won't let Injuns in," I observed to Eve. She shuddered.

There was a rough fireplace at the end opposite the door, just some flat rocks stacked straddling a hole in the wall with a mud and stick chimney built up outside. That chimney didn't have any trouble drawing. The fact was that we could hardly feed it enough wood to keep it going. The first thing Ma had us doing was to dig a small trench around the inside of the wall. We mixed that dirt with water and chinked the bottom logs to the ground.

"Makes it snake proof," Eve observed.

"Any snakes out in this weather'll be drillin' under that lookin' for warmth," I growled.

Snap had been acting funny and we knew her time to whelp was near. The girls pulled grass and piled it near the door for her bed. She seemed content with it and settled on it for the night. Next morning, she had moved all that straw over by a corner of the hearth where the rock was warm.

"How did she move all that grass?" Mary asked.

"She didn't move *all* of it," Eve said, looking at the trail of grass across the floor.

Ol' Dan came in and trotted over to nose the bed where Snap lay. She growled and snapped at him and he retreated.

"Tha's 'Nap's bed, Dan," Martha lisped. She sat on the hearth to guard Snap from further intrusions. We were all busy chinking when she squealed, "Mother, Mother, rats are eating 'Nap!"

It took us a while to convince Martha that those were not rats, but puppies; then she and Mary took over the care of them. Snap would not let any of the rest of us get near them without a warning growl.

Noah grinned. "Let 'em go, she'll be beggin' us t' take 'em when they get their milk teeth."

As they grew, we could tell that there were at least three sires to the bunch and we had many an argument about whether one of them was a coyote or a wolf. When that dog was full grown, it was obvious by her size that there had been a wolf behind the woodpile. Noah claimed her, but she claimed me and was my constant companion when the girls were inside. Somehow she sensed that Eve was special kin to me and she looked after her too. The girls named them Mary, Martha (without regard to gender, since Mary was a male), Grunt, Sleepy, Fatty, and Dapple. When Ma got tired of the "confusion" of calling "Martha the Girl" or "Martha the Dog," she decreed they had to be renamed. Mary the Dog became Blinky and Martha became Spot. My wolf-dog was a dappled gray with a wolf's head and ears, somewhat rangy body, and huge feet. Her name was shortened from Dapple to Dap.

Dap loved Mary and Martha — the girls — and became their guardian. Her second greatest preference was to be with me and she was indifferent to the others.

CHAPTER 3
THE CHARM OF
THE THIRD TIME

1867

We spent that whole winter chinking cracks and thatching the roof. When we were through chinking, there wasn't a fist-sized rock within a hundred yards of the house. By the last of March, the house was done and it was warm enough that we wished we hadn't chinked up all the cracks. A thunderstorm rolled through one afternoon and the driving rain washed the chinking out of the west wall.

"I can see right now we will never be through chinkin'," I griped to Eve.

"Push the clay to the back, then fill it with rocks, maybe then it won't wash so bad," Noah suggested.

"Go get us more rocks, Mr. Know-It-All," Eve retorted.

"Think I'll do that, you just keep on muddin'." He tried to dodge the mud ball Eve threw at him and it hit him between the shoulder blades. "Just for that, you can wash my shirt." By the time that was said, he was out of range. "Mary, Martha, come on and help me pick out the pretty rocks for the house," he called.

"They're *all* pretty, Noah, just you get a sackful," I called.

Making a farm out of virgin land was hard work. We were up before daylight and didn't quit until dark drove us to the house. We never passed through the door without an armload of wood and we hauled until the hearth was holding enough fuel for the next day. Sometimes we were almost too tired to eat and often I awoke rolled up in a blanket by the hearth, without any idea how I got there.

Two or three times a week through the summer, Ma would make us go to the creek or the river and wash. I suppose if she didn't make us, we would have turned black. We got pretty rusty as it was. When Panther Creek stopped running on top, we spent our time in the Llano. We had a little more leisure time after the crops were laid by and the truck garden was up good. Noah and I spent a lot of evenings in the river. The long pool under the red bluff was deep and clear and we never saw it go dry. We spent a lot of time jumping off the bluff, seeing what was the highest point we could jump from and not hit bottom. We were two-thirds the way up the bluff before we had to stop because we were hitting the bottom too hard. Cannonballing just exposed our backsides to the rocky bottom. We didn't try that high point too often, but jumping from lower places was a lot of fun.

"I think we could go higher to jump without hitting bottom," Noah said one day as we swam.

"How's that?" I asked. "I'm not gonna try anything that bangs my feet up where I can't walk. Pa would have my hide." With the river falling, we were not able to jump from halfway up the bluff.

"When you jump, as soon as your feet hit the water, kick them forward as hard as you can and see what that does for you."

The first time I tried it, I kicked too soon and liked to busted my butt.

"Kicked too soon, didn't you?" Noah grinned at me. "Here's how you do it," and he jumped. I watched and when he hit the water instead of going straight down, he shot almost horizontally across the pool. His momentum still pushed him to the bottom, but not nearly as hard and fast as just straight jumping would have.

It didn't take us long to perfect the jump

and we were able to jump from higher up without damage. "River gets full, I bet we could jump from th' top," Noah surmised.

"Maybe," I said, "but I doubt it."

The river rose with the spring rains and we gradually could jump from higher and higher places, but we never did jump from the top of the bluff.

The Indians didn't bother us much that first summer, though Pa heard they had a lot of trouble east of us and up around Jacksboro.

"Jacksboro is too close to Indian Territory for my comfort," he would say.

We hadn't dug a root cellar, so that first fall, we hilled the potatoes right there in the garden. They held pretty good that way, but we near run out before spring. The corn did good, but that hominy got awful tiresome. It was too far to a gristmill and we missed our cornbread after we ran out of meal.

We put up a lean-to agin the east wall of the house and that's where we kept the stock. Comanche Moon nights, one of us always slept out there. Trouble was, Comanche Moons was near every night, so we had a regular bed by the wall. At least the rain couldn't get to the chinking under that lean-to.

I remember it was the first week in March

1868 and the creeks were running, even Bain Creek. The river was bank full and had that blue-green color that told you it was cold as ice. Pa sent me and Noah up on the Panther Creek bluffs to cut cedar poles. The girls were grubbing out roots from the garden behind Pa's plow.

Me and Noah saw them at about the same time, three or four Injuns sneaking through the trees after Pa and the girls. Pa had his back to them, plowing another row and didn't see them.

We set up a howl, "Injuns, Father, Injuns are upon you," I screamed.

Eve didn't even look back, just grabbed Martha up and dragging Mary by the hand beat a path to the house.

Pa had his rifle across the plow handles and whirled, bringing it up to sight. He fired and the lead Injun fell. The girls were nearing the door, but a big buck was near on them. Just as he got close enough to grab the girls, Ma fired from her sighting hole by the door and he fell. As the door was closing behind the girls, Pa yelled, "Hold the door" and drove Sol right into the house. The plow handles were too wide and they stuck in the doorway. Pa turned with that Colt's revolver and fired at the closest Injun, who ducked to the ground. His second shot convinced the others to seek cover.

There was some conversation at the house we couldn't hear and Pa pulled the plow out of the doorway. Arrows were flying at him thick and a couple of the Indians fired rifles. The door slammed shut and Pa rounded the corner to the lean-to where King and Amigo were. Ma's rifle fired again and the Indians quit scratching for cover where there was none and ran back up the divide.

Some movement to our left caught my eye and here came three of those savages lined out in an arc to catch us. "Run, Noah!" I pushed him towards the river, nearly running over him in the process. We streaked for the bluffs, those Indians gaining about every step.

"We haf-t' jump," Noah panted. An arrow whizzed past my head and like magic, one appeared, stuck through Noah's coat sleeve. "Missed me," he muttered. I cursed my short legs as Noah pulled ahead.

We were still fifty yards from the brink and they were gaining on us. By the time that distance was halved, I could hear the nearest savage panting. I dared not look back. Ten yards, and the devil pulled up beside me, grinning at his victory. He wasn't looking where we were going and as he began the swing of his war club, I leaped as far out as I could. The buck disappeared with a scream and we fell almost together, only the Indian was bouncing off rocks and ledges and got a little behind me.

Noah's splash caught my attention and I almost missed my chance to kick out. It probably didn't matter, the river was deep enough, but it helped to shoot us away from where we hit. Still, an arrow shot by me in the water and floated toward the bottom, point down. I grabbed it and shot for the top, lungs bursting after that run and jump.

"Here, under the ledge, Ad," Noah called in a quivering whisper. His lips were already blue and face pale as death. We both were freezing.

"Don't move around much and the clothes will hold some warmth," Noah advised.

I hung to the rocks and panted as we watched the Injun float past, facedown in a cloud of bloody water. "Why's he floatin'?" I asked as much to myself as to Noah.

"There he goes," Noah said, and the body kind of rolled and slowly sank through the bloody cloud, the current still taking him along.

"Ain't . . . gonna . . . see me . . . swim . . . in' . . . inhere . . . 'tillthat'sgone," I stuttered through chattering teeth.

"We . . . gonna . . . diein . . . thi' . . . water," Noah chattered.

I started to climb the bluff, but saw that wasn't good. We needed heat and fast. Pa and Ma were still shooting, then it got quiet a moment before we heard Eve screaming our names, "Noah? Adam? It's safe now, come out of the water." She must have been standing on the point above Panther Creek Falls.

Noah nodded toward the far shore and we swam across the river, clothes and all. I got to wading first and pulled Noah up to me. We stumbled out of the water weak as kittens. The air hitting us was cold enough to make us want to turn around, but that wasn't good either. We sloshed up on the bank and sat down to take our shoes off.

"Come up this way, Pa's comin'," Eve called. She was standing as far out on the point as possible waving us up the bank. Moving helped and we moved up opposite of her. "Take those clothes off and wring them out," she called over the sound of the falls.

"Turn around," Noah motioned with his hand.

"No, you turn around, I've seen hind ends before." Bossy girl.

We turned around and pulled soggy clothes off of blue bodies. "Oh, my Lord help me. Noah, I've turned into a girl," I whispered, horrified.

Noah looked at me in horror and felt between his legs. "O-o-oh . . . it's all right, Ad, we just got so cold we went inverted. Bet they come out when we're warmed up. I hope so," he added.

We wrung our shirts out and put them back on. They were long enough to hide the place where we used to hang out and when Pa called, we turned around. I could almost hear Eve tittering. "I'm gonna get her," I vowed.

Pa was standing there with a bow and an arrow with rags wrapped around it. "I am sending you some fire, get ready."

We hustled up the bank and gathered leaves and twigs at the edge of the brush. "Ready, Pa, send it on," Noah called.

Pa unrolled the rag a little and Eve poured coals from a pot. They quickly rolled them up and tied the bundle. He nocked the arrow and fired it high in the air. Even as it fell, it began smoking and when it hit near us, we grabbed it and hustled it to our fuel where we soon had a little flame. Noah nursed it along while I gathered more sticks and we soon had a fire going. When we turned to signal it was going, both were laughing and we realized our shirts didn't cover the subject behind when we were stooping over. "Git back over here as soon as you can," Pa called, "I will put the ladder down." He motioned to the Bain's Creek side. We had a notched pole ladder about halfway up the creek that we kept pulled up on top. It saved a lot of walking when we had to go down that side. He turned and pushed a reluctant Eve up the hill.

That was one of those times we didn't keep our fire low and it wasn't long until it was roaring and we were warming ourselves, turning like pigs on a spit. Our clothes were close enough to steam as they dried and we had to be careful they didn't scorch.

"Better put those shoes on before they dry like rocks," Noah observed, and we did. Our dried socks didn't stay that way long.

"You think the shoals is too deep t' wade?" I asked. We hadn't seen it since the last rise.

"For sure it would be waist deep by now," Noah replied.

"Sometimes when the river's full, th' current slows some, don't it?"

"Sometimes."

"Maybe thisun'll be thataway." I threw another stick on the fire.

Another hour and we were ready to get

home. Our clothes were dry and it was after midafternoon and we hadn't eaten since breakfast. We slogged up the river beyond Bain's Creek to the place where the shoals had been. It didn't seem the river was moving as fast, but it was certain it was deeper.

"I'll try it, Ad, and see if we can make it over right here."

"If you make it, I'll be behind you."

"Give me your clothes and I'll carry them for you."

That made sense since Noah was taller and heavier. The clothes had a better chance of staying dry with him. We bundled the clothes up and tied them on the end of a long stick with our shoelaces, and Noah waded in. The current was stronger than it looked and soon it was up to his chest. Another step or two and he was up to his neck, the stick held high in the air. He sort of bounced along in the current until he got to shallower water on the other side.

"That's swimming water for you, Ad, better go upstream a little more and come across on an angle," he called when he was out.

There was a big boulder on my side of the river up a ways and the water was fairly calm below it. I could wade out there and angle across as far as I could walk and not

56

have far to swim. Noah unwrapped our clothes and dressed quickly. He kept the long pole with him and signaled for me to start across. Two steps past the boulder and I was swimming as fast as I could for the other side. When I had drifted down to where Noah was, he lowered the pole to me and pulled me to the bank. First thing I did was look down and what progress I had made coming out had reversed and I was almost as smooth down there as a girl.

"Don't worry, Ad," Noah said, grinning, "he'll be back when you warm up."

He was right. When I woke up the next morning, everything was back to normal.

Since we had missed dinner, Ma cooked the big meal for supper and served it early. It was a quiet supper for a change. The two little ones picked at their plates, their eyes red and cheeks tearstained. Ma was still pale and shaky and teetering on a good temper fit. We stayed out of her way.

Pa eyed her a while, then said, "Fannie, you will never guess what Eve and I saw across the river this morning . . ."

She slammed her bowl on the table and said, "You saw my two sons run off a cliff into the river and . . ." Her teeth were clinched as she said it.

"*We* saw not one, but *two* pale moons

peeking out from under linsey-woolsey clouds." Pa raised his voice a little to interrupt her and possibly cool her a little.

Eve giggled and I kicked at her and missed. She had drawn up her feet in anticipation of what was coming.

"Jumping off that bluff was not bad with the river full, Mother. It was just awful cold," Noah said.

"Besides, Mother, Eve would not turn away when we took our clothes off," I added.

"You had your backs turned so I could not see your business," Eve said, then giggled. The corners of Ma's mouth turned up a little and the fire went out of her eyes.

"Would not have mattered much anyway, Mother," Noah said, "the business side was all but disappeared. Guess they did not like that cold water."

Eve giggled and Pa laughed. Ma couldn't help grinning, then we all started laughing. The possibility of a storm had passed.

After supper, we eased outside with Pa to look at the bodies. "Looks to me to be Kioway," Pa said of the one nearest the door. The one up by the garden was taller and dressed differently — if you can be different with only breechcloths on. "He is Comanche, for sure," Pa said.

"They will make nice scalps," Noah observed.

Pa shook his head, "Taking these scalps would be an open invitation for every Indian in the country to come after us and the end result would be a burned down house and bodies scattered all around; the girls carried off to become a slave or some buck's wife. We're gonna give these bodies a proper Indian burial. Noah, go saddle Sol, and Ad, you go get the axe and that coil of sisal rope. I will go see Mother."

We finally had to blindfold Sol to get him still enough to load those dead Indians and carry them one at a time up the bluff above Panther Creek a couple of miles from the house. While Noah cut some cedar poles, Pa and I got the bodies ready for burial. For some reason, the Comanche still had his blanket around his waist and we rolled him up in it and laid his bow and quiver on top, tied to the body. We made a platform in an oak tree and laid him out on it. In the next big tree nearby, we laid out the Kioway the same way, only wrapped in one of our blankets. Next to both bodies, we laid a small bag of jerky and biscuits.

"Maybe if the Indians see we treat their warriors with respect, they will not concentrate so much on running us out of the country," Pa said. Even then he knew it was a futile hope.

"Third time's the charm," Eve whispered as I bedded down by the fireplace.

"That don't mean there won't be a fourth or ninetieth time, Eve, we gotta stay sharp — if Ma ever lets us out of sight agin."

Chapter 4
Fort Bain and the Cyclone

1868

We lived in that shanty the first two winters Pa brung us out here, but after the crops was laid by and through that second and third winter, Pa cut big logs and we shaped them up to fit tight with almost no chinking necessary. Some of the chinking on the old house was almost as wide as the logs. Got so we hated to see it rain because it washed out the chinking and piled lots of it inside the house.

"Why can't we be watered by a mist that comes up from the ground like before the Flood?" Pa would ask.

It took all that third winter to get walls up on the house and Ma moved in that spring before the roof was on. We went to making white oak shingles. Me and Eve and Noah made shingles until we could make them in our sleep. Noah kept saying, "Ain't this enough, Father?" and Pa would just shake his head no and keep splitting white oak logs. Come spring, he loaded up a big batch of shingles and left for the settlements. He came back with provisions and a keg of blacksmith nails. We kept making shingles. When we had another good load, we took them to the Beaver Creek mill and traded them for wood planking. Pa hired a man to come over and build us a rock chimney. Noah and I had hauled up a bunch of rocks and they were not enough, so we hauled some more 'til he said he had enough. Pa paid him by letting me and Noah out to him to gather rocks for a big house he was building in Beaver. He had a sledge and span of mules to pull it and we hauled rocks from Beaver Creek clear up to the Llano River. Before we were through, we had a reg'lar road from the settlement to the river. Folks used it for years.

Our roof had a big overhang over the front and back doors and we floored the loft for two bedrooms divided by a canvas, one side for boys and the other for girls. Pa bored holes in the floor of the overhangs so someone could cover the doors with their guns.

That summer, as time allowed, we began nailing up shingles, but it was winter before the whole roof was finished. We got in a race to see who nailed up the last shingle and I got the last one in the last row. "I won," I called.

Noah nodded and stepped back to look things over. "Well, would you looky there, I skipped a space." He took a shingle and nailed it in place. "And that's the last shingle."

"Not quite," Pa said at supper. "Now you can start shingling the barn."

"What barn?" I asked "We do not have a barn."

Eve kicked my leg and Pa looked at me a moment. "We do since Mother moved out of it."

I ducked my head and concentrated on my plate.

"We are going to put a shingle roof on the barn, Father?" Noah asked.

"Not now, Son; I want you to make the shingles longer and nail them to the walls to cover the cracks. You be sure they are chinked good before you shingle over them."

"Yes sir," we all three mumbled and it was quiet while we thought over that chore. Noah was the first to speak, "We are going to need more nails, Father."

"More blamed shingles, too," I grumbled.

We always suspected the folks put that shingling chore on us to keep us close to the house in case we had unwanted visitors.

The only break in that routine was when one of us watched with the Colt pistol while Pa plowed with his rifle across the plow handles. Pa said Eve made the best watcher, I was the best shingle splitter, and Noah was the best talker. I never had aspirations to be the best splitter *or* best talker.

The Injuns seemed to appreciate what we did with the two we killed. They didn't bother us for a while, though we found sign they had been by the burial trees and left things for the dead. Gradually, Ma and Pa allowed us more freedom and if we were careful enough, we could sneak out even farther than allowed and not get caught.

"What they don't know won't hurt them," Noah said.

"Yeah and what they find out *would* hurt us," I replied.

Mostly, we kids were left to ourselves; Ma or Pa would give us our chores and let us learn for ourselves how to best do them. Sometimes when things weren't turning out like they intended, we would get hurried and emphatic instructions and maybe a knock on the head or lower. I couldn't blame them very much; they were busy with their work from daylight to dark. We all worked hard and few were the days of rest. It seemed we could see them grow older by the day — especially Ma.

The only time Dap wasn't with me was when Mary and Martha were outside. She stayed between the girls and anyone else around and if the girls strayed apart so that she couldn't guard them both, the dog would herd them closer together. It never seemed to bother the girls. Ma grumbled sometimes that she had to ask Dap before she could approach the girls, but she took a lot of comfort that the dog was on duty and alert.

We were back up on the Panther bluffs cutting poles one hot afternoon when I looked around and Dap was gone.

"Girls are outside," I said and when we peeked over the ridge, there were Ma and the girls picking peas in th' garden. Dap lay at the end of the row, on watch.

Noah was chopping trees down and I was limbin' them with the hatchet when the sunshine disappeared. When we looked up, a big and black thunderhead climbed for the stars. We could hear the distant rumble of thunder. As we looked, the whole cloud from tree line to top lit up like its whole insides was on fire.

"Storm's comin', Noah."

"Sure looks threatenin', don't it? We better mosey for shelter. I shore don't want t' be up here on this bluff when lightnin' starts our way."

We heard the girls squealing and looked to see Dap hurrying all three toward the house. She seemed to nip at Ma's skirt, then ran ahead to grab Martha's gown and drag her toward the house. Ma grabbed Mary up and ran behind.

"Dap may be in trouble," I said. Noah grinned.

We bundled up what poles we had and with Noah on the big end and me on the other, shouldered the load and headed up the ridge to the path to the bottom. That cloud moved fast and was over us before we could get down. A bolt blasted a tall oak not fifty yards from us and instantly we both threw off the bundle and scrambled behind it as it rolled down the steep rocky bluff.

"Stay out of the water," Noah shouted above the roar of the cloud. I tried to jump the creek and nearly made it, but landed knee-deep. The water stopped the momentum of my legs but not the rest of me and I went down. Something big splashed into the water next to me.

"Hail!" Noah yelled and grabbed me by my overall galluses and jerked me to my feet. "Run!"

We ran, trying to hunch up under our hats

and the hail and rain peppering down on us. An occasional hunk as big as a hedge apple hit with a big thump or exploded on a rock. If one of those hit us, we would have been done for. Mary was holding the door open and we dove through the door, ending up in a pile on the floor. Mary slammed the door shut and Ma set the bar. Dap had herded Martha into a corner and yapped for Mary, who ran to her. That dog pushed the two girls into the corner and lay against them. Something slammed into the loft floor. A hailstone had come through the roof. Noah and I grabbed the table and set it over girls and dog and I pushed Ma under it. Another stone came through the roof and slammed into the stairwell. It broke a rung on the ladder and slammed against the wall, breaking into a hundred pieces.

"Where are Eve and Father?" I shouted over the roar of the storm.

"They took Sol to the barn," Ma replied through her shivers. It was the coldest rain I had ever felt.

The hail let up and then the rain slowed and I headed for the back door to see about Eve and Pa. "Father," I yelled. The house had been dark as night; but when I opened that door, it was just as dark outside — dark enough to need a light. The sudden very stillness of all things was scary.

"Eve, where are you?"

The cloud looked low enough to touch, all bumpy and raggedy and swirling, but not a leaf stirred near the ground. It seemed hard to breathe.

"Over here in the barn, Ad, where are you?"

Noah stepped out with a lit candle and held it high. "We're at the back door, Eve, is Father with you?"

"I'm here, Noah. Hold the light, we are coming." The ice was so deep it sounded like they were walking on glass. We heard a low rumble like it was a long way off and getting closer. "Cyclone's coming. Into the house." Pa herded us through the doorway. "Fannie, where are you?"

"Right here, Rogers." She was lighting another candle.

"Where are the girls — hold that light here, Noah." He was doing something with the leather door hinges. When I saw he was cutting them, I grabbed the bar seat and handle and held the door up.

"They are in the corner with Dap under the table." I saw Eve crawl under the table and Pa pulled the door down. "Noah, you and Ad make a wall with this door on one side of the table. Fannie, bring the light and help me." He ran to the front door. It was only a moment until it was down and they were dragging it across the floor. He leaned it against the end of the back door and between the end of the table and the hearth at the wall.

"Look, girls, we are building a fort — Fort Bain," I said to ease their fear.

"Go under the table, Fannie, and cover you all with those quilts," Pa said.

I had pulled the bedclothes off Ma's bed, ticking and all, and we stuffed them over them all. There was a whimper behind me and Snap crawled across the floor, puppies all around her. Noah held the door open a crack and they tumbled in, rooting under the covers.

The roar had been growing louder and louder and Pa hollered, "Here, boys, and help hold up these doors."

We crawled under the table and held the doors and waited — it seemed a year — while the roar grew louder and louder. It sounded like it was coming from the northwest of the house and the wind blew a hurricane through the back door and out the front. All the chairs blew to the door where two that had fallen over, jammed in the doorway. Other stuff piled up against them. Something thumped hard against the door I held and I was glad Pa had made it thick and strong. I ducked and closed my eyes, struggling against the pull of the wind on the door.

There was a sudden crash and boom, northwest of the house, and right after another kind of explosion seeming northeast of us—and just as sudden as the snap of your fingers, the wind quit. We could hear the roar fading off to the east.

"The storm is gone," Pa said and stood up. I stood and rubbed the dirt off my face. Ma was beside me and sighed, "Look at that mess," she said, more to herself. Martha tugged at my pants leg and I lifted her up. "Yook a' 'at mess, Ah, yust yook," she said in disgust. She hadn't conquered the "d" sound and so my name became Ah.

"Going to take a lot of work to clean up, is it not, Martie?"

"It's Mar*thuh,* Ah, an' 'ou no's it." She thumped my chest. She was still shaking from her fright, but the mess was a good distraction for her.

"Let's go see what is still here," I said and stepped over the doors. Dap's littermates tumbled over the top and danced around our legs. One saw the jam at the front door and growled, hackles up from ears to tail. "Be kite, B'inky," Martha demanded.

The house was a mess, nothing was untouched. The jam at the front door caused by the chairs getting stuck caught a lot of things that would have blown away. The little table we kept the Bible in had skidded across the floor and against the jam. When Eve opened the drawer, the Bible was still there, dry and untouched.

"What in the world . . . ?" Ma was staring at the fireplace. It had been cleaned as slick as if someone had swept the ashes and washed the stone down. The crane was pulled into the fireplace and the chains the kettle hung from were sucked up the chimney. I looked up the chimney and when my eyes got used to the dark, I could see the kettle stuck upside down on the rock walls. Trying to pull it down by the chains did no good and we left it there for the time being. The Dutch oven and skillet were gone.

Water dripped to the floor in a hundred places, it seemed, and when we looked up, we could see blue sky. I groaned, "Shingles gone."

Ma called from the front door, "Ad, you and Eve climb up and get the bedclothes. We have to hang them out to dry before night."

I had thrown the bed from the boys' side down when Eve called, "I can't get these

71

blankets off, Ad." There were two gaping holes in the roof over the girls' bed. In two places, the covers and ticking had been pushed through the rope net foundation, making a sort of pocket, and inside each pocket was a chunk of melting ice. I had to throw the covers over the holes and stand on the floor through the netting to free the bedding. Part of the trouble was that the melting ice had swelled the mattress ticking. We threw the bedclothes down the ladder well and followed them.

The brush was soon covered with drying bedding and we went to look at the barn. The thatching on the roof was all gone, but the bare framing was still in place with only one or two broken. The whole building had taken a decided lean to the east. Pa and Eve had gotten the horses inside before the storm hit and they were bruised and scared.

"The thatching was springy and thick enough that those big hailstones just bounced off and did not come through," Pa explained. "Adam, take Amigo and ride down the hill and see if we have any cattle left."

Amigo was awful skittish. I gave up saddling him and jumped on bareback. That seemed to please him more and we trotted down the hill. The ground about a quarter mile from the barn was swept clean in a wide swath all the way across the land from Bain's Bluff to the Panther Creek Bluff. I could see a pile of trees and stuff in Panther and determined to look things over after I found the cattle. They were scattered about and considerably nervous. By my count, there were five head missing and I hoped to find them on my return to the house. When I started back, the whole herd followed.

The cyclone had left a path of destruction a hundred yards wide. Sitting in the middle of it, I could see its path in both directions. Mostly, it was a jumble of tangled and broken timber, but in places, the ground was swept clean. Even small rocks were picked up and some big ones had been moved. Where the twister had hit the Panther Bluff, it had dropped its load and all kinds of trees and limbs and gravelly dirt fell into the creek. Already, the water was backing up behind that dam and it looked like we would have a pretty good tank. The same thing had happened at Bain Creek Bluff and that stream was dammed up too. From the looks of things, we were going to have plenty of firewood for the next few years.

Riding through the brush and trees along Panther, I found a steer with a broken leg.

He tried to follow with the cattle, but couldn't. Pa went down and shot him and we butchered him. There was a lot of bruising on the meat. That poor feller had taken a beating in the hail. We eventually accounted for all the cattle except one that we never found. "She could be under that Panther Creek dam or clear to Fredericksburg, for all we know," Pa opined.

Our next chore was to clear the chimney so we could build the fire back. Pa hoisted me up on the roof and handed up a long pole. "Go see if you can push that pot loose. If you have to, tap gently and try not to break the pot. I will try to catch it when it falls."

I scrambled up to the chimney, only putting my foot through the roof once. "Ready, Pa?"

"Ready," he called.

The thing was really jammed and it took a long time and a lot of tapping, some not too gentle, to get the pot to move. Something fell with a metallic clink and I groaned. I had broken the pot.

"That's alright, Adam, keep tapping, I can see it move," Pa called.

I tapped softer. That broken piece must have been what held the pot, for it was giving with each tap. It fell without warning and Pa grunted as he caught it. "Got it, boy, see if you can get down without coming through the roof."

The chip was from the rim and the pot didn't crack, so no real damage was done. Eve tied a string around it and hung it on my neck. The kids called me "Chip", then "Ship" in accord with Mar*thuh's* way of saying the name.

We spent the next few days gathering up our scattered things, fixing broken chairs, and rehanging doors. The thump I felt during the storm was a peeled stick driven into the door. We couldn't pull it out and ended up cutting it off. The Dutch oven was tangled up in the stuff at the front door, but we never did find the lid. Enough of the skillet was left around the handle that Ma could use it to fry in if she didn't use too much grease. She used it that way a long time. It hung on a peg beside the fireplace. Our tool chest sat against the wall and we used it as a bench and sideboard when needed. It was watertight and we never could explain how it got so wet inside. Me and Pa spent a lot of time drying and waxing the tools so they wouldn't rust.

That beef was all the food we had since the garden was ruined and the dry goods were dry no more — those that hadn't been blown away. We were lucky that the storm came early in the season and we could replant the garden. To our surprise, some of the beans and peas came back, some even from the roots. The corn was gone completely and Pa had us soak the seed before we planted to give them a head start. It seemed to work well, as they were sprouting in no time.

We were in a pretty fix for a while and spent our time making shingles for trade, knowing they would be in high demand at Beaver Creek — if the storm had left anything standing there. When we had a load of shingles, Pa took Ma and the little girls to Beaver Creek with him. While he was gone, we made more shingles and started patching our roof. They drove in with two mustangs tied to the tailgate a few days after we expected them to be back. We were relieved to see them.

"They did not have the things we needed and we had to go up to Hedwig's Hill," Pa explained. "Our shingles were more valuable to them than at Beaver Creek and we made good by going up there. I had to take these horses in trade for some of the shingles. They might amount to something with a little work."

"Did they have much damage at Beaver,

Father?" I asked.

"Not to the houses, but the mill got a little and the race got filled with trash. They will be back in business soon."

"What was Hedwig's Hill like, Mother?" Eve asked.

"They have a nice store there and it was a little larger settlement, I believe. We got a new Dutch oven with a lid and everything else we needed for now and I got you some underthings."

"Mother!" Eve turned red and Noah and I grinned.

"Looks like you need some more wood," Pa said. "I will see what the storm blew down tomorrow. It's getting to be quite a distance to good white oaks."

We were proud of what we had done while he was gone, but he didn't mention anything about it. I guess it wasn't any more than what he expected of us. If he had looked, he would have seen that it was quite a bit more than usual. We had worked hard.

Chapter 5
Mustangs and Rustlers

Fall, 1868

Those two geldings turned out to be half-broke and a handful of trouble for a time. One was a lineback dun and the other was roan with a blaze face and white stocking on his right foreleg. Noah, Pa, and me spent a lot of time taming them down, and when it came to *riding* them, we had to start all over again.

Pa taught us how to gentle-break the horses. I found out later the only difference between rough-breaking and gentle-breaking was the amount of time it took for each; the methods were pretty much the same. Gentle-breaking takes a few weeks and rough-breaking tries t' do it all in a couple of days.

There were not a few empty saddles. "That dun must be half jackass," Noah opined as he beat dust out of his hat on his leg. Amigo and King were kept busy run-

78

ning one or the other down. The strange thing about both of those horses is that they acted tame around Ma and Eve. They would come at their call and behave around them. Dap seemed to understand that, but she would never let Mary or Martha near either of the animals.

The two little ones were the official animal namers in the family and they had to be consulted any time there was a christening. They had a hard time thinking up names for the horses, having used up all the names they knew on the puppies. We kept suggesting names, but none of them met with their approval. Things had come to a head and one night after supper, I picked up Mar*thuh* and Eve followed us with Mary in hand. We walked to the corral gate and I sat both girls on the top rail. Dap had a fit and I thought she would bite me before I could get both girls down where she could lie down between them and the horses. An occasional soft growl kept the horses at bay.

"Now, ladies," I said, "we have to name these horses tonight or they told me they are going back to their old home."

"So get to thinking and come up with names before bedtime," Eve ordered.

Mary considered a moment, digging a trench in the dirt with her big toe. "We could call that one Spot . . ."

Eve shook her head. "We already have a dog named Spot and neither horse has got spots; it has to be something new."

"But I like Sp—"

"No, Mary." It was time to be firm. "That one has a blaze face, he has one stocking and he's a roan color," Eve said.

Martha's brow wrinkled in thought. "Where him yose him boot?"

"Lose his boot?"

"Him haf fhree boots 'n' one sock, Ah; where him's *ofher* boot?"

"I guess he must have lost it, Martha."

"We call him Yost Boot, Mary, until him find it."

With that settled, the namers turned their attention to the dun. He was maybe a little younger than the other horses and more playful. His favorite joke was to catch one of the horses unawares and nip him, then whirl away with a sound more like a laugh than a snort. The other horses responded as the mood struck them, sometimes in anger, other times playfully. As we watched, the dun crept up to King, who was thoughtfully chewing a mouthful of hay. He nipped King's flank and whirled away as King's hind hooves kicked at empty space.

Mary jumped up and down in glee, "He's

the Joker, Martha."

"Yes. *That* is Joker and that one is Yost Boot," the junior namer proclaimed. And so it was. Mary and Martha always referred to the roan by his full name, Yost Boot, but the rest just shortened it to Yost.

"It is time we got some more cattle to keep grass and brush down," Pa announced one morning that fall after the '68 cyclone.

I groaned. That could only mean more shingles. We had dragged out the white oak logs from on top of the two dams the storm had dumped on the creeks and we had plenty of wood to work with.

Pa grinned at me. "Not more shingles, Ad, we are going to rustle us up a herd."

Now, let's get this straight right now: we were not going to *steal* cattle. That's an animal of another stripe completely. *Rustling* is gathering unmarked cattle that run wild on the open range and are owned by no one. Taking branded cattle is *stealing.* If a man wanted to build a herd from wild unmarked cattle, he would *rustle* up a bunch, slap his brand and notch on 'em, and he was in the cattle business.

Some of those early open range fellers tried to claim that unmarked cattle on what they called their range was their property, but that reasoning never held water so long as the range was public land. A brand on a cow's hide was the sure sign of ownership, *wherever* the cow was found. But even that didn't stop the arguing — and sometimes a man's argument was punctuated with knuckles or lead.

"We are going over west of here and gather a little bunch of cows and put them on our range," Pa explained to the family. "I want to be leaving here this time next week with Adam and Noah. Parson Engle and his wife have agreed to come stay with the girls while we are gone. The Indians have gone to hole for the winter and will not be bothering us until spring. I plan for us to be gone four to six weeks. With a little luck we should be able to gather thirty to fifty head and drive them home."

I could have yelled and Noah just grinned. Eve wiggled in her chair and I moved my legs in time to avoid her kick. She kicked my chair leg instead and jammed her toes.

We busied ourselves and got everything set to go. "The three mustangs will be our cattle horses and we will use Sol as our pack mule," Pa explained.

We would leave King in the corral for Ma and the girls in case they needed him. All was ready and we waited for the parson and his wife to show. It was two whole days of waiting and they rattled into the yard before noon on the third day.

"Get things ready and load Sol as soon as we eat and we'll be leaving here," Pa whispered to me and Noah as the wagon stopped at the house. "Welcome, Parson, Mrs. Engle. Boys, take the horses to the corral and pour them a feed after you rub them down."

We handed down the Engles' baggage and drove the buggy around to the corral. The horses got a little grain and a little less rubbing and we checked our gear, which had been ready to load for three days.

"All's ready 'cept guns an' food," Noah said for the tenth time.

"I'm gonna saddle Amigo," I said, and I did. Noah saddled Yost and we put Pa's saddle on Joker. Eve called dinner and we kids ate outside while the grown-ups ate in the house so we could be through at the same time.

"I'm through," I said as I got up and stuffed meat wrapped in a biscuit in my pocket.

"You can't be through, I barely got started," Noah complained.

"I'm gonna be loadin' Sol," I replied.

"It's gonna be an hour afore they're

finished in th' house," said Eve.

"It's not like Sol's gonna be loaded all day; we'll be stoppin' afore sunset," I replied as I left. Sol hadn't packed for a while and it took him a while to be resolved to the fact. I hadn't packed an animal before and had to do it three times before I thought it might stay put and not swing under his belly. I left him tied in the barn out of sight. Mary rode while I led the horses to the hitching rail in front of the house and Mary ran to tell Pa they were there. It served us well to remind him that "time's a-wastin'." And still they sat and talked.

"Told you so," Eve scolded, and I threw a ladybug in her plate.

Noah grinned at me. "Little bit anxious, ain't you?"

"Tell you what, Noah, if you ain't int'rested in goin', Eve'll take yer place an' you can stay here an' entertain th' Parson. He'll be glad t' practice his sermons on yuh."

"Jist 'cause I ain't wettin' my pants t' git goin' don't mean I ain't wantin' t' go." He turned back to take a drink and I shoved his elbow so that the water spilled in his face and all down his front. He grabbed me afore I could get out of reach and we rolled on the ground.

"Fight! Fight!" The little girls squealed happily.

Noah was on my back rubbing my face in the dirt with Martha on his back hollering, "Let go, Noah, let go."

Something hit Noah so hard I heard the thump and the air go out of him. When I looked up, Dap was standing on Noah's chest, her nose not two inches from Noah's. Her soft growls sounded like a kitten purring — a big kitten. Noah was frozen in place, his eyes squeezed shut.

"It all right, Dap, it all right," Martha was saying, her arm across the dog's shoulders.

I had to spit dirt out before I could talk, "Dap, come here." The dog saw me and relaxed. She moved off Noah and gently pushed Martha away to where Mary and Eve sat watching.

Noah sat up. "I think if I had opened my eyes, she would have eaten my face off."

"Don't think she wants you messin' with me," I said.

"It ain't you, dummy, it was Martha she was protectin'."

"Don't think so." I was pretty sure he was right, but it wouldn't hurt a bit for him t' think it was me Dap was protecting.

"Adam, you and Noah load Sol and bring him around to the front." Pa stood in the back door. He didn't sound happy. "And Adam, *wash your face.*"

Noah headed for the barn, his front dripping water and his back shedding dirt and leaves. Dap sat beside the girls and grinned. I scratched her ears. "Good girl, Dap."

Eve felt left out. "I should be goin' too."

"There's not enough cow horses an' Ma needs King here in case you need t' git out in a hurry," I said. Still, I would have felt better if she could go with us. Eve is a lot of help around cattle and the camp.

"When we come back, we'll slip off an' git you enough cows t' trade for a horse. I promise."

"An' I'll hold you to it," Eve vowed.

Noah was ahead of us with Sol and we hurried around the house after him. I was trying to find a clean place on my shirt to dry my dripping face.

"Shame on you boys, leaving here as dirty as two pigs." Ma was embarrassed and Pa was mad.

Mary began, "It was a fight, Mother —"

"— An' Dap beat!" Martha finished, arms spread.

"Blessed are the peacemakers." Parson Engle smiled. He must have grown up in a big family where fighting was common.

Mrs. Engle smiled and patted Ma's shoulder. "Boys will be boys, Fannie, it is the same all over."

Pa checked Sol's pack and tightened a few ropes. "Time to go. With good luck, we will be back in four weeks. If we do not have enough cattle by then, we will stay a little longer."

Except for the company, Ma would have kissed all of us; instead she waved and said, "You be careful, *all three of you.*"

Pa grinned and tipped his hat. "Make yourself at home, Parson and Mrs. Engle." To the girls, he said, "Goodbye, my ladies."

The young dogs were closed up in the corncrib and set up a howl when we started out of the yard with Dan and Snap. "Stay with Mary and Martha, Dap," I called.

We rode out and I was so excited I forgot to wave before we were out of sight. We spent the first night on the west side of the James River across from where Salt Creek comes in. Pa chose a spot in the trees up above the river on the slope of a hill. The sunset was longer on the west side and as it got darker, we noticed bats flying around us. Their chirping got louder and louder and we followed the sound until we could see where millions of them were shooting straight up out of the ground. "Bat cave," Pa explained. It took more than half an hour for the flow of bats to slow.

"Let's go see that hole," Noah said and we crept over and peeked into the cave.

"Cain't see nothin' but blacker black," I said.

The bats had dispersed to their hunting grounds and we spent the evening watching them dive around our fire catching moths and mosquitoes. As our fire died, they moved off to better hunting grounds.

"Better tie Snap up or she will probably head back home," I said. I had been watching her and she kept glancing back the way we had come.

"You can almost hear her thinking, 'After dark, I am heading home.'" Pa chuckled. I got a rope and tied her to a tree. Snap and Dan slept on the foot of our bedroll. There was a nip in the air when we got up. In the open places, the ground was covered with light frost. The bats must have been coming in for a long time, for there were just a few going into the cave at sunrise.

Chapter 6
Under the Blue Mountains

"Sol must be a little sore," Pa said. The mule fussed when we loaded the pack on him. We found a pass through the hills that lined the west side of the James River and rode around the northeast end of the Blue Mountains, a range running southwest along the southeast side of the Llano bottoms. We could see the river across the bottoms against another range of hills.

Late that evening, Pa rode up a narrow valley a ways and picked out a campsite. The valley turned out to be almost due east of Yates Crossing of the Llano River. "We're pretty well hidden here and this will be a good place to hold the cattle," he said.

By dark, we had set up a decent camp and cooked supper.

"First thing in the morning, we will check out the bottoms for signs of cattle," Pa explained as we rested before turning in. "I want to see what is here. We want to catch cows and calves and let the bulls be."

"With the calves in tow, most of the mamas will follow us along," I said.

"The trick will be keeping calves interested in going some place without mamas," Noah observed.

Pa agreed. "Mama will follow her young calf a ways, but not necessarily a long ways for older calves. We can get them up here by bringing the calf along, but we will have to drive the cows home and let the calves follow them."

I tied Snap and lay down. She settled behind my knees on top of the covers. The howl of a wolf echoed up the valley from far away. Dan growled low, but didn't move. Conversation lagged and it was warm with the dog lying against me . . .

I woke when Snap stood up and shook. The fire was already stoked and coffee getting hot. The clouds overhead were showing the red of sunrise. *Red sky at morning.*

Dan sat at Pa's elbow supervising the frying of bacon. "Ad, bring in your horse and saddle up," Pa called. Noah was leading Yost and Joker and I hurried to get Amigo. Breakfast was salt-cured pork and coffee and we were soon on our way down the valley. We could see cattle grazing and there were a lot of calves. When we rode into the open, those cows disappeared like magic. They were close to the foothills and disappeared into the brush with hardly a stir. In less than a minute, all we saw was little wisps of dust where they had to run a ways to their hiding places. There were lots of tracks in the bottoms. The cattle had worn several trails across to drinking places on the river, and the banks were pretty muddied up where they drank.

"Lots of calf tracks, Father," Noah observed.

"I see that," he replied, "but I do not see any cattle."

"They must be night grazers," I said.

"And we are going to have to be night catchers," Noah added.

I had a feeling our experience herding milch cows was going to be of little use here. Our roping skills hardly existed and wild cow experience among the three of us stood at zero. Pa must have been thinking the same thing. We rode into the brush and it was a long time before we saw hide or horn — and little of that. A disturbance in the brush caught our attention and we rode into a clearing to find a heifer standing over her calf trying to fend off six or eight coyotes. The calf lay bloodied and still. Dan and Snap caught the last coyote as he slinked into the brush and tore into him. When he ran into the brush, the two ran after him despite my calls. There was an uproar and both dogs scampered back into the open, tails tucked.

"Found an ambush in there, did you?" Noah asked.

Meantime, the cow turned to face this new threat and Pa studied the situation. "If we could get a couple of ropes on her, we could get to the calf and she would follow us." He rubbed his chin in thought. "Adam, that Amigo has been a cow horse, do you think you could get a loop over those horns?"

"I think so, Pa, what then?" Anyone could see that one rope was not gonna hold that cow. It would take two ropes and two horses to hold her.

Noah rode to one side and shook out a loop. "Try roping her, Ad."

This must be what suicide feels like. I shook out a loop and as Amigo trotted by threw it over the cow's head. Noah's rope missed and Amigo and I became her prime target. As the cow lowered her head to use her horns, Dan came out of nowhere and clamped down on her nose. The cow skidded to a stop and whirled as Snap nipped her heels. Amigo turned near the end of the rope and I looped it over the saddle horn just as it came taut. Noah threw his loop on the ground and when the cow danced her hind legs into it, jerked it closed. Without her hind legs, the cow fell and Amigo kept the rope taut. Pa was down and tied the cow's front legs. To my surprise, Amigo stepped forward and Pa loosened the noose some. He stepped over and examined the calf. "Does not seem too bad. They chewed an ear a little and bit off its tail. I can not tell if it has ever stood up."

Pa picked up the calf and tried to hand it to Noah, but Yost would have nothing of that. He brought the calf to me and Amigo stood still while I slipped behind the saddle and we laid the calf across it. Pa built a fire and branded the cow while she was down, then hoppled her front legs. He removed our ropes and hustled to his horse before the cow could get her feet under her. She tried to charge me and fell to her knees. I turned and rode into the brush and she followed as fast as she could.

We took a slow ride back to camp and when Pa and Noah lifted the calf down it wobbled to mama and nursed as the cow watched us. Dan and Snap circled at a safe distance. An occasional rustle in the brush told us the coyotes were still with us. "They smell the afterbirth and blood," Pa pointed to a bloody mass hanging from the heifer's rear. We kept the calf near and that kept the cow close, though you could tell she didn't like that idea at all. When the afterbirth finally fell, Pa had us pick it up with sticks and carry it 'way up the valley. It sounded like the biggest dogfight as the coyotes devoured the stinking mass.

"Ought t' shoot 'em all," I growled.

"One down, forty-nine t' go," Noah crowed.

"That's not a likely thing to happen." Pa was stirring up the fire and setting the coffee pot to work. "It's going to take a lot of people and them more skilled at handling wild cattle than us to gather any amount of stock. I think we should set our sights on maybe a half dozen head and be satisfied with that."

"They catch wild horses out here by building long wings that funnel the horses into a pen at the end. Maybe we could do something like that to catch cows," I said.

"Even if we catch them in a pen, we would still have to handle them, then keep them secure while we worked the others," Pa said. "The fact is that we do not have enough help." He shook his head, "I should have known."

"These cows go plunging into the brush any time they see danger. If we could make the brush so thick they couldn't go in and put a pen behind the first small opening, they would dive right in and we would have them," I persisted.

"We could handle one or two at a time, Father," Noah added.

Pa lit his pipe and thought a moment. "It might work, but we only brought hatchets when we need an axe for that job."

"You have to work with what you have." I quoted a saying Pa used all the time on us, and grinned at him.

Pa grinned. "My bread cast upon the waters has returned. If you two are up to it, we will try building a pen and one wing."

Noah cooked dinner while Pa and I honed the hatchets and after we ate, we rode down to survey the catching grounds.

"That clearing we found the cow in would make the start of a good corral," Pa said. "We can expand it and weave a brush wall around it, then build two walls out to the open land. If one wing works, we might want to build up the second one on the other side."

The clearing was about twenty yards inside the brush and we went to work clearing the brush around it and weaving it into a wall. We left the larger trees in the pen for shade. It was hard work and even with the cool weather, hot work. We closed the walls up by the middle of the third day.

"My blisters have blisters," Noah complained.

Pa was studying the path to the open bottoms. "Let us angle walls both directions from the gate and we will put a wing a ways to the north. We might add a wing on the south side if this works."

"Maybe we should just thin the brush between the wings so the cows will not get too suspicious," I suggested.

"The less brush chopping the better," Noah agreed.

By sundown we had made good progress on the two wings and by the end of the second day they were finished out to the bottoms. It took the rest of the week to build a wing we thought long enough to catch a cow. Pa declared a day of rest and we spent it around the camp and our captive cow. It was before daylight when we rode down to the trap the next day and as we approached, there was a stir in the mouth of the pen and a cow turned and ran through the gate.

Noah laughed. "Do we want to keep

dumb cows, Father, or should I turn her out?"

"We are catching cows so they will have calves; it does not matter how smart they are." Pa chuckled. "Maybe by being dumb, they'll get bred easier." I understood the broader application of that thought after I became more worldly-wise.

The snort of a bull down by the river alerted us to the other cattle, scattered over the bottoms, that hadn't seen us. We circled around to the river and scattering out, slowly rode toward the north wing. I was at the end of the wing to the north, and when a couple of cows flushed my way, had to ride hard to keep them from running around the end of the wing. They must have had some knowledge of the barrier. Noah was in the middle and kept them against the wall. When they got to the opening, Pa hazed them into it. Both dogs nipped at their heels as they fled from us.

We all crowded them into the pen and closed up the opening with poles and brush.

"We got three cows, a yearling, and a newborn," I called.

"Now comes the hard work," Pa said.

"How we going to do this?" Noah asked.

"Maybe they would lay down and hold their hooves together if you asked them."

The voice, speaking German, came from behind us and we whirled to see a figure still shadowed in the dark. A packhorse stood beside his horse and regarded us with interest.

"We tried that, but these cows do not know the language," Noah replied.

The man rode closer and we could see his teeth as he grinned. The rest of his face remained in the shadow of his sombrero. By the dress we could see he was a vaquero, probably through with work for the winter and headed for the settlements.

"We have discovered that we are ill-prepared for the capture and taming of these mav'ricks," Pa said. "We are woefully short of manpower and ability."

"What do you aim to do with those cows?" the man asked.

"We have a place over on Panther Creek and need to stock it," Pa answered. I could tell he was being cautious about this stranger. It was a necessary caution.

"I saw signs someone was around there last spring when I came out," the stranger said. "Figgered you were down toward the Llano between the bluffs."

"Yes, we are," Pa answered.

"Indians do not bother you?"

"Not much," Noah replied. "They found

out Mother and Father are good shots."

"Putting those two bucks in the trees tells them that, and it also tells them you have some regard for their dead." The man seemed to agree with our approach to the Indian situation.

"How would you tame these cows to drive?" Pa asked.

The man rode closer to the pen and peered over our wall. "Small corral for branding and taming. I think the best thing would be to let one critter out at a time, rope and hopple and brand her out here. When you get two done, neck them together and go for the rest. Keeping those calves close will keep mama close, too."

"We are not good ropers," Noah said, "reckon you could give us a lesson or two?"

"You figger out how to let one cow out at a time and I will shurely give it a try." It was getting lighter and we could see that the man was young, probably not more than eight or ten years older than me and Noah. His German was good enough, but he spoke with the idiom of the American language we had learned. Our "American" was far from the proper English language.

"My name is Rogers Bain and these are my sons, Noah and Adam."

"Two good Biblical names." The man

grinned. I wondered what this man would think if he knew about Eve and Mary and Martha.

"Folks mostly call me Sandy; the other names they use in refering to me are common and best left unsaid in polite company. Start a fire and get your iron hot, we'll try this." He rode off a ways, unloaded his pack, and tied his packhorse to a sapling while we built a fire.

"Well, let's see if we can get *one* cow out of that pen for you," Pa said. He lowered the gate poles and I rode into the corral. The cattle congregated on the far side of the pen and I rode Amigo around the wall toward them. They ran and we chased them around the circle. By the second circle, they were strung out good and Noah opened the gate when all but one cow had passed. I turned on her and she ducked out the gap, the smaller calf behind her.

I rode through the gate in time to see Sandy rope her front legs and bust her. The dust was still rising when he was off his horse and on the cow. Grabbing her tail, he pulled it up tight between her legs and sat on her hips. His horse kept the rope tight on the cow's front legs. "Iron," he called. Noah was already running to the cow with the branding iron. Pa notched her ear, put the hopples on her front legs, and shook off the lariat. It was over in a minute and Sandy released the cow and ran for his horse.

Bossy rose with a grunt an' beller, looking around for the culprits that attacked her. Seeing Pa still trotting to his horse, she charged, only to plow a furrow with her chin when her front feet wouldn't work. It only took another fall to convince her the effort wasn't worth the pain.

A bleat and beller drew our attention to the pen where the calf was standing and her mother on the other side was attempting to get to it. "Well, is not that the cat's meow? We got an open invitation for that cow to come out on her own," I said. I drove the calf off a ways and Noah opened the gate. Mama crept out and, getting her bearings, trotted toward her calf. Sandy's rope ran true and Noah had the cow down, tail tucked before she could get her breath. I had the iron and Pa notched her ear and applied the hopples.

"Do not burn that too deep, son," he warned.

"Hold that cow there," the vaquero called, and he rode up to the fire dragging the calf. While the iron reheated a little, Pa notched his ear and made a steer out of him.

"Save those oysters," Sandy called.

101

Pa gave him a puzzled look, but laid the "oysters" on a leaf under a bush.

We got all of those cows branded and hoppled by high noon in spite of our fumbling around. The last cow had a crumpled horn that she had kept rubbed shiny and we named her Tinhorn. Sandy had two more "oysters."

Noah was grinning. "Bet I know what he's goin' t' do with 'em."

I fed more wood on our fire and rode to the river with the coffee pot. Pa was pretty bloody and came down with Sandy to wash.

"Don't scoop up a minner, Ad, they make the coffee taste fishy." Sandy grinned. He was washing the cojones. At the fire, he skewered them on a green stick and set them to roasting on the fire. Pa eyed the proceedings with doubt.

"Best meat in the country," Sandy declared.

We shared our meager lunch with him and he gave each of us an oyster. Pa still doubted and Noah hesitated. Mine was hot but it did smell good and I took a small bite. "It's good." I took another bite and rolled it around until it was cool enough to chew. Noah was watching me and ventured a small bite. "I like that, lets go get some more."

"Not today, Noah, we have to get these back to camp," Pa said.

It was an education to us what a competent roper and trained horse could accomplish with the cattle. I'm sure we would have spent several days getting this much done. And it would have taken a lot of luck to get it done without someone getting hurt. I could tell that Amigo knew a lot about handling cattle, but none of us were good enough ropers to use him efficiently.

After we had driven the cattle to camp and eaten supper, Pa spoke to Sandy, "We could surely use your help catching more cattle, but I do not have anything to pay you."

Sandy eyed the toothpick he was carving and said, "I been thinkin' on that myself an' there might be a way we can work out a deal without cash money. I got too much o' that a-ready. Maybe we could catch cows on shares."

"That's a possibility," Pa said. "What do you propose?"

"I was thinkin' about, say, I get every third cow, calf-by-side, and found."

Pa thought a minute, just to be polite. "That seems to be a lot since the three of us will be doing most of the hard labor. What about every fourth cow?"

There was another polite pause, though I could tell Sandy was favorably disposed to the proposition. "Every fourth cow and her calf if she has one — with found — and we got a deal."

It was a full minute before Pa nodded and said, "That sounds fair." They shook hands and we got ready for bed.

Sandy Sanderson told us a lot about ranching in west Texas and how they lived out there. He talked a lot about the Indians and Mexicans and why the Indians stole cattle and horses. "There is a high demand for cattle in New Mexico Territory what with needing to stock the rangeland, feed soldiers and Injuns on th' reservations. And there ain't a better source than th' Texas ranges.

"Th' Kioway-Comanches have a treaty with the Mexicans and Pueblos an' you won't see those tribes attacking or robbing them. It was just natural that they would team up agin their common enemy, Texians. 'Fore long they hit on a scheme where th' Injuns'd raid down into Texas and steal cattle and horses and drive them to the Llano Estacado where Mexican-American comancheros would meet them to trade guns, ammunition, Taos Lightning, and trinkets for stock."

"They do a lot o' killin' an' scalpin' an' stealin' *people,* too," I said.

"Yeah, an'those comancheros do a lot of slave tradin'," Noah added.

"Believe it or not, killin' Texians an' stealin' women and children are secondary goals. Young bucks expecting to establish themselves as warriors make raids simply to kill, destroy, and steal anything that strikes their fancy, including women and children, but the main object of the older warriors is t' trade cattle for guns and powder.

"Sometimes the comancheros would show up at an Injun camp and call for the number of cattle and horses needed to complete a trade. Then the Injuns would steal the required stock. More than once, Mexican-American comancheros have been seen in those raids."

"Don't seem like th' ranchers and army would want stolen stock," I said.

"Truth is, them New Mexico ranchers and cattle traders don't see no Texas stock brands," Sandy said. "Them that do, don't even bother to rebrand the stolen cattle they buy."

"No wonder these American Texians hate New Mexicans as much as the Injuns," Noah said.

Sandy nodded. "An' don't think it's only

th' Mexicans that participate in the coman-chero trade. Damnyankee merchants and ranchers provide goods and money for th' trade. Even U.S. Army soldiers finance them.

"The Goodnight-Loving Trail has proved a boon to the Indians. All they have t' do now is wait 'til the herds are anywhere near th' Pecos River, then take 'em. While part of the party gathers horses and cattle, another group goes after Texian scalps."

I thought about it all a moment or two. "I guess German Texians have gotten thrown into th' same bucket as American Texians."

"Fer better or worse," Sandy agreed.

Several things became obvious to us as time went by; first, we were never going to get fifty or even thirty head of cattle in the time we allotted ourselves; second, we didn't have enough rope for hopples for half that count; and probably the biggest thing was that the free cattle got very wary of the trap.

We weathered one little storm, but the lateness of the season made us all nervous. Even the animals seemed more restless. The captured cattle grazed the valley down and it was getting harder to keep them close, even with their hopples. Every night, we kept the horses within a rope corral we slept in, hoping that any prowlers would happen into the rope and warn us. The day we caught only one cow, we decided to quit and start the drive home. Twenty head wasn't half what we planned on getting, but more than half of them had a calf. We made it so all of Sandy's cows had calves or would drop one sooner or later. Still, five head seemed small pay for what he had done for us.

It would have taken forever for us to drive the cattle with the hopples on, not to mention the damage they would cause the cattle. Our only alternative was to neck them together in pairs, and that was a struggle in itself. The result was amusing and satisfactory for driving them.

"This is going to be a slow drive and once we start, we can't stop until we get home," Pa said.

Instead of going down into the Llano bottoms, we drove the cattle east over the divide into the James River bottoms. It was easy enough herding them in the open country, but crossing the river was tricky. We had to find a wading crossing and give the cattle time to drink; then keeping them together in the woods on the east side of the river was nigh impossible. Man and horse were already tired and the hassle of herding pairs of wild cattle through the woods and brush only wore on us more.

By the time we got to the open prairie above the James breaks, it was pitch-black. We closed the herd up close and used the clack of horns to keep track of the pairs should they happen to get out of sight. The half-moon was welcome when it rose and Salt Creek was dry when we crossed it near sunup. We had one more stretch of woods after crossing Bain Creek, then we were between the bluffs of Bain and Panther Creeks.

All four girls were out in front of the house when we passed and there was a lot of waving. Ma and Eve disappeared into the house while we were still in sight. It was a sure thing there would be food on the table when we got back there.

One by one, we loosed the cattle and kept them ahead of us down the divide to well within our range. They were thirsty and very tired. After drinking and grabbing a few bites of grass, they lay down to chew cuds and rest.

Noah was counting on his fingers: "Thirty . . . forty . . . forty-two hours without sleep or stopping, Ad. My butt's so tired it's numb an' my brain's not far b'hind it."

"I drove a herd eighty miles without water or stoppin' with Charlie Goodnight when we broke in the Goodnight-Loving Trail. We still argue about how many hours that took with only stopping long enough t' switch from an exhausted horse to a tired one and not a wink of sleep out of the saddle," Sandy said.

We were walking back up the divide to the house and leading our horses. It also served to keep us awake until we got home. "I'm gonna eat half a cow for dinner, then sleep for two days," I declared.

Our last chore was to unload the horses, then feed and rub them dry. They were so tired, only Sol and Sandy's packhorse rolled in the dust. They all ate a little, then stood or lay down to rest and nap.

"One thing's for sure, we need more than one mount t' catch any more of those wild ones," I said.

I don't remember much about that meal, only that I ate a lot and woke up some time later rolled up in a blanket by the fireplace. It was dark and I had no idea what time it was — or what *day* it was for that matter. The lid dropping on the new Dutch oven was the next thing that woke me and I sat up. Ma was cooking and whatever it was smelled real good.

Eve kicked my feet. "Get up, Rip Van Winkle, you're gonna sleep your life away an' you're in our way."

I stomped my boots on and threw my blanket on Ma's bed. The sound of voices outside told me Pa and Sandy were up. I stepped out and wished I had kept my blanket on. It was dark and really cold. The wind was blowing out of the north and the clouds were low. It felt wet. Even on the south side of the house, it was blowing strong.

"Storm's coming, Ad; we got home just in time," Pa said. "We got the stock in the barn and the cattle are in shelter down by Panther. All you need to do is get Noah up for breakfast."

I ducked back into the house. "Where's Noah?"

"Still in bed, I imagine," Ma answered. "Go get him up for breakfast."

"Yes, ma'am."

There was no sign of any human occupation, only a lump in our bed, but Noah grunted when I shook it. "Time to get up, Noah, supper's on."

"Supper? What time is it?" The lump sat up and flailed until Noah's head emerged.

"How would I know, I don't even know what *day* it is. How come I had t' sleep on th' floor?"

"Sandy got your place. Is he still here?" Noah scratched his tousled head.

"Him an' Pa are outside watchin' th' storm."

"Storm? What's happenin'?"

" 'Bout a foot o' snow's all."

Noah groaned and lay back down.

"Come on, Ma's fixin' t' call supper." I scrambled down the ladder and got pounced by two girls and about a hundred puppies. We wrestled and rolled around on the floor.

"I swear, Adam, all you can do is get underfoot," Ma complained, but I saw her smile.

"It's not my fault, Mother, these girls sicked their dogs on me."

"Those dogs should be outside," Eve scolded.

"Too cold," Mary retorted.

"Iss, too cold, Eve," came the usual echo.

"Mary, call down Noah. Martha, call your Father to breakfast," Ma ordered. The puppies scattered in confusion about who to follow. Martha held the door open wide and we could see a few flakes of snow blowing by.

Noah missed the last rung of the ladder and stumbled. "Did not mean to sleep all day, Mother. Sorry."

Ma wasn't paying attention to what he said. "It is all right, Noah, you and Ad wash up."

Eve glanced at me and I shook my head. "Feller stays up forty-two hours straight chasing wild cows ought to get to sleep all day," I said.

She turned away to hide her grin. When she turned back to us, she whispered to Noah, "So now, you're going to stay up all night?"

I offered him a solution: "You can stay down here and pretend to sleep on the floor and I'll sleep in the bed."

"O-Oh no —"

"Are you still sleepy?" Eve asked.

"I-I guess not."

"Then Ad ought to get to *sleep* in the bed and you can sit by the fire and whittle and keep it going," Eve commanded.

The biscuits and sausage gravy were hot and the coffee steaming. Ma even set the molasses jug on the table. It was getting low by its heft and that was another reason for a trip to Fredericksburg in the near future. We needed seed for spring along with a long list of things Ma was keeping. The big worry was how to find the money to pay for the provisions.

Noah and I planned to trap through the

winter and that would be a cash crop. The cattle would be another small source of income, but they would have to be a lot tamer to ever be driven to market.

The clouds kept Noah from seeing the sun and determining what time of day it was. When it didn't get dark, he knew it was breakfast he ate and not supper. He vowed revenge. Sandy left that morning for his folks' home near San Antonio. He spent the night with us in the spring when he returned to the ranch.

Spring, 1869

We decided to trap a couple of miles up the river on two or three creeks there and did pretty good through the winter. When the animals started shedding their winter coats, we determined to pick up our traps and quit. Two days later when we ran the lines, we had two 'coons and the remains of a possum that had been trapped and then partially eaten by coyotes.

"Leave that trap alone and we'll set traps around it and catch a coyote or two," Noah instructed.

"They're shedding a lot, Noah, you sure you want the pelts?" I asked.

"Even if we can't use the pelts, we'll be rid of a nuisance or two."

"All right," I said, "you can run 'em, I'm tired of comin' up here." But I couldn't let him go by himself and we made one last trip to the traps.

We had already seen signs that the Indians had come around and several nights the dogs had raised a ruckus. Pa, Noah, and I began taking turns sleeping in the barn with the horses. I was there the night of Monday, March 8, when the dogs raised a ruckus. Dan and Snap were in the barn with me because Dap insisted on sleeping at the foot of the ladder while the two little ones slept in the loft.

It felt good to have Pa's bird gun with me. We had loaded one barrel with bird shot, and the second barrel had a load of rock salt. Close enough, the bird shot could be deadly and farther away, it would repel any advances. The rock salt could do about the same thing except the results would hurt a lot longer under the skin.

The horses were restless and Dan and Snap ran to the back door growling and barking. The young pups were outside and raising a big fuss when the strangest thing happened. Every dog shut up in an instant and my two dogs whined and ran to me. The stock stood perfectly still, ears erect and listening. I couldn't even hear them breathing. The hair on the back of my neck stood up and I cocked both barrels, taking care to keep it pointed away from any creature, for it had hair triggers.

There wasn't a sound outside and peeking through the cracks, I could detect no movement around either door. As I watched the house, two shadows came around the corner to the back door. When I heard them working on the door latch, I aimed through a knothole and fired the rock salt barrel. The shadows ran. I reloaded.

Pa fired his pistol from the front door of the house and I heard Ma's Long Tom boom.

"Adam, are you hurt, Adam?" Eve was calling from the loft.

I growled, "No." I durn well didn't need a conversation at the moment. All was quiet for several minutes and I couldn't hear a sound. The animals were still in a state of fear or something like that. It was strange the horses didn't move and the dogs stayed either side of me, touching my legs. No one made a sound.

There was a rustle in the thatch overhead and I watched as stars appeared. A figure rose and dropped through the hole. I shot him as he fell and he hit the ground in a heap. Another shadow dropped through the hole to the floor and I fired again. The horses were going crazy and I couldn't see a thing through the bodies and dust they raised. Dan and Snap had disappeared. Why were they so cowed?

Someone loomed at me from the right and I grasped the gun barrels and swung. It struck with a satisfying thud and the stock broke off. Something hit my head and a thousand lights exploded behind my eyes. That was the last thing I remembered of that night.

Meanwhile, Eve had troubles of her own: The little girls huddled in the bed listening to the fight while I pulled my dress on over my nightgown.

"Someone's up there." Mary pointed to the roof and they heard hammering and wood splintering.

"Run to the ladder," I whispered and herded the two to the ladder. I was helping Martha down when someone grabbed me from behind and shoved me through the hole in the roof where someone else shoved me off the roof.

I turned my ankle when I landed and got the breath knocked out of me. I leaned up against the house trying to catch my breath. Pa's repeater was firing in the house and I prayed he got the ones that came through the roof. The one that shoved me off the roof landed beside me. He jerked me up and shoved me down the hill toward Panther Creek. I heard the barn doors slam open and the horses came out in a run.

"Over here, Adam, I'm over here," I screamed. The stock rushed by me, someone riding King. I tried to catch his leg as he passed, thinking it was Adam, and the rider quirted me across the face and shoulder. It wasn't Adam.

Near the creek, other figures caught and calmed the horses and I saw that someone was draped over Joker, hands tied to feet under his belly. "Adam," I cried and limped to him; but it wasn't Ad, it was an Indian. Blood dripped from his face and hair. He groaned softly when I raised his head.

"Here I am, Eve," Adam whispered from where he sat on Amigo. He rode to me and I scrambled up behind him. His hands were tied together and by the way he rode, I could tell his feet were tied together under the horse.

"Hold on and kick Amigo for me," he whispered and we made a run for it. There was a cry behind us and I kicked Amigo harder. We leaned low and ran up the divide. In a moment, we could hear a horse galloping up behind us.

Chapter 7
Captured and Adopted

"King!" Adam spat. "King's in the race." I could just see the horse's shadow as he gained on us and the slap of a quirt told me he had a rider.

"Duck," Ad hissed and we hugged the horse as close as we could — and none too soon, for he ran under the trees, limbs slapping at us and scraping down my back. I heard a grunt behind us and in a moment, King caught up with us, riderless. "Can you catch him?" Adam asked as we slowed to a walk after we had put some distance between us and the Indian.

"Here, King," I called and he came up close enough for me to grab his halter rope. We stopped and I hopped to the ground.

"Can you untie me?" Adam asked. He slurred his words and I knew he was hurt. The leather thong around his wrists was tight and had cut off circulation to his hands. I found the knot and wrestled with it as fast as my shaking hands would let me. Finally, it came free and Ad pulled it off with his teeth while I fought the bindings around his feet. He was finally free and when I looked, his chin was on his chest and he tottered precariously. I shook his arm, "Adam, what now?" He flinched at my call and slurred, "Got to . . . run . . . go west to James Riv . . ." His head slumped and he fell over on Amigo's neck. I retied his feet under the horse and scrambled up on King's back.

With Amigo's halter rope in my hand, I led him up the divide. The James River; where was it? It had to be west of us and when I thought we had gone far enough, I turned right. We rode that direction until King stopped on the bluff above Bain Creek ten feet below. We had turned too soon and had to follow the bluff until it petered out and we could continue west — I hoped it was west. We climbed up from the creek and over a hill down into another bottom that had a dry streambed. *The James?* I wondered, and just as I was about to ask, Adam mumbled, "Salt Creek, Ev," and heeled Amigo across and up the opposite bank. Light was chasing away the dark and at the top of the hill, I could see a dark streak in the valley below us. *Let it be the James River,*

I prayed. When the horses stopped at the water's edge to drink, Adam sat up and studied the area.

"Down there . . . a cave." He pointed down the river. We rode in that direction and he sank back down. The stream was low, but still flowing. About a half mile down the river, we came to a rock shelter in the bluff across the stream and I crossed to it. If this was Ad's cave, it wasn't much, but I guessed it would have to do. Adam told me later that the shelter wasn't the cave he meant, but it was just as well, I would never have entered a hole full of bats. The fear of capture wasn't that great.

I tied the horses under the brush in front of the bluff. I untied Ad's feet and tried to waken him. "You can get down, now, Ad, come on." He would only moan a little.

"Come on down, I need to bandage your head." I pulled him and he fell on me. We fell in a heap, Adam's head cradled in my arms.

There was a gash in his head and the top of his right ear was missing. Both places had reopened and he was bleeding again. I struggled out from under him and turned his head so I could see his wounds. Both were seeping blood and all I could do was part his hair along the gash and pinch it together. The severed top of his ear was matted into his hair and I threw it away. I tore strips from my nightgown and wrapped his wounds as best I could. It seemed to stop the bleeding.

He mumbled something I couldn't understand and I saw that his lips and face were caked with dried blood. The water was cold when I dipped another strip of gown in it. As I washed his face, he licked the moisture and I realized he was thirsty. There was nothing to carry water in but my cupped hands and that soaked rag. Adam swallowed as the water trickled into his mouth. It took three trips to the river to slake his thirst.

The back of the shelter was bare dry sand and I had to find some way to get Adam there. I tried and tried to waken him, but he wouldn't stir. It scared me. Was he dead or dying? He was still breathing and all I could do was sit by him and cry.

Both horses grew restless and I knew they wanted to feed, but I couldn't let them go free. I gave them a couple of armloads of dried grass and let them drink all the water they wanted.

The sun set early under the bluff and it was getting cool. All we had for cover was dried leaves and I spent some time gathering them and piling them over Adam. It was nearly full dark when I quit and crawled under the leaves against him. Maybe I could help keep him warm. With my back against his side, I laid my head on my arm and drifted off to sleep, sounds of gunshots and splintering wood, little girls crying, drifting through my mind. Sometime in the night, I awoke with my arm asleep and my shoulder aching. I had to move.

Ad was on his side. *He moved; he's not dead!* I thought, and I felt his bandages to see if they were still in place. They were and didn't feel wet, so he wasn't bleeding. He groped for my hand and held it tightly. Pinning my arm under his, he gripped my hand and we slept.

I awoke with the startling knowledge something was nosing through the leaves. As quietly as I could, I moved the leaves aside until I could peek out. All I could see was gray fur as the animal nosed toward Ad's head. The animal whined and I whispered, "Dap, is that you?"

The wolf-dog's head popped up. His tail almost wagged and I sat up. "It is; it's Dap, Adam." I swept the leaves from Adam's face and Dap licked his nose and whined. He also had a bloody ear and there was blood from a cut on his shoulder. Adam scratched the big head between his ears and the dog lay down beside him. My thoughts ran to Mary and Martha. *If Dap is here, it must mean that the girls are safe — or beyond hope,* I thought with disquieting alarm.

"Eve, I'm hungry." Adam's voice was gravelly, but he didn't slur so much.

"Me too," I replied, "I'll go hunting."

"Thirsty," he whispered as if to himself.

"I'll get you a drink." I hurried off to the river.

The water was cold and Adam drank eagerly. When he was satisfied, I returned to the river to drink and wash Adam's blood off as best I could. As I sat up, there was a splash at the riffle above the next pool and I saw a fin above the water. As quietly as possible, I waded behind the fish and pounced on him, trapping him under my skirt. He made a great struggle, but my own urgent hunger drove me and I got him up the bank far from the water before I let him go. He must have weighed a couple of pounds or more. His mouth was large and angled downward from his head; by that, I knew he must be a bottom-feeder. His scales were large and rough; but beyond that, I didn't know what kind he was. All I knew was that he was food.

It was lucky in a way that Adam had been in the barn, for he was dressed and had flint and steel and his folding knife in his pocket. I finally got a fire going in a trench left by a rotting tree root. While it burned down to coals, I cleaned the fish. He was awful boney. Dap found the entrails and after eating them lay down and gnawed on the head while half of the fish broiled over the fire. When it was done, I peeled the skin off and threw it to Dap.

"Dinner's ready, Adam, open up." I fed him a bite and took a bite for myself until the meat was gone. The meat had lots of fine bones and a musty taste like muddy water. I got most of the bones, but we ate some too. When we were done, I got water for Ad and cooked the other half of the fish. When done, I wrapped it in green leaves and moss.

We couldn't afford the luxury of a fire for fear of drawing attention, so I filled the trench with small sticks and laid a flat rock over the fire. The sticks would go to charcoal and burn good when we needed the fire again.

There was a prickly pear nearby and I peeled the skin and needles off a pad and laid it against Ad's wounds to draw out any infection. I wondered about the rest of the family, if they were still alive and where they might be. I prayed they were safe. Still, it didn't feel like it was safe for us to return. Besides that, Ad was too sick to be moved.

Blood had run from Adam's head down Amigo's shoulder and dried. In the afternoon when Ad was sleeping and Dap was guarding him, I took Amigo to the river and washed the blood off. He seemed to enjoy the washing and attention. I had never before seen a horse shake himself like a wet dog would. When he was tied to the tree again, I gathered a big bait of hay for both horses. King was quite restless and I thought he was wanting free. "Can't do that, King, we are going to need you soon," I told him.

That dappled wolf was restless also and sniffed the air often, a silent snarl on his lips. I warmed the fish on the hot rock and we ate. Darkness was welcome and I covered us with leaves, and we slept with Dap on guard. He was a good watchdog, much more so than his littermates. Late in the night, I heard him growl and move away.

Something was shuffling softly through our pile of leaves. It rooted within a foot of our heads. *An animal would have smelled the blood and rooted until it found us,* I thought. A breeze sifted through the leaves and I caught a faint odor. Indians! Gradually, the shuffling moved away and it was an hour or so before Dap returned. Neither of us slept the rest of the night. I dozed off as the sky lightened and when I awoke, Dap was gone. It made me sit up in alarm and I heard a grunt behind me. Sitting there wrapped in blankets leaning against the rock wall were six or eight Indians.

Two arose and quickly tied my wrists and hoppled me like a horse. One of them stumbled over Adam and exclaimed, "Ai-i-e-e." The others laughed as the startled one flipped leaves away and revealed Adam. He tried to rise and couldn't, falling back with a groan. One of the men kicked Ad in the ribs and said something I could not understand. When he prepared to kick again, I lunged at him, forgetting my bonds, and fell across Ad into the man.

"Leave him alone." I shoved him away and lay over my brother to protect him. Rough hands jerked me up and the man I had shoved slapped me hard across the face. The words he said were just gibberish to me. Blood dripped from my nose.

The man aimed another kick at Ad and to my surprise, Ad dodged, caught the foot, twisted it sharply, and shoved the man hard enough that he fell. "*You* leave my sister alone," he growled at the man. The men sitting against the wall laughed and nodded. One, who must have been the leader, said something sharp to the captors and they grudgingly pulled Adam to his feet and tied his hands and feet like mine.

Another gruff order from the leader and the men shoved us to the wall and made us sit. They turned to the firepit and tipped the rock away. More sticks were added, and they began to prepare a meal with a pot of coffee and meat they roasted on sticks.

"These aren't Comanches or Kioways, Eve," Ad said low.

"If they aren't," I said, "who are they?"

These Indians were smaller than the Comanches, their dress quite different. They wore knee high leggin's or moccasins and the usual breechcloth. But instead of wrapping a blanket around their bare shoulders, they wore long-tailed shirts tied at the waist by a belt or holster and ammunition belt. Their black hair touched their shoulders, for the most part, and they wore colorful headbands or turbans. Even the younger men were tanned and wizened. It was obvious the older men were teaching the younger ones about raids and scouts.

"Must be Lipans," Adam guessed.

Even that didn't quite fit these men and we studied them more. One of the older men rose and stood before us. He spoke in two languages, neither one of which we understood, though the second was obviously Spanish. I replied in German and American to no avail. The man shrugged and spoke to a young cook who came to us and asked, "You speak Tejano, you Texians?"

"No!" Ad said vehemently, "We *Germans.*" To admit to any Indian we were Texians was a death sentence at our age. Younger children were treated differently.

"Ah-h-h-h, Ger-*mans,*" an old man exclaimed. The other old men nodded, satisfied. The young man was disappointed. This possibly meant there would be no torture on this trip. I fervently hoped so.

The meat done, the men shared a cup of coffee and ate their shares of meat. "They won't feed us," Adam whispered, "We'll have to fend for ourselves."

"How?" I asked.

"Probably by tightening our belts and going hungry."

Adam's prediction was correct; we were ignored while the men ate. They lounged around the fire, talking in low tones. Presently, they arose and prepared to leave. Two men retrieved Amigo and King and, as if by afterthought, one came to us and prodded us up with a stick. He indicated by gesture that we were to follow the horses. Our hopples prevented us from taking large steps and the guard prodded us along with his stick, but it was no use. We couldn't keep up. At a curt order from one of the elders, our guard removed the hopples. We were better able to keep pace, though Adam had to struggle. He seemed dizzy and disoriented, sometimes muttering to himself.

We came into a small clearing where their horses were being held by two young boys, and all mounted. The senior elder chose King and had quite a struggle to mount the frightened horse. We were prodded to a nag with one eye, obviously quite old, and told to mount. I got up behind Adam and the Indians tied our feet under the horse's belly over his objections. His lead rope was handed to a man already mounted and we were pulled into line. At the river, men and horses drank, but no one offered us any water.

"Don't ask," Adam demanded. He quietly heeled the horse deeper into the water, and I allowed as much of my skirt that could reach to get soaked. As we rode west, we sucked the moisture from the cloth. No one paid attention to us until the nag began to lag in spite of our guard's merciless beating. When the poor horse could go no further, we were put on two fresh horses and the nag was left to his own devices.

It was noon when we reached the Llano River at present day Yates Crossing. There was a camp across the river with several more Indians there, including women. I let my skirts soak again and Adam was able to submerge his boots as we crossed over.

There was a lot of excitement at the sight of us and we were examined closely. At the curt demand of the leader, the women returned to their chores and we were left alone. We sat as far under a bush as we could get and sucked moisture from the clothes. Ad took off his boots, being careful not to spill the water, and we both drank what little was there.

"From now on, keep your feet cleaner," I demanded, and Ad chuckled. He put the boots back on and dug his knife and steel from the sand to deposit them back in his boot.

A woman approached and dragged me out from under the bush by my hopples. Chattering angrily, she untied my hands and shoved me toward the fire where she made me turn the spit. She made sure I understood that there would be dire circumstances if the meat burned. The creature cooking seemed to be either lamb or goat. It smelled wonderful. The meat was fatty and dripped tallow constantly. I caught some when it dripped and, in spite of the burning, licked my hand clean.

There was a lot of traffic around the coffee pot and one of the tin cups rolled off the rock. I picked it up and set it in the coals under the dripping fat. When it was near full, I hid the cup under my skirts and filled another cup in its place. Nobody questioned my activity, probably thinking I was acting according to instructions.

The men began gathering to be fed and I hid the cooler cup of fat in my bodice. It burned a little. Two women came and, shoving me aside, lifted the spit from its cradles. Another woman grabbed the cup of fat. In the bustle of activity, I stole away to our refuge under the bush.

Adam was asleep so I drank half of the hot fat before waking him. He eagerly drank and we both cleaned the cup with our fingers. Presently, a woman threw a bunch of bones at our feet and we made ourselves content to brush sand away and gnaw them. Adam crushed two of the bigger leg bones and we dug marrow out with sticks and ate.

I wouldn't say that the Indians ate; it was more like they gorged themselves. It wasn't long before the squaw came scolding after me, and I scrambled out from under the brush before she could grab my hopples and set my scalded ankles bleeding again. There was another critter on the spit to turn. Though this one was not as fat, I was still able to gather more drippings and a pinch or two of meat. It became the pattern of our lives on the trail, and for a while in the camps, that Adam and I had to scrounge and steal what little we got to eat.

Adam slept a lot, whether on the horse or on the ground. His wounds were healing, but the blow to his head must have affected his mind. He seemed disoriented and dizzy and his vision was diminished. It was fortunate for him that the Indians traveled at a leisurely pace, seemingly unafraid of pursuit. He improved gradually.

Both of us were small for our age and that was fortunate. Even so, one night I was dragged from our sleeping place by a young buck and it was clear what his intentions were. It was one time I was glad I wore those hopples. He was turning me over on my face when I heard a thump and my attacker slumped to the ground. Adam dropped a fist-sized rock and helped me up. The Indian lay there completely naked except for his moccasins. His breechcloth was lying where he had discarded it, and Adam wrapped it around his face, tying it with his belt. He helped me back to our ragged blankets and went back to sleep without saying a word. I lay awake the rest of the night terrified that the Indian would awake and attack again.

The camp began to stir and the old squaw came chattering and scolding for me. I sat up about the time she saw the body of the young man. "Ai-i-i-e-e!" she screamed, and there were calls from the other women and much chatter. They came running and gathered around the man, whispering. He groaned and sat up, fumbling with the cloth on his face. Some of the women giggled and his eyes flew wide when he saw his circle of witnesses. Covering his nakedness, he stumbled off, the relative whiteness of his bare rear seeming to glow in the morning light.

The women laughed and chattered, and my tormentor pulled me to my feet. She lifted my gown and examined my legs and crotch. My bloomers were still in place and she shook her head, indicating that I had not been molested. More laughter. More chatter to me, though I understood not a word. Someone said something and the group took up the phrase in a sort of chant. In order for me to understand, several of the women lifted their skirts, revealing bare bottoms, squatting, and then making the motions of flipping sand into their crotches.

This must be the way they avoided unwanted sex or rape. I smiled and nodded my understanding.

A gruff call from the fire brought them back to the work at hand and we all hurried off to our morning chores. All this time, Adam had not stirred. I doubt that anyone suspected it was he who had knocked the Indian down. They knew he was hurt, and from their attitudes, I think they thought he was crazy and they avoided him. His blazing red hair fascinated them, and this fascination, I suspect, was what led them to keep him instead of setting him free. My hair was an auburn color and not as much a wonder to the Indians.

I feared we had made an enemy, but we didn't see my attacker after that and learned later that he and a friend had ridden off together and made their way back to the tribe on their own. It seemed that the woman who supervised my work had adopted me and she kept urging me to stay with her, but I refused, choosing to stay and care for Adam. His recovery was slow, most likely due to the lack of nourishment and constant moving from place to place. He pretended he was sicker than he really was so we could stay together and look for a chance to escape.

King hated Indians and gave them a lot of trouble. They mounted from the wrong side and they smelled bad to him. Several times he threw his rider until the man quit riding him. King was never allowed to run free with the other horses because the Indians knew he was a racehorse and could be the source of much wealth for the tribe.

One day he was giving much trouble and the man handling him began whipping him mercilessly. When he could stand it no longer, Adam rode over and pushed between the man and King. The horse recognized him and calmed immediately. Adam took his lead rope and rode away, King following quietly.

That was the moment the chief took Adam into his family and we stayed together no more. I was taken in tow by my adopted "mother." From then on both of us enjoyed more freedom. Still, it was very obvious we were watched every moment, and with us separated, any opportunity to escape became much more remote.

I was soon immersed in the daily work of the household, learning the things expected of a woman of the tribe. My adoptive mother, Rosita, a Mexican-Apache, was for the most part kind and patient except when her husband was present. We spent many hours together and, in the process, learned each other's language. The Apache language was well infused with Spanish words and phrases, and in later years I learned that I had gained a fair knowledge of that language. She treated her husband, Two Bears, like a king and he demanded it. I learned to despise him.

Adam seemed to take to his new family quite readily. His "parents" were Elkhorn and Little Bird. Elkhorn spent much of his time teaching Adam, and it wasn't long before he had shed his pants for a breechcloth. He tied his shirt with a belt and wore a headband and high-topped moccasins. His Indian name was Rojo Pelo, which is Spanish for Red Hair.

When Rosita heard his name, she turned to me and said, "Castaño Rojizo," which is the Spanish name for Auburn.

"Ah-h-h-h," the other women said, and nodded. Around the camp, we were called Rojo and Rojizo. It pleased me that we were given similar names. To me, it was a recognition of our kinship.

ADAM RETURNS

I don't think I could have survived without Eve's nursing. Even with her help, I suffered a lot. Years later, a doctor told me that the blow had bruised my brain and the best treatment known was complete bed rest. The back of a horse was far from that. I can only credit my youth, God's grace, and Eve's care for my survival. Even after many years, the slightest bump on my head will trigger a terrible headache.

Even though I was taken into Elkhorn's family, my trials were not over. I still had to fend for myself for food and endure the abuse of Little Bird and her mother, Wounded Deer. Wounded Deer was my main antagonist, usually preceding her orders with a sharp rap with the cane she carried. She had some kind of leg injury that caused her to limp and she used the cane to aid her walking, though I came to believe its primary use was to beat on me — and any dog that got within reach. The dogs learned to keep their distance, but I could not. Elkhorn observed my treatment, but did not interfere.

I was allowed the run of the camp when we were not traveling, but every night my hands and feet were tied and I was made to sleep outside the tipi, tethered to a post or tree. Whenever Wounded Deer tied me, she made the rope on my legs so tight it cut the circulation to my feet. She delighted in waking me the next morning and beating me while I tried to hobble on benumbed feet.

Her primary job was to abuse me while I did chores that were her responsibility. There were only two young boys near my age in the group herding the horses and they would laugh and poke fun at me for doing women's work. I got my fill of her abuse one day while hauling in a particularly large load of wood and enduring frequent blows from that cane. Dropping the wood, I turned in time to catch the cane before it struck and wrench it out of the woman's hand. I took her by the arm and pushed her to the pile of wood.

"Pick up," I demanded in her language. She started to protest loudly, and I struck her across the shoulders — rather sharper than I had intended.

"Pick up." When she started to protest, I caned her again. "Pick up." I was so mad I hardly noticed her difficulty in bending and picking up the sticks. As she was rising with her load, I struck her soundly on the bottom. "Go," I ordered in her language. And we proceeded to the tipi. Little Bird saw us coming and hurried to meet us, scolding me in words I could not yet understand. She made to take her mother's load and I warned her off with the raised cane. Wounded Deer limped on and deposited the wood beside the fire. I broke the cane over my knee and threw it in the fire. "Go," I said to the woman and she turned and limped away. I almost felt sorry for her.

Little Bird grabbed up a large stick and advanced on me. I stood my ground and when she swung the stick, I caught it and wrenched it out of her grasp. My conscience was returning as my anger played out, and I took the stick to Wounded Deer, motioning that she should use it for her cane.

Now it was my turn to wonder what I was to do. Elkhorn had watched the goings-on from where he was making arrows, without interfering. There might have been a small glint in his eye as he motioned me over. Showing me how he was rubbing bois d'arc shoots in a grooved rock to make them perfectly straight and round, he gave me the job while he shaped steel heads from a scrap of wagon-wheel iron. The rest of the afternoon was spent making arrows and learning the tribe's language.

The next day, he took me to a bois d'arc thicket and showed me which limbs would be suitable for making a bow. We cut two limbs and on the way out of the thicket, I found a dried limb on the ground that I thought might serve my needs. Back at camp, Elkhorn showed me how to begin the process of making a good bow. As he worked on one of the limbs, I was to imitate his work on the other. We worked the rest of the day on the bows, with the man instructing and reproving with a sharp word or a rap on the knuckles when I erred.

The next few nights were spent working on the dried limb I had picked up. Soon, I had a rough cane with a handle. I smoothed it and tapered it down to the end, then fire-hardened it. I made a stain by boiling walnut hulls and soaked the cane in it until it was good and dark. A lot of polishing brought out a sheen that was pleasing. It made the cane look like it was very old. When it was ready to my satisfaction, I gave it to Wounded Deer as a peace offering. She was very pleased with it and laughed when I signed that she was not to ever hit me with it.

One night, a scout came and reported to the elders. It was decided that the camp would move the next morning, and we spent several days traveling, generally northwestward. The hills receded behind us and the land became gently rolling or very flat. Occasional mountains with flat tops arose out of the plains. Each hill seemed to have a name and Elkhorn gave them to me as we passed. I made it my business to remember the things he told me, for some day I would be returning this way. The land became progressively dryer, trees thinning until there were none, just grass and cactus.

Elkhorn explained to me that they were Mescalero Apaches from the Mescalero Apache Indian Reservation at White Mountain in New Mexico Territory. The tribe had found that they could continue their traditional culture and lifestyle on the reservation with little or no interference from the Anglos. With one or two exceptions, their agents had no interest in their charges. As long as they gave no great trouble, they let the Indians come and go as they pleased while the agent plundered the government supplies meant for the welfare of the tribe.

Chapter 8
A Waterless Passage

Summer, 1869

The day I rebelled against the women was the day I entered into training to become an Apache warrior, though I didn't recognize it at the time. Elkhorn began teaching me to make arrows and bows and training me as he would have trained his son. I had much to learn.

The women were packed and ready when the horses were driven into camp. Elkhorn pointed out the horse he would ride and motioned for me to catch him. It proved troublesome, for Indian ponies are just as shy of Anglos as Anglo horses are of Indians. I finally caught him and led him, reluctant and white-eyed, to Elkhorn. He then pointed out the horses the women needed, and I caught them. When I would have caught the horse I normally rode, the Indian stopped me, signed for me to follow, and then rode off with the other men, leaving the women to load and follow. I trotted along beside Elkhorn's horse, dodging bushes, cactus, and rattlesnakes. If I lagged too far behind, one of the following warriors would give me incentive with his quirt to catch up. My legs were numb, my lungs burned, and my shoes fell apart. By the midafternoon stop, I was exhausted. Little Bird gave me some jerky and a little water and Elkhorn sent me to the horse herd to get my horse.

We rode well into the night before we came to the Mustang Water Holes and stopped. I couldn't eat the little jerky I was allowed until I drank, and I couldn't drink until after the horses were watered. I wrapped in my blanket and was asleep before I finished my jerky. Wounded Deer's sharp toe roused me to another day just like the day before.

That night we made a dry camp in a range of sand hills, and as we rested, the setting sun reflected off something bright atop a dune. I walked up to the object and found a half-buried bottle. It had been leaning against a board of some kind and after a few minutes of digging, I realized with a start that I was standing in a buried wagon bed. I studied the ground with renewed interest and beheld relics of household

144

furniture and wagon parts. A wheel protruded from the sand and every hump of sand I dug in held relics of what was surely a wagon and its scattered contents. A wagon tailgate protruded from the sand a dozen steps west of that wagon, and I discovered it was attached to another wagon bed buried in the sand. Even the smallest lump in the sand cast a long shadow in the setting sun, revealing the resting places of at least a half dozen wagons. It is likely there were more hidden in the sand.

I wandered back to camp in the dark. Rolled up in my ragged blanket and nestled into the warm sand, I dreamed of a wagon train under attack by Indians. Another dream revealed wagons mired in the deep sand, animals and men exhausted and waterless, succumbing in their thirst. The thought that I had found no bones made my dreams think that the wagons had been abandoned and the people had left to find water. No other possibility came to my subconscious mind and I slept until Wounded Deer punched me with her cane.

There never was an explanation of what happened to that wagon train and years later there was no sign of it when we searched the sands.

The third day was different. It seemed that

preparations to depart were more carefully attended to, and the women filled bladders with water for the first time. The horses were driven to the water three times before we left. If anything, this land was hotter and drier than any we had come through. Hardly anything grew but stunted cholla and withered prickly pear. Elkhorn had me ride and catch King and keep him with me.

We had seen an occasional dead cow or horse, mostly bones, sometimes with hardened hide still clinging to them. As we progressed, the bodies became more numerous until one was hardly out of sight of a carcass before another one was passed. Twice I saw human bones, one a shriveled mummy with scraps of cloth clinging here and there. Farther along, we passed a skull, staring with open sockets. A hundred yards further along lay the headless body, bones scattered about and a pack rat's nest in the body's rib cage. Little was said in the crowd, each realizing that they could be the next set of bones scattered and bleaching in the sun.

It was good that my feet were toughened up from going barefoot most of my life, but that last day of running barefoot was really hard on them. I rode along with one foot across my knee and dug cactus spines out with my knife. The callous on one big toe was split away from the quick and I wrapped it tightly with a rag from my shirt.

"Aren't you gonna run again today?" I jumped at Eve's voice and realized I had been dozing. King was nuzzling her and getting his ears scratched.

"No, I guess they decided that if they couldn't run me to death, they would have to try something else," I replied.

She was on a nag of a horse, being led by the woman she served, her wrists tied. I eased over and we rode together in spite of her mistress's objections.

"Are you eating well?" I asked. When no one was paying attention, I reached over and cut the thong holding her hands.

She smiled. "They give me a little along, but when I cook, I can steal more; how about you?"

"Pretty slim pickin's, but I get along."

"Where are we going, Adam?" Her face clouded and her worry showed.

"I don't know, Sister. I hope it isn't anywhere near here."

"Do you think we could get away from them?"

"Not out in this desert. We need to stay with these people if we want to live."

"I want to go home, Adam."

I nodded. I couldn't tell her that on the whole, I liked these people in spite of my ill treatment. Elkhorn seemed to take a real interest in me, and he took the time to teach me things. It was more than I had gotten from Pa; he was always too busy. I noticed bruises on Eve's arms and one bare shoulder.

"Eve, if you fight back, that woman will quit beating you. Her old man probably won't interfere and if he does, I'll interfere with him."

"Why would I fight back? She would only beat me more."

"You have to show her that you won't take it anymore and she will stop," I said.

"I don't know —"

"It's the difference between being a slave and being a part of the family. If you don't show some spunk, they won't want to have you; then everyone will mistreat you until you're dead. You have to show you are *somebody.*"

"It's like they're testing me?"

"Yes, they want to know what you are made of. If you add up, they'll take you in."

"I don't want to live with them."

"No, but you want to *live* — and be more comfortable and fit to escape. Just assert yourself; you wouldn't let Ma or even Pa mistreat you, don't let these people." I chuckled. "Now, that old woman's gonna know I put you up to it."

"Most of the time, she's nice to me . . ."

"You don't have to embarrass her, just let her know you aren't going to take any more beatin's."

We rode along without talking a long time.

"All right, Ad, I'll try it." Eve grinned at me, and I felt a lot better. It was nice to *speak* with someone for a change. Living among people you couldn't talk to got pretty burdensome after a while. We didn't talk much after that. It was too hot and dry. The sun felt like a load pushing down on our shoulders and back. A mirage appeared far ahead of us and we saw a man riding a horse. They looked to be a hundred feet tall. He stayed ahead of us nearly to midday, then faded away.

When the sun was at its zenith, we turned southwest. "Why did we turn, Ad?" Eve's voice was hoarse, hardly above a whisper.

"Maybe to get the sun out of our eyes? I don't know."

Midafternoon, we stopped for a while and I found my family sitting under the shade of the horses, eating. Wounded Deer tossed me a strip of jerky. She poured a scant cup of water and gave it to me, motioning that I should drink it all down. I chewed the meat without much desire for it. Soon we were on our way again, walking into the sunset and beyond. Wild China Pond was dry, only a mudhole to indicate its location. There was no stop that night and the sunrise replaced the chill of a desert night with oppressive heat.

We plodded on, only stopping once to drink a little water. I washed my horse's mouth out and wiped dust from his eyes. King got the same treatment, but didn't seem as affected by the heat and travel. His Arab bloodline served him well in this desert.

I wondered how Eve was getting along and dropped back to see her. She slumped over the horse and when I spoke and cut her wrist bindings again, she only shook her head and said, "He gives us no water."

I looked sharply at Rosita and was surprised that she didn't seem any better than Eve. The water bladders were not on her pack where they should have been. I found them hanging from Two Bears's saddle and they held more water than any other water bags in the group. Two Bears and his horse had been watered.

I studied the situation a moment and approached Two Bears, acting friendly. He eyed me with suspicion and I stayed just out of his reach, talking to him in German as if he knew what I was saying. When I finished talking, I dropped back by Eve. Both women were suffering more than the rest of us. Two Bears's chin dropped to his chest.

"Eve, get Rosita to go talk to him on the far side." When she understood, the woman rode up to Two Bears and they had a conversation that soon became heated.

"Hold my horse, Eve," I said and dropped to the ground. I approached the man from behind, knife in hand, and when he leaned over to strike his wife, I cut the straps holding the water bag on my side of the horse. The shift in weight caused the saddle to slip and Two Bears almost lost his seat. While he fought to keep from falling, I grabbed his lance and backed off. Rosita had dropped back beside Eve and, as they passed, I gave the wife the water. A whelp was already rising on her face and her nose bled.

I barely had time to turn when the man rode his horse into me and I fell. Two Bears turned to ride over me and I rolled away, bringing the lance up and causing him to veer off.

Suddenly Elkhorn was between us and

several of the other men surrounded me. There was no escaping. The men dismounted and the lance was ripped from my hands. Other hands grabbed me and forced me to the ground. Two Bears had to be restrained from attacking me and he was forced to back away.

There was much talk for a moment and Elkhorn called for quiet. The men then sat in a semicircle around me and the whole group gathered behind them. I was satisfied to see that Rosita and Eve were sharing a drink. At least I wouldn't die for nothing.

There followed a long discussion of the event and recitation of tribal law that would govern in this matter. It seemed that they had come to a conclusion, and it was obvious I had lost the case. Just as Elkhorn was about to rise with the elders' judgment, one of the women called out, *"Hermana."*

Another voice called, *"Hermana Gemelo."* "Hermano" is Spanish for sister and "gemelo" means twin. In the Indian world, the birth of twins rarely occurs; both babies surviving infancy is an even more remote occurrence. The Apache people are aware that twins have a special bond attributed to spiritual gifts.

One of the customs of the tribe is that only a parent or sibling can interfere in the relationship between husband and wife, which gave me the right to intervene in my sister's behalf. The fact that she was my "gemelo" made that right even stronger.

Elkhorn relaxed and there was more discussion. In a few moments, a consensus was reached and the council adjourned to resume their trek. Two Bears motioned to his wife and she removed the second water bag from his horse and tied both to her saddle. She and Eve looked much better and I suspected they had taken their full allotment of water all at once. Neither man nor wife seemed to take notice that Eve's hands were not tied.

Elkhorn motioned to me to follow and when I started to mount, he called a sharp "No." It had been ordained that I was to be punished, not for doing wrong, but for doing the right thing the wrong way. I walked all afternoon leading both horses. I cut a prickly pear pad, peeled it, and sucked on it, but it gave little comfort and no moisture.

Just before total darkness, Elkhorn motioned for me to tie Little Bird's rein to his horse's tail, Wounded Deer's horse to Little Bird's, and my rein to her horse's tail. Motioning for me to mount up, he continued our march. I could tell that other groups were also tied together. In our present condition, to stray would be a fatal mistake.

We plodded on all night, man and beast suffering from the lack of water. My tongue began to swell, and I spit out the pebble I had been sucking on. There wasn't room for it anymore. Moonrise made visibility better, and watching our progress, I could see that we were strung out too much. People were delayed when a horse failed and they had to change mounts. The spare horses and their drivers were not visible in the dust and distance.

Just before sunrise, we stopped and Little Bird gave us the last of the water. I couldn't swallow mine and just held it in my mouth until it was gone. The last half of my cup I gave to my horse. It was going to be his job to carry me and to find water.

A tall mesa arose far ahead and we were headed directly for it. "Wieck-pah," Elkhorn said. Of course, I didn't know it was a Comanche word that meant "gap-water." A couple of miles from the foothills, the animals perked up and picked up their shuffling pace.

We were approaching from the northeast, and near the foot of the mesa, rounded a point of the mountain where we found a side cañon that was full of green trees and bushes. The animals crowded into the brush and found water. It was stagnant, the spring that fed it having dried. The water was fit only for the horses to drink. They weren't allowed to drink their fill, and were driven away to the south around the base of the mountain. I watched the mountainside, hoping to see another patch of green that might offer water fit to drink.

The little foothills opened and we came to a dry wash that seemed to run straight into the mountain. A gap through the mountain appeared, its brooding cliffs rising hundreds of feet on either side. The cañon had cut the mountain in two. The smaller mountain on the right was called Castle Mountain by the Americans, and King Mountain was on the left. A passable road led through the cañon, which sometimes narrowed until only the streambed could squeeze through. There were burned wagons in places, reminders of these troubled times. One very old wagon wheel still mounted on its axle held a withered arm and hand tied to the rim.

The lesser slopes of Castle Mountain were covered with boulders, some as big as barns. Above that, the bluff rose vertically at least a hundred feet. King Mountain rose more steeply from the stream and the slopes were not so rocky. About a third of the way up was a bench likely a hundred feet wide or more. At the back of the bench, the solid rock cliff rose above an overhanging shelf several feet thick that ran most of the length of the bench. Under the overhang were several caves and shallower shelters. From that overhang, the cliff rose three hundred feet to the mesa top.

It was a fantastic place and I hardly noticed the horses picking up their pace. The gap opened up onto the plain, flat and sere as far as the eye could see. The most beautiful thing I saw that day was a spring that flowed out of the foot of Castle Mountain and into a large, hollowed cedar log. It was cool and clear water and I couldn't wait to get to it.

Elkhorn sat on his horse watching the surrounding hillsides. He made no attempt to get water, and I realized this was an ideal place for an ambush. Instead of quenching my thirst, I sat with Elkhorn and kept watch as the others drank and watered their horses. The sharp rap of that dang cane on my leg announced the presence of Wounded Deer and she poked a cup of water at me. I could only hold little sips in my mouth and let it trickle past my tongue. Wounded Deer

led my horse and King to the trough and
they drank.

Chapter 9
Horsehead Crossing

The trail through Wieck-pah and further west past Horsehead Crossing was called the Comanche Trail, and that made our captors nervous, for the two tribes were not friendly. Nevertheless, our horses were not in shape to travel and the group chose to stay there a day or two and recoup. There was a rock house and a rock corral that we camped in. Water bags were filled and carefully stored, everything done in preparation for flight or fight. That night, the horses were driven into the corral with us, and guards posted on the walls. There was no comfort in thinking about what would happen if that herd stampeded inside the corral.

The night was uneventful and I was glad to leave the confines of that corral and drink my fill at the trough. Eve came out for a pot of water and we talked while she filled it and hurried back to the gate. "They aren't tying me up, Ad."

"Why should they, you aren't going anywhere," I replied.

"What is this place?" she asked nodding toward the house.

"Best I can figger is it must have been a stage stop." She hurried through the gate and I was left to my own devices. The house was empty save for a pack rat's nest in the fireplace. Around behind the house were lean-to stalls where the replacement horses were kept, and a dilapidated old wagon was parked under the shed, its tongue missing. There was a wrecked stagecoach pushed into a gully. The faded name above the gaping door was Butterfield S . . .

North of the spring was a prairie dog town on the flats. It was full of dogs, and the rattlesnakes living with them convinced me to keep my distance. The rest of the day I spent with Elkhorn and the women working on my bow and learning their language. It was good not to get too far from the water.

Our second night cooped up in that corral with those horses was our last night there, the men being nervous about staying longer and the possibility of encountering the Comanche/Kioway warriors.

As we rode, again southwest, Elkhorn taught me words. He leaned forward and held his horse's head with both hands, saying a word I took to mean horse's head, then he crossed his fingers. The third time he signed, he added "Pecos," and I understood what he was trying to say — Horsehead Crossing of the Pecos River.

Our wild cow catching partner, Sandy, had told us about the crossing and the river, about the many horse carcasses around the crossing. "Me and a friend picked up a bunch of those skulls one day and lined them up cheek by jowl along the bank. That line of skulls ran for a hundred feet an' if we hadn't tired of th' game could have been a hundred *yards* long.

"I've counted thirteen graves there, all except one th' result of gunfights. People that know the crossing say that when a bad man dies, he gets th' choice of goin' t' hell or th' Pecos country. So far, no one has chosen th' Pecos."

I was anxious to see this river and crossing, but as far as we could see, the land was flat, not any sign of a river valley. Elkhorn indicated that it was most of a day's ride to the river. The grass was higher here, and knowing there was water at the end of the day, the horses were allowed time to graze as we moved along. I could tell by their behavior that the horses sensed water, but still, there was no sign of the river. I had allowed my horse to stray from the bunch in his grazing, and he apparently decided it was time for a drink and struck out due west. Less than a hundred yards away we came upon the high vertical banks of that river. The water was brown and murky and flowed with a good current. The rest of the band was at the river crossing and we turned downriver to join them. While my horse drank, I knelt and dipped up water with my cupped hands. It tasted muddy and slick and I remembered that Sandy had called it "Alkie, don't drink too much at a time and you will get along good enough. Best to let it settle in a jug some before you drink; makes terrible coffee."

People had been watching for my reaction and I disappointed them. Elkhorn gave me a slight nod of approval.

"Horses'll die if they drink too much at a time," Sandy had said, so I pulled my horse away from the water and led him back to the grass. "Drinkin' it will make you scour, but you can git by 'til better water comes along." Already my stomach was rolling just from what little I had swallowed.

We moved up the river a ways and camped without fire or water worth drinking. The camp was restless with people moving about all night. It was wise to watch where you stepped in the surrounding bushes — when there was light enough to see. I filled the jar I had found in the sands and let the water settle all night. A full one fourth of the bottom was filled with mud. The top water didn't taste so muddy, but it was still slimy. After watering the horses again at the crossing, we moved up the east side of the river. There was more grass on this side for some reason.

As we rode I realized why we had come so far south to the river. There were very few places to safely get down to the river and Horsehead was the closest access to water when coming from the east.

No valley, the river has no valley! Riding across that flat plain, one came suddenly upon the river, a ditch with tall vertical banks and with water so thick and muddy you had the idea you could walk on it. I never saw a river so crooked. In places there were loops where at the neck there weren't ten yards separating the streambeds, yet some of these loops held fifty to a hundred acres inside the circling stream. A man could travel ten miles along the river only to gain a few yards on his north to south path.

The second morning after we had eaten,

Wounded Deer pointed to her horses a couple hundred yards upstream and sent me after them. I walked toward the horses until I came to the riverbank. *How did they get across the river?* I wondered. Wounded Deer called and waved her arms impatiently; I was well acquainted with the Indian word for "go on and hurry about it."

There was nothing to do but to swim the river, so I stripped to my breechcloth and jumped in. The water was surprisingly deep and cold and the far bank steep and slick. It took me a while to climb and I was covered with mud and dirt when I rolled out on top. I lay there catching my breath while Wounded Deer stood on the far bank yelling her "Go on and hurry" and throwing rocks at me.

I got up slowly, just to show her that I wasn't afraid of her rock throwing. Another rock arched across the river and I caught it and hurled it back at her. "You missed, try again," I yelled, even though I knew she wouldn't understand. The rock came close enough that she dodged and I turned to the horses. A cut across my path appeared and I suddenly realized that it was the river again and that *I* was the one on the wrong side of the river. Those horses had been on the east side all along and that woman had known it.

Retrieving those horses now became secondary to spoiling that old woman's fun. Instead of going straight toward the horses, I turned left and followed the river to the western bend of the next curve. A little clump of bushes hid me for a moment, and it was here I jumped into the river. The bank I had to climb was just as steep as any other, but there were roots exposed that I could climb without getting as dirty. It didn't take the horses long after seeing me rise up out of the grass to decide it was time for them to go to camp. They slow-walked ahead of me, snatching a mouthful of grass now and again, and showing their disdain for my urgings. "You're just like that old woman, mean as a snake," I gritted and smacked the laggard horse's rump with a rock. It hit with a pleasing thump and laggard became leader. I was sure he was telling Wounded Deer what I had done when I got to camp.

The old woman came chattering to me while I dressed, and by motions and drawing the river in the sand, she showed that there were two river crossings between camp and the horses. I pretended not to understand for a moment, then as if I caught on, I shook my head and erased one loop of her drawing, which made the horses on the west side of the river. I indicated that I had ridden one horse across the river and that the water was only hock deep and I had swum the river only once.

Wounded Deer paused and considered, *No, that couldn't be.* She shook her head and redrew her picture, signaling with her fingers: two crossings.

No, I shook my head, *one* crossing. She knew I was lying and it was making her mad. Two! Her extended fingers became a fist shaking in my face.

I smiled.

She stomped off muttering. Elkhorn and Little Bird were smiling.

Much of the travel urgency of the last few days was gone and our trip up the river was almost leisurely. The usable crossings of that river were few and trails from several directions converged on them, not only for crossing, but these crossings were also the only places man and beast could reach the water to drink. The next crossing we came to was called the Salt Crossing; not because it is salty, but because this is where the Salt Trail crossed the river to the salt flats around a large lake. (*Called Juan Cordona Lake today. Ed.*)

Eve and I were given the run of the camp since no sane person would attempt to escape into this waterless land, and tracking down any escapee would be an easy task with very unpleasant consequences. Nevertheless, we were under constant observation.

We were walking together a couple mornings after Salt Crossing when Eve pointed to a dark object in the sand, "What's that, Ad?"

The object seemed familiar and strangely out of place and I kicked up the withered remains of a man's boot. "It's a boot."

"What's it doing out here?"

I noticed that the Indians had moved away from the track and us. "The boot must have been owned by someone who died, from the way those people are acting." I dumped sand out of the boot and the bones and dried skin of a foot appeared.

"Ai-e-e-e, a foot, Ad, throw that thing down," Eve exclaimed.

That deed was a thing of the past before she had finished talking. "I don't see any other sign of a body, do you, Sis?"

Eve scanned the area and shook her head. "Don't see anything, an' don't want to neither."

I scooped out a shallow hole in the sand and kicked the boot into it. "Likely, this is the second buryin' of this foot," I said.

"An' likely not the last, in this blowing sand," Eve replied.

Catching up with the camp, we found the grave of the boot's owner by watching the Indians avoiding the spot.

"Who do you suppose that was and what happened to him?" Eve wondered.

"Any one of a hundred things, I imagine." I didn't have to mention that most of those things would not be at all pleasant.

That evening, I helped the herders steer the horses into one of those loops of the river and the rest set up camp in the narrow neck. We had passed up a loop that had some curious mounds in the narrow neck, and after what these people called a meal, I walked back to inspect the place. The mounds covered the burned out remains of a wagon. I could see the outline of the unburned doubletree and tongue under the sand. The fire had done a thorough job and not much more than the iron was left. These signs of previous travelers and their violent endings left me wondering. What would become of this country and these people, red *and* white? Their conflict was far from settled and no doubt would continue until its final solution. I couldn't help but think that there was still much bloodshed to come.

"Was this a wagon, Ad?" I hadn't seen Eve approach and she startled me.

"Yes," I said. "You can still see where the tongue is buried." I wandered around toward the back of the ruins. Sometimes useful things can be found in places such as these.

Nothing was left of the wheels except rims and partially burned hubs. Something in the water's edge caught my eye and I stepped over to see a wagon wheel half buried in the mud. A rope tied to it trailed off in the current. Right between my feet was a groove in the lip of the bank. It pointed straight to the nearest wagon wheel.

"Well, I'll be — Eve, come here," I called.

"What is it?" Her face betrayed fear that I had found another body.

I pointed to the groove in the bank, "You see this groove? It points straight to where that wheel burned. Now, look in the river."

"That's a wagon wheel," she exclaimed.

"Yeah, see the rope? Someone tied that wheel to the wagon and I'm guessing they hid by standing on it under the bank."

"It wouldn't do them any good if they were attacked in the daylight —"

"So they were attacked at night," I finished.

"The rope burned in two when the fire

got to that wheel and they fell into the river."

"Or they climbed up before the rope let go." I wanted Eve to see the positive side as well as the tragic.

"And if they didn't?" Eve questioned.

Actually, the way the wheel below was trampled into the mud, I could tell that whoever was standing on it had fallen with it, but I didn't want Eve to know that. "Then they could have floated down the river and climbed out somewhere else."

"You think so?" There was hope in her voice that my imaginings were true.

"Yep, I think so," I said and then turned her away. A noise at the wagon drew our attention to Elkhorn pulling a wheel rim from the sand. "Iron," he said and laid it on my shoulder to haul back to camp.*

*An explanation of the events surrounding the boot and the subsequent burned wagon can be found in author Patrick Dearen's novel, Dead Man's Boot. Ed.

Chapter 10
A Parting

Now in addition to King, I became custodian of that danged tire rim. It couldn't be packed in any fashion because of its shape and weight and I actually carried it tied to my saddle, banging my poor horse on shoulder and flank and dragging ground in high spots. That night I built up a hot fire and heated the rim white hot in three places and mashed it flat. That put it in a shape that could be carried on the packhorse — and that's where it went over the protests of the women. The extra weight proved taxing on the horse and from then on, that rim had its own packhorse.

River crossings became farther apart and we sometimes had two dry camps between them. The women refused to carry that river water in their water bags because it would ruin them, so we had dry camps and throats.

It was impossible to follow the twisting river and sometimes we were a mile or more from the stream. Elkhorn drew a map in the sand showing the river flowing south, then turning east. "We are here." He stuck his stick in the ground near the end of the eastern leg of the river where we were camped.

"We will go this way," he said, drawing a line straight from our present place to the upper end of the north-south leg of the river. "There is a lake here where we will have water." He drew an elongated circle about halfway along our proposed route. Leaving what was later called Emigrant Crossing, we struck out across country as much as ten miles from the river.

Soda Lake was dry when we got there. Around the edge of the lake were shallow wells dug through the hard crust, and there was water in them that the horses could drink. The best I could do was wet my throat with the stuff.

We were back to the river the next day and with a lot of work could get the stock down to the water at three places as we traveled. The camp began the fourth dry day with a lot of enthusiasm that gave Eve and I hints that better things were coming.

There was much chatter among the women when we came in sight of some red sandstone bluffs late in the afternoon. We arrived at them after dark and discovered that all the excitement among man and beast was a pool of the sweetest water ever imagined. It came from a freshwater spring and I was ready to build a hut and stay there a while.

We did stay three days at that campsite on the west side of the river, and there were no tears shed when we left the Pecos for the Delaware River. Little Bird pointed to the western mountains, "Sierra Guadalupe," and I saw the mountains that would become my home. It was then and there that I realized my captors were Apache — in this case Mescalero Apache, I later learned.

There was water in the Delaware River, and it was not near as alkie as that Pecos. The first few miles it flowed, then dried to pools that became less numerous as we climbed. Finally they were no more, but a hole dug just a few feet deep would fill with water. These wells were numerous in the upper stretches of the river. The lower riverbed was flat and wide and, in many places, had two separate streams. An occasional deep and steep-sided arroyo cut into the plain and opened into the stream. High up on the river another stream came in from the left, "Wild Horse Draw," Elkhorn called it.

We stayed with the Delaware right up to near its head, then cut across country uphill to a spring on the side of the mountains.

"Pine Spring," Elkhorn explained, as we watched the women set up camp not far from the spring.

Now our route swung north and east along the foothills. Two days later we turned northwest through the wide mouth of a cañon into the mountains. The cañon walls gradually crowded us into the streambed and we climbed a narrow trail that wound about and through a jungle of huge boulders and rocks. Sticks and limbs marked a high-water line above our heads. There would be no escape up those steep mountainsides if it flooded.

As usual, Elkhorn was in the lead of this single file parade, and as required, I was right behind him leading King. "What if it rains up there?" I asked.

"No clouds." Elkhorn pointed skyward with his nose.

"No clouds, we go; clouds, we no-go," I said.

Elkhorn did not reply.

High in the mountains, we came to a long narrow meadow on the left side of the wash and entered a small village of about a hundred people living in brush huts they called wickiups and tipis. While Elkhorn conferred with several men of the village, Little Bird and Wounded Deer hurried to the pole frame of a tipi and began spreading their buffalo hide cover over it. I moved to go help but a sharp word from Elkhorn stopped me. He intended for me to listen while the men discussed the trip and events that had gone on in the village in Elkhorn's absence. I could understand enough of their talk to get the gist of it. Nothing much had happened in the village; game was getting scarce; the women had harvested all the berries, nuts, and yucca nearby; water holes were drying. The village would have to move soon.

The men admired King and the rest of the stolen stock as the herd was driven in, and Elkhorn motioned that I was thrown in with King. The horse was more interesting.

The council came to the consensus that the village would move on the morrow, and Elkhorn and I moved on to the now-completed tipi, where he told the women of the plan. No mention was made of the destination of the move, and by that I assumed that the location had already been settled upon and everyone knew what it was — everyone except the two captives who would have been no wiser had they known.

Eve found me after we had eaten a much better meal than on the trails. "The village is moving tomorrow, Ad. Do you know where we're going?"

"Somewhere up there." I pointed up the wash that was little more than a very small brook. A spring fed it and flowed less than a couple hundred feet before sinking into the ground.

"Ad, Rosita says they are not a part of this village and they are going to take me away from here soon."

This was very disturbing news; Eve and I had grown up very close, and the last few weeks were the times when we had been most separated. "I will talk to Elkhorn; maybe he will buy you."

"I'm not a horse or dog to be bargained for," she stormed.

But with these people she was, and it would be a hard lesson for her to learn. I gently shook her shoulders. "Eve, you are no more valuable to them than a horse, right now. You *have* to show that you are more valuable than that or your life will be short and full of pain and sorrow. You *have* to do that even if we are separated for a time. I will find you eventually and somehow we will get out of this situation."

She leaned her head against my shoulder,

"Promise?"

"I swear on my life."

Rosita called and Eve hurried away to her chores. I sat by the tipi and thought — of short nights of rest between long days of work on the farm that never seemed to end; of our capture and flight across a country full of wonders and hardship. Elkhorn had taken me under his care and taught me more things than Pa ever had. His training was harsh but I saw the benefit of it in this harsh and unforgiving land, which gave very few second chances. By the time we reached the village, he had me toughened and trained so that I joined the other young men in their strict warrior training on a mostly equal footing.

The entire village was packed and moving up the valley when the sun found us. Gradually, the land flattened out at the foot of a tall peak with steep slopes. The trail squeezed between the mountain and a drop-off on a narrow rock shelf. Two thousand feet below us, the cliff tapered off into a steep rock-strewn hillside that sloped another two thousand feet to the bottom of the valley. There was no time to enjoy the view. I paid all my attention to where my horse and King stepped.

Turning away from the cliff, the trail

entered a large bowl-shaped valley, and midafternoon we rode into a large meadow where the women began setting up camp.

Eve found me picketing King and said, "The others are leaving in the morning and I will go with them if Elkhorn doesn't buy me."

I found Elkhorn sitting in front of his tipi. "Elkhorn, I have three horses of my own I would give Two Bears for my sister. He will not trade with me, but he would with you. Would you help us?"

"You would give all your horses for this girl, and walk?"

"She is my *Hermana Gemelo,* is not blood more valuable than riding horses?" I could tell Elkhorn was reluctant to talk to Two Bears, but he could tell that I was intent on trying to buy Eve. After several minutes, he said, "I will talk to Two Bears after we eat."

I nodded and returned to my chores.

After we ate, Elkhorn went to talk to Two Bears. He was gone only a few minutes and when he returned, he said, "Two Bears will take only one horse for the girl."

My heart sank. "Which one does he want?" I asked.

"King."

King wasn't mine to trade and Elkhorn would never trade the horse for another mouth to feed, no matter how helpful Eve was to his women. "I thank you for helping, Elkhorn." I turned away to hide my frustration.

Eve got angry enough to cry when she saw that Two Bears would not trade. Rosita was happy. The next morning the clan left before daylight. I rode with Eve a ways and then watched them climb the trail to Dark Cañon, their next camp.

The next days were very dark for me and I hardly remember them except for the sadness.

There was no discussion about what I was to become in the tribe. Elkhorn had adopted me as his son and all sons were to be warriors. So it was that I was thrown into the group of boys of the village to be trained as a warrior. The training was hard — sometimes harsh — and failure was not acceptable.

There were six of us, all about the same age, only I was the oldest. Tio was named after his Mexican mother. Paisano — The Roadrunner — was the swiftest runner. Sees In The Night had the best night vision of anyone I have ever known. When no others were around, we called him Owl. The bird was an ill omen to the tribe. One Who Saw The Star Fall had a name too long to use so we called him Beto. Wolf Pup was the hothead of the group and got himself — and us — into all kinds of trouble. They called me Rojo Pelo or just Rojo because of my red hair.

There was no formality or regularity in our training. We were left to our own devices most of the time; but when the opportunity came, one of the warriors took us in hand and taught us various things.

White Wolf taught us about the bow and arrow and good hunting skills. I was proud of my bow and the half dozen arrows I had made. One of the women had made me a quiver and I thought I was fully equipped.

"Where is your knife, Rojo?" Wolf asked one day as we were hunting. We had gone into the mountains for a few days and had to hunt for our food.

"I don't have one," I answered. He would have laughed at my pocketknife and I didn't want it generally known that I had it.

"How would you skin your kill without a knife?"

"The women skin my kills," I replied.

White Wolf smiled. "Do you have a woman in your quiver? Will she go with you on the hunt or warpath? It seems you need a knife or you wouldn't eat when you are away from your tipi."

Tio snickered and the others were smiling behind their hands. They all had knives that were well-worn cast-off butcher knives the traders called Green River knives. Most of them had lost their original shapes from multiple sharpenings. Beto's knife had fallen into the fire and the wood scales of the handle burned off. His mother discarded it because after burning it would not keep an edge. It still had the original shape.

"You cannot borrow a knife from the others," White Wolf said to me, "you must learn to live without a knife until you get one."

That gave me something to think about while I hunted. *I could use my pocketknife, but Wolf would most likely take it away if he saw it.* My only option was to make one of my arrowheads into a knife. We divided into pairs and went after our suppers. Wolf Pup and I hunted among the bushes and Pup killed a tough-meated jackrabbit. I got a cottontail rabbit. It would have better meat, but less of it.

"We can skin them here and you can use my knife," Wolf Pup said.

"No, I will play the game as White Wolf ruled. I can sharpen an arrowhead and use it for a knife," I replied.

Back at camp, I selected my longest steel arrowhead and sharpened one edge. It worked well enough, but the shaft was not strong and was clumsy to use. After we ate, I found a stick that would work for a handle, and when it was shaped to my liking, I removed the arrowhead from the shaft and drove it into the handle. I used the gut tie from the arrow to tie the knife handle to the blade. After a day or two curing, I cut the rabbit skin into shape and made a sheath.

"We've killed all the rabbits and ground squirrels around here," Beto declared one night. "We need to move to another spot."

"No, we will not move from this camp," White Wolf ruled when we asked him.

"Then we have to learn to eat grass and bark," Wolf Pup muttered.

"Would you become a Digger?" White Wolf asked.

There had been a people in the hills and desert who lived by digging roots and eating rats and other small animals when they could catch them.

"Their highest ambition was to steal the things they needed, and if they could, they would bash your head in with a rock and eat *you*," White Wolf added.

"Wolf Pup is too tough to eat," Owl declared.

The Diggers had long disappeared from

this region, but there were stories that they still lived in the deserts north and west of us. They still served as an example of laziness and general no-goodness among the people.

"We can either go naked and dig roots or kill bigger animals," I said.

"Tomorrow, I will kill us a deer," Sees In The Night vowed.

"An elk has more meat," Wolf Pup muttered, "kill one of them."

"Kill your own elk, Pup," Sees retorted.

"Any large animal caught will be shared with the whole camp," White Wolf said. "You have many things to learn about hunting and preparing large animals."

Six hungry campers slept fitfully that night, and well before daylight, I woke my partner for the day, Paisano, and we slipped away to our assigned area.

"I could have eaten the morning meal," Paisano complained.

"Mice or ants?" I asked.

"Huh!" he grunted.

Deer are night browsers and the best times to catch them is early morning or late evening when they go to water. It would be hard to find them after they had bedded down for the day. We went to a spring several miles from camp and were hidden well before sunup. Our vigil was in vain, for no animal appeared. Near noon, we went to the spring for a drink.

There, near the water, was the faintest paw impression of a large mountain lion. "Here is the reason no one came to drink," I said.

Paisano knelt and searched for more sign. "He went this way," he said, moving toward the thick brush.

"You don't suppose he is still near, do you?" I whispered.

That brought Paisano to a halt before the thick brush — a place that could easily hide a predator. "You think so?"

"I *don't* think I would go hunting for him in there. Most likely, he's lying out on some stout limb or atop a rock taking a nap or watching for dinner," I said.

"Well, I'm hunting for dinner too." Paisano eyed the brush, but still hesitated to go on.

"If no one drank last night or this morning, the spring will have a lot of business tonight. Let's hide again and see what happens."

"Let it be so, but I'm likely to kill the first thing that shows," he said.

Hunger and the warm afternoon soon had me drowsy and I napped until sunset. Our first customer, a porcupine, came grumbling in fear as the gloom deepened.

"Not him," I whispered.

"Porcupines only drink when there is no dew," Paisano reasoned, as if to himself.

Our next customer had a white stripe down her back and four little stripers toddling along behind. Paisano shook his head.

A parade of little people came to the water and still we waited. It was almost totally dark when the bushes stirred, and after what seemed an hour, a young buck with nubbin horns eased into the open. We hardly breathed as we drew our bows and waited as the deer cautiously approached the spring.

"Now," Paisano breathed and we both shot.

The deer whirled and bolted across the opening in front of us. "No you don't." Paisano leaped up and ran an intercept course. He grabbed the deer around the neck and jumped on his back. The animal struggled on and I caught up and tried to throw him down. A sharp hoof caught my leg and made a long cut down the back of my calf. The deer fell over on his side on top of Paisano, legs flailing and still trying to run. I heard the two arrows snap in two.

"Slit his throat, Rojo," Paisano gritted

through clenched teeth.

I jumped on top of the deer and slit his throat with my knife. Paisano grunted. "Hurry, I can't breathe."

The deer kept struggling and his throat didn't bleed much. My blade was too short. "Give me your knife."

"Only have . . . twohands . . . andIwon'tturn loose . . . ofthisdeer," he said.

The deer was flailing and both of us were getting cut up by those hooves. I tried to find Paisano's knife and only found the scabbard, the knife had fallen out in his struggles with the deer. Frantically, I felt around with one hand while holding the deer's horn to keep him from flailing with his head and beating on my partner.

"I can't find it, Paisano."

The deer jerked in a final convulsion and died. I got up, still holding that horn in case the animal was not dead.

"Roll him off me," Paisano demanded.

I pulled the carcass off, the two embedded arrow shafts scratching across Paisano's chest. "Ouch, Rojo, be careful."

"What's the matter?"

"Those arrows scratched me." He sat up and felt his chest, "I got blood all over."

"How much of it is yours?"

"Don't know, but we got us a deer."

"We sure did. Let's get him to camp before we're too weak to carry him."

Paisano laughed. "We could just cook him here and eat."

"You think they would notice if we went back with only a deer hide to show?"

"Likely; let's get going before that lion takes a liking to our meat."

Paisano cut a sapling pole while I slit the deer's legs and pushed one hoof between bone and tendon of the opposite leg. We put the pole between his bound legs front and back, tied his head up so it wouldn't drag, and shouldered our load. I led until we stopped to rest about halfway there, and Paisano led us to camp very late in the night. We stopped well short and Paisano gave the owl call. It was answered in a few moments and we carried the carcass the last fifty yards into camp. Beto appeared from the brush and pushed more sticks into the fire. "What have you there, Rojo?"

"A mountain of venison," Paisano said, rubbing his raw shoulder where the pole had ridden.

The others were rousing and coming to see the deer. White Wolf appeared from the path we had walked and said, "You were being followed."

I looked at Paisano and we said almost in

unison, "That lion!"

"He ran when I hissed at him, but he won't go far. We need to get this carcass safe for the night."

There was a rope dangling from a limb high on the fir tree we were camped under. We tied the hind legs of the carcass to it and hoisted it up so White Wolf could gut the animal, then we hoisted the carcass high in the tree and tied the rope off. I found my blanket and rolled up and slept until Paisano's yell woke me. Before I could move, something big and heavy pounced on me and leaped away into the brush, tearing my blanket.

"How are you, Paisano?"

"I am well, I think; something was sniffing and poking me."

"He jumped on me with all four feet and ran away," I said. "You must smell good with all that blood on you. Want us to hoist you up in the tree too?"

"No, Rojo, go to sleep."

"You don't have to be grumpy, and don't scare that critter on me if he comes back." He only grunted and I slept until sunrise.

Paisano sat up and everyone stared at him. Dried blood covered him from his chin to his legs — and some portion of it was his own. Beside his bed were lion tracks. When he had yelled, the lion jumped over him and landed on me. Only a few bent grasses indicated where he had gone.

After a big steak breakfast, White Wolf set our chores for the day and took Paisano to a pool he knew of to wash.

We spent the next two days working on that carcass under White Wolf's supervision. Each of us skinned a portion of the hide and found that my short blade was the best skinner. I decided to keep it like it was and get another larger knife also. We collected musk glands, pegged the hide down and scraped it, and cut jerky meat to dry. Best of all, we had venison aplenty. I wondered if the hams could be smoked like we did pork back home.

CHAPTER 11
THE SALT RUN

The perception that the Apache is a desert-dwelling race is not accurate. They are mountain dwellers who love the high mountains, with their forests and alpine meadows, their mountain game such as deer and elk, and the natural nuts and berries that grow there. They have learned to survive the hot, waterless deserts that intervene between the mountain ranges they inhabit, but they do not live there.

Now that we were not on the move, our training became more frequent and more intense. One Antler took us to the cliff overlooking the salt flats one evening, and while we sat on the slope behind the bench, showed us the landmarks spread out before us.

Flat Top Mountain was the north end of the Sierra Diablo that ran south from there. He told us where in those mountains we could find water and where we might graze our horses, where hidden places were that would offer safety.

Far down at the south end of the Diablos, we could just make out another range the white man had named the Baylor Mountains. One Antler told us where to find the only water available in those mountains. It was just a seep and would not sustain a long stay. In the desert halfway between the Baylors and the Apache Mountains to the east was a small pond that held water in the wet season. Sometimes when it was dry, you could get water by digging.

To our far left and reaching the base of the Guadalupes at Guadalupe Pass were the Delaware Mountains. One Antler spent some time relating the features of the Delawares, especially Wild Horse Draw.

When he was finished with his lesson, he asked each one of us questions about what he had talked about. If we misspoke or forgot some detail, he would throw sand in our eyes and then explain again the answer to his question. There were no bragging rights among us, for all of us blinked sand at one time or another. Patiently and with great care and detail, he taught us about the land spread before us. Our knowledge of the land would more than once mean the difference between life and death. This was indeed the land of no second chances.

Beto found us stalking marmots in the rocks one morning and called, "It's time for us to run."

Paisano grinned, "I will be your teacher."

"Paisano, I will show *you* how to run today," Wolf Pup said as we followed Beto.

Various men of the village undertook different portions of our training. Nava taught us to run long distances without rest or water. "Our camp is out of salt," Nava said as we gathered around him. "You have to get the salt bags from your mothers and run to the salt flats and get a bag full of salt and be back here by sunset tomorrow. Now go."

I ran to the tipi and found the salt bag lying by the fire. There was something in the bag and I looked at Wounded Deer. "Something to eat as you go," she said.

I grabbed the bag — it seemed awful big — and ran back to the center of the village. Owl shook his oversized bag at us, "We will have enough salt for a lifetime."

"They must be full," Nava warned, "or you will have to return to the flats."

"Which way?" I asked as we trotted toward the cliffs.

"The way we came is the shortest and easiest," Paisano called. He was already in the lead.

Tio trotted beside me. "The Pine Spring is about halfway to the salt flats, Rojo. The flats are below the sunset side of El Capitan."

I nodded and calculated in my head. It must be a good thirty miles to the spring, so sixty miles total one way. "We have to run a hundred twenty miles in two days, Tio. That is more than we have ever run." Tio had a puzzled expression but didn't say anything. Distance was never measured in increments, but in time.

"The run back will be with this big bag full of salt," Wolf Pup puffed.

"And mostly uphill," Beto added.

"We must plan our run carefully," Owl said.

"See how that Paisano is so far ahead," Wolf Pup growled. "Hush and run."

We spread out a little and ran on around that four-thousand-foot-high bench and on down the valley. It would be four thousand feet down and four thousand feet up on the return. "We have to make our best time on the downhill run and reserve extra time for climbing back up the mountains," I said. "There will be little sleep this night. Where's water?" I asked.

"Only Manzanita Spring after Pine

Spring," Owl replied.

Beto was running next to me, "Rojo, you are panting too much; fill your lungs and hold your breath a moment, then breathe again."

I tried his suggestion and to my surprise, my panting stopped and I was no longer dizzy. From then on, I would occasionally hold my breath with my lungs full and I got on better. That was the last we talked. After that, we concentrated on closing the gap with Paisano. Down we ran, reaching the mouth of the cañon midafternoon.

I walked the last fifty yards to the spring at our first camp. By the time I got there my breathing was normal and I took several swallows. "No more than three swallows," Nava had said. The others had passed me by. *This is a race for endurance, not about speed, so I will pace myself and be sure to finish — on time or not.* I could smell the campsite — ashes, offal, and horse manure and a half dozen other scents gave evidence of the earlier occupation by our group. Later, I learned to gauge the length of time a camp had been abandoned by the smells and age of the horse manure.

Past the ruins of the old stage station, we arrived at the pool at Manzanita Spring where we stopped to rest a moment.

"Is there water between here and the flats?" I asked.

"No, this is the last," Paisano said. Already, he was up and preparing to run.

"We have to run thirty miles without water, carrying a bag of salt half of that way," I said.

"What's a mile?" Wolf asked.

"About the distance from here to that point of rocks," I said. "We will run sixty miles from the camp to the salt."

"Then sixty miles *up* the mountain with that bag of salt," Tio said.

I opened my bag and dumped out the snack Wounded Deer had packed. "Hickory nuts!" I exclaimed, "That woman sent me hickory nuts." The others laughed. "My bag is new, so I am going to fill it with water."

"*All* our bags are new," Wolf snarled. "No one has ever had a salt bag this big."

We filled our bags and struck out after Paisano and Owl. I put my arms through the pull string loops and ran with the bag of water bouncing against my backside. The water dripping down my back felt good.

We rounded the point of El Capitan well up on the slope and saw the salt flats shimmering in the late afternoon sunlight. Down the hill we ran and out on the crusted salt.

"Here is a hole someone has dug," Paisano called.

We sat by the hole and drank our water, half of which had leaked out. There was a lot of water left when I was full and I washed my face and removed my moccasins and washed my feet. I turned my bag wet-side out and filled it with salt. It must have weighed ten pounds.

"We must run all night to get there on time," Owl said.

"Yes, Owl, you will have to lead us until the moon is high," Tio replied.

We helped each other put the bags on our backs and pad the drawstrings with our headbands.

"Now, my hair will be in my eyes," Beto complained.

"You won't be able to see much in the dark anyway." Wolf Pup grinned.

"Tie it up like a horse's tail," Paisano suggested.

It was easy to run across the flats, but we only trotted up the hill to the bench that ran around the point of the mountain.

"Run downhill, trot uphill," Tio quoted our running instructor.

"Gonna be mostly trotting up that mountain," I muttered. We ran along the bench and up to Pine Spring where we drank as much as was advisable. "Now, Owl, trot us along," I said.

Owl led and we followed single file, sometimes trotting, sometimes walking. We made Paisano bring up the rear, much to his frustration and our amusement.

"We put you last to know how that feels," Wolf Pup said. "Besides that, we'll always know you are with us by your eternal complaining." Paisano didn't laugh with us.

On we went, mile after mile with little downhill running and much uphill trotting and walking. The moon rose behind us and gave a good light to our path and we spread out again. Paisano ceased his complaints and again took the lead.

Sunrise found us at the old campsite. "How many of your miles do you think we have left?" Wolf Pup asked me.

"About twenty, I would guess. It would take us about half a day to get there."

"Plenty of time to rest," he proclaimed and lay down, his salt bag his pillow. We drank our fill and slept in spite of the hunger that gripped our stomachs.

Someone was kicking my foot and I awoke to see the sun shining straight down on us. With a start, I realized we had slept almost four hours. It would be a challenge to make those last twenty miles in time. *You got us in trouble again, Wolf Pup.*

Not a word was said. I got my salt loaded and grabbed a good drink before following the others up the hill. Now it was *run* uphill, across the bench and around the point past midafternoon. We could see the smokes of camp still a good three miles away.

"Gonna make it fine." Wolf grinned.

"No thanks to you," Tio said.

"Ah-h-h, but you slept just as well as I." Wolf couldn't be blamed too much.

Nava was not at his wickiup so we lay our salt bags at his doorway and went our separate ways. Those bags of salt were hidden around the mountains in various places where the people camped and supplied them with ample salt for several years. The biggest problem was keeping animals out of them, especially the porcupines.

Nava was not pleased with our time, saying that it should have been much shorter. We didn't tell him about our four-hour nap. Taking that away and factoring in the bags of salt, we were much nearer his estimation of the time needed to make the run.

Little Bird had a kettle of stew with fresh venison and she was cooking a large steak as I entered the tipi and sat by the fire. My feet were sore and felt swollen; my legs ached and I knew this would not be a good night.

Wounded Deer handed me a bowl of the stew. "How was your snack?" She leered.

"Very good, Wounded Deer, I cracked them with my teeth and ate them as we ran. That was a good idea, only not enough of them."

Her smile faded and she growled at me and returned to the fire.

"Your moccasins are in shreds, Rojo, give them to me and I will repair them," Little Bird said.

"He must learn to do that himself, Little Bird. Tomorrow you can show him how," Elkhorn said as he stood at the tipi door. "How did you run, Rojo?"

"Well enough. We should have been here sooner." I didn't mention to them that I had made my own moccasins for some time, now. I wanted to learn how they made this style of moccasin. They were better for running than the ones we made at home.

Wounded Deer took a kettle of water from the fire and poured in a generous amount of salt and some dried herbs. She stirred it a moment and set the steaming concoction before me.

"Soak your feet," she demanded.

I eyed that steaming pot and took my time slipping off my moccasins. I suspicioned this would be more of a scalding than a soaking.

"Put them in," she demanded.

"Would you cook my feet, Wounded Deer?" I pulled a half of my headband from my belt and dipped it into the water. It was almost too hot to wash my face.

"Feet in," she demanded and I reluctantly obeyed and at once became aware of four sensations: my toes cramped up, the bottom of my feet drew up, the blister on my right heel stung, and the water was too hot. Out of the kettle they came, beet red, and I rubbed them.

"Back in," my tormentor demanded. Gradually, the water cooled until I could keep my feet in the water and it felt real good.

My steak came to me on a forked stick and I ate and soaked. Another bowl of stew followed the steak and I became very drowsy. Wrapped in my warm blanket, I slept right there by the fire. Several times in the night, one leg or the other would cramp and I would have to rub it out. Once, both cramped and I had to stand to get relief.

The next day was spent learning how to make Apache moccasins and the inactivity was good. My footbath was reheated and I sat and sewed and soaked.

CHAPTER 12
BRONCO APACHES

It is hard to account for all the forces that made Adam as Rojo Pelo embrace the Apache culture. Certainly, the acceptance and attention he received from his captor had much to do with it. As Barnabas Sackett said, "Man is not far from the wilderness and it takes him but a short time to go back living with it." In Rojo's case, it was more accurately a lateral step from one culture to the other.

The training of the six young warriors continued apace. Lolo and Red Horse taught us the arts of trailing and moving without leaving a trail for others to find. When we could detect the passage of a man by the bend of a blade of grass or the age of a trail by the tracks of a crossing lizard or beetle, the two warriors decided it was time to put us to the test. Tio, Paisano, and I were given a secret destination to attain by means of concealing our trail, and half a day later, Owl, Beto, and Wolf Pup were assigned the task of finding and following the trail.

The contest was played enthusiastically, and the two warriors were satisfied with the results. Now, the spare times of the six were used in the game of tracking and trailing, still under the close observation by the adults. It was without warning that their skills were put to the test in deadly earnest.

A runner from Two Bears trotted into camp one afternoon with the news that they had been attacked by a band of Apaches escaping from the San Carlos reservation. "When they could not persuade the clan to go to Mexico with them, they stole several women and young people and escaped eastward. When pressed hard in pursuit, the fugitives broke into several smaller groups and scattered. One group going south along the Guadalupe foothills is not being pursued."

Elkhorn nodded, "Tell Two Bears we will follow this band and return his people to him." He addressed the others around him and said, "Prepare to go."

In the space of a few moments, the men were back, our six novices included: fully prepared to take the trail of the renegade band.

201

In answer to Elkhorn's hesitation, Red Horse spoke, "These young men have proven to be good trackers. They could learn much and be of help finding the band."

"Very well, but they are not to go into combat, should that happen," Elkhorn decreed. Nevertheless, the boys carried their bows as the party rode out and down the cañon of their entry into the mountains. It took very little hunting to locate the fugitive trail and follow it to Manzanita Spring.

Again, this group split up, some going southeast apparently to intersect the Delaware River; the other continuing around the foot of the mountain to turn south somewhere along the way. Elkhorn split his troop, sending Red Horse, Nava, and Wolf Killer on the eastern trail, with Beto, Owl, and Rojo as trackers. He took the rest with him after the westward trail into country more dangerous and harder tracking.

Trailing the eastern-bound band was easy. They obviously had several hostages who took no trouble to hide their progress. After a couple of hours tracking, Red Horse called the scouts in. "You have been on the trail long enough to know. Where do you think the enemy is going?"

Beto spoke, "It does not seem likely that

the band will try to circle around and go back to the mountains with their hostages, but it would be in their greatest interest to go south and get into the Sierra Madre as soon as possible."

"I believe the trail may be older than we think and we will only get closer to them, and not catch them," Owl said.

Wolfkiller looked at me. "What does Rojo think?"

"They can get a little water from the riverbed, but they are going to have to let their horses rest and graze soon. I think they will go to Red Bluff and rest there. If we follow their tracks, we will always be behind and we'll never get to rest if we are to catch up with them."

Beto drew in the sand, showing the Delaware flowing east to the Pecos River. "We are here and the band may be somewhere between here and the Pecos. If we cut across here —" he indicated a line from our present position southeast to the Pecos "— we stand a good chance of getting ahead of them."

"If not, we at least would cut off several miles of tracking and be closer to them," I added.

Red Horse nodded. "It is important to think like your enemy and anticipate his moves, then you can catch him. We should go more to the right than I drew; then we are more assured of getting ahead of them."

We crossed the dry river and when on the south bank, Red Horse pointed the path he wanted to take. Spreading out in a broad line, the scouts led, watching for signs. Their shadows stretched far to the east when Owl on the far left struck the fugitive trail.

"We have gained on them and now we must continue as long as we can see," Red Horse said. Our pace quickened, the scouts now ranging out farther ahead.

At sunset, we came upon an abandoned horse in a draw, standing with head down. Red Horse called a rest. "Where are they going?" he asked us.

"They will go to the spring at Red Bluff," Beto said.

"Then where?"

"Other horses are faltering, so they must care for them or abandon them," Owl said.

Beto surmised, "With the captives, they can't afford to walk. They will keep the horses."

"I would think they would at least stay a day at Red Bluff," I added.

"So they rest at Red Bluff," Wolfkiller concluded.

"How far are we from Red Bluff?" Nava asked.

"About ten mi—" I caught myself before the question "What's a mile?" could be asked, "— two hands if we hurry."

(With no timepiece, the Indians measured time by the day and half day. If they needed to break it down any further, they would measure the number of hand widths the sun was above the horizon. It turns out that one hand width at arm's length approximates one hour on the white man's clock. Ed.)

"That could take three hands if we do not hurry," Red Horse said.

I thought a moment, "In three hands, it will be completely dark and before moonrise."

"That is correct, Rojo, ideal time for a raid. We must plan. First, we will take a sip of water, and give the rest to the horse. We will need him."

When that was done, Red Horse said, "We can use the horse to get into the camp unseen and find the hostages. If they are free to run, they can get away while we distract the guards."

The horse seemed to regain some of his strength with the water we had given him and when we were ready to go, came with us. At sunset, Owl with his night vision led us toward Red Bluff. The horse smelled the river when we neared it and we had to hold him back.

Red Horse sent Owl with Nava to scout the camp. They covered their heads with grass and limbs and crawled to the top of a dune. From there, they could see the people sleeping. It was easy to locate the prisoners. They lay in a bunch on one side of the dead fire, but not a single warrior could be seen.

"They are scattered around keeping watch," Nava whispered. "We must find them if we can."

Owl nodded at the base of a boulder behind the prisoners, "There is one."

"I see him," Nava said after a moment. They began searching the circle of the camp and soon Nava nudged Owl, "There under that bank."

Owl watched a long time before some tiny movement caught his eye, "I see him."

"There should be more here and another warrior will be across the river with the horses," Nava whispered.

They searched without success until a figure arose from a bush near the river. "Watch him," Nava hissed. He continued to scan the area, paying no attention to the standing man. Owl watched as the man sank back to the ground.

"He stood to draw our attention away from other movements around us," Nava said. "Now he will move to a new place. Watch for him."

The faintest clink of a rock indicated that the man was moving to the right of his old position, and Owl watched until he made a darker shadow under a bush near the ford of the river. The man under the bank hadn't moved, but when they searched for the man by the boulder, he was gone. The faint glow of the rising moon showed on the horizon.

"He may have found us," Nava whispered. "Lie still." A moment later, he backed away down the slope and Owl lay still, listening and hardly breathing. There was the faintest sound behind him, like a sigh, then nothing else. A long, long time later, someone pulled Owl's foot. He slid backwards, knife in hand, praying it was Nava.

"He sleeps," Nava whispered. "I will return to his place under the boulder and you crawl to the captives and cut their bonds if they have any. Tell them if any fighting starts to run behind the boulder and hide. Red Horse will be above the man under the bank and Wolfkiller stalks the other man with Beto. Rojo rides to the herd. When you see me by the boulder, crawl to the prisoners."

"He disappeared and I crawled closer to the sleeping group. I don't know how long he had been sitting there before I saw him — he just appeared — and I began crawling to the people," Owl said later. "The moon rising was causing problems and I slithered in amongst the little group. To the nearest people, I whispered, 'Do not move, we are here to free you. Have you been tied?' "

" 'Yes,' the mound to my right replied, 'the adults are tied but the children are not.' "

As was the custom of the Diné, the people slept with their feet to the fire. I had crawled in from above, head toward the fire. I cut the ropes around the feet of the ones either side of me, then slowly retreated until I could free their hands. "Don't run unless there is fighting, then go behind the big boulder." Moving through the crowd was very·slow, and I was not through when the full moon was halfway up and I had to stop moving. I pretended to be a sleeping prisoner.

"Red Horse is on top of the bank," Nava murmured to us, "be very still."

Owl continued, "I heard the horse approaching and when he came into my vision, I was sure I could see a heel hooked over his shoulders. It had to be Rojo."

I barely had time to slide down with a handful of mane and hook my heel over that horse's back before he proceeded to the river and bowed to drink. It took a pretty good kick to get him to start across. That rifle propped under my right arm was getting heavier and heavier. Soon, he was at the spring and drinking. When he was satisfied, he moved on to the herd grazing on the plain. I could see the night guard moving toward us.

I told the man to stop twenty yards short of us and told him what Wolfkiller had instructed me to say: "You can ride away and live or stay and die with your friends." The man hesitated a moment and I knew I could not shoot him with that old flintlock hanging from my horse's neck. I swung to the ground, cocked, and propped the gun over the horse's back. The man grunted and cursed me, then heeled his horse toward us. I aimed and pulled the trigger as my horse spun to face the charge. My shot went wild and the horses collided, knocking my horse over on top of me. Pain like a hot poker shot up my leg from my left foot, and my head slammed into the ground. The world went black for a few seconds, then slowly spun around and around. The old familiar pain came back to my head.

The man hesitated a moment, deciding whether to kill me or ride to the rescue of his friends. A shot from the camp and my horse's feeble struggles to rise convinced him to leave me until later and he raced for the ford.

My horse couldn't get up, and if he would, it could only be by stepping all over me. Fortunately, I was under his shoulder and could reach the reins. I pulled them tight and talked until he calmed down and lay still. The next thing I did was retrieve the rifle, check the flint, and reload it. If that Bronco came back and found me still here, he was going to get a surprise. I lay the gun aside and took stock of my situation. My legs were pinned just behind the horse's right shoulder and there was no way I could pull both of them out. If I could get the horse to roll up in a semi-sitting position, it might be possible to move my right leg forward enough to be out from under his body and just behind his elbows where my leg would be free enough to pull clear. Then by pushing as hard as I could with my free leg, I might be able to pull my left leg out or move it forward and get it clear.

He was calm and breathing easy and I began to talk to him. "All right, fellow, let's see if you can get up." Loosening the reins, I pushed his head up and he rolled upright on his forelegs. Twice he tried to rise, but couldn't get his hind legs under him. Both times, I could move my leg forward. On his third attempt, my leg came free and before he could lie back down, I planted my foot on his shoulder and pushed as hard as I could. My left leg moved a little. On the second push, my knee came free. Before I could push again, the poor horse gave up the effort and lay back down. I barely had time to raise my right leg out of his way. With my left knee again under him and my right leg atop his left shoulder, I was astraddle him backwards. By pulling his head toward me, I could scratch between his ears and talk until he calmed. Darkness and dizziness settled over me again.

The campground was quiet — too quiet after that one shot. Now, the fighting would be with bow and arrow and hand-to-hand. I really needed to be helping instead of lying here under this horse. I put my foot against his withers and pushed as hard as I could. The horse took this as a signal to try to get up and rose on his forelegs enough that my leg slid free. My ankle was swollen and discolored, the moonlight making it seem darker than it really was. When I stood, it told me in no uncertain terms that it would not carry me one single step. Very carefully, I sat back down and scooted back until I could lean against my horse, who had once again given up on standing. Any fighting would have to come to us.

My whole foot swelled to twice its normal size once it was freed from the confines of the horse's body. Each toe stood out swollen and separate and the skin was so tight I thought it would tear. Just to move it a little shot pain up my leg.

My backrest must have been pretty hungry, for he gathered his hind feet under him and jerked upright and onto his feet. He teetered there a moment and I thought he would fall on me again. I crawled away, disregarding the stinking pain. Everything went black.

I guess he didn't fall, for when I awoke, he was gone and the moon was low and in my eyes. The black figure of a man approached from the ford and I scrambled back for my long gun. It felt like it weighed a ton as I tried to aim through a dark tunnel at the approaching specter.

"Do you wish to shoot a friend?" Beto called, and I lowered the gun.

"We have the hostages safe. There is one dead Bronco and three are walking to the

Sierra Madre with one horse," Beto re-counted with satisfaction. "You are hurt. What is wrong?"

I tried to say "my ankle," but the words sounded funny and far away.

"Let me see," Beto said and began at my feet, feeling my feet and legs. "Bi-i-ig foot." He continued his search, commenting as he worked, "no broken legs . . . ribs good . . . arms are well." He grasped my head with both hands and rotated it, "Neck is stiff." Carefully feeling, his hand found a large bump and blood on the back of my head. "Ah-h, the problem is found. You have hit your head hard enough to split the scalp and your senses are leaking out. We have to bind it up."

"Who have you found, Beto?" I recognized Red Horse's voice and the sound of a horse approaching from far away.

"Rojo. He has a bad foot and his head is hurt on the back."

"Horsh f-ell m-e." My tongue seemed very thick.

"This horse will take him to camp and the women can treat him," Red Horse said. I remember being lifted onto the horse and I felt cold water splash on my feet when we crossed the river, but that is all until I awoke in the light of the rising sun.

"He awakes," an unfamiliar voice said. I beheld a woman unknown to me leaning close. Another face appeared, then left.

Owl's face came close to mine, "Have your senses returned, Rojo?"

"I have not lost them."

"Then you are telling us that you only *slept* these last two days?" a grinning Beto asked.

"I do not sleep when there is danger about, Beto. You are playing with me."

"Go away, you two, he has been very sick and you will make it worse bothering his mind," the woman said. The two left and the woman asked, "Are you hungry?"

"Yes."

Another face appeared and handed the woman a bowl. "This is good broth. You must sit up a little."

Pain shot through my neck and shoulders when I tried to lift my head, and Owl knelt beside me, slipping his arm under my shoulders and lifting me up a little. The woman lifted the bowl to my lips and I drank the hot broth.

"You have slept two whole days and two whole nights and we did not think you would ever awaken," the woman standing over me said.

Wolf Killer peered at me over the woman's

shoulder. "There is danger in staying here too long, Rojo, do you think you could ride?"

"Yes," I said, but I was very doubtful. There would be no refuge in this open place if an enemy found us. We had to move. I slept until I heard the horses cross the river, then by rolling to my side, I was able to lift my head and sit up. Strong arms lifted me to the back of a horse and I lay my head on his neck. Someone took the lead rope and I closed my eyes again. I remember very little of that ride, except the relief of lying down at night and sleeping without motion. I do remember getting home and my Indian mother taking charge of me. After that, I got better.

The other party came in from the salt flats, having lost the fleeing Broncos in a sandstorm south of Hueco Tanks. Tio, Wolf Pup, and Paisano were praised for their scouting skills.

CHAPTER 13
VENGEANCE AND BLOODY NOSES

It began to get cooler in the mountains and the nights were downright cold. The council met the morning we awoke with snow on the ground and decided it was time to move from the high mountains. Dawn of the next day found us heading north to the reservation. I took note that Eve's village had already left Dark Cañon. It gave me hope that I would see her again soon. I really missed her.

Our pace was almost leisurely as we traveled northeast along the foothills of the mountains. Several times along the way, when we came to a place where the mast was plentiful, we would camp for a day or two while the women gathered nuts or grapes and plums. At a grove of white oaks, they gathered baskets of the mast. They would use the acorns to make a kind of flour and mix it with the dried fruits and nuts.

They called the river we found Rio

Peñasco and we followed it northwest along a well-defined trail right into the Mescalero Apache Indian Reservation. We left the Peñasco and crossed over into the Rio Felix Valley and from there to the place where three creeks came together to form Turkey Creek. Here, we made our winter camp. Some white man from the agency visited the camp and I hid from him.

Not long after he left the village, three Mexican traders drove their carts loaded with goods into the village. Their chief trade good was Taos Lightning and there was a brisk trade for the stuff. Almost as soon as the carts entered the village, I noticed Beto, Paisano, and some of the older children beginning to gather the youngsters and captives and herd them away from the trading.

"Help get the babies away, Rojo. You must hide also or they may kill you," my friend whispered. The women were so intent on getting some of the whiskey, they left their children. They gladly gave up papooses on their backs to the young girls who took them away.

As the Indians grew drunk, the price of the whiskey rose to exorbitant heights and the village was plundered of their accumulated wealth. The effect on the Apaches was extreme. Even the women joined in the debauchery. Their violent emotions ran the gamut from lust to rage and fights broke out with the participants wielding knives and lances.

This situation was not new to the children and even the toddlers ran to us, their faces contorted in terror. We crowded into a wickiup on the far edge of the village. Tio, whose mother is Mexican, sat just inside the door watching. Paisano and Beto stood guard somewhere out of sight outside the hut. We didn't see Wolf Pup or Owl.

Some time after dark, we heard the carretas with their wooden wheels and axles squeal out of the village. The violent celebration continued for some time until the whiskey was gone and the exhausted participants sank into their alcoholic stupors. The anger and fear in the wickiup was palpable and I had to get out of there. Tio silently went with me and we stood taking in the fresh air.

"We have to feed the children," Beto spoke from the gloom. "Rojo, you and Tio make us a fire and we will see what can be found in the village." I heard their footsteps fade toward the dark huts.

We found live coals in the firepit on the east side of our hut and it didn't take long to have a fire going and the abandoned kettle of stew warming. Two or three of the older girls disappeared into the darkness and returned with bowls and spoons and another kettle of food they had found. The light of the fire attracted the children and they gradually emerged from the hut, their dingy faces streaked with tears. They huddled around the fire in tight groups, drawing comfort and security from their companions. Three hungry babies in their papooses fussed and cried. A young mother who heard her child's cries staggered into the light, and ignoring the pleas of the girls, nursed her baby. She passed out while nursing and the baby got sick and threw up his milk all over the unconscious mother. One of the girls took the infant, and Tio and I dragged the woman into the darkness. Tio kicked her hard in the back and we left her there.

While the children were being fed, Beto and I gathered what bedding we could find and made the wickiup one big bed. The fire died, the cool air settled in, and the children sought warmth and sleep in the hut.

"It's time," Beto growled, and without another word, the five of us dispersed to gather our weapons. We met at the upper end of the village and followed the carreta tracks up the valley. Even without Owl, we could see by the moon well enough to follow the carts.

We found the Mexicans' camp on the divide between Turkey Creek and Rio Felix. They were sharing a jug of that whiskey and celebrating their successful venture. One man was dancing around the fire with the jug, imitating an Indian dance to the delight of his two companions.

He stopped and raised the jug high to drink. My arrow burst the jug, showering the vile liquid all over the man and spilling into the fire where it immediately flared, catching the soaked clothes of the dancer. At first, he stomped as if to kill the flames climbing his legs. When he reached down to fight with his hands, his coat sleeves caught fire and he immediately became a flaming torch screaming and running into the darkness.

Whether by indifference or torpor, his companions sat and stared, not moving to aid the man. He became an eerie light passing through darkness until he fell and the flames gradually died. My second arrow into one of the Mexicans was unnecessary, for Paisano's arrow had already found his heart. We stood in the darkness and stared at three dead men.

"Now, we have the goods back," Piasano said.

"No, Paisano, they do not belong to us or the village," Tio said. "We must not take what has been traded to others."

"Then what do you propose to do with these things — and those horses out there?" Paisano asked.

"We can send them to hell after their owners," I exclaimed.

Beto objected, "But our people will go hungry and cold."

"Wasn't that determined when they traded these things for the whiskey? They are already staring at hunger and cold. If we restore these things to the village, we will become killers and thieves and the comancheros will not trade with us again," I said.

There was silence for a few moments, then Tio said, "Rojo is right. We do not want to become common thieves who kill from ambush and steal from others."

"You would kill the horses, Rojo?" Paisano asked.

"No, he would not," Beto interjected, "but they no longer belong to the village."

Tio had been thinking and said, "The children will suffer without robes this cold season and they are innocent. We can keep enough robes for them and burn the rest of the goods."

"I am thinking the horses could be turned loose and take care of themselves," I said.

"Turned loose far from here where they would be hard to find," Paisano added with a grin. "We should keep our horses. We will need them to herd away the others."

"— And outrun angry warriors," I added.

"We have to hurry if all this is to be done by morning," Tio said. "Rojo and I will gather our horses and you three get as many robes as you can. We will pull the carts together and build a fire to send these to the afterlife."

Finding the right horses in the dark was hard and took some time. When we finally drove the stock to the camp, Beto and Paisano had a goodly pile of robes separated from the carts. We pulled the carretas together with the oxen and piled the dead Mexicans on top of them. The whiskey made good fuel and soon the pyres were aflame. We watched only a moment or two, then returned to our chores. Tio and Beto piled the robes on two travois and headed for the village while Paisano and I gathered the horses and oxen and drove them to Rio Peñasco and up the river to the northwest where we turned them loose.

"I will stay and push them on a little

farther," Paisano said.

On my way back to the village, I cut across above Rio Felix and down one of the creeks to the village. The sun was up and I circled around out of sight of the village to the wickiup. Only a few of the children were awake, the rest sleeping off the fatigue that comes after terror. The older girls had taken over running things and we saw to it that they had sufficient food for the group.

The village was quiet as death, only a few people stirring but too spent to do anything more. As I walked through the village, I saw several unmatched couples sleeping off their debauch together. The violent results of the whiskey were not over. There would be several noseless women in the coming days. Long association with alcohol must have conditioned the Anglo somewhat against the ravages of drink. Even though the Apaches brewed and drank tiswin, they did not possess this preconditioning and the effects of strong drink were magnified in their systems.

As I approached Elkhorn's tipi, I became aware of soft keening coming from within, and brushing aside the curtain, found Little Bird and Wounded Deer with arms slashed and bloody sitting beside the cold body of Elkhorn. He had been stabbed many times.

Little Bird was pale and faint from the loss of her own blood and leaned heavily on Wounded Deer. It was a few moments before they noticed me standing there. Wounded Deer exclaimed, "You must avenge this, Rojo Pelo."

"Who did this?" I asked.

"Yellow Spots." Wounded Deer spat the name as if it were filth in her mouth. Elkhorn and Wounded Deer had been careful to observe the taboos the Apache held about contact between son-in-law and mother-in-law, but it was plain that she held much affection for her daughter's husband. "He tried to force Little Bird and when Elkhorn interfered, he killed him."

It was a point of honor that the family of a murder victim take revenge on the killer. The negative thing about that is that the killer's family in turn felt obligated to seek like revenge. The whole thing could and many times did become a vicious cycle of murder and revenge. The Anglos have a name for it: feud.

Yellow Spots had not gotten far from the tipi before the effects of the alcohol overcame him. He lay facedown in the dirt, spread-eagled and naked save a carelessly folded breechcloth. His bloody knife was still in his hand.

There was a willow bush nearby and I cut a limb the size of my little finger and sharpened the end, leaving the leaves in place. I looked around to see if anyone was watching while I honed my castrating blade. The cuts of a sharp knife are not felt as much as that of a duller blade. When I could shave with the blade, I cut a slit through both sides near the edge of his scrotum and pinned it very firmly to the ground with the limb. Yellow Spots didn't move. I took the murder weapon and washed it. Little Bird would wear it on her belt as long as Yellow Spots lived.

I hurried back to the refuge wickiup to get my horse. "What are you up to, Rojo?" Beto asked.

"Elkhorn is dead. I go to bury him."

"Dead?" Beto was disturbed.

"What happened?" Tio, who had emerged from the hut, asked.

"Yellow Spots killed him."

"Why?" Beto asked.

I stared at him, *"Why do you think, Beto?"* My anger surprised me and I realized how much I had admired and depended on my adopted father. Tears stung my eyes and I turned away to untie my horse. Beto put his hand on my shoulder and murmured, "We will go with you, friend."

The four of us watched for our two companions as we rode through the village.

"There is Owl." Tio's exclamation brought us to a halt and we beheld Owl's feet with his fancy moccasins lying in the doorway of a hut. Pushing the curtain aside, we beheld the naked body of our friend sleeping away, the woman of the household as bare, cradled in his arm.

"O-o-oh no-o-o," Tio whispered, "vengeance and a bloody nose."

I pictured that pretty face without her nose and said, "Not if I can help it."

Tio slipped into the hut and removed Owl's arm from under the woman's head, and Paisano and I dragged Owl outside. When Tio didn't emerge, Beto peeked into the hut, then motioned for me to follow. There on the bed lay the husband.

"Help me move the woman," Tio whispered.

We lifted the robe she was lying on and carried her to the man. Gently, we rolled her off the robe and against his back. Beto threw the robe over the two and we crept out of the wickiup to find Owl sitting, elbows on knees and head in hands.

Beto bent close to his ear and said in a little louder than normal voice, "How are you feeling, Owl?"

Owl winced and clapped his hands over his ears. Beto looked at us and grinned.

"Where are your clothes, Owl?" I called.

As if for the first time, the boy noticed his nakedness. "I-I-I o-o-oh," he groaned.

"Get up, Owl, you must go with us," Tio demanded. We lifted him by his underarms and Beto, mounted, led him by his hand as he stumbled and groaned beside the horse.

"Don't let that horse step on your pretty moccasins," I warned.

"Where . . . going?" Owl slurred.

"To a funeral," I replied.

"Whose?"

"It might be yours," Tio growled.

At that moment, I agreed.

We didn't see Wolf Pup on our way to Elkhorn's tipi. "Probably sleeping it off in the arms of some man's wife," Paisano said.

Two of my companions noticed the body lying by the path. Number three was holding on to Tio's saddle and walking with his head down.

"See that? A tree grows out of his ass," Owl exclaimed. He stumbled over to take a closer look. "Ah-h-h, not from his ass, but from his bag." Yellow Spots groaned. Owl sat beside the man, shamed by his nakedness to go any farther. He eyed Yellow Spots's breechcloth until he noticed it was pinned by the stake.

Elkhorn had been washed and dressed in his best clothes. His shield lay across his body and his bow and arrows lay beside his rifle, ready to accompany him on his journey.

"Will you take him to the place his fathers lie in the Guadalupes?" Little Bird pleaded.

I hesitated, not knowing that place and Beto spoke, "I know the place, Mother, and I will show Rojo where to go."

"Thank you, Beto. We will not go," she said, indicating herself and Wounded Deer.

"We must find Elkhorn's horses," I said and we rode to the Rio Felix and caught the horses we had just turned loose. "Wish I had known," I said.

We returned midafternoon to find the body wrapped and bound into his robe and two fresh travois poles by the tipi. The two women had washed and dressed in their finest and Owl had found clothes to wear. Yellow Spots was gone, though the stake that held him was still in place. Drops of blood marked his path and his breechcloth was still pinioned to the ground.

"He screamed when he got up," Owl said with a grin, "then walked off holding himself so his cojones wouldn't fall out."

"Owl, I swear on the bones of my fathers

that you will receive the same cure if you ever drink the white man's poison and lie with a stranger again," Tio vowed.

Owl watched his toe make circles in the sand. "You will never have to keep your oath, Tio." He was sincerely ashamed of what he had done.

We determined to start right away in spite of the lateness and had the travois in place and the body secured. Others would have gone with us to pay their respects to their fallen leader, but they had no horses and were in no condition to walk. I was glad they didn't come.

As we passed the edge of the village a shot rang out and I felt a tug on my blanket over my shoulders. A cloud of smoke betrayed the shooter's position and I raced there to find Yellow Spots desperately trying to reload his rifle. As I jumped from my horse, he dropped the rifle and charged. I fumbled for my knife and dodged. His slashing knife caught in my blanket. My knife came clear, and with a desperate swing I caught the back of his shoulder as he swung through. He whirled, swinging his blade at arm's length. It was easy to duck and my knife found its mark in his lung. I jerked the knife back and swung at his neck. He fell, his heart pumping out the last of his life.

"We must go," Owl said, handing me my rein, and we rode away. I glanced back to see Elkhorn's tipi flaming brightly. Two other wickiups were casting their white smoke to the sky. It was a terrible sight and the last vision I have of that village.

We got to the burial cleft of Elkhorn's fathers about noon on the third day. I climbed to the cleft and pushed bones and other contents to the back to make room for Elkhorn. It took all four of us to lift the body over our heads and into the little shelter. Owl handed up Elkhorn's shield and I laid it on his chest. Paisano passed up the weapons and I laid them on the opposite side of the body near his right hand. Next came a ham of venison for his journey. I turned to jump down just as Beto killed the travois horse. "Not your best horse, Elkhorn, but all we have right now," he said.

The thought struck me: *that should have been King.* We camped and cooked thick venison steaks. After we had eaten and were resting before sleeping, I said, "I cannot return to the village."

There was silence for a moment, then Tio said, "I understand, Rojo. To return would only prolong the fight you had with Yellow Spots. The ending would not be good. This way, the killing will end unless his kin come to find you."

"What will you do, Rojo?" Beto asked.

"I will stay here with Elkhorn for a while, then it may be that I join another village. I will not return to my white family."

"Perhaps you may join your *Hermana Gemelo,*" Owl suggested.

"Perhaps, I don't know." I knew I couldn't do that; it would be too convenient for my enemies to find me. After a day's rest, my four friends bade me a fond farewell and returned to their village.

It was good to be alone and think about what was and was to come. I shivered through the night without a fire, finally falling into a troubled sleep. Visions of Elkhorn passed before my mind's eye, teaching me how to make arrows or showing me the track of mice in the sand. Once he laughed and the sound of it woke me up to find only emptiness. Sleep left me and I ate some jerky, said goodbye to Elkhorn, and left to search for King.

CHAPTER 14
ALONE

I aimed for Rio Peñasco at the mouth of Elk Cañon. As I had suspected, the horses had not reached that point and I began my search moving downstream. Eventually, I began to see tracks and I searched among them to find King's shod hoofprints. Even in the short time they had been free, the horses had become shy of men and I could not have easily caught any of them. The more I studied the signs, the more puzzling the lack of *any* shod prints was to me. There were several in the herd when we released them.

Late evening found me at a long hole of water after a riffle and I camped there. I caught several trout and ate them without bearing the disapproval of my Apache friends. It was good to have a fire to warm my feet as I slept.

Another day of fruitless searching and I began to suspect something had interfered with the normal dispersion of the herd. That interference could only travel on six legs. Before dark, I left the river and spent the night hidden in the hills. The object of my hunt changed from four-legged animals to that of the two-legged variety. If someone were gathering horses, King would be sure to be his primary quarry. That pet would not be hard to catch.

Covering the valley was more effective up near the divide, and my vigilance was rewarded near sunset with the discovery of smoke in the trees across the river. There was a good crossing a mile downstream and I crossed into the woods and up the hill to the opposite divide in the dark. This placed me downwind from the camp. When I smelled the smoke, I tied my horse and crept down the hill. Our friend had caught all of the shod horses and King was among them. I stayed away from the horses, for King was sure to say something if he got wind of me.

There was not enough light from the fire to see the man's face. When his head turned so I could see his profile, the "friend" became that rascal Paisano. *Ah, making yourself rich at the expense of your village, are you? We'll see about that,* I thought.

My spot was comfortable and secure if

the wind didn't change. It was just a matter of settling back to wait. Soon the fire died to coals and Paisano stopped weaving his rope and checked the horses before lying down. Waiting had given me time to think and I had come up with a plan, such as it was. I had taken one of Elkhorn's arrows as a reminder of him and now I would use it to try to discourage Paisano from pursuing me, for I didn't want a confrontation with him.

Eight horses were on a picket line and also hoppled. I shot Elkhorn's arrow deep into the tree at the end of the picket line nearest to the camp; then began removing the hopples and laying them in front of the horses as if they had just stepped out of them. I tied the horses head to tail and coiled the remnants of the picket line and hung it over the arrow. The thick carpet of pine and cedar needles muffled the noise of our passing, and we climbed the hill to where my horse was tied and made good our escape.

When Paisano found the arrow, he would know it was Elkhorn's. Hopefully, he would think he was being warned by Elkhorn's spirit not to pursue the horses and not to steal any more and the rascal Paisano would become the honest Paisano.

We returned to the Guadalupes and Elkhorn's grave. Something with the paws of a panther had pulled down the venison ham and made off with it, but the body was undisturbed and very likely to stay that way. Snow and cold crowded me down into one of the deep cañons, and we spent thirty-five days there before we had to move to better grazing. It was easy to lose track of time spent alone in the mountains, and it was a long time before I felt any desire for human companionship. I missed Eve the most.

They weren't as nice as Little Bird could make them, but the buckskin suit I made from less than perfectly tanned deerskin met my need for winter wear.

To occupy time, we began to explore the mountains around us. I would saddle up one of the horses and ride to a certain area to explore and spend the day looking for caves and shelters and water where there might be signs of people. There were a surprising lot of signs — paintings, hand-prints, rock carvings and such. There were lots of flint chips and some shells that could have only come from some ocean. I didn't find any quarries of flint, so it must have also come from outside the mountains.

My strangest finding was a cave that had appeared in the side of a bluff when heavy rain had caused a large flat rock covering the mouth of the cave to slide down the slope. I could barely reach the rock lip of the ledge by standing on the edge of the fallen door. Pulling myself up with my elbows and scooting on my belly, I got on my knees and crawled through the small opening. The smell of age was heavy on the air and I almost backed out until my eyes became accustomed to the dark and saw light reflected off of something shiny.

Three more yards on hands and knees and the tunnel opened into a large room high enough to stand in. The light was reflected from a small piece of mirror tied to decorations on a rifle that stood in a stand with several other rifles. All were very old. Someone had left a torch of weeds tied together and when lit it cast a very good light. A candle in a bottle sat on a wooden shipping box with Butterfield painted on the sides. That candle made a steadier light. On the ceiling above it someone had smoked the date of 5 May 1860. The wall to the right of the opening held the usual blown handprints and carved spirals. This is the only place I found in the mountains that had Kokopelli pecked out. The back of the room was filled with loosely piled rubble. There was the slightest breeze coming through them. As the candle was sputtering down to its last light, I opened the box and there in the bottom wedged under one side lay a silver Mexican peso blackened with age. The date on it was 1803.

The Butterfield Stage route skirted the foot of the Guadalupes and there was a way station at Pine Spring. A coach loaded with riches of all kinds traveling through this remote and lawless area drew outlaws like flies to carrion. This cave must have been the home of a gang who abandoned it when the line stopped running in 1861. The stacked long guns, which were unrifled, were old and must have been considered too heavy to carry across that desert; so here they remained.

The next time I passed that way, a mud-slide had covered the cave entrance again and only a corner of the rock slab showed at the bottom of the slide to hint at the loca-tion of the cave.

Even high in these mountains, the weather was getting milder and it would not be long before the Mescalero would be making their spring trek from their reservation to the mountains. The likelihood they would find me ran about a hundred percent and the likelihood some of them would want to kill me ran just as high. Those two likelihoods came together unexpectedly one morning when I rode out to check on the horses I had left grazing in a small ravine. King suddenly stopped and snorted his "I smell Injun" snort as we approached the mouth of the ravine. I sat very still, looking all around us, but could detect no more than the fact that there was not a horse in the little cañon. King moved forward cautiously at my insistence and I studied the ground. There among the shod tracks of my horses were the unshod tracks of two horses — Indian ponies.

They hadn't been gone long and King and I discussed our options. "Catching them would be no problem —" he began.

"— So long as they run in a straight line," I completed.

He snorted his disgust.

They must have known about my campsite and that made me wonder why I wasn't still lying in my blankets with a slit throat. Also, they hadn't taken King, which was a strong indication the thieves were not Comanche, Cheyenne, or Kiowa. The logical conclusion was that they were Apache — who were not so interested in how good a horse could run — thus leaving King alone.

"They expect us to follow, King, and

that's how they will get you and eliminate me," I said.

He nodded his head.

"Our best approach is to get ahead of them and surprise them. That means you are going to have to do some hard and fast riding and I have to figure out where they are going."

He turned his head and eyed me as if to say, "Well get to figuring."

The Indians had come down the valley from The Rim, that high, impassable cliff that runs the length of the western edge of the Guadalupe Mountains. That meant that they had not passed the arroyo where the horses were to find my camp. It may be they happened on the horses accidentally and took advantage of the opportunity. I never saw an Indian hesitate to take something he wanted. Most likely, they figured that there were at least as many men in the party as horses. Being just two, they didn't want to stir up eight or more men against them. The prudent thing to do was to take the horses and run.

If I were to be sucessful in heading off the thieves and horses, I would have to figure which direction — north or south — they would take at the top of the cañon on the Rim Trail. It wasn't hard to guess they would turn north, back toward the reservation and sanctuary from white men trying to retrieve their horses. They would be in no great hurry, knowing they had left men afoot who were not likely to follow. Thus, they would stay in the valley until reaching the top.

This is where my exploration of the mountains paid off, for I knew a place where we could climb out of the cañon and reach the ridge on the north side of this valley. The Indians might know of the shortcut also, but could not drive the herd that way.

"Well, King, they might not know of the shortcut since it's hidden by the brush. We'll take it and see what happens."

We followed the herd up the valley and I watched the tracks to see if there was anything I could determine about the riders. A tiny scrap of calico hanging on a thorn told me that they were not dressed for war. One of the riders rode steadily behind the herd, but the other was everywhere, from side to side, up one side of the herd, and back behind to cross to the other side.

"Acts like a kid without a lot of experience stealing horses and with a tired horse between his knees, King."

He nodded and huffed his sympathy for

the horse.

"Other rider is older and has experience —"

"— *And* a fresher horse." Sometimes I think that horse could talk.

We left the trail and pushed through the brush to the base of the washout we would climb. I got down and led King. It was a scramble and there were a lot more rocks and gravel shoved down the hill before we reached the top. Both of us needed a rest and it was painfully apparent that no water was available on the mountaintop.

"All right, boy, let's go see what we've gained on our friends."

We both walked up the ridge to the Rim Trail. King snorted his disgust before I saw that the horses had passed and were still ahead of us.

"Wily Injun knowed about th' shortcut, didn't he? Well, ol' boy, we still got some riding t' do."

The only thing that shortcut had done was give both of us cuts and scratches and fatigue. I remembered what old Zesch had said about King not having any endurance and wished I had Amigo instead. Our only hope now was to follow along and wait for an opportunity to retrieve the herd. They moved at a steady pace, not leisurely, not

241

hurriedly. Either the Indians didn't think they were followed, or they were stringing me along until they could take care of me. My bet was on the stringing along.

King and I suffered the most in those next two days without food and water . . . well, the horse got food, but I didn't get any nourishment out of eating dried grass. It was to our great relief that early the third day the herd was driven off the trail and down a watershed for a rest and water. We wondered how we could do the same without being detected.

"Now, King, we are about to turn from the hunters to the hunted." It would only take one man to watch the horses and free the other to hunt us. "We have to find our own water, and fast."

I turned around and hurried back to the nearest drainage down the slope and followed it a long way with the hope of finding water. What we found was a seep where someone had scooped out a small basin below. I got a drink before King drank it dry. He began grazing on the greening grass while I watched the seep fill the bowl again. About sunset, the bowl was full for the third time and we began to feel relieved of our thirst. There was a bench up on the slope of the south hillside and downstream a ways, we found an easy way up to it. I staked King on some grass out of sight from below, and tight against the back of the bench made a little fire to warm by. I slept and dreamed of a sizzling venison steak.

It wasn't a noise, it wasn't a smell, but I awoke in the predawn dusk and knew something was amiss. King hadn't said anything, but he was standing staring toward the seep, ears pricked forward. I crawled to the edge of the bench and stared down into the gloom. If he hadn't moved, it would have been a long time before I saw him squatting at the basin.

"Dang it, King, he's drinkin' our water. Guess we're gonna have to go drink his."

When it got light enough, the man would see our tracks and follow on down the dry streambed until we climbed to the bench. I wondered how long it would take him to realize that we were between him and the stolen horses.

I set a record saddling up and we rode up the bench until it met with the bottom of the ravine. When we were on the Rim Trail, I heeled King into a run. Down the watershed toward the herd, we slowed to a walk. I could tell by watching him that King smelled the other horses and I got a whiff of smoke. The camp was around a curve in the arroyo and I rode close enough to see the camp with the other Indian tending the fire. It was a woman — a familiar woman. When she turned toward the sunrise, I could see that it was Rosita, Eve's Mexican-Indian mother. There were only two people here, Rosita, and I supposed her husband, Two Bears. Where was Eve? My throat tightened and my eyes stung. I was on the verge of calling to Rosita when King's attention was drawn up the trail. We barely had time to get hidden in the brush before Two Bears raced by.

There was a sharp exchange between the two and the man jumped down and struck Rosita. She fell and Two Bears was on his knees atop her, striking her again and again. He was so intent that he didn't notice my approach from the back, and when I was close enough for a sure shot, I let my arrow fly. It pierced through the left buttock, crossed his crack, and penetrated his right buttock. Don't assume that I missed my mark.

The bully screamed and fell away. Trying to grasp the shaft of the arrow only increased the injury and pain. I nocked another arrow and walked toward the two. Rosita sat up and stared at her husband.

"Don't be afraid, Rosita," I called. "It is

Rojo Pelo. I won't hurt you."

She wiped blood from her face. Her left eye was beginning to swell and her lip was split. I suspected her nose might be broken. It didn't take long to do all that damage and I regretted not moving faster to stop it.

Two Bears lay on his side and groaned, the feathers on the arrow shaft waving like a flag. Rosita watched a moment before comprehending the situation. With a grunt of pain, she rose and examined the man's wound, clucking and talking low.

Two Bears growled like a cornered animal and cursed us. He rolled a little and pulled his knife from under him. Waving it awkwardly with his left hand, he slashed at the woman, who dodged and wrenched the weapon from his hand.

King and I rode to gather the horses and drive them back up the hill. When I returned to the camp, Rosita was cooking her meal as if nothing untoward had happened. Two Bears lay where he had fallen, his hips and legs knotted in cramps. His wife had done little to aid him and I noticed a long cord tied to the exposed arrow shaft between his buttocks. Every time he cursed or threatened, his wife would give the cord a tug. I wondered how long he would kick against the pricks.

"Rosita, where is Castaño Rojizo?"

She handed me the bowl of stew and said, giving the cord a yank, "*He* sold her."

"Where did she go?"

The woman shrugged, "Comanche take her away."

Sold to a Comanche? I shuddered at the thought. Then and there, my mind was made; I had to go to the Comanches. I ate and thought and Rosita filled my bowl twice before I was filled, though I cannot recall the taste of the food.

"I go with you," she said, and began packing the things she would need while Two Bears watched and cursed. The only time he was quiet was for a few moments after Rosita tugged the cord. Soon, all she had to do to quieten him was show him the cord. He was learning.

I caught her horses and she loaded her pack on one while I saddled the other. When she was ready, she turned to Two Bears and said, "I go to my people now, the others will find you soon. Do not remove the arrow, you can't stop the blood."

He stared at her and began to speak between clenched teeth, but stopped when she shook the cord in his face. It took her three attempts to mount and she followed me up to the Rim Trail where we turned south.

We got to Pine Spring late and camped for the night. Rosita cooked and we talked until late. She told me about Eve and that she was like a daughter to her. It was a black day when Two Bears sold her to the Comanche for four horses and a bag of powder. The man's wife had no child and he bought Eve to be his wife. The news was very disturbing.

At Guadalupe Pass, I pointed out the way she should go to the Hueco Tanks and on to the settlements along the Rio Grande. She seemed assured and I watched her ride down the old trail. Snow melting off the high places and several rains ensured that the streams across the desert would be running. Rounding up the fat horses and driving them before me, we ambled and grazed to Rio Pecos. It was bank high and roaring and we loafed along its west bank for several weeks. We were almost to Horsehead Crossing before crossing seemed possible. A large party riding unshod horses had passed over recently, heading southwest. Comanche raiding season in Mexico had begun. We crossed the river and hurried northeast while the tanks and wallows still held water. A couple days later we saw an early cattle drive aiming for Horsehead. With the horses hidden in an arroyo, I rode Amigo into their camp after the first night riders had gone to the herd and before it was dark.

CHAPTER 15
A COMANCHE ODYSSEY

Here is a crossroads for our hero. He could become Adam Bain again and return to the white man's way, or he could remain Rojo Pelo the Indian. The search for his twin sister would be much easier if he had easy access to the villages of the Indians, but his choice was much more complicated than that. He had gone too far down the Indian pathway to turn back. It would be good, here, to look at this young man through another man's eyes.

Name's Sutter Lowery, but most folks calls me Sut. Me an' Gus Bell been ridin' for Jake Meeker's outfit, seems like a lifetime. That's not far from wrong, considering I was thirteen an' Gus was only twelve when we first hired on with him. Both of us lied an' said we was fifteen, but Jake knowed better from th' start. A man can't be choosy when he has t' put two thousand head of longhorns on th' trail an' he's shorthanded. Me an' Gus come along at th' right time an' just like that, we was "twenty-five a month an' found," bound for Abilene, Kansas. Can't say we was top hands, but we carried our weight. Jake says twenty-five a month was too much, considerin' how much "found" we ate. Anyhow, we got through it an' Jake kept us on at the ranch that winter, roundin' up an' brandin' mavericks. Me an' Gus each have our own trail crews now an' generally take a herd north ev'ry year. What I'm tellin' you about now is a happenin' on our fourth trip with Jake as foreman. He had contracted to deliver a herd of three thousand to Fort Sumner for the army an' we was on th' Goodnight-Loving trail south of Big Spring.

First thing we knowed he was around, this feller hales th' camp from th' brush. He's speakin' Spanish an' Jake calls him in. Well, sir, in rides this feller on a mustang mare. You can bet that causes a stir on th' picket line. Even geldin's got feelin's.

Cookie's layin' out a cup an' slappin' steak an' beans on a plate.

It took us a while to see it, but this feller's a youngster, maybe fourteen or fifteen. He's wearin' a rough suit of buckskin, turned black with wear. A strung bow an' arrow lays across his lap. His red hair hangs ragged to his shoulder blades, tied back with a dirty red sash. At his sight, two o' th' boys fades into th' brush an' me an' Gus stands up, plates in one hand, an' empty hand near our gun hip.

Jake stands up an' says, "Light down, friend, an' have a cup with us."

"Gracias," he says an' gits down *on th' mare's right side.* He drops th' rein an' that little mare stands right there th' whole time. Jake don't offer t' picket th' horse, knows th' commotion that'd cause. "Our horses aren't used to a mare in camp," he says right easy an' sits down.

Cookie sidles up an' hands th' man his plate an' a cup of coffee. This feller cross-legs on th' ground, bow an' plate in his lap.

"I'm Jake Meeker an' this is Cookie, Gus, an' Sut." He waves his hand at us an' frowns us t' sit.

"My name is Roho Pelo," he says through a bite of steak. He eats slow an' thoughtful-like, seemin' t' like coffee th' most. Cookie refills his cup, sumthin' he don't do fer us. Gus grunts an' glares at him.

This Roho Pelo finishes eatin' an' says polite as a gen'leman in th' parlor, "Thank you." Knows American too.

Gus cocked his head sideways, "Seems t'

have a German accent, don't he?" he whispered.

"German accent? He ain't said ten word an' yo're hearin' accents?" I whispered back.

"Yuh know anythin' 'bout th' trail t' Horsehead?" Jake was always about business.

"Tanks are drying up but you should have enough water to get you to the river. Rio Pecos was swimming, but passable three — maybe four days ago," he says in Spanish. "Big Comanche party crossed going southwest, to Mexico, likely."

Gus punched my ribs. "He *is* German," he hissed.

"Water's plentiful goin' east," Jake offered. It ain't perlite to ask personal questions like "Where you goin'?"

"Your horses are ganted," this Roho Pelo said.

"We lost half our remuda to thieves and can't afford to let these left graze at night or we would be hoofing it to New Mexico," Jake answered. He didn't mention that we had a runnin' fight with th' thieves an' that they was mostly whites. We had buried Ep Ross an' left one o' th' thieves swingin' from a cottonwood limb.

This feller scratches in the dirt with a stick a minute and says, "I have some horses that could help you if we could make a trade or two."

"I'd be interested, for sure," Jake replied.

Act too interested an'it'll cost yuh more.

"I need a gun and a pistol with ammunition and a bowie knife," Rolo Pelo says.

Jake Meeker gives that some thought, rubbing his stubbly chin an' knowin' all th' time we've got poor Ep's outfit right down to his saddle an' extra shirts. "We can scratch around an' maybe come up with something," he allows.

"I will bring my horses to your camp when you stop after the morning march," this feller says, and he leans forward and lifts himself up just with his crossed legs.

"Yuh see that, Gus, can *you* do that?"

The feller takes his plate to the wreck pan. Damned if Cookie don't hand him another steak rolled up in a newspaper. You'd think they growed on trees, and us with only a half dozen heifers in th' lot t' git us to Sumner.

Pelo speaks to his horse and the little mare perks up.

"Bet he can mount that horse from either side," Gus Bell allowed.

"How's come?"

"He's talkin' German to him."

Shore 'nuf that feller mounts from th' left

and rides slow upwind of th' picket line. I thought for a minute those geldin's was gonna uproot th' mesquites they was tied to. "Done that a-purpose," Bell growled. The other hands eased back into the firelight.

"Now ain't that spookier'n a horse on loco weed?" One of them asked.

"Think I'll bed down up by th' picket line," I said.

"You could have solid men sleepin' head t' toe around that remuda an' he'll still git away with them horses," Jake said, "an' leave you sleepin' like a baby."

Even so, he put an extra man on th' night herd crews and kept his night horse tied to a chuck wagon wheel — over Cookie's protests. You can bet there was some sleepy discontent amongst th' crew. No one complained about breakin' th' monotony of a long hot cattle drive, though.

Twice th' next morning I nearly fell off my horse when he took after a stray while I was dozing. Sometimes I think he does it a-purpose. "One of us has t' stay awake, ol boy, an' you have t' see where you's goin'. You kin sleep on th' picket line while I's ridin' herd." He shook his head an' made his ears flop like a mule's. "I *knowed* there was some jackass in yore lineage sommers."

Even rubbin' terbaccer juice in my eyes didn't help.

Our shadows had tucked up under foot when we saw th' smoke of Cookie's fire an' before we got there, we run on to this Pelo feller. He had seven horses b'sides his mare tied to bushes. We noted that only two of them had th' same brand.

"That grulla come from th' Lazy C outfit up on Salt Fork," Gus said.

"Huh," Tom said, "I rode that dun for th' Half Moon Xes."

Jake looked at Pelo, expectin' an answer.

"I took these from the Apaches because they were stolen and still had their shoes. They will be useful to you and you can return them to their owners when your drive is over."

"What's t' keep us from just takin' them an' not payin' a thing?" Gus muttered.

"Tell you what, Bell, you take th' first one an' we'll git th' rest," Tom answered.

Cookie throwed his hat up an' first crew rode in to eat. Jake an' th' Injun scootched up under a bush an' palavered.

Pelo insisted on dealing one horse at a time an' by th' time they were through, he had 'most all of poor ol' Ep's outfit, including his extra shirts. We rode in to eat and that feller rode with us. First thing he did was strip off his buckskin outfit. The shirt kept th' same shape as it did when he wore it. "Coulda been bullet proof." Gus chuckled.

There he stood, knee-high moccasins an' breechcloth. He pulled one of those white shirts on and wrapped the gun belt around his waist — cinched to th' last notch — and stuck th' bowie sheath under the belt.

" 'Cept fer his hair, there stands a 'Pache warrior," Jake observed.

"My father was Elkhorn, the Mescalero chief, and my mother was Little Bird," Pelo said.

"Who were your white folks?" Jake asked.

"I do not remember them, they are dead." The Injun in him said it without a sign of emotion.

"Injuns don't talk about dead folk," I whispered to Gus.

He elbowed me in th' ribs. "I knowed that."

"You knowed that like you knowed Adam."

The Injun inspected his firearms and noted Ep's name carved into the rifle stock. "White men would hang me if they found me with this gun. I would trade anyone for one without a name." He spoke Spanish; seemed more comfortable with it.

"I knew Ep and his family well," Gus said. He went to his horse and pulled his rifle out of its boot. "I will trade you my no-name rifle for it." The guns were just alike and both traders seemed satisfied. When we got back home, Gus gave that gun to Ep's middle boy. He made points with one of Ep's girls and squired her for some time — until he run out of jingle. Preached many a sermon about fickle greedy women after that.

"I knowed 'bout fire 'thout gettin' burned ever' time I built one." I mentioned it to him only once. Seems th' thought was painful for his heart and for my shoulder an' ribs.

Roho Pelo ate with us an' that Cookie wrapped up another steak for his greasy sack.

"Hope I done read those papers," Gus said loud enough for Cookie t' hear.

"Your 'reading' only extends to pictures in ads for women's union suits an' corsets an' I wrapped that grub in th' front pages that's only got words an' which you never look at," Cookie retorted, waving his iron poker in a threatening manner.

"I'm gonna throw that poker in th' next river we cross," Gus muttered.

"Won't do no good, th' nex' river's Rio

Pecos an' th' rod'd float just like Moses' rod in th' Nile."

"Didn' throw his rod in th' Nile. That's heresy."

"Well he coulda," I retorted. Who made *him* a Moses expert, anyway.

They were in need of horseflesh and I was able to trade off five of my seven for a rifle and Mr. Colt's revolver and ammunition. I thought it wise to put a lot of distance between us for my own safety and the continuing possession of King and Amigo.

Two days later, we watered at Big Spring and rode to the top of the mesa to study the land. To the north, the plain rose to the breaks below the Llano Estacado. Even though the land was semiarid, there were lots of natural tanks and wallows and this time of year they were all full. There would be fewer tanks and lakes on the Llano. Travel there would have to be more carefully planned.

The east and west views were much the same, with the westering sun reflecting off hundreds of tanks. Sandhill cranes loafed around the water, biding time before their migration north for the summer. The south view was disturbing, for a thin column of dust could be seen. The path it was taking could only mean company was coming.

The trail down off the mesa on the north side had to be a one-way trail, for nothing short of a goat could climb it. It led straight to the breaks of the caprock and we took it, not bothering to hide our tracks. I began to worry as we approached the foot of the caprock, for there was no trail to the top. In the valley below the north side of one of the last hills, the trail split, one running east and one running west along the base of the bluff. We turned west without hesitation and about a mile along came to a solid rock shelf. Just what I was hoping for.

The Apaches had made leather booties for the horses to hide their trail and I put them on the two horses. King didn't like them and when I was wrapping Amigo's front hoof, the mustang reached around and nipped my butt. She was shocked when I slugged her on the jaw and stood quietly while I finished.

That ledge ran for a long way both directions from the trail crossing and we went east above the junction of the trails. Night came early on the east side of the mesa and when the ledge petered out, we made a dry camp. I tied the horses close to be my watch while I slept and had to promise them a good long graze on the morrow. At dawn, we scrambled down through the shinnery brush to the trail. I took the booties off Amigo's unshod hooves and rode King with his booties on. At noon, we found a tank well off the trail and I removed his booties and let them graze the afternoon away.

My arrow pinned a fat turkey hen to a tree and I got to her just as she broke the shaft. Making a new shaft filled the time she took to cook. I found two eggs in her — enough for two breakfasts.

We bypassed one cañon that cut into the caprock but the extra wide mouth of the cañon they call Yellow House fooled me and I was several miles into it before I realized what I had done. The wide trail of a village on the move gave me pause and I hid in the brush and thought about my situation. The tribe could only be either Kiowa or Comanche, not likely a combination of the two. If they found me, my life might be short and painful. I couldn't afford to let that happen. My options were to turn around and evade detection if I could, or gain the village without challenge and seek the safety of being the chief's guest.

It was highly unlikely that I could hide and escape detection by the hunters and warriors, as they would have to cover a very large hunting ground to provide for a village as big as this one. *You wanted a chance to join the Comanches and here you've stumbled into them. Take the opportunity.* I admired the Comanche. Though they were a bloodthirsty people, their riding skills were not equaled by any people I had met. The Apache didn't respect the horse and what he could do for him. He would ride his mount mercilessly, drink his blood when he couldn't get water, and kill and eat the horse when he could go no farther. Kiowa/Comanche warriors cared for their horses, saw to their welfare and breeding. A horse was intelligent but would be compliant even to his own death. If an intelligent and concerned man would give his horse his due, the horse would lead the man out of trouble nine times out of ten. The wise rider was his horse's partner, not his master.

I decided to enter the village late in the night and camp at the chief's door until he discovered me. Late that evening, I had the luck to kill a deer. It would stand me in good stead to offer it to the chief's wife. When the dipper indicated the night half over, I muffled the horses' hooves and rode up Yellow House Cañon.

The myth is that it would be impossible to sneak up on the wily and ever-alert Indian, but that is not the case. Where they felt secure, the villages didn't post watchers at night, depending on the watchfulness of their dogs to warn of things unusual. There were always two or more boys herding the horses, but they were far from the village and as likely to be under a bush sleeping as not. I had learned a trick or two from the Apache about keeping dogs quiet; the main one was to keep them well fed.

By judicial use of morsels of meat and bones, I was able to keep the fuss to a minimum and of a nature not to alarm. I found the chief's fancy tipi in the middle of the camp with a fine horse saddled and tethered outside. An idea struck and I transferred the chief's saddle to King and tethered him in place of the chief's horse. The chief's horse gladly joined the camp's grazing herd when I shooed him up the valley. I hung the deer on the meat rack, threw a couple of sticks into the firepit, and rolled up in my blanket and dozed — lightly. Amigo almost snored.

There was a faint glow in the sky when a noise at the tipi awoke Rojo to see an old crone emerging, muttering to herself. She glanced at King, took a step or two, and stopped, "Aie-e-e, you are not Thunder; who are you?" she muttered in Comanche. Turning back to the fire, she saw Amigo dozing there and in shuffling over to examine her, stumbled over Rojo. "Aie-e-e," louder, and she delivered a swift kick in the ribs. Now, grandmother was fully awake and trotted squawking into the tipi.

I stood facing the door, in nothing but breechcloth and moccasins (in case I had to run), my empty hands open. There was excited chatter inside; another woman's head popped out of the curtain, surveyed the scenery, and disappeared to more chatter. A male voice spoke sharply and the chatter ceased.

In a few moments, a man stooped through the door and straightened to his full six-foot-plus height. His hair was freshly combed, a scarlet blanket draped over his shoulders. Beaded moccasins covered his feet.

"I am the Apache Rojo Pelo, come to serve you, Chief," I said in Apache.

He examined me up and down and a smile tugged at the corners of his mouth. "When did the Apache grow red hair?" He spoke American, to my surprise.

"I was a captive who became Apache," I stammered. The language seemed foreign on my tongue.

"Well, my Apache friend, why do you come here?"

"I have killed the murderer of my father,

Chief Elkhorn, and left to avoid a feud among the Apache. Now, I wish to become a Comanche warrior."

The head of a younger woman emerged through the curtain and said something to the chief. "I am Quanah, headman of the Quahadi, come, let us eat." He turned and stooped through the door.

I hesitated. *Only a fool would stick his head through that curtain to get it crushed by a war club,* a little voice said.

Quanah held the curtain back and said a little impatiently, "Come, Rojo Pelo, it is safe."

THE IRON JACKET

Here, it seems, is a good place to tell what Rojo Pelo learned around many campfires about Quanah Parker, the last hereditary chief of the Quahadi Comanche. And to do that, I must go back several generations, for the uniqueness of Quanah Parker has more to do with his Comanche ancestors than it does with Cynthia Ann, his white mother.

Many generations ago — no one knows how many — one of Quanah's forefathers — we will call him First Man — found a mail shirt in the sands of the Swift Fox (Arkansas) River. He immediately saw the advantage of an iron shirt that could repel arrows, lances, and later, even bullets. The shirt was badly rusted and some of the rings were fused together. Every day the man worked on his new shirt, neglecting his duties until there was no more meat in the tipi.

"Give me the jacket and I will have it bright and shiny before you can return with meat for the family," First Wife said.

"Hah, woman, you think it will take me days and days to bring you venison or buffalo hump and tongue? I shall go tomorrow and be back before the sun sets with both and you will not have the first circle shiny. I will take your pony away as punishment and you will gather wood afoot as the poor widows do."

"And if I have the jacket shiny on time you will give me that white filly?"

First Man smiled; this was no wager. "Yes." Nothing more was said and the faithful wife served his supper with meat borrowed from her mother's kettle.

As was his custom when hunting, First Man left well before daylight with intentions of getting a nice fat doe from the foothills west of the village. The buffalo would be easy to take on the way home. First Wife, too, as soon as he was on his way, arose, and taking the shirt of mail and a stick she had laid aside for this occasion, mounted her pony, which had been tied behind the tipi, and rode for the river. She crossed the frigid river with her skirt held high and her feet on the pony's back. While the pony shook himself, she chose a large water-smoothed granite rock from the riverbank, and balancing it on the saddle rode over the first sand hills.

There, out of sight from the river, she ran the stick through the arms of the shirt and laid the rock on the body. With a rope tied to the stick ends, she and the pony dragged the shirt through the fine sand. After a mile or so, she examined the shirt and found a satisfactory shiny spot, but only under the stone. "Oh pony, we have a long day ahead of us." First Wife moved the rock as far back on the shirttail as she dared, and making a wide arc, dragged the shirt back to the beginning of her pull. There was progress, but it was too slow a rate to get the job done in a day. Another rock helped a lot and by the time she had made four circles, one side was good and shiny.

The day was far spent by the time she had turned the shirt over and polished the other side; then she turned the shirt wrong side out and finished those sides. Still, it was hours before sunset and she hurried back to the tipi with the shiny coat of mail. At the tipi, First Wife hung the shiny shirt behind her husband's lance and shield displayed by the door. The neighbor women were quick to take notice and nod in satisfaction that another man had been bested by his wife.

It had been a long day for First Man. He had no trouble getting a fat deer in the foothills but when he returned to the plain, there was not a buffalo in sight. Not one. It was slow going with his horse carrying the added burden of the deer carcass. Near midafternoon, he found an old bull lolling about in a wallow. First Man grunted in dissatisfaction; the meat would be tough and strong but it would have to do, he decided. He would have to stalk the bull afoot because his horse was too tired for a chase. It took longer than he wanted, but his arrow ran true and the bull died where he lay. He butchered the carcass with one eye on the sinking sun, taking as much of the meat as he had time to get and the horse could carry. Leading the laden horse, he raced the sun for the village.

Aha, Father Sun, I have beaten you! First Man thought as he reached the village just before the sun touched the shoulder of the Far White Mountains. He waded through hungry sniffing dogs to his tipi and called to his wife to take care of the meat. It was good to sit again on his cushions and partake of his mother-in-law's stew. First Wife busied herself with the meat and soon had a large venison steak roasting for her tired husband.

"Well, woman, I do not see my iron shirt, did you get it shiny?" he asked.

"Oh, you did not see it hanging with your shield at the door?"

First Man sat up in alarm; that rusty thing hanging with his shield would make him the butt of many a joke from the other men of the village. He hurried out to the stand to be stopped short by the shiny jacket hanging there. *Oh no,* he groaned inwardly, *she has shined it.* It didn't bother him so much that he had lost the white filly as it did that he had lost the bet and the whole village knew he had lost. Someone snickered in the dark, but he couldn't see who it was. Realizing that many eyes were watching him, First Man returned to his couch.

First Wife brought the sizzling steak to him and returned to the fire. "I have named the filly Shining Shirt," she said.

Great controversary arose over the strange tracks young men of the village discovered in the sands south of the river. Many theories were proposed, but the mystery remained. Those who knew kept the knowledge to themselves.

Soon, enemies of the Comanche noticed a new warrior on the battlefields. This man wore a shirt of shining rings and no weapon could stop him. Legend had it that he blew arrows and lances away from him and it was later testified many times that bullets had no effect on him. He became known as Iron Jacket and his prowess in war and vicious cruelty became legend. As years passed and Iron Jacket became stronger, the belief that he would not die grew with the legend. It was a secret the Comanche kept that the jacket was handed down from father to son for many generations. There had been four Iron Shirts within present Comanche memory.

Sometime around 1850, the jacket was handed down from his father to Pohibits-quasho, a young man in the Comanche tribe. In 1858, John (Rip) Ford and his Texas Rangers invaded Indian Territory to punish the Comanches who were preying on Texas citizens.

The Battle of Little Robe Creek, on May 12, can be divided into three engagements. The second engagement occurred when

Ford attacked the village of Pohibits-quasho and Iron Jacket led his warriors to battle. Iron Jacket's horse was shot from under him, and as he stood by his horse, Jim Pockmark, the Anadarco scout captain, raised his Sharps buffalo rifle and killed Iron Jacket. The coat of mail could repel ordinary bullets, but not a Sharps .50 caliber bullet.

The Comanches fled in panic and left Iron Jacket on the field, and if it were not for Peta Nocona, Iron Jacket's son, rescuing them, the people of the village would have been destroyed.

Later that evening, the victorious Rangers retrieved the jacket and broke it into many pieces for souvenirs. The Tonkawa Indian scouts, known as Man-Eaters, ate some of Pohibits-quasho.

Peta Nocona married Cynthia Ann Parker and they had two sons, Pecos and Quanah. A third child, Topsana, was a girl. I leave for others to tell the sad story of the recapture of Cynthia Ann and Topsana.

CHAPTER 16
A CALL TO RAID

Spring, 1872

Quanah's tipi was spacious and neat. The chief motioned me to a couch of robes and when we were seated the women served us breakfast. Giggles came from one of the robes to the side and a child stuck her head out and stared. She crept to her father's side, and reaching behind his back, stroked my hair.

"She has never seen a red-haired Apache," Quanah said with a chuckle. The child whispered something. "Now she wants me to get her red hair." He reached around and pulled the child into his lap to her delight; then standing her up, he sent her to the robes with a fatherly spat on her bare bottom.

Quanah pulled his pipe from a pouch and filled it with kinnikinnick. The young woman brought him a burning stick and he lit it, offering a puff to the four corners.

271

After another puff or two, he handed it to me and I conducted the same ceremony.

"You have brought me the gift of a fine horse?" he asked.

I nodded, "His name is King and he is very fast — for a short distance," I added. The "gift" came with strings, for I knew I would be the only one who could ride him.

"The other horse?"

"He is mine," I replied.

A very dark man entered the tipi and stood just inside the door. "We have an Apache visitor, Crier. He wishes to become a Comanche; we should call the council."

The man nodded, and not having said a word, left. Soon I heard Crier calling through the camp.

A few minutes after the crier quit calling, Quanah said, "We must go."

There was an arbor in the common ground in front of the chief's tipi and people were gathering from all directions. Everyone was anxious to see this redheaded Apache, and the calling of a council was a break in the everyday routine of village life. Quanah sat in the semicircle of men and motioned me to sit facing them across the firepit in the middle of the arbor. Again the pipe was lit and the ceremony repeated by Quanah. Then he passed the pipe and each man took a puff. My turn came last and I returned the pipe to Quanah. A man who knew the Apache language sat beside me to translate.

When the pipe was safely stored, Quanah said, "This man is Rojo Pelo of the Apache. He has come to join us to avoid a blood feud among the Apache." There was the usual long silence as the council members considered the topic at hand.

A wizened old man with a wispy white mustache sitting at Quanah's right hand spoke; "We must verify his story."

"Hou," agreed several of the council.

After several moments of meditation, a dark-skinned man with a scar from his nose to his left ear said, "The Apache seems to be young to be a warrior, perhaps he is a little too ambitious." There was the least hint of humor in his voice.

Quanah nodded to me and I responded, "I have trained with the other young Apache men and know the skills of a warrior and have become proficient with the bow and lance." I waved at the deer hanging from Quanah's meat rack, "I hunt the meat to feed my people.

"With the other young men, I tracked wife stealers from the Sierra Madre and fought them. We recovered the women and children safely.

"Comancheros brought Taos Lightning to the camp and the Apache had a debauch. When the Mexicans left, my friends and I followed and killed them and burned their wagons with the booty they had gotten from the villagers.

"A crazy-drunk Yellow Spot would have his way with my mother, Little Bird, but my father, Chief Elkhorn, prevented him and was killed. Later when Yellow Spot would also kill me, we fought and I killed him with this knife." I held the knife for all to see. "Now, Yellow Spot's kin will try to kill me. I am not afraid, but a feud would be very bad for Elkhorn's clan. That is why I come to the Comanche."

"You do not go to your white family?" another asked.

"No, I do not know them. Some Apaches said they were dead. I wish to be a warrior."

After a long silence, the old man with the mustache spoke, "He must prove himself to be a Comanche warrior. Perhaps he should go with the men to Mexico." There were nods and "hous" of approval and when no other comments were made, Quanah stood and said, "Rojo Pelo, you will go with Raven on the raid and be his helper. He will see if you are qualified to be a warrior."

Raven, the dark man with the scar, smiled, "I must learn to speak less in the councils."

"Hou," came a chorus amid chuckles from the crowd. It signaled the end of the council and the meeting broke up. I stood, not knowing what else to do.

Raven approached and said in Spanish, "Rojo, there is not room in my wickiup for another. You may sleep in the bachelor wickiup and take your meals with me." I groaned inwardly, knowing the squalor and pestilence residing in a bachelor's wickiup where no woman dared cook or clean. When things got bad enough, either a bachelor or neighbor set the hut afire and the occupants built again among the ashes. The skill of bachelor wickiup builders drew many a disparaging comment.

"Perhaps I could sleep *outside* Raven's wickiup instead of *inside* the bachelors' hut."

Raven grinned. "*Perhaps* you do not care for the tiny residents the bachelors live with?"

"I have knowledge enough of them," I replied.

Raven laughed. "Come, let us see if there is anything left to eat."

Raven's darkness was only skin deep, for

he was a bright, talkative, and friendly man. As is the case most of the time, his wife, Rosebud, though as friendly as her husband, was a quiet person who seldom had the opportunity to speak when Raven was present.

The reasons for the crowded condition in the household were a number of tykes from two to six years of age that kept the household in a state of confused activity. I never knew which children belonged to Raven and Rosebud, and the number present varied from four to six or eight at any given time, including bedtime. Their comings and goings were seemingly at each child's whim. In the village there was always an adult nearby watching them, and they were free as long as they stayed within its confines. Mischief abounded and as likely as not, Raven would be in the middle of it. It seemed to me that Rosebud's patience was as bountiful.

When a couple of the older boys discovered I was sleeping outside, they insisted on sleeping with me. I didn't mind, for each brought a buffalo robe and we made a quite comfortable bed. I slept well as long as I was out of reach of flailing arms and kicking feet. It wasn't long before I discovered the robes held tenants not conducive to peaceful rest. A periodic daylong visit of the bedclothes to a large — and well fed — anthill kept unwanted visitors to a minimum.

The Comanche relationship with the Old Mexico population was vitriolic in the extreme. For a long time, the Comanche/ Kiowa raiders held the advantage over the Mexican peon, but that advantage would gradually erode with the arming of the peons and the increasing efficiency of the Mexican Border Rurales under the command of Col. Emilio Kosterlitzky. He made war on any and all Indians, whether the bronco Apaches of the Sierra Madre or visitors from north of the border.

A man named Sun Rise had called for the raid and, as was the custom, was the leader. Men of the tribe had the choice of following Sun Rise or staying home. The fact that fourteen men had volunteered indicated that this warrior had some success in previous raids.

Raven kept me busy making arrows while he made metal arrow points. We tested and adjusted until each arrow ran true. Our lives depended on them. Though most of the men had rifles, they still depended on the bow because it had a more rapid-fire ability than the muzzleloaders or even their few needle rifles. The problem all of us had was the chronic lack of adequate ammunition for our guns. A lot of attention was paid to the care and welfare of our horses. Each of us would have two mounts. Any further need would come from what we could find and steal on our raid.

There were to be six apprentice boys along with the fifteen warriors on this raid. The jobs of the apprentices were to care for the horses, keep camp, and any other chore a warrior might demand. Sometimes these were demeaning, but few duties would include participation in activities or exciting dangers reserved for warriors. It was our secret desire that the Mexicans or Rurales would attack us, for then we apprentices would be expected to fight as much as a warrior, and thereby possibly gain the status of warrior by our courage and fighting.

Our departure was abrupt and stealthy. I had noted that the village horses had been divided into two herds, one going up the cañon and the other the opposite direction. I took notice that the herd sent up the cañon consisted only of those horses designated for our raid. It couldn't be coincidence that the two herders were apprentices designated to go with the raiders. As a consequence, I gathered my packs just inside the hut after dark, where I could get them on a moment's notice.

Needless to say, my sleep was light and wakefulness often. Still, there was no tap on my shoulder, no whispered summons. Near sunrise I became anxious that the raiders had left without me. There was a gray streak in the east when I gave up and slept soundly until rooted out by three scamps.

Raven looked up from his bowl and grinned. "How was your sleep, Rojo?"

"Just fine," I growled.

"You must find an anthill for your blankets; I fear your sleep has been too much disturbed." He couldn't hide his amusement even with that bowl in his face. Later on, when we were alone, he said, "We must be careful about our movements, Rojo, the rocks have eyes."

Great clouds billowed up far away and high above the rim of the cañon. By nightfall, the lightning was flashing too far away to hear thunder. Later, a soft rain fell and the lightning died away. A slight rustle at the door roused me to action. Without word or sound, we followed the horses up the cañon, joined by other shadows. I was surprised; we must have walked two miles or more before we were up with the herd. The darkness under lowering clouds and rain was almost complete. There was no way to find our own horses, so each caught a horse and mounted. A disturbance on the other side of the herd hinted that someone had tried to mount Amigo. I hoped it was Raven.

We rode up Yellow House until it was only a shallow swale and turned south on the Llano. A flatter plain cannot exist. Midmorning, the rain stopped and the clouds broke up. We followed the southward path of yesterday's storm, keeping to the thickest sod. Our pace was almost leisurely.

When my mount indicated thirst, I let him wander to a tank and drink. "Only one or two horses may drink at a pool, just like the wild horses do," Raven instructed. I walked my horse into the water far enough that I could reach down and get a palmful or two of water for myself.

Late evening, we came to Twin Lakes and stopped to change to our own horses and eat a little pemmican and jerky. After dark, we rode west a few miles and slept. It was nice to hear the sounds of the prairies, piping frogs in the water holes, yipping coyotes, and once the lonesome howl of a lobo wolf.

Our pace the next day was purposeful. We left the path of the storm and spread out wide to keep dust to a minimum. There were still plenty of wallows and tanks with water, but the fourth day the land became very dry with no surface water. Our pace slowed in the sand and dust and heat. We rode through the night and just before dawn, the horses smelled water, picked up their pace, and scattered to several tanks where the party rested while the horses drank and grazed.

Raven pointed to a shadow on the horizon far to the south, "There is the mountain with the gap. We go west of it to the crossing of Rio Pecos."

It was Horsehead Crossing and Sandy's Castle Gap. "I know the place," I said.

"The land is very dry after Rio Pecos and we will suffer for water some," he said.

I had never been south from Horsehead, but the Apaches had told me about the land and the lack of water. King Mountain rose on the horizon as we approached it the next two days. We came down the west side of the mountain, avoiding passing through the gap, and camped at the foot of the mountain near the spring. I drank from the log trough for the second time.

There was a well-beaten trail that ran southwest from Horsehead Crossing, but we turned right almost due west. "Soldiers have built forts on the trail and we will take a new trail to avoid them," Raven said.

The trail we followed was invisible for the most part, and far from smooth. The dust and heat took a heavy toll on man and horse. The last half of the second day without water, most of us walked. The whole band grew more and more cautious as we progressed. Raven told me that we were only a short ride north of Fort Stockton and its soldiers. Just before sunset, a scout rode in and reported that the springs at the head of Leon Creek were safe to approach; no soldiers were around. The springs were low, but by digging downstream, we found enough water for the horses.

It seemed there was nothing good in the land ahead of us. Grass was sparse and already turning brown. We spent a restless night scratching around for adequate grass for the stock and watching for the Buffalo Soldiers. Well before dawn, we watered the horses and left the spring. Sand hills slowed us, and beyond them, the alkali flats choked man and horse. Many a curse was called down on the curly black heads of the soldiers who built Forts Stockton and Davis on the Comanche Trail and forced us to travel these waterless wastes.

The afternoon after we watered at the spring, we encountered a fresh trail of shod horses that crossed our path in a northwesterly direction. The men gathered and decided to send scouts to follow the trail a ways. Raven allowed me to ride with the scouts and near sunset we smelled smoke. Creeping forward, we came quite suddenly upon the bluff of a ravine and down below saw horses. The twinkle of a fire through the leaves of trees that lined the ravine bottom told us where the men camped. My companion, Little Horn, whispered, "Buffalo Soldiers."

"Where?" I asked.

"I know by their horses," he replied.

I looked closer, but aside from the horses looking old and skinny, couldn't see any sign that might tell me who rode them. "Not very good horses."

Little Horn nodded. "That's how I know who rides them. Buffalo Soldiers never have good horses."

This was my first encounter with the Buffalo Soldier, but in all the years I knew them, I never saw a decently mounted squad. The reason being that the army only gave them condemned and retired horses. Yet the Ninth and Tenth Cavalries were the best and most active units in the Indian wars. In spite of the prejudice of the white army, they fought more battles and engagements and had the least desertion rates of any other army units. Name almost any battle on the southern plains and Buffalo Soldiers would have been there. Many of them were awarded the Medal of Honor for their bravery.

An owl hooted softly and we gathered with the other scouts. "They are not a threat to us, we will let them go on their way," Little Horn said and the others agreed. Without another word, we mounted and rode to intercept the trail. We found our party's passing and followed. "They won't stop tonight, but will ride until they get to Balmorhea Springs," Little Horn explained, and we rode on through the night. Again, our horses were exhausted and again we walked. Our long, long shadows at dawn had almost disappeared under us when the horses smelled water and picked up their pace. We let them go ahead and stumbled into camp at our own speed.

Concern about the welfare of the horses seemed to be on the minds of all the men, and Sun Rise called a halt to allow them to recruit a little. I took that to mean that there was more waterless travel ahead. Balmorhea Springs was an oasis in the desert and the marshy places around it had plenty of green grass. The horses did very well there, and they left the grass cropped two days later.

From there, we followed a well-defined trail southwest into the Davis Mountains. The cool Madera Cañon with its thousand-foot-high cliffs became an oven in the noontime sun. It was midafternoon before the shadow of the western cliff gave us any relief. We reached the divide in time to see the sunset, and a little ways down the other side, made a dry camp.

South of the pass between Mount Livermore and Bear Mountain, we dug wells for our horses at Medley Draw. The water was barely fit for them and not fit for us.

Raven drank too much and scoured in his breechcloth. "Take this and wash it out in a well," he demanded. I hesitated, refusal on my lips, and he raised his war club. Guess he anticipated my reluctance. The cloth got an angry, perfunctory washing, and I was on the verge of rising when movement on weed leaves near my face caught my eye. The leaf was covered with tiny red dots, and when my hand drew near, the dots raised up on edge. Closer inspection revealed hundreds of tiny seed ticks. Each time my hand neared the leaves, the ticks rose as one on hind legs, anticipating a transfer to a traveling meal. With no thought of hesitation about it, I scraped a good number of them into the folds of the cloth.

"Ah-h, that feels cool," Raven said as he tucked the damp cloth under his belt. Later, he experienced intense itching in his crotch. Though he had dark suspicions, he never figured out how those ticks got on him.

Our water bags were getting low. Mile upon mile of hot, dusty trail brought us to a dry lake, and we trudged on southwest to a point north of Capote Peak where we found stagnant ponds the horses could barely stand to drink. They were not allowed their satisfaction, for the water was heavily alkaline. Even at that some of them scoured and we only allowed them a small drink in the morning.

"Water is near, Rojo," Little Horn said as we rode through the pass between Capote and the Sierra Vieja. At the end of the Sierra, we turned sharply north up the west side of the mountain to a spring bubbling out of the mountain. The horses stopped to drink from the little stream before it sank, and I walked on up to the spring, anticipating a long cool drink on this hot day. No one else seemed anxious for a drink, so I knelt and dipped my hands into the water. It nearly scalded my hands and I jumped back to the laughter from my companions.

"The water is too *frío* for you, Rojo?" Raven asked.

"Caliente," I replied and splashed some on his legs. He hopped back laughing. "The horses are wiser drinkers than Rojo."

Chapter 17
South of the Border

We crossed the Rio Grande at the arroyo north of the village of Candeleria. The valley was wide and well watered, broken into fields, and farmed by villagers living in the edge of the hills west of the valley. "We will visit the village upon our return," Raven said. "Now, we have other places to visit."

The change in the band was notable. Where they were furtive and cautious in Texas, they now rode openly with the demeanor of conquerors. Even as they rode, they painted faces and bodies for war. When we stopped to rest and eat, more time was spent applying war paint and dressing for battle than eating or resting. Even the noncombatant helpers applied paint to themselves and their horses.

The Apache laughed at the Kiowa/Comanche custom of painting themselves for war, calling them vain women. I only adopted the custom to appease my companions and as many times as not "forgot" to paint myself.

Beyond the river valley, we reentered rough hills devoid of any water except the occasional stream or spring in the valleys where the Mexicans huddled and scratched out an existence just above starvation. They were terrified of us and hid when we rode into sight. There were more abandoned ranches and villages than occupied, a testimony to the devastation caused by the invading Comanche and Apache warriors. Around the campfires, there was talk of the time they had invaded the city of Chihuahua and the desire was strong to return there, though not with this small a force. The western side of the mountains was better watered and populated by a more prosperous people. It was here that we began our depredations, gathering horses, looting, and stealing women and children.

As the newest helper, I was given the most menial of tasks, which meant gathering firewood and herding the growing caballada. As it grew, it required more and more helpers to keep the horses gathered. We were watching them feed in a cornfield while the warriors attacked the nearby village when a posse of Mexicans armed with old guns, pitchforks, and clubs ran from the trees yelling and waving blankets, intent on stampeding and stealing the horses.

"See to the horses, Dog Fat," I called, and turned to meet the mob. I charged them from their right side, firing arrows and yelling. They were so bunched that my shots nearly all took effect of some kind, and I charged right through the middle of them.

A man with an old blunderbuss fired at me, but he was too far away for the pebbles he fired to do more than sting. It was enough to give my mount added incentive to run and we bowled over the men in our path. I lay low on the horse and slashed left, then right with my bow. Another man fired at me, his bullet passing harmlessly overhead, but the nearness of the shot made my ears ring for days.

I cleared the crowd and turned for another charge when the posse scattered into a panicked retreat. Only the two men with the guns remained in the field of battle, reloading their guns. They slowly retreated along the paths of their companions, guarding their backsides until they disappeared into the woods. There were no bodies left behind and I took it that my arrows had only inflicted wounds that would heal.

The horses had panicked and run and it took us a while to get then calmed and gathered. By that time, they were in an oat field and the feed calmed them down enough to graze again. Since this was farther from the woods and surprise attacks, we left them. I was sweaty and sticky and when I wiped my face, my hand was bloody. One of the herders rode up and exclaimed, "Rojo, you are covered with blood."

There might have been a dozen bleeding places on my right side. I hopped down and rubbed my horse's side and he had as many places on him as I had. His fur had given him more protection and there weren't as many bleeding places on him. I wiped down my face and side with my headband but it didn't help much. Most of the places ignored the wiping and continued to bleed. Blood caked in the coat on the horse and caused his bleeding to stop before mine. We plastered my spots with mint leaves found growing along the roadside and it stopped the bleeding. The next trick was to peel the leaves off without restarting the bleeding. This split in the edge of my ear is where a pebble cut it.

The two old rurales sat dozing against the wall, out of the cold wind and warmed by the sun. Long past their prime and crippled by the rheumatism that afflicted the old, they were content to while their days awaiting *la puerta de muerte* to open and beckon. Their rest was disturbed by whispered conversation beyond the wall and a shower of sand on their sombreros.

"They are here, Lupe, we have found them." The boy pushed backward from the wall and fell in the gravel with a grunt. The sound of running feet faded as the boys ran for the gate. Soon, around the corner they came, their bare feet stirring little clouds of dust as they ran.

"Grandfather, Grandfather, tell us the story of El Rojo," Lupe puffed.

"Tell us, tell us," young Picho implored, hopping on one foot and pulling sand spurs from the other.

"We are very busy here," Grandfather Gabriel said as he peered from beneath the rim of his sombrero, "and many of the world's sorrows remain to be solved."

"You say the world will always have sorrows, Grandfather," Lupe said.

"This is true, Gabriel." Fernando, his companion, tapped Gabriel's knee. "But we will not have the *chiquitos* long; they will grow up and find other things to do. We must tell the stories while they will listen."

Gabriel shifted his back against the wall, seeking a sun-warmed spot to ease his aches. "Very well, boys, sit and we will talk of these things." He sat a moment, reaching back in time and arranging his thoughts. "It was many, many years ago when we were young men —"

"How many years, Grandfather?"

"Ah-h-h . . . this many." Fernando flashed his ten fingers — though one was just a stub — five times and then held up the five fingers of one hand.

The boys' lips moved in counting and Lupe's eyes grew wide, "You are *that old,* Grandfather?"

"That and much more." Gabriel chuckled. After a moment, he resumed his tale. "The Indians were very wild and cruel back then and they would come down across the border and raid our villages, taking our horses and corn and killing and burning our homes. First, the Apaches would come and then the Comanches and Kiowa would come. The people fled to the bigger towns, only the brave —"

"And foolish," Fernando interjected.

"— stayed. Our village would not run from the invaders.

"The Comanche came suddenly one day and according to plan, the young men grabbed their weapons and ran into the woods. We were not cowards, but we had the intention to gather and attack the Indians as an army. While we were gathering, someone saw that the caballada was destroying our cornfield and it was decided that we would attack there before the crop was ruined."

"If we captured their horses, the Comanche would be helpless in our hands," Fernando added. "We crept to the edge of the woods and on the signal charged, yelling and waving blankets. The animals ran and all the herders ran after them in terror."

"All *except* El Rojo," Gabriel corrected. "He was a very large man with blazing hair that fell below his shoulders. When he rode, his hair flowed out behind, making him seem to be ablaze. His horse was large with feet of iron that struck fire when he ran.

"El Rojo charged us, loosing arrows so fast a dozen men were hit before he plowed into us, slashing left and right with a huge club. Many fell before him and his great horse felled many others with his hooves and teeth."

"Your grandfather had a blunderbuss loaded with smooth river pebbles and as El Rojo passed, fired into him," Fernando said. "An ordinary man would have fallen, but not that *Diablo*. He drove right on as if nothing had happened. At the edge of the posse, I fired my rifle, my muzzle almost touching the man. He did not stop, but ran through and turned to attack again."

"This was the moment that our *Capitán* called for a retreat and the company returned to the woods," Gabriel continued. "As planned, Fernando and I, the only two with firearms, stayed behind to protect our retreating comrades. We were quickly reloading when a warrior called to El Rojo and he left the battlefield. There on the ground was the rifle ball that I had fired at El Rojo. It had bounced off of him.

"We had won the field, and though we failed to capture the caballada, the horses had stampeded and were lost to the Indians for a time." Gabriel shifted to a warmer spot on the wall.

"But it was won at a terrible cost," Fernando continued. "Many men were wounded by El Rojo's arrows and club, and it was many days before all the wounded were healed."

Gabriel had settled against the wall again. "You have seen the lump in Señor Sebas's back where El Rojo's arrow struck. The head remains there to this day."

"El Rojo struck terror in our land and many times he invaded Mexico, but he never returned to our village. Our bravery was too much for him," Fernando concluded the tale.

The two boys sat wide-eyed and silent, savoring the image of the battlefield and the terrible El Rojo. Shaking himself from his reverie, Lupe commanded, "Gather your army, gather your army, Picho, I, El Rojo, return to avenge my defeat."

"*I* am El Rojo, and *you* must call *your* men to arms," Picho countered. The two scrambled away to find their "blazing capes" and mount their fiery stick steeds and argue the afternoon away.

Gabriel sighed and lowered his sombrero over his eyes. There was a long silence as the two returned to their naps.

"They whipped our asses, you know," Fernando's lowered sombrero muffled his voice.

"It is not good to burden the boys with too much truth," the other sombrero replied. "I will confess my sin when Father O'Brady returns."

Word came to bring the horses into the village and when we did, several were loaded with the loot taken from the houses. There were silver and gold items taken from the church, but no precious metals or coins were found in the houses.

I heard crying and found a child in the house, crying over the body of his mother. A man lay nearby, several arrows piercing his body.

"Take the child or kill him," Raven said as he passed, carrying loot from another room. I picked the boy up and he kicked and squalled until I slapped his face. He was covered with blood but I found no wounds on him. Sun Rise called and we scrambled to mount and ride away.

The boy sat in front of me and sobbed quietly. It wasn't long until he slept, overcome by fear and grief. He was small, maybe four or five years old. His only clothing was a dirty shirt or gown that reached to just above his bare feet. He smelled of sweat, blood, and old urine, and I saw a louse crawl through his close-cropped hair. *What am I going to do with you?* A bath and nit picking were the first order of business, for sure. I avoided thoughts of what came after that.

Sun Rise led us up into the mountains on a trail that gradually faded into nothing and on through the trees until we came to a stream that flowed out of a rock passage so narrow that it scraped our legs as we passed through. The passage opened into a narrow meadow surrounded with towering cliffs.

We rode nearly a mile through tall and thick grass to a shelter under the left wall. Buildings made of shaped stone and covered with mud lined the back of the shelter from floor to ceiling. On the old plaza in front were two mounds that covered pits the Apaches called kivas. They seemed to be places where the people gathered for some kind of ceremony or possibly a secret society or worship.

Though the Comanches seemed to show no fear of the place as the Apache did, they were subdued and quiet as they unloaded their packs on the plaza. Fires were lit in two of the firepits and the captive women were put to work cooking meals.

The child clung to me, dry-eyed but still with an occasional sob that shook his whole body. After my chores were done, I took a blanket and one of the shirts I had traded for and led the boy downstream to a small pool where I washed, then stripped and scrubbed him clean to the tune of his loud protests. I had to apply a hand to his bare bottom to convince him to sit still while I combed nits from his hair. It was good his hair was short. Wrapped and warm in the blanket, he slept as I carried him back to camp and my robes.

Sun Rise set the watches at the pass and

Raven's was from noon until sunset the next day, which meant that I would be the watcher while Raven slept. My chores ended, I joined the boy in the robes . . . as did the warriors with their whiskey and captive women. The sounds of weeping and violence precluded any sleep or rest, and I took my bed, child and all, and removed to the helpers' camp far from the noise. *It may have been a blessing your mother died in her house, little one.* Even so, the sights and sounds of violence echoed in my mind and wrenched away sleep and drove me from my robes. I tossed a stick on the coals and the flare of the flames revealed the helper Dog Fat, son of Howeah, sitting across the fire from me. He nodded without speaking and we sat staring at the fire, each lost in our own troubled thoughts.

Howeah was one of the most enthusiastic raiders, showing no mercy for his victims. Twice, he had captured women, only to slit their throats when a more attractive woman was encountered. He slept with a young woman no older than Dog Fat.

The boy was muttering to himself and the words gradually came to me, "He dishonors my mother, he dishonors my mother," over and over, as if he couldn't think of anything else.

Activity in the main camp died away with the fires and relative quiet settled over the valley. We could hear the horses grazing across the meadow. I pulled my knees up, and with my head cradled in my arms, slept.

Some small stirring across the fire disturbed my sleep and I glanced up to see Dog Fat settle back down. He had gone to get his robe. He seemed much calmer and lay down with his feet to the fire and slept. I thought I saw a spot of blood on his cheek.

A dark figure swung his machete at me, and I flung my arm up to deflect the blow. The loss of my arm pillow caused my head to fall, pinching my injured ear against my knee and it bled anew. It took a moment for me to remember where I was. Dog Fat snored softly and the fire needed tending. The golden sunlight on the cliffs high above announced sunrise and I put the coffee pot on the fire. The aroma wafted over the sleepers, arousing them from their rest. Even my little captive shuffled into the firelight and found my lap. I named him Janos after his village. The warrior sleeping ground was still very quiet, so we commenced cooking a meal of our own. The morning wore on toward noon and I played with little Janos, keeping his mind off his sorrow and fear.

People began to stir up at the main camp and the women began to prepare a meal. A disturbance and scream drew our attention to Howeah, who was beating his slave woman to the amusement of the other men. The woman broke free and ran away. Howeah took a few steps after her and gave up the chase. His face and chest were bloody, and it was apparent he had been injured. As we approached, he clamped his headband to his face in an effort to staunch the blood flow.

"She has cut my face," he exclaimed. When he pulled away the cloth, we saw that a goodly portion of his nose had been cut away. "I will kill her."

"She did not cut you, Howeah, I did," Dog Fat said, and he tossed the severed piece of flesh at his father.

Howeah stared at the bloody mass in his hand a moment, then at Dog Fat, his anger building. "Then it is you I will kill," he shouted and charged the boy.

Hands of several men reached out and restrained the man before he could reach Dog Fat. This killing was doubly forbidden by the tribe, which forbade the murder of an offspring. The murder of a fellow warrior would cause the raid to cease immediately and the men would have to return to their village.

Sun Rise grabbed Dog Fat and shook him, hardly containing his anger. "Why have you mutilated your father?" he demanded.

"He has been unfaithful to my mother and lay with another woman. He is no longer my father." Dog Fat jerked free of Sun Rise and returned the man's stare. "Is it not said that the unfaithful one shall have their nose cut off?"

"That punishment . . . is for the woman . . ." Sun Rise stammered.

"The man is just as guilty as the woman," Dog Fat insisted. "I have done this thing in defense of my mother. Her faithfulness to Howeah has been betrayed."

Sun Rise realized he had been holding his breath and slowly exhaled. *The boy in his ignorance does not realize the husband's right to seek restoration is the offending man's "punishment."*

"The son has the same right as the wife's brothers to seek retribution in this instance," Hojoso, an old warrior said. "I have seen it so."

"Ah-h-h, but to cut off one's nose, is it not a new thing?" another asked.

"I have seen this once before," the old man replied. "But is it not better than cutting off the horn?"

Several in the crowd grinned and nodded. There were rare occasions when the offended wife removed the horn of temptation from a husband sleeping off an alcoholic debauch.

"Then it is the right of the son to seek revenge on the unfaithful husband, but is it right he should remove his nose?" Sun Rise asked.

Hojoso shrugged. "It is his choice."

"It is a thing one cannot undo," a warrior observed. "We cannot punish the son for standing up for his mother."

"Howeah has been punished for his trespass," said another. He could not help but notice how many other men, including himself, could receive the same punishment were there someone to stand up for their wives. The council was very quiet.

After several moments of quiet, Sun Rise spoke, "This thing is a family affair and not a fight or crime against the band. We will continue our raid." The men returned to the fires and their meals. Howeah glared at Dog Fat. "This is not over. I will seek you at another time." He turned and strode away. When the band gathered to plan their next raid, Howeah was not there.

Chapter 18
Ghosts of the Sierra Madre

I do not think the Indian is bothered too much by a conscience. His actions seem to be more of a reaction to the events of the moment. It seemed that all the enthusiasm for the raid left with Howeah and the consensus of the men was that they return to the rancheria with what plunder they had. Sun Rise was still hungry for a more successful raid and set our route north, intending to go into New Mexico Territory. There was a Rurales outpost at Ascension and we stole their horses. The soldiers shot at us long after we were out of range.

"El Capitán will tell all about the battle with us and how he repelled our attack and ran us off, *'But ¡ay!, they stole our horses.'*" Little Horn laughed and laughed.

"We are going northwest, Little Horn; I thought we would be going north or east to the reservation," I said by way of asking.

"We go to the Valley of Playas. There is a

gringo rancho there that has many horses, much cattle. Soon you and I will go there to spy."

This was good news to me. I was ready to be away from this bunch. The whole band had become sullen and their dark mood led to short tempers and much abuse of the helpers. We were crossing a large flat plain and had stopped for the night when Little Horn motioned for me to join him, "We go, now."

I barely had time to take Janos to one of the women to care for him while I was gone.

Little Horn rode ahead, northwest toward the mountains, and I trotted to catch up. Soon, there was only the faintest glow behind the peaks and we rode on into the night. We rode single file, and I was expected to keep up without notice of any change of pace, for we did not speak. Soon, horse caught on to our intentions and I left the keeping up to him. He did a good job. At the foot of a mountain, we ran on to a stream and watered in one of the few pools left.

"Now, we put the boots on the horses," Little Horn instructed.

When he was ready, he mounted and turned right along the east base of the mountain, leaving me struggling to tie the last boot while horse fussed, *"Hurry, we are being left behind."* When at last the tie was made, he hurried off, not waiting for me to mount. I was lucky to get my left foot in the right stirrup and for a moment considered mounting the nag backwards. Hoss's pace never slackened until he was in position behind his leader. By lying on my belly across the saddle, I was able to squirm around and take my proper seat.

I leaned forward and whispered in the horse's ear, *"If you say one word about that, I'll geld you."* He snorted and nodded his head. Promise of another sunrise gave us enough light that I could see the little cove in the mountain that Horn turned into.

"We leave the horses here where there is enough grass . . ." Horn jerked his horse to a stop and stared. The grass was mostly gone and what little was not grazed down was trampled. Little Horn carefully stepped down and stared at the ground while I pulled my rifle and stood guard.

"A few horse tracks and many, many moccasin tracks and some boots. Much confusion here." He wandered across the cove and disappeared into the bushes. When he didn't return, I picketed the horses where there was a little grass and hurried after the scout. He had wandered up a well-hidden path, reading sign and ignoring the danger of not having a lookout. "Blood here . . . and here . . . much blood here." He pointed the spots out as he passed. I chanced a glance now and then and noted that the path — where it wasn't bare rock — had many tracks. An occasional splash or stain of blood gave testimony that there had been violence along the trail. A boulder had a large stain on the east side of it and scars of bullet strikes on the west side. The blood had turned black, indicating that time had passed after it was deposited. Cool air flowing down the mountainside carried the stench of death and our pace slowed as our caution redoubled.

At the top of a ridge, the trail forked, one branch running to the right and climbing the steep hill. "Lookout point," Little Horn nodded toward the peak of the ridge. We heard the low growls of wolves while the vultures sat on the rocks patiently waiting to pick bones. Little Horn searched up the hill a way and returned. "Boots and moccasins go up, only moccasins come back down," he muttered as he passed, continuing over the ridge and down the main trail.

Here we found twigs clipped by bullets and bullet impacts on both sides of the boulders along the trail. A leg bone protruded from a boot lying in the path. It took us a few moments to find the body lying face up, partially held in the branches of a bush. Little Horn studied the ground a few moments. "No tracks where he walked in there, and there were two people close behind that rock; one was small." He pointed to a boulder on the right side of the trail and walked around to the west side of the rock, and pointing to scuffs in the moss said, "Ah-h-h, he climbs the rock." Walking to the east side again, "He leaps; hider shoots him on the fly and he lands there. Hider and little one run up the trail."

Removing his headband and tying it tight around his face, he crawled under the brush. With a stick, he stirred the gore on the ground under the body, disturbing a cloud of flies and bugs. We hurried down the hill out of the cloud of bugs before removing our masks. "Dead only four or five days, Rojo. There was quite a battle here."

And so it was. We continued down the mountain with Little Horn studying the ground and commenting on what he found while I stood watch over him. I was able to learn a lot about tracking that day. Once, I saw the Sierra Madre across the valley. "We are not on the Sierra," I exclaimed.

Little Horn smiled. "That is right, this mountain is called El Medio because it is alone in the middle of the plain. The placita we seek is hard against this mountain below us and we will have to leave this trail soon or risk being seen."

Indeed, we didn't go a hundred yards more before he ducked into the brush on the right side of the trail. It seemed we crawled a mile under that brush, pushing our rifles before us. We soon could hear occasional sounds below us; a man calling, a horse walking along a stone path, a rooster crowing. Little Horn finally stopped behind a huge flat-topped stone as big as a house and stood up. Holding a fist full of grass in front of his face, he stretched to peek over the top of the rock and exclaimed, "Well look at that."

I beheld a rock wall built along the far edge of the rock. "Someone built themselves a fort," I whispered.

"Give me a boost up," he grunted, and without waiting, stepped on my thigh and rolled on top of the rock, leaving me to struggle up as I could and crawl across the rock behind him. The wall was crudely built, testifying to the haste in which it was constructed. Still the builders had left several holes for shooting through and the number of shells lying about proved they had shot many times. I smelled one of the shells, "These were fired recently, Little Horn."

He sniffed several shells and nodded, "Two, maybe three days ago."

The placita lay below us, all except the far sides of the walls open to our view. The shooters had an excellent spot for covering the streets and flat roofs of the houses below. A dark stain down the inside of the wall above the roof of the nearest building indicated they had at least one victim. Heavily armed Anglos and Mexicans stood, marched, or sat everywhere around the plaza.

Little Horn elbowed my ribs, "Look here." He picked up a broken arrow shaft with the point missing. "Apache. They built this wall, most likely overnight before they attacked the placita at dawn."

I pointed to the stain on the wall, "They had a lookout there."

"Yes, and one is likely there now," he replied. We watched closely for a time and at a call from below, a man who had been sitting in the shade under the near wall of the house stood and strolled to the front of the house and answered.

Little Horn grinned. "Lazy man makes

poor lookout."

We could see only three or four horses in the corral, and they were nothing special.

"Good horses over there." He pointed to the northwest across the plain where a house sat in the edge of the foothills. For the first time, we looked over an empty plain. Not an animal of any kind was visible, no cattle, no horses. The largest thing on the plain was an arbor far to the south. Little Horn nodded toward a similar arbor in the middle of the northern plain, *"Åbolir."* He looked over the whole view before us carefully and abruptly said, "We go."

We wriggled off the rock and Horn struck off east through the brush until we intercepted a dim trail that led up the mountain. Several hot and very dry miles later, we reached the main trail and hurried over the ridge and down to the horses. No grasses survived within the circle of their pickets, and we rode southeast to the stream and all of us drank. To my surprise, Little Horn turned north along the eastern foot of El Medio into the night. I ate the last of my jerky and contemplated eating the leather pouch it was stored in, but decided to wait until I could boil it a while first. Well above the north end of the mountain, we turned west and hurried across the open plain to

the foothills of the Sierra Madre. Behind
the first hills, Little Horn found a dim trail
and followed it south until it ran under a
bluff, and in an open space we stopped. We
rolled up in our blankets and slept until the
rumbling of our stomachs woke us. There
was a firepit close that had been recently
used and we cooked with the wood left
there.

Little Horn drew in the sand. "We are
here; the horse pasture is here. It has a *jacal*
for the keepers in this corner," he said,
indicating the southwest corner of the
pasture. "We will go to see if there are any
horses there."

We rode south on the trail, noting that it
had been used by unshod horses only a few
days before. I worried that the Apache
might still be lurking about and spent as
much of my time looking behind us as in
front. Twice, Little Horn stopped and
climbed the hill that rose between our trail
and the plain. Each time, he returned looking grim. "No horses in pen," he said.

We tied the horses in a small clearing and
followed the moccasin tracks to the shanty
in the edge of the woods. It was empty and
there were two fresh graves behind the
building. We could see from our hiding
place that the bars of the gate to the horse

pasture were down.

Little Horn pronounced a curse on the Apaches that had beat us to the placita and its treasure, "May your horses go lame and your wives be barren."

"That seems harsh, Little Horn, why do the wives have to be barren?"

"I have said what I have said," and he headed for our horses.

At least we were closer to the south plain and our band. When we mounted, I led the way south on the trail. "No, no, no, Rojo, we will not go that way." He turned to retrace our trail back north.

"Why, Horn? Isn't it closer to go south and cross the plain there?"

Little Horn stopped and turned, "It is closer except for the *espíritu.*"

"Espíritu?"

"Yes, the Black Robe espíritu."

I thought a moment; "Do you mean ghost priests?"

"Yes, Rojo, espíritu of Black Robes. They come and build a church down there," he indicated the trail south, "and their espíritu guards it."

"They built a church up here in these hills when there is plenty of flat ground down there?"

"Only a small church; only two Black

313

Robes. Water is there. They plant beans and corn."

"What happened to them?"

"Apache kill, leave bones; espíritu cannot go to spirit world. They guard the church and bad things happen to those who go there." He turned back to the north trail and I followed. *If part of scouting is that you starve, I will not be one.*

There was much consternation and anger when we reported our findings at the camp on Rio Casas Grandes where the band had waited for us. To show our contempt of the Anglo ranchers, we burned the south arbor and its occupants; and in full daylight made a leisurely march up the middle of the plain, camped at the north arbor, and left it burning the next morning as we rode north to pass between the Big Hatchet and Little Hatchet Mountains.

We could get water by digging wells in the Hachita Valley. A scout that looked at the country west of the valley found a prospector's camp. It had been hastily abandoned and they plundered the camp. By the time they returned to the main body, the whiskey they found was gone and they were roaring drunk.

That camp was the last any of us saw of settlement of any kind until we began to

find a few ranches as we neared the Rio
Grande. A few scalps were taken, but the
smoke of burning houses and barns warned
people of our approach and we found their
places abandoned. The stock had been
driven off so that there were few to take.
There was much plunder to take, but without horses to carry it, we had to destroy it.

The villages along the Rio Grande were
our last targets, but before we got there, a
posse of Anglos and Mexican-Americans
met us. They were a determined bunch, and
after following us for some distance, attacked. The women captives ran for safety
and I caught Janos as he was being dragged
away by the woman caring for him. I
shielded the howling boy from the bullets
and ran for cover.

Sun Rise found a deep arroyo, its sides
covered with heavy growth. It was a good
place to make a stand. I found a log that
made a good prop for my long muzzle-
loading rifle and sat down behind it, my
back against the bank and Janos lying close
against the log. The brushy overhang above
us prevented any attacks from behind.

The posse was forced to make their attacks afoot and would creep up on the edge
and fire a volley into the arroyo. Though
they fired blindly, they were effective in

wounding and killing warriors. I was almost covered with twigs and leaves brought down by their shots.

Dog Fat crawled in beside me. "I will help you, Rojo. How do you know where to aim before the men appear?"

"They send a sign before them when they attack," I replied. "Wait and watch."

We watched the edge of the ravine bank and in a few minutes a tall-peaked sombrero crept into view. I shifted my aim to it.

"Ah-h-h, the sombrero announces the man." Dog Fat chuckled. When another sombrero appeared, he shifted to aim his arrow at it.

The two heads beneath the hats appeared at the same time as if on a signal and we both fired. "Now, we duck, Dog Fat," and I lay behind the log.

Dog Fat followed after a moment. "In his eye," he said.

When the enemies' guns were empty, they retreated and I reloaded as quickly as possible with a one-eyed specter staring at me, an arrow shaft protruding from his right eye. Someone pulled the bodies away from the brink and we awaited the next attack. Many times, my shot was the first one heard — and they were effective, as were Dog Fat's arrows. He began to delay ducking to see if his shot had taken effect or sometimes would get off several arrows before ducking. Once he was struck in the stomach but poked a rag into the hole and continued fighting. Almost everyone in the arroyo was wounded or dead from the repeated attacks. I had a couple of grazing wounds along the back of my exposed arm and wounds from flying gravel. Sun Rise had wounds in his left arm and leg but still fought. Tahkuh, the son of Peta Nocona's brother, got shot in the back.

Toward evening, Sun Rise moved through the arroyo giving instructions. "When it is nearly dark, I will go out to meet the enemy and while he is occupied, those that can, escape."

By the time we had sustained another attack and it was dark enough, there were only six of us left alive. I had run out of bullets and my last two targets got the taste of my arrows. One of my shots hit a man in the chin and he was able to retreat.

"Now is the time for us to go," Sun Rise said. "I will go out to meet the enemy and you escape down the arroyo to the water."

"No, you must not do that." Tahkuh rose up from his bed, pain contorting his face. "Sun Rise, you have wives and children to think of. Don't leave them in poverty. There are more honorable things you can do to redeem yourself."

"I will go to save you and the others," Sun Rise said. The shame of his failure lay heavy on his soul. He knew he must do something to give the survivors a chance to escape.

"I will go with you, Sun Rise." Dog Fat rose by climbing his bow until he had his feet under him. He could not stand up straight for his wound. Already his stomach was swelling and he faced a very painful death from his wound.

That left me, Janos, Tahkuh, and a woman camp follower who had a broken leg and could not run. I started before Sun Rise and Dog Fat went out and moved Tahkuh down the ravine to the river and told Janos to stay with him. I had just begun returning to get the woman when the two warriors began singing their death songs. A rattle of gunfire from the posse ended their song and I turned back. There was no way to help the woman and we had to hide.

The yelling and shooting posse entered the arroyo and the woman's scream of defiance was answered by multiple shots; then all was quiet except for low murmuring talk. We lay in the water and rushes an hour before the murmuring ceased, and shouts and the rumble of horse hooves told us the posse had left to go brag of their victory.

Tahkuh was in bad shape and I had to find a safe place and treat his wound. He told me of a rock shelter under a bluff on the river and we were fortunate it was close by. After I bandaged his wound and wrapped him in a robe I had gathered from the arroyo, he lay on a shelf at the back of the shelter and I built a fire to reflect off the wall and warm him. We were there several days and Tahkuh was improving. It wouldn't be long before he would be ready to travel. Game was getting scarce around the bluff and I had to range out farther to get meat. I had been away for half a day when I returned and found Tahkuh dead and Janos by the fire crying. When I went to move the body to bury him, a rattlesnake warning made me decide that the cleft was a good burial spot.

There was mild surprise when we returned to the village. Two of the apprentices had escaped before the fight began and it was believed I had died with the rest. My story of Sun Rise and Dog Fat's sacrifice so we could escape and Tahkuh's death renewed the mourning in the village. Quanah seemed quite affected by the news. He had been close to his cousin.

There were some whispered doubts about

my story, but Quanah believed me and put
an end to the gossip.

CHAPTER 19
PORTENTS OF CHANGE
(MACKENZIE'S BATTLE OF
McCLELLAN CREEK)

Fall, 1872

General Ranald Mackenzie, that most promising young officer, was given the task of bringing the Comanche and Kiowa into their Indian Territory reservations. His early forays into the field proved that cavalry and infantry could successfully cross the Llano Estacado. Frustrated that he had not engaged the Indians, he planned a fall campaign on the Salt Fork of the Red River. When his scouts found a fresh trail on the banks of McClellan Creek, the army followed it to a Yaparika village, which McClellan promptly attacked.

Quanah's grandfather, Lean Elk, had been visiting the Quahadi and wished to return to his tipi with the Yaparika Comanches. Quanah appointed four young men, Otter, Sleepy Eye, Red Dog, and I to escort Lean Elk. We found the Yaparika on what the white men called McClellan Creek.

Red Dog set his eye on a comely young lady and was reluctant to leave so we stayed a few days to visit. We were by the creek late one afternoon talking to the girls when soldiers attacked the village without warning. Firing and shouts from the Kiowa village nearby confirmed they were under attack also. Though the Comanche and Kiowa were allies, they always camped separately.

The girls ran to the bushes and we mounted and raced to the village. Lean Elk was standing outside his tipi calmly reloading his gun and firing at the soldiers. He directed us to a hollow down by the creek where the tribe was gathering. We needed no more urging than the buzz and whine of bullets flying about us, and by no small miracle we reached the gully without injury. I tied my horse out of danger and joined the warriors at the edge of the arroyo, returning fire from the soldiers and giving fleeing people from the village a chance to reach safety. A man and woman emerged from behind a tipi running toward us. "It's our headman, Kahwohtseep, and his wife," someone called. The warriors called encouragement to the couple as we fired and reloaded as quickly as possible.

The pair was within a hundred feet of safety when Kahwohtseep fell wounded. His wife was in the act of kneeling beside him when she was hit also. Two warriors dropped their weapons and ran to help the couple while the rest of us kept up our fire. The headman rose, and taking his wife's hands began dragging her toward the arroyo. The rescuers grabbed up the woman and jogged toward safety while a third warrior helped Kahwohtseep.

His wife was dead and it was only a few moments before the headman joined her on their journey to the spirit world. Gently, the men laid the couple out side by side. Already, the women were keening and crying.

"Stop that crying and get to the bottom and make the children safe," Otter Belt, the remaining headman, demanded.

The Buffalo Soldiers faced the Indians in the middle of the skirmish line but were reluctant to attack them in the brush. Twice, Rojo rode out between the lines and challenged the soldiers. Though he drew much fire, he was untouched.

"What on airth do dat Injun got on his head?" Private Thomas Cregan, who was a little nearsighted, asked.

"Dat ain't no headress, darky; dat Injun's got red hair," Private Isaac (Ike for short) Casey replied.

"Be a white man?"

"Shore as I'm shootin' at 'im," Ike fired and grunted. "Das bullet jes bounce off'n him."

"If it did, it bounce off'n a rock fust," his partner retorted.

Lieutenant Baldwin crept up and lay beside the two soldiers. "I saw a redheaded Indian, men. How many of those 'Indians' are white?"

"We done counted three, Suh," Private Cregan answered. "An' thet don't count th' Mixicans, nuther."

"Doesn't count the captive women, either, Cregan." The officer grunted as he backed away and ran crouched down the skirmish line, encouraging his men.

There followed a kind of deadly dance between the combatants. The Indians would ride forth in a line as if to charge the blue-dressed Buffalo Soldiers and the soldiers would retreat. With too much open land to cross, the charge failed, and the Indians would return to the hollow. Then the soldiers would advance to their former positions. While they were so occupied, the women and children had time to gather and find secure places to hide.

As darkness fell, the warriors in the hollow rode to join the rest of the warriors on a hill not far away, and the soldiers gathered more than 120 women and children from the bushes, marching them away from the burning village to the army camp where they were closely guarded.

"Lieutenant Baldwin, ride over the ground and give me a body count of the Indians killed," General Mackenzie called. He never estimated the numbers of combatants killed but stated actual counts in his reports. "Pay close attention; I want to know if any of them are white."

"Yes, sir."

The general called to the head of the Tonkawa scouts, "Lieutenant Boehm, you and your scouts take charge of the horse herd. Don't let those Indians get them back."

"Yes, sir." The lieutenant gave instructions to his scouts and in a few minutes, they had rounded up the unneeded army horses and the captured Indian horses and moved them out of the camp. They found a shallow depression and drove the herd into it.

This was the worst defeat the Kiowa-Comanche alliance had suffered since before the Civil War, and it demonstrated a strong commitment by the army to force the tribes into the reservations.

Doctor Rufus Choate worked into the night treating the wounded while the rest of the camp attempted to sleep behind a strong cordon of guards. Mackenzie kept his staff busy checking and rechecking the camp security and a hundred other details. It was precisely 1:18 — for the good doctor had just checked his watch — when bullets clattered through the hospital tent, aimed at the only light in the camp.

In any other army unit, the orderly who stood and doused the light would have been awarded the Medal of Honor, the only medal the army had at the time, but General Mackenzie hardly recognized any action in combat as being "above and beyond the call of duty." Since the target light hung high in the tent, the only injuries were from flying splinters from the center tent pole. They counted seventeen bullet holes in the tent fabric.

The attack on the light was only a diversion for the real objective: the release of the prisoners. Indian cries came from the darkness for loved ones to run. They were answered by the prisoners, but no one was able to escape.

At daylight, Mackenzie sent out two strong patrols to reconnoiter the area and determine the strength of the enemy. The longer they stayed there, the more likely the Indians would be reinforced, and the last thing the general wanted was a defensive battle. Still, the surgeon insisted that the wounded could not be moved for two days. A strong detail was sent back to the village to collect tipi poles for travois.

The patrol reports were encouraging. They did not find any signs of reinforcements and the warriors were short of horses, the majority being afoot.

Private Casey was instructing the "new" recruit Cregan on the fine points of Injun fightin'. "Don't mean hardly nuthin' them Injuns is afoot. S'long es dey has moccasins, dey'll run just 'bout es far es dey would ridin' on a hoss. We gonna have a fine Injun *ex*cort all da' way t' Concho — an' sommers 'long da way, dey's gonna git dem ponies back. I seen it a hunnert times er more."

"Ef you seen it a hunnert times, you musta seen ninety-nine dat year you was in afore I jined." Cregan snorted

"I seen it shore."

"Not no hunnert times, Ike Casey, not no hunnert times."

The "hunnert and first time" came that very night while Casey and Cregan were on guard duty at the herd. Lieutenant Boehm and his Tonkawa scouts made an outer ring around the herd some fifty yards out from the inner circle of soldiers.

Otter Belt called the warriors together. "We must retrieve our horses," he said, drawing a circle in the sand to represent the depression and the herd. "The Tonkawa guard is out here," he drew another circle some distance from the herd, "and the soldiers ride here in an inner circle. We have to get through the Tonkawa without alarming them and then attack the soldiers and herd. Red Dog and Sleepy Eye will try to pass the lines here." He tapped the northwest side of the Tonkawa circle. "And Otter and Rojo will try here." He tapped the northeast side. "The rest of us will wait down here, on the opposite side, and when the horses start, we will attack the Tonkawa and gather the horses."

"And how does Otter Belt say we can get by the Tonkawa without being scalped?" Red Dog asked as we waited for dark to settle.

"He left that for us to figure out," I answered. "I don't have any ideas."

"It would do no good to try to sneak through their line, they would be sure to catch us," Otter said. "We will have to create some distraction so some of us could sneak by their line."

"I know, Otter, we can give them your liver and while they are eating, slip past them," I said.

"Huh. They much prefer white eyes' livers, so we will give them yours."

"Do they like it better raw or cooked?" Sleepy Eye asked.

"Hardly ever wait for the cooking, only when they have whiskey to occupy them while they cook," Red Dog observed.

"Aw-w, if they had whiskey, the liver would likely burn and never get eaten," Otter said.

"In that case, I'll keep my liver and gladly give them whiskey," I said — and that's how we stumbled into a plan.

"Where would you get that whiskey, Rojo?" Otter asked.

Red Dog snorted. "Why, he would just walk up to the whiskey wagon and trade his silver for a bottle."

"Or maybe I would sneak into the back of the wagon and get as much as I wanted," I said.

"It would have to be darker than this," Otter observed. "We should ride and find the wagon before it gets too dark."

"I will tell Otter Belt our plan and that we need a man who can speak Tonkawa well," Sleepy Eye said.

"We should ride." Red Dog was always impatient to move.

We rode to the soldiers' camp and found the whiskey wagon out on the edge of camp. Guards were already out and we noted their positions. The whiskey man acted as if he had taken a lot of his own medicine, and we watched him roll up in his blanket under the wagon. While Red Dog kept watch, Otter and I approached the wagon. I cut the end panel canvas and crawled into the wagon. There were all kinds of bottles of whiskey filled from small kegs that lined the sides. Gathering bottles without noise was hard, and after a few tries I gave up and picked up a keg. Otter grunted when I handed it down to him. As I crawled out of the wagon, Otter crept up to the sleeping man and lightly touched him with his lance, counting coup. I hoisted the keg to my shoulder while he gathered the few bottles and we left.

Otter Belt had our Tonkawa speaker with him when we returned. Wuyake was a Lipan Apache who had lived with the Tonkawa until he could no longer stand their filthiness and cannibalism. He had dressed himself like a Tonkawa and we rode to our assigned place in the ring of guards. Wuyake poured whiskey on his clothes and took a swallow — or two. He approached the line, softly singing a Tonkawa song, the bottles clinking in their sack and the keg on his shoulder. We gave him a good start, then followed, crouching low. Soon we would have to crawl past the line.

"Belcher, where are you?" he called in a hoarse whisper. "Where are you, my frien'?"

The nearest guard stepped toward Wuyake and shook his arm, "Be quiet; Belcher is over there somewhere."

"I have something for him, will you call him to us?"

"No." The scout sniffed. "What is it you have?" He lifted the sack and felt the bottles within. "You have brought us refreshment, yes?"

"Iss for Belcher," Wuyake slurred slightly, "but you could have jus' one bottle. He wouldn't mind."

The adjacent guards approached cautiously. "What is it?" one asked.

"He searches for Belcher to give him bottles of whiskey." The first guard had already pulled the stopper and taken a drink. Wuyake handed each new man a bottle. "Belcher won't mind," he said confidently. He set the keg down with a sigh of relief and sat on it, pretending to drink from a corked bottle. As planned, the four young men split into pairs and crawled through the line either side of the drinkers. It wasn't long until they were safely away.

Wuyake arose rather shakily. "Have to find Belcher," he whispered to his companions and stumbled away. No one mentioned he had forgotten the keg.

The soldiers rode their horses around the herd, half riding clockwise, the others counterclockwise. They conversed in low tones as one passed another. "I seen lightnin' up dere to da no'th," Ike Casey said to Private Cregan as they met.

"Gen'ral run southeast out here. Not likely t' git here," Tom Cregan muttered without opening his eyes.

"You be keerful ya don't snore; start a stampede, shore."

"Uh-huh," Ike mumbled. He had only ridden a short distance when a figure came up and shoved him out of his saddle. Before he hit the ground, something hit his head hard and Tom Cregan slept again. His buddy Ike never heard any commotion, for he was also laid out and "sleeping." The two had aching heads for several days. Even more than before, they believed in the Buffalo Soldier motto: "When you see Injun sign, be keerful; when you don't see ary sign, be mo' keerful."

Our four young men on two cavalry horses rode into the herd shouting and shooting over the herd, which obliged by stampeding the other way, scattering soldiers and sending Tonkawa scouts running for their lives. It was a credit to the mounted soldiers that they were able to split the herd, thus saving part of them. Rojo was rewarded with a painful kick in the leg by an army mule. It gave him great satisfaction to enjoy a large steak from that mule the next day.

General Mackenzie regretted the loss of the Indian ponies and a few army stock. The Indians never failed to retrieve their captured herds. *That will never happen to me again,* he vowed to himself. His vow would have grim consequences.

Now, the surviving warriors had sufficient mounts to follow their wives and children with the retiring army. The trip to Fort Concho was closely followed by the Indians and more than one attempt to free the captives was foiled by army vigilance.

The captives were kept at Fort Sill for trading for white captives; Parra-o-coom, a Quahadi chief, came to the fort for the first time and exchanged four captives for four of the captive Indians. The capture and holding of the women and children had a telling effect on the Indians' behavior.

Indian depredations declined noticeably for a time.

"I'm getting very tired of following the army in the hopes they will let their captives go," Red Dog said one day as we rode along.

"It sure is a chore, following a bunch who take all the water holes and eat all the grass so that we have to move way off the trail to find forage," I said.

Sleepy Eye pointed east with his chin, "Big Lake is there and the village will be along Sweetwater Creek up there beyond Rio Colorado." He looked north. "We could water at the lake and spend the night at the Colorado, be home tomorrow."

"What are you talking about?" Otter rode up.

"We are talking about the Sweetwater camp," Red Dog explained.

"I am ready," Otter turned his horse north.

"We were going to water at Big Lake first," I called.

"Bad water; horses don't like it," Otter returned over his shoulder.

Sleepy Eye shrugged and grinned and turned his horse to follow Otter.

"We should tell Otter Belt," I said.

"Told him this morning," Otter called.

Red Dog and I heeled our mounts into a lope and followed our two companions.

"Sweetwater, beware, here come your warriors," Sleepy Eye sang.

Raven died at the Rio Grande fight. I had decided that when I returned, I would seek my own home. I think Rosebud was reluctant to let me go, and I continued to provide meat for the family. Raven had been rather lax, knowing his wife would visit her mother's pots if he didn't produce. It made for troubled waters at times.

There was a young widow named Bubbling Water, a captive Cheyenne, living in the village. The dead husband's family refused to help her, as she had not produced grandchildren for them. I had helped Quanah by seeing that she had plenty of meat. When we left to escort Tahkuh home, I left Janos with Bubbling Water.

The only words Quanah had for me as I rode into the village were, "Rojo Pelo, it is time for you to act like a responsible *Comanche* warrior." He turned and reentered his tipi.

Now, what do you mean by that?

"Shall I take your horse now, Rojo?" Janos stood holding the reins close under Amigo's muzzle. The boy led Amigo away to Bubbling Water's tipi and I followed for want of anything else to do.

Bubbling Water was cooking on the outside fire and looked up as I approached. "Hello, Rojo Pelo, I have a roast almost ready if you are hungry."

"That would be good, Bubbling Water." I opened my blanket to her and she stepped into the folds, deftly pulling the edge over our heads. She pressed her body to mine. We stood there a long time, me holding the blanket around us and whispering things only a lover would tell his sweetheart. Janos came chattering around the tipi and stopped suddenly as he saw us. I opened the blanket and Bubbling Water stepped away, a blush on her cheeks. She was a pretty woman and I suppose the only reason she hadn't married before is the reticence of the young men to assume the responsibility and their families' reluctance to allow a marriage to a woman who might be barren. Comanche women were not as pretty as the Cheyenne women and their beauty faded fast. I didn't care about having children — though I didn't object either. Time would prove that Bubbling Water was not the barren one they thought.

You would think Crier had announced it in the night the way the whole village knew of our marriage even before the sun rose the next morning. The teasing of both of us was raucous and bawdy. I was able to hold my temper, but Bubbling Water was brought to tears and anger a time or two.

CHAPTER 20
THE ENCIRCLING CEREMONY

1874

Springtime in the Indian culture was known as the "Starving Time" because the winter's food storage was getting low — or gone — and nothing in nature had produced fruit. So the first order of activity was to find food. After food was secured, the warrior's thoughts turned to the warpath. Grass, the king of all things, was green and the horses were getting fat. One couldn't have too many horses, and a raid on enemy tribes or Texians could garner more coups, scalps, and slaves in addition to livestock. Soon, the comancheros would come with their goods, seeking cattle for the New Mexico Territory markets.

Reservation life changed the dynamics of this life cycle by providing food for the people. Now, the warrior was freed from the imperative of the spring hunt and his restless mind turned to war. The tribes collected their spring allotments; the women dumped the spoiled flour on the ground and kept the sacks; and they now had food to sustain them on the reservation or on their clandestine trek west to the buffalo grounds — or to war.

One by one or in small groups to avoid detection, they left the reservation and gathered at the villages along Sweetwater and Pecan Creeks near the North Fork of the Red River. Quenosavit, White Eagle, began to tell of his experiences. "I have ascended above the clouds and spoken with the Great Spirit who granted me great powers," he proclaimed. "I have raised the dead and healed the sick. I can send lightning and hail on our enemies. I blow away bullets fired at me and they fall to the ground. I can make all warriors safe from bullets, and the triggers of the enemies' firearms will not work."

Quanah smiled. "I find that fantastic, White Eagle; what proof have you of this?"

White Eagle frowned that anyone, even the headman Quanah, would doubt him. "You have seen The Star-With-A-Tail, have you not? Within five days it will disappear. And because there is doubt among you," he addressed the council and spectators, "I will withold the summer rains and the grass will wither."

"Hah," I said to Otter, "already the grass withers before he curses it, and Star-With-A-Tail has been sinking. I can make that prediction also."

"Perhaps you can, Rojo Pelo, but can you vomit a wagon load of cartridges suitable for any gun as Terheryaquahip says?"

"— And raise the dead?" Red Dog asked.

"So you two believe this White Eagle's tales?" I asked.

"We shall see if his predictions are true before we decide," Otter replied.

On the fourth night, Star-With-A-Tale could not be found in all the sky, giving White Eagle greater credibility, and when the drought continued and the streams began to dry, he gained even greater popularity. He decreed all Comanches must come to a Medicine Dance to be held on a certain day in the white man's calandar in May. It was held on the Red River near the agency boundary. For the first time in their memory, portions of all the Comanche bands were present, some by almost all of their people. White Eagle gave them a song to sing. He directed the mounted people to gather around a tall pole set in the ground with the top in the form of a cross and instructed them to circle the pole while singing. The innermost circle walked around the pole, while the ones on the outer circle had to run their horses. The dust became so thick the people couldn't see.

After the dance, the prophet preached that the Great Spirit had pointed out that the settled tribes on their reservations were miserable, declining in numbers and goods. If the Comanches followed the white man's road, their lot would be the same. "To remain prosperous and powerful we must eliminate the white man wherever he is found," he proclaimed.

When many of the Indians who had come out of curiosity realized that the celebration was dominated by the war party, they eluded those trying to prevent them from leaving and returned to the reservation.

Quanah and the Quahadis moved their camp to Elk Creek, called Sweetwater by the Anglos, and several other villages followed, some settling along Elk and Pecan Creeks and some along the North Fork of the Red River. All of the Comanches gathered around the Quahadis. There was a large Kiowa camp and a Cheyenne village nearby.

"We won't be here very long," Red Dog declared. "The horses have already eaten the grass nearby and they have to range out farther and farther to find good grazing."

"There would be plenty of grass if White Eagle would remove his curse," said Otter.

"The drought was here before his 'curse' and will still be here after he removes it," I said.

"Is it your white blood that speaks these things?" Otter asked. We had argued about White Eagle's powers before.

"I will believe when I have seen him vomit a wagon load of cartridges that fit all guns. If he swallows them again, they do us no good."

"It is true, Otter," Sleepy Eye said, "Terheryaquahip says that he has raised one from the dead, but we do not find a witness or a resurrected person."

"White Eagle has called a war council tonight, perhaps he will convince you that he is a profit from the Great Spirit," Red Dog said.

I nodded, "Perhaps, Red Dog, and I will be there to see if he does. Now, I go to find my wife. She goes among the Cheyenne to find her family." I found Bubbling Water at our tipi. Her face was stained with tears and she told me that her family had all been killed when she was taken. "I understand how you feel, Bubbling Water, my family also has been destroyed. Only my sister Eve and I remain and she is a captive among the Mescalero."

I stayed with my wife all afternoon until Crier announced the council was to begin, and we all went to the council fire. Bubbling Water and Janos sat with the women and children. I found my friends and sat down just as Quanah passed the pipe to the other council members. The ceremony over, White Eagle rose and spoke. His speech was much the same as before; he had risen above the clouds and spoken with the Great Spirit who said the Comanche must not go the white man's road, but must destroy him so that the people could live the good life. He had given White Eagle the power to stop bullets and his power could prevent the warriors from being shot. He again urged us to destroy the white man and drive them from our lands.

There was quiet for a few moments, then one of the warriors seated behind the council called, "The bluecoats cannot find us without the Man-Eaters (meaning the Tonkawas) showing them the way. We should destroy them; then the army would be at our mercy."

There were "hous" and nods of agreement. There followed a long discussion of the proposition, little of it making sense, and I realized that the warriors speaking were drunk.

"We have been struck by Taos Lightning," Otter the clown hissed.

"I have heard enough," I said and rose to go.

White Eagle raised his staff and called, "No one is to leave until all have spoken."

Two members of the Tedapuknuu Society, the appointed village police, rose behind me, their quirts ready.

"I have heard the warriors speak and I am ready to go kill the Man-Eaters, White Eagle; but now firewater is beginning to talk and firewater's council I will not follow."

"Hou," several warriors nodded, while others under the influence growled their displeasure.

Quanah rose and spoke above the murmuring. "We have heard enough for the night. Tomorrow, we will come together to plan our war against the Tonkawas."

One of the Tedapuknuu approached me, "Only warriors are allowed to speak in the councils."

"I have counted coup on the living enemy and you may come to my tipi and see my scalps," I replied and moved on to where Janos and Bubbling Water were waiting.

"You have chosen a hazardous trail, Rojo Pelo; I do not wish to become a widow

344

twice." Her smile betrayed her words and we turned for our home. My three friends casually followed us in case Taos Lightning should seek revenge for my words.

Those that slept that night arose with headaches and clearer minds; those that drank the night away slept the day away to find that clear heads had realized the Tonkawas lived at Fort Griffin, and the bluecoats would have no trouble finding us at their fort. Thus it was that the council met not to plan a war, but to find another enemy to make war with.

"Sentiment runs hot for Texas," Sleepy Eye said as we found our seats.

"Will you object to that, Rojo?" Otter asked with a grin.

"I will go where Quanah goes," I replied. Still, it would be to Texas with regret.

There followed a near repeat of the night before; much talk, most of it very repetitive. White Eagle drew much attention. His promises touched the hearts of the people. Despite its hardships, the free life of the prairies and mountains were their greatest desire. When an obviously drunken warrior rose to speak, Sleepy Eye on my left and Red Dog on my right grabbed my arms to the amusement of those around us. Again, Quanah rose and dismissed the council.

The following night was not productive, for it seemed that the people were not of one heart. It ended without any plans made and questions about who would lead the war. The council broke up without coming to a decision. It seemed the war was not to be. In spite of the policing of the Tedapuku-nuu, small groups were sneaking away to carry out war on their own. The big war party was in danger of falling apart.

The next morning, I found Quanah performing the first part of the pahpanahn ceremony. The pahpanahn or encircling ceremony is the request of a warrior for the help of a village, band, or tribe in a war. His ride completely around the village requires any warrior so encircled to accompany the performer of the ceremony. I saddled his warhorse and mine and when he rode the encircling, I rode with him. We circled the entire Comanche camp and the Kiowa camp also; then we circled the Cheyenne camp.

"Every man inside the circles is required to join us in war, Rojo," he explained. Back at his tipi, he instructed Crier to announce a council for that evening.

"Tell us, Rojo, what does Quanah intend to do?" Sleepy Eye demanded.

"He did not tell me what his plan is,

Sleepy Eye. I will say this; his plan will be better than any plan the council comes up with."

"I, for one, will be ready and eager to go," Red Dog vowed. Indeed, the whole camp was eager for activity and by evening every warrior was prepared to go to war at a moment's notice.

When the people had gathered, he spoke: "I will go to war against the white-eyes and Texians, to avenge the deaths of my kin. With all of us together, we could regain our hunting grounds. There will be no hunting except for the good of all." It was here that White Eagle rose and proclaimed that the Great Spirit had set the day and hour for the attack. He announced it to the gathering, and it became well known among the tribes of the reservations.

A late spring had delayed the northward migration of the buffalo herd, and scouts had been sent out to find them. The men of one scout returned with disturbing news and Yellowfish sought out the headman. "Quanah, Beaver has returned from his scout and tells me there are many hide hunters south of Swift Fox River. They have built a city at Adobe Walls."

There was much anger among the people when they heard of the invasion by the hide hunters. Quanah and the council agreed that the hunters must be driven out of our hunting grounds. "It is as always, the white-eyes have broken their treaty. Ten Bears and Silver Brooch have touched worthless paper. It is decided, then. I will get my vengeance at Adobe Walls. We leave before the second sunrise."

There was little hurry to prepare, for that had already been done. It is normally the custom that the newly married warrior does not participate in war the first year of marriage, but the pahpanahn ceremony required all men to respond above all other customs. Thus, I was required to go on the war. It was fortunate that it happened that way, for I was intent on going without regard to any customs. Word had gotten back to the reservation that we were going to war, and we gained fighters all the way across the plains to the hunting grounds.

Quanah's warrior society, the Tedapuku-nuu, was put in charge of the enforcement of the encircling ceremony rules. The police were strict and overbearing and Quanah had to call them down a couple of times.

"It's hardly past sunset and people are taking up the warpath," Sleepy Eye complained.

Otter laughed. "Sleepy Eye has *two* sleepy eyes."

"Go get some sleep, Sleepy Eye, and you and I will catch up with them in the morning. Our horses will be fresher and so will we," I said.

"I will wait also," Red Dog said.

So it was decided that the four of us would get one more night's rest in our village and leave just before sunrise. The Tedapukunuu police would have compelled us to go with the main band had they found us, but in the dark, it was not hard to avoid them. We followed their trail at a leisurely pace and joined the camp early in the afternoon. Where the North Fork runs south, they had crossed the river and camped in the hills west of the river. Most of the men were asleep.

Quanah called a council at sunset and the entire camp gathered at the council fire. "The buffalo have finally moved north and the hide hunters are at work killing as many of them as they can. They are scattered in little camps all over the plain from here to the Swift Fox. Here is where we will break up into small groups and kill all the hunters we find. Kill them all except one man a day and let him escape. He will run to the city at Adobe Walls. Perhaps they will run back north of the river.

"Lone Wolf will lead the Kiowa and Stone Calf will lead the Cheyenne. They will tell you their plan in your camps." He pointed to the half-moon in the eastern sky. When next the moon looks like that after the full moon, we will gather where Red Deer Creek meets the Canadian River. Then we go to the Adobe Walls city and destroy it."

The volume of the "hous" startled me and I looked around.

Red Dog stared around him, "Rojo, how many are there?" he whispered.

I thought a moment, then flashed my fingers, "This many ten times is one hundred. Ten times one hundred would be the number of warriors here." I could tell he would have to think on that before he understood.

Next, White Eagle stood and preached his standard sermon. At the end, he said, "I go now above the clouds to speak to the Great Spirit. He has promised to give me power to stop bullets without harming me. When we gather at Red Deer Creek, I will give you this power."

With that, the council was concluded and we went to our several camps.

In 1873, the slaughter of the buffalo north

of the Arkansas River had continued un-
abated until the northern herd essentially
was no more. The Medicine Lodge Treaty,
which Quanah and the Quahadis had refused to attend, forbade white hunters to
hunt south of the river. The southern herd
remained intact and was a major source of
Indian subsistance.

The herd became too much temptation
for the hunters, and little by little, they
began to trespass Indian hunting grounds.
The rewards in hides were great, but the
danger of Indian attacks raised the risk of
hunting. There was only one fate awaiting
the captured hunter and his skinners, and
often that fate was slow and very painful. It
tended to hold back a wholesale invasion by
hide hunters.

Hide men south of the river listened for
the boom of his neighbor's Sharps .50.
When it was joined by the pop pop pop of
smaller caliber rifles, he knew Indians were
about and scampered for safety. Buffalo
hated the Indian scent and when the herds
grew restless and moved about, the white
hunter knew Indians were near. The scent
of the white man did not alarm the animals,
and in a calm herd, the hide man could set
up a stand and kill as many of the buffalo
as his skinners could handle.

So many hide men had determined to cross the Arkansas and hunt the southern herd that it seemed to be a profitable thing to set up a camp somewhere in the area. In the spring of 1874, the merchants Myers & Leonard, James Hanrahan, and Thomas O'Keefe, a blacksmith, left Dodge City, intent on setting up business at the old Adobe Walls. They found a good site about a mile from the Walls on East Adobe Walls Creek.

Myers & Leonard built a twenty by sixty picket house, while Hanrahan built his twenty-five by sixty saloon out of sod. Thomas O'Keefe built a picket blacksmith shop fifteen feet square. A little later, Charles Rath of Rath & Wright brought merchandise down and built a sixteen by twenty-foot sod store.

Lee and Reynolds were the sutlers at Camp Supply where the Southern Cheyenne got their government allotments. They learned of the planned attack on Adobe Walls and the day and time of the attack. Being friends with R.M. Wright, the Fort Dodge sutler, they told him of the Indian plans. Wright and Charles Rath were partners in the store Charlie had set up at Adobe Walls.

The Camp Supply sutlers hired Amos

Chatman, a half-breed Cheyenne army scout, and prevailed on the Camp commandant to send a sergeant and four privates to escort Amos to warn the men at Adobe Walls. One of the soldiers garnered the anger of the hide men at the Walls by stating that they were looking for horse thieves.

Amos had a secret meeting with Myers, Rath, and Hanrahan and told them the day and hour of the planned attack. That night, hiding in John Mooar's wagon from the hide men who wanted to hang him, he told John of the attack. The next morning, John drove to the hide camp of his brother, J. Wright Mooar, to warn him. They were chased back to Adobe Walls, being saved from an Indian attack by the sudden rise of Red Deer Creek between them and the Indians.

At the settlement, they immediately loaded their wagons for the trip to Dodge City. It was here that the three merchants prevailed on the Mooars to keep the attack a secret so there would be men left at the town to defend their stores and supplies. The Mooars drove their wagons out and two days later, Myers and Rath joined them. Myers had left Fred Leonard in charge of his store, and Rath turned his store over to his clerk, James Langton.

■ ■ ■ ■

Quanah's plan was to break into many small groups and cover the plains, attacking every hide hunter's camp we found. It would not be hard to find the hunters and their camps. If we didn't hear the boom of their big guns, we could follow the smell of drying hides. Coyotes, wolves, and other scavengers gathering around the abandoned carcasses also told of the nearness of a hide camp.

"Where the flies gather, there lies the carrion," Otter said, fanning at the millions of flies that infested the hunting grounds. So many warriors had joined Quanah's party that we had chosen to go with a smaller group, Rattle, and his three companions, No Hair, Rock, and Black Knife.

"We will go south to the Salt Fork and turn west until we get to the buffalo herds. There will be hide men there," Rattle explained. Our first camp was at the head of Oklahoma Draw on the river. Two days later and far up the river we found a few buffalo. It was clear the main herd had already passed.

We followed the herd. "Soon we will hear the big guns boom," No Hair said.

As we rode, we began to encounter more

animals and we found two abandoned hide camps. Wide tracks of a loaded wagon drove north and we followed. The sun had set when we smelled a campfire and decided to join the hunters for their meal. Riding abreast, we galloped through the camp yelling and scattering men, equipment, and animals. The horses and mules panicked and ran ahead of us, two of them dragging picket pins.

"Now, we have their horses and they will be helpless before us." Black Knife was jubilant. We drove the animals a safe distance away and drew stones to see who would have the care of them. Otter lost. The rest of us returned to the hide camp to see what the whites were doing.

"There were five of them around the fire, and all our shooting managed to miss every one of them," Rattle growled. "Now they have had opportunity to build a fort and we will have a time getting them."

Just as he predicted, the hunters had turned the wagon on its side and dug in behind it. We surrounded them and spent the night keeping them stirred up. Rock crawled up and knocked on the wagon bottom. When a head popped over the side, he struck coup with his quirt and escaped safely in a cloud of flying lead.

"How are we going to get them?" I asked.

"Let us go to the herd and talk," Rattle said.

"They will expect us at sunrise," No Hair said.

"We will let them worry about that and visit them later."

"Rattle's smile means he has a plan," Black Knife said with a grin.

Otter had a tiny fire going and the stock had scattered in the moonlight, hunting grass that might have been left by the grazing buffalo. We rested and ate our jerky and pemmican.

"We can sleep and visit our quarry later in the morning," Rattle said and rolled up in his blanket. The sun was well up when Otter rode out and brought a fresh horse to me. We spent the next hour rounding up horses and mules.

"My mouth waters every time I see one of those mules," Otter called.

"Maybe tonight you will taste one of them," I replied. The sun was halfway to the zenith when we got the herd back to the fire.

"We should go see if the hunters have risen," No Hair said.

"Keep the herd bunched and ahead of us," Rattle called. "Perhaps we will give them back to the hide men."

Faster and faster, we drove them until they were galloping right through the camp. The wagon toppled over, exposing the hunters. That Sharps boomed and No Hair's horse fell. The man tumbled over his head and lay still. Other rifles joined the fight. That .50 boomed again and someone on the other side of the dust fell with his horse. No Hair ran into the corner of my vision straight for the hunter as he desperately tried to reload his Sharps. I yelled and charged the fort to draw attention away from No Hair. The Indian hit the hunter just as he was swinging his rifle up, and he crumpled. Another white fell as he was swinging his rifle toward No Hair. My rush carried me too close and instead of turning, I quirted my horse over the wagon bed and through the rifle pit they had dug. As I passed, I slung my lead rope toward No Hair and he grabbed it. I dragged him to safety away from the fight.

No Hair sat up and groaned. His chest was a mass of scratches, fast becoming red with blood. "I do not know if I should thank you or shoot you, Rojo." He grinned and spat trash and blood out of his mouth.

"That was the bravest or most foolish thing I have ever seen," I said to No Hair. "Maybe a little of both."

"You would not call charging a horse through the fort full of shooters foolish?" he asked.

There was no more shooting at the fort, and I could see the others riding for the stock. It was Rock who had fallen, and now he was sitting against his horse's carcass. I hoped he was not hurt too bad.

I got down and helped No Hair to his feet. He was scratched from shoulders to feet. One of his moccasins was missing. He pulled his breechcloth back in place.

"Get on the horse and we will go find your moccasin." I helped him mount the horse and led it back toward the fort. His moccasin was halfway to the fort and I slipped it on his foot. We went to where Rock lay. There was a bloody rag tied around his lower leg. "Shot through my horse and my leg," he said. His paleness showed through his dark skin.

Rattle and Otter rode up behind the winded cavvy. Rattle had a couple of bloody scalps. He tossed one to No Hair, "You deserve the hunter's scalp, No Hair."

"Thank you, Rattle," he replied. He had been anticipating harvesting it himself.

Black Knife and Otter joined us. Otter had a long cut along his jaw where a bullet had grazed him. Black Knife appeared whole and unharmed. "Do not invite me to hold your rope, Rojo." He glanced at No Hair and chuckled. "You should take a bath before you go to bed tonight."

No Hair could only grin.

No one knows how many battles such as this were enacted over the expanse of the Llano Estacado, but there were many. And though they tried, the Indians did not clear their hunting grounds of hide hunters. They missed more than a hundred men scattered around the herd. In later years, Rojo Pelo could recall only three camps his party found.

Rumor spread among the hide hunters of a warrior of exceptional ability and bravery. It seemed he was invincible — and he had flaming red hair.

The first time the men at Adobe Walls knew Indians were in the area was when Joe Plummer rode a fagged-out mule in to tell that his partner Dave Dudley and their skinner, Tommy Wallace, had been killed. Joe had driven his wagon to the stores for supplies and had found the two men dead when he returned to his camp on Chicken Creek. Wallace had been killed outright, but Dudley had been tortured. They had cut his gut open and driven a stake through him and into the ground.

When Joe saw what had happened, he cut a mule out of his harness and rode straight ahead into the brush, giving credence to the old Mountain Man's adage: "Don't return the same way you left." By making a big circle, he avoided the ambush the Indians had set for him after he had seen what had been done to his partners.

Right on the heels of Plummer's adventure came news that two more hide men had been killed on a tributary of the Salt Fork. They were John "Cheyenne Jack" Jones, an Englishman, and "Blue Billy," a German.

Billy Dixon was driving to the settlement for supplies when two hard-riding men told him of the attacks. He lost his wagon and guns in the flooding Canadian River and led his surviving mule the several miles to Adobe Walls. The only gun he could buy was a Sharps .44, a little light for good buffalo killing.

Neither merchant nor surviving hide man had seen an Indian.

Rock studied the waning moon, "Tomorrow we must start for the Canadian if we are to be there on time."

"How far away are we?" I asked.

"Two long days if we ride hard."

"It may take longer if we find another

hunter's camp."

Otter laughed. "You are ever hungry to fight, Rojo."

"We have found enough carcasses to feed all our people for many moons, Otter. The meat is spoiled and wasted by the white man's greed and our children will go hungry," Rock said. "We must make them stop the slaughter."

"Where is the best place to leave our horses?" Otter asked. The party had gathered quite a herd of animals from the three hide camps they had found.

"There will be water in McClellan Creek, about a half day north of here. They shouldn't scatter too much from there," said Rattle. "Come, let us cache our treasures before dark."

The loot from each camp had required a packhorse. There were several rifles including four Sharps .50's, and an abundance of much needed ammunition. They had teased No Hair for seeking shirts to wear over his scratched-up chest. Rojo made him wash each night and put on a fresh shirt. By washing time the next night, the shirt was ruined. The first several nights, the shirt had stuck to his wounds and had to be peeled off. He would remove the buttons and burn the shirt.

The bullet had gone through Rock's leg without hitting bone and he could ride well enough to fight, but he had developed an aversion to being near a Sharps in battle.

The warriors had changed their tactics after the first battle and waited to catch the other two camps when they were unprepared to defend themselves. No more major injuries occurred, and they wore their minor scars with pride.

They sat on the ridge above Red Deer Creek and surveyed the camps on the flats below. "There's the council fire, Quanah will be near," Rojo said.

"That is the Kiowa camp." Otter pointed to the camp east of the Comanche camp.

"I see Stone Calf's tipi." Black Knife pointed to the Cheyenne camp up the Canadian River a ways.

We rode down into the Comanche camp where apprentices took our tired horses and turned them into the herd on the hills. Red Dog and Sleepy Eye sat by the fire watching their steaks cook. A fresh scalp hung from Sleepy Eye's lance.

"You have had good hunting, Sleepy Eye," Otter observed.

"Yes, we found a big camp, Red Dog counted coup, and I got the kill."

"Many of the small parties didn't find any

camps," Red Dog said. "Did you find one?"

Otter smiled, "We found one — then another — and another." He turned his face so the two could see the long wound on his face. "Rock and I got shot the first fight and Rojo dragged No Hair across the ground with his horse."

"Ah-h, I hear a story coming." Quanah stood behind us. "What is this, Rojo, that you would drag one of my best warriors behind your horse?"

"No Hair charged the hunters' fort and I rescued him," I explained.

"And the only way you could do that was to drag his skin off?" Quanah must have already heard the story, for he was smiling and not angry.

"No Hair didn't know whether to thank me or shoot me," I replied.

An apprentice brought up Quanah's warhorse. "I must hear the whole story, but now I must go to the Kiowa camp. Satanta and Lone Wolf have joined us from the reservation." He mounted and rode off, the apprentice trotting along behind.

"Satanta and Lone Wolf, hou," Sleepy Eye whispered. "Our Big Bow came in from the reservation yesterday with Little Robe and White Shield of the Cheyenne."

"Now, we have more than your ten times

one hundred, Rojo," Otter observed.

"This must be the biggest army of the People ever," I said.

"Grandfather said there were many, many more when the Comanche made war on the pueblo people," Sleepy Eye said. "That was a long time before even he was born."

Other groups were coming to the camp, some from the plains and some still from the reservations. There was a scattering of Arapahos and Lipan Apaches in the camp. Two days after our arrival, Crier rode through the camps announcing a council set for that night.

After the opening smoke, Quanah rose and spoke: "Tomorrow we begin our journey to the city at Adobe Walls. We will travel south of the setting sun to Chicken Creek, where the Kiowa and Cheyenne will camp. The Comanche will go on to White Deer Creek so that we all may have enough water. Do not let any white man escape to warn the city. The second day we will gather and ride down White Deer to arrive at the Canadian after dark. We will cross the river in the dark and hide in the trees until we attack at the set hour on the third morning. It is very important that we have complete surprise, we must take them on the first charge while they sleep."

"We ride farther so our guests get the first camp," Sleepy Eye whispered.

"But we gain by having fresher horses when we attack," Otter answered. "Quanah is a sly one."

Quanah sat and White Eagle rose to speak. There was a stir in the huge crowd; then it got deathly still. One would hardly breathe. The seer waved his feathered rod over the crowd. "I have come from the Great Spirit above the clouds. He has given me authority to take the power from the white man's guns so that their bullets will not be strong enough to break the skin. Their guns will become impossible to fire." White Eagle waved his staff again, "You are now covered by the power of the Great Spirit and no bullet will harm you. We must attack the morning of the third day from today, the day set by the Great Spirit. You will find the white-eyes asleep and you can kill them with your clubs. Go, and overcome our enemies." He sat down and lit the pipe. It was very quiet while the council smoked. When the council rose, the crowd scattered to their own camps where the drums beat well into the night.

I pushed the sticks into the fire and rolled up in my blanket, feet to the fire, and slept.

A hand touched my shoulder. "Rojo Pelo,

wake up."

I started to rise, but the hand held me. "Do not rise; I have something to tell you." I tried to turn to face the speaker, but the hand restrained me. "Be still and listen. Castaño Rojizo lives with the Kotsoteka. She has married a warrior and borne him a son. She is treated well and seems happy; her only sadness is that she cannot be near you. Now, do not move."

The hand lifted and I heard the stranger move away. The fire had died and the night was black. I looked but knew I would see nothing. I sat up and pushed the sticks into the fire, then lay back down. There was no pretending to sleep and I lay and thought of Eve living with a Kotsoteka warrior. It was better that she didn't have an Apache husband — but not much better — and she had a child. I lay on my back and stared at the stars a long time.

CHAPTER 21
THE SECOND BATTLE
OF ADOBE WALLS

In 1864, Colonel Kit Carson attacked a Kiowa village on the Canadian River. Chief Dohasan's warriors held off the army until the women and children were safely away. Carson's troops pressed the retreating Indians until they were joined by hundreds more Kiowa and Comanche warriors at Adobe Walls. There, the retreat stopped, and if it were not for the mountain howitzers holding off the Indians while the army retired, the results of the battle might have been very different. This was the first battle of Adobe Walls.

June 27, 1874

The whole army stopped at Chicken Creek and Quanah called us all together. "We have a warrior who has a bugle and knows the signals of the army. Because we are so many and will be spread out, we will use the bugle to signal our orders." A captive Mexican from the Kiowas stood by Quanah and played tunes on an army bugle, and then he taught us three bugle signals. The first one was for "attention," which he would play before the other ones. Then he played two signals, one for "charge" and the other for "recall." Recall was to gather out of the battlefield and receive instructions for the next charge. With so many of us and as scattered as we became, the bugle signals were very helpful.

"Didn't Quanah say that we must win on the first charge?" Red Dog asked as we rode to White Deer Creek.

"He did, but it sounds like he isn't sure that will happen, doesn't it?" I answered. "If the hunters know we are coming, it will be very hard to beat them in their houses."

"We can burn the picket houses but only the roofs might burn on the sod houses," Otter said.

"And bullets won't pass through the sod walls," Sleepy Eye added.

"With more than ten times one hundred warriors, we will far outnumber the white-eyes at the city with only five buildings," Otter asserted.

"You should ask Rock and No Hair what those guns that go boom can do," I said. "I think it would be very hard to beat them if they get a chance to use those big guns."

"But we are so many more than they are," Red Dog said.

"Their bullets will reach us well before we would be close enough for our bullets to reach them, Red Dog. I have seen it so." Otter remembered our first little battle.

"It doesn't matter if we find them in their beds," Red Dog replied. "After tomorrow, you may call me Many Coups." He slapped his war club in the palm of his hand.

So many warriors on their horses crossed the swollen Canadian at one time that the water turned dark and the current slowed. We stayed bunched behind the brush at the edge of the woods, most of us standing by our horses' heads to keep them quiet. Quanah and White Eagle sat in the middle forefront of our army.

The men at the settlement noted the many owls calling in the woods down by the river, but put no significance to it.

James Hanrahan had help — most likely from his barkeeper, Shepherd — rousing the camp at 2 a.m. that morning. When his helper fired a pistol outside the saloon and woke two men sleeping there, Hanrahan yelled, "Clear out, the ridge pole is breaking!" They recruited several others to help prop up the two-foot diameter cottonwood with a slender pole that by some miracle lay at the woodpile and fit perfectly. It couldn't possibly hold up a broken ridgepole. With the roof lightened by throwing off some of the sod and the saving pole in place, Hanrahan invited the workers to the bar for a drink on the house.

The real cause of the alarm was kept secret by an oath taken by the men who knew about the attack. Nearly sixty years later, J. Wright Mooar, the last survivor of the party, told the true tale of the cracking ridgepole to his biographor, James W. Hunt. No doubt, the five men, John and J. Wright Mooar, Myers, Rath, and Hanrahan would have feared for their lives if it became known that their selfish and cowardly act had exposed twenty-eight men and one woman to sudden and violent death. The deaths of the Shadler brothers and Billy Tyler should have weighed heavily on their consciences. For years, the mystery of why the hunters were awake at this hour could not be explained by the Indians.

The muffled sound of a gunshot came from the city and I heard Quanah say softly, "We have lost the surprise."

"I have made the hide hunters sleep soundly. They hear no noise," White Eagle replied. The sky grew lighter over the far eastern mesa. "Time draws near." White

Eagle and Quanah moved out of the trees a ways and the warriors mounted and sat a few yards behind the two men. The Kiowa bugler rode out to join them. There was no sound save an occasional snort or stamp of a hoof from an eager warhorse. I could feel my heart beat in my temples and I dried my hands on my breechcloth for the hundredth time. Sweat dripped from Otter's nose and he took in a big breath. Even Sleepy Eye's droopy eyelid was wide open. The hunters' horses were grazing between the buildings and us. A man emerged, walking toward the herd. Another man walked out to where a horse was picketed. Every eye was on White Eagle. He looked east, then spread his arms and looked to the sky, muttering something. We only heard the sound of his voice, but no words. The bugler sat watching intently, the horn a few inches from his lips.

"Now," White Eagle said aloud, and the bugler blew the charge without the attention song. Quanah heeled his horse into a lope and our eager warhorses joined without prompting. The lope quickly became a run and as we gained room on the prairie, the army spread until we were all one line. Faster and faster we ran, overtaking White Eagle, but Quanah and the bugler still led. Again, the bugler played the charge and his music was drowned by the war cries from a thousand throats.

Billy Dixon had decided to stay up and gather his stock to move out to the killing fields early. He was going for his horse when he spied the charging Indians. He witnessed a charge like no one had ever experienced, and those that were there still remember and dream about it. A long line of hundreds of charging horses, their manes and tails plaited and decorated with ribbons and feathers, their shoulders and sides painted yellow or crimson, seemed to emerge from the glow of the rising sun. Scalps dangled from their bridles. The thunder of thousands of flying hooves shook the ground and made a rumbling background for the war cries of the warriors. Their naked bodies were also painted for war, their best brass and silver ornaments reflecting the rising sun, their hair plaited with feathers or covered with warbonnets flowing in the wind of their running. They were armed with guns and lances and brightly painted shields. Their quirts beat a rythmic tune on a thousand flanks. Though he had at first assumed the Indians were after the horse herd, Billy soon realized they were charging the village and he ran for safety.

The horse herd scattered and the second

man, Billy Ogg, turned and ran for his life.

"I will be the first to count coup." Red Dog's voice was shrill with excitement, but no matter how much he urged his horse, he could not pull ahead of the charge.

I could see the man would make the buildings before we could overtake him. The second man had grabbed his horse and tied him to a wagon. He grabbed up his rifle and fired at us, then ran for the buildings. He banged on a door and just as it opened, the runner dove through amongst the angry whistle of dozens of our bullets. The man with the rifle ran in and the door slammed shut.

I saw Quanah's shoulders sag. Far behind the charge, I saw White Eagle sitting still and watching.

"The surprise is lost," Otter called.

The single shot of the man who tied his horse to the wagon was the only shot from the buildings and we charged right up to them. Warriors banged on the doors and shuttered windows. Someone shot the horse. Cries of anger and frustration filled the air. A warrior at the window fell dead from a shot we didn't hear, and we began to retreat, some carrying the body. Two men (the Shadler brothers) were caught sleeping in their wagon and they were killed with their big dog. All three were scalped.

Our bugler signaled recall. Word spread that the dead warrior had not been in the crowd when White Eagle had blessed us and the warriors took heart. I held my tongue; they would find out soon enough.

"You do not speak, Rojo," Otter said as we gathered and gave our horses a rest.

"You will see soon enough, Otter, just be wise in the things you do in the next charge. I would be very sad if you were the next one to find that their bullets break the skin." I said it to my friends and the warriors that overheard grunted their disapproval. My hair marked me as a captive white, and the warriors who didn't know me might do me harm in their frustration. From then on, I held my tongue and stayed near Quanah. My three companions were subdued and quiet. Maybe my warning would preserve them. Rattle, No Hair, and Black Knife joined us and conversed with Otter in whispers. They looked at me, and Black Knife nodded ever so slightly. I wasn't sure what that meant, but I determined to be extra cautious until the Indians perceived the truth. Then there would be time to fight.

The war chiefs conferred with White Eagle, then returned to their warriors. "We will lead the charge on the houses from the middle," Quanah called, and we mounted our horses and waited the signal. In a few moments, the other war chiefs rode out in front of their tribesmen and the bugler played attention and the charge. Away we went, the charge almost as determined as the first except for the tiring horses.

Puffs of smoke now came from the buildings. The hide hunters had recovered from their surprise and were prepared to meet us. A horse on our left screamed and fell headfirst, his rider somersaulting over his head. The warrior's body was still in the air when a following horse hit him with his legs and knocked him aside. The man huddled there a moment, then sprang into the shelter of his horse's carcass.

A man to our right threw up his hands and fell, his horse charging on. Two more warriors fell in quick succession. The men around me were shocked and pale, but they pressed on in the charge. Sleepy Eye caught my attention and nodded. I had been right.

White Eagle's horse was shot and he stood among the flying bullets. Two Cheyenne warriors rescued him and threw him out of harm's way. I am not sure exactly when Quenosavit got his new name. The two Cheyenne warriors may have renamed him as they carried him to safety. By the time the bugler blew recall and we returned to Quanah, Quenosavit had become Isatai'i, his influence forever gone.

(The Comanche word "Isatai'i" refers to the nether end of a female coyote or wolf. Therefore, for the sake of decency, the man is referred to by the Comanche word, its meaning hidden in the unfamiliar language. Ed.)

Billy Ogg and Billy Dixon had stumbled into Hanrahan's sod saloon to find Hanrahan, Bat Masterson, Mike Welch, Shepherd, Hiram Watson, McKinley, and Carlisle scrambling around to find weapons to defend themselves with. The banging on the door and shutters was most disturbing, but there was no panic among the men.

Dixon shoved a cartridge into the breech of his .44, "Had to leave a whole case of ammunition in Rath's store, didn't I?"

Hanrahan grinned. "That rifle won't be too useful if those savages break through that door. Better tend to your six-shooter, Billy."

Bat, the youngest of the bunch, fired his pistol through a crack in the shutter and we heard a scream. "That's one." The pounding stopped a moment, then resumed with increased vigor. He fired again, but apparently didn't hit anyone.

Others had found guns and portholes and begun firing. They heard a distant bugle and the pounding stopped. "Mike, was that a bugle blowing recall?" Hiram asked.

"Damned if it weren't. Almost got up to run for my hoss," Mike replied.

"They're all leavin'," Bat called, his eye on the shutter crack.

"Give 'em one t' go by, Bat," someone called.

Dixon looked around at his companions and laughed. Only Ogg and Hanrahan were fully dressed like him. The others had rolled back into their blankets and were asleep when the attack came. "You fellers gonna fight in your underwear?" he asked.

"Might's well," Shepherd said, "things'r gonna git hot, looks like." None of the men moved to dress and fought that way all day. They heard another bugle call: "Ready up, boys, that's a charge." Hiram peeked out of his loop, then aimed his .50 and fired. "Got 'im." He scratched a mark in the sod wall. The men had time for only one shot with the big guns before the Indians were close enough for their handguns. Everything was noise and smoke to the tune of Indian yells. The charge seemed to last forever, then the Indians were forced back and the bugle recalled them.

"Grab your rifles, boys, let's send them off big," Hanrahan hollered above the ringing in his ears. The answering booms of the .50's was satisfying; Billy Dixon's .44 was not quite so loud and he cursed his luck at losing his .50.

"Y'got any water in this place, Hanrahan?" Carlisle asked. He had the morning-after thirst.

Hanrahan shook his head, "All my drinks is 90 proof."

"Phoo," McKinley exclaimed. "None o' that got t' my glass, Hanrahan, where'd ya keep it?" The banter carried on as the men busied themselves cleaning and reloading their weapons. Hiram Watson added two more scratches to his wall record. All was quiet for nearly an hour, enough time to call between buildings and find that there were no serious injuries.

Hanrahan's barkeeper, Shepherd, had grabbed up Jim's Sharps when the fighting started, but was too nervous to be effective. Billy Dixon was the best shot there and needed a big .50, so he gave Hanrahan his gun, "Here, Jim, take my .44 and let me have the .50, Shepherd." The man was so eager to get rid of the gun, he nearly dropped it.

Jim Langton called across the alleyway,

"Hey, Dixon, I'll send your cartridges first wagon heads your way."

"Do that, Jim, an' I'll send one 'er two back your way without the hulls on 'em."

"Too far fer them .44's t' do any damage," someone called from behind the sod wall.

"Who was 'at?" Dixon called.

"Who was what?" Langton replied, "I didn' hear anythin', me ears is ringin' so."

"Ya got any water in 'at 'ere sal-loon?" Andy Johnson called. "Let Bat dip his finger in it an' come cool my tongue for I am tormented in this hell."

"Torment's th' same over here," Hiram replied.

The music of the bugle echoed off the hills. "Here they come agin," Mike Welch called, and the guns boomed their welcome.

Billy Tyler and Fred Leonard had gone into the Myers & Leonard stockade and were forced back into the store by the attack. Just as Billy got to the door, he turned to fire and a bullet hit him in the lung. He only lived a little while.

"There he is agin, Bat," Dixon called.

Hiram Watson looked up from his reloading, "Bat got a buddy out there?"

"A redheaded buddy," Bat gritted as he fired.

Hiram aimed and fired. "Got 'im. Seen one over here, too, recon there's two of 'em?"

"He's over here, now," Hanrahan called. "Shore is an active feller."

Masterson fired, "Got his horse; he's down b'hind it."

Another warrior rode by the downed horse on the run, and at the last moment, the redheaded warrior stood and vaulted onto the horse. Bat fired again, "Hit *that* horse, I'll be danged." Blood streamed from the horse's leg as he three-legged out of sight, the two riders beating him with their quirts.

"Don't worry, he'll be back, Bat," Hanrahan called over the near continuous firing.

The men had been watching the grass moving where an Indian was crawling toward them, but their shots were ineffective. Searching for a better position to shoot from, Dixon noticed the transom over the barricaded door. He climbed the precarious pile of flour and grain sacks and aimed at the crawler. The recoil of his shot was enough to loosen his toehold and he tumbled down the pile of sacks into a tub of pots and pans, making a fearful racket.

"Noise don't scare those rascals," Masterson called as the others laughed and offered other useless advice.

Billy climbed the barrier again and saw that he had missed. Bracing himself better, he fired again — and missed a second time. *You're a disgusting shot, Billy Dixon; can't hit a target less than a hundred yards away,* he thought. His action became very slow and deliberate: *Reload. Set your feet. Rest arms on the transom frame. Sight target. Inhale and hold breath. Sque-e-e-eze trigger slowly.* The boom of the shot startled him, and if he hadn't had his elbows hooked over the frame, he probably would have fallen again. He stared through the wafting smoke at his target. The grass moved no more.

The Indians fell farther and farther back after each charge, never quite getting out of the Sharps's great range. Quanah's horse was shot four or five hundred yards from the buildings, and he took refuge behind a buffalo carcass that had been built in by wood rats. As he watched the battle, something he could never explain hit him a terrific blow between his shoulder blade and neck. When he recovered enough, he ran to a plum thicket and hid. His right arm was nearly useless, and another man rode by and took him from the battleground.

Our charges became less and less frequent

until they ceased about midafternoon. There were many grim faces around us.

"We should kill Isatai'i," Red Dog growled.

Otter nocked an arrow, "I can get him from here."

We were told to attack one side of the town while others tried to rescue the dead. In this way, we were able to gather several of them. The warriors' devotion to this act was noble, for they believed that a scalped or otherwise mutilated body would prevent the warrior from entering their "Otherworld." This belief would explain the mutilation of their enemies. We were unable to rescue thirteen of our dead that were under the very noses of the hunters. To attempt to rescue them would only have added to the dead.

All of the hunters' horses and oxen were killed and the hunters had no way to escape. At first, we thought to starve them out, but realized they could most likely hold out until soldiers could march from Fort Dodge to rescue them.

By late afternoon, we had fallen back to the hills at the foot of the eastern mesa. We divided into two groups, one on the east and the other on the west side of the buildings. There was considerable running back and forth between the two groups until the hunters began shooting the riders. Their circles got much bigger.

When the bugler was killed running away from the dead men's wagon with a tin of ground coffee under one arm and sugar under the other, it deprived the hunters of any warnings.

We sat around the fire eating our supper and talking. Red Dog was leaning against a tree asleep, his food in his lap.

"Already, many have left the war party," Otter said.

"With Quanah hurt, we do not have great leadership," I said.

"We should stay with Quanah and see him home safely," Sleepy Eye said.

I agreed, "That is what we will do." We spent the night watching the city to prevent any hunters escaping. Early in the third morning, about twenty of us rode out in the plain and were sent scurrying back into the woods by those buffalo guns. From there, we rode to the top of the eastern mesa and watched the Adobe Walls village. Isatai'i sat beside Quanah. "It is so bad my medicine failed. A Cheyenne warrior killed and skinned a skunk and broke the charm."

We were near enough to hear this and Sleepy Eye put his hand over his mouth to indicate his disbelief. A few minutes later, we heard the slap of a bullet hitting skin and the warrior sitting beside Isatai'i fell from his horse. It was a second or two before the boom of the gun rolled off the bluffs. We turned and raced out of sight.

Isatai'i turned his horse and peered through the trees at the settlement. "Buffalo gun shoots today, maybe kills tomorrow."

We heard the man on the ground moan, and Otter and I ran out and dragged him to shelter. He had a big red spot on his chest, but otherwise was not badly hurt.

After the battle, the Indians scattered over the plains killing whites in Texas, Kansas, Colorado, and Indian Territory.

Billy Dixon made that remarkable shot of some 1,538 yards — one shot and no more. It ended the siege of Adobe Walls — and more than anything else tolled the end of organized resistance to the white man's occupation of the Great Plains by the Kiowa/ Comanche–Southern Cheyenne alliance. By the next spring, all the Comanche divisions except the Quahadis had surrendered and settled on their reservation.

In 1876, J. Wright Mooar talked to the Cheyenne chief Whirlwind at the Cheyenne Agency. When asked about the Adobe Walls fight, Whirlwind said there were 1200 warriors there and that 115 men were killed. This number probably accounts for the many wounded men who died later. Whirlwind said that the defeat was because the Comanche medicine man was "no good."

CHAPTER 22
THE RED RIVER WAR

1874

There is a gap in Rojo Pelo's narrative here. We know that the plan of the four young men was to escort Quanah to his Quahadi village, somewhere on the plains of far west Texas. However, there are dependable witness accounts of a redheaded Indian leading a band of Indians on raids of isolated ranches and farms. In one incident, they attacked a whole settlement and burned most of the buildings there. They captured a sizable herd of cattle and horses in this raid. Rojo picks up his narrative in the fall of 1874 when the U.S. Army waged a coordinated war on those Indians who refused to voluntarily return to their reservation.

After we had escorted Quanah to the village, Sleepy Eye, Red Dog, and I joined with Rattle, No Hair, Black Knife, and Rock to spend the summer ridding the plains of white settlers. In the fall, we drove a considerable herd of cattle and horses to the Quahadi camp in Palo Duro Cañon. They were camped on the flats where the Cita Blanca Cañons join Palo Duro. There was a Cheyenne camp to the east across the Prairie Dog Town Fork. The Kiowa camp was upstream a half mile or so.

Bubbling Water and Janos were happy to see me back safely and I gave each a fine horse I had captured. Bubbling Water was heavy with child and we anticipated a quiet winter and the arrival of our first child — after Janos.

"That Kiowa medicine man, Maman-ti, has declared that the bluecoats would not disturb us in the cañon," Sleepy Eye said.

"It's a safe prediction, the bluecoats don't know the cañon exists and have never been this far into the Llano — and lived," Otter answered.

"I might feel safe, but not because some seer mumbled over some ceremony and said so." Rojo was skeptical of all medicine men.

Bubbling Water's time was very near and Quanah had ordered Rojo Pelo to stay with her, charging his three friends with keeping him there. They spent their time making arrows and preparing for the spring warpath.

■ ■ ■ ■

General Ranald Mackenzie continued his campaign into the winter and camped above Tule Cañon. The Indians found them and about thirty Indians tried to entice pursuit. Lieutenant Boehm rode up to where Mackenzie was watching the antics of the Indians. Saluting, but not dismounting, he said, "Sir, permission to pursue."

"Yes, Boehm, take two companies, but remember Fetterman and don't get trapped. Go no farther than two miles."

"Yes, sir!" came the reply of the receding officer.

Sooner than you would expect, the two companies were riding in pursuit. The Indians, on fresher horses, stayed just out of carbine range and the chase continued. The Indians were slowing, and the soldiers were closing the gap by the time they had gone two miles.

Boehm's scout called to him, "I don't like this, Lieutenant, they're lurin' us into somethin'."

"No, they aren't." The lieutenant threw up his arm and halted. "Blow our friends a kiss, men, this is as far as we go today." Amongst the expressions of dismay of the newer recruits were many an approving nod from the experienced soldiers. The companies returned to camp, Lieutenant Boehm putting them through several maneuvers on the way and ignoring the cries of the Indian followers.

"Very good, Boehm," was the only reply Mackenzie gave when the lieutenant reported. His mind was on other things and his staff knew something was afoot. At the officer's call, the general gave his orders for the night, "See that your men are fed before dark. I want the horses hobbled, picketed, and sidelined. Place the men in a circle around the herd; they can sleep in uniform and armed. We'll have a surprise for those Indians when they come to steal our horses."

Lieutenant William Thompson and his scouts returned in the night and he reported to the general. "We found three camps in the Palo Duro at a place they call Cita Blanca. My scouts say they were Kiowa, Comanche, and Cheyenne."

The expected assault on the horse herd came, but was repulsed, though the Indians kept up a harassing fire all night. At dawn, Mackenzie ordered out two companies of cavalry to run off the Indians, who retreated south away from the cañon. In the afternoon, Mackenzie ordered his entire command to take up the trail of the attacking Indians. At evening, they camped for the night. After dark, he ordered the troops to break camp and they hurried back north.

It took Thompson's men a little time to find a well-traveled path down the thousand-foot bluffs the next morning, and when they did, the general said, "Mr. Thompson, take your men down and start the fight!"

They were halfway down a trail so steep they had to lead their horses before they were detected. Instead of attacking the single file of soldiers exposed on the trail, the warriors prepared to protect the women and children as they escaped up the cañon.

"The bluecoats are in the cañon, grab your guns!" Rojo yelled at his sleeping friends. He was almost out the tipi door when Otter called, "Wait, Rojo, wait, wait."

"Come on," Rojo called, hardly pausing. He met Red Dog, who was on his way to the tipi.

"Grab him, Red Dog," Otter called, and the larger Red Dog grabbed Rojo from behind, pinning his arms at his side. He carried the struggling man back and held him at the door. "What should I do with him?"

Rojo could just barely reach the ground

with his extended toes. He finally relaxed. "What do you want, Otter?" Sleepy Eye took the redheaded warrior's rifle and shield and stood ready to help Red Dog if needed.

"Quanah has said you must stay out of war until Bubbling Water delivers."

"But —" he gestured at the line of warriors forming in the lower end of the villages.

"He didn't say *where* the fighting would be, he said to stay away from it," Sleepy Eye interjected.

"In our own camp?" Rojo yelled the words, incredulous at his friends' stand.

"Look at the trail, Rojo; they still come. The camp will not be ours much longer; we have to take care of Bubbling Water."

How could Otter be so calm when there is fighting to do?

Sleepy Eye held up his hand to stop Rojo. "Look at your wife, Rojo; already the pains come. She cannot run with the others. We have to hide her."

Bubbling Water had emerged from the tipi, a large bundle on her back. Janos was equally laden. Rojo saw her pale face and all thoughts of fight or flight left his mind. Sleepy Eye took her bundle. "The Stone Tipi, up North Cita Cañon."

"Take them, Sleepy Eye, and Otter and I

will stay behind and hide your path," Red Dog said.

Sleepy Eye shouldered the bundle and turned for the cañon, Janos struggling along behind. Rojo held Bubbling Water's arm and guided her through the pathless brush. The climb was steep and rocky, and the woman had a hard time. She stopped as water gushed from her womb. "The child comes soon," she whispered to Rojo.

"Soon, Sleepy Eye," he called. The next hundred yards were extremely slow and Bubbling Water said, "Now. Janos, a robe and the blanket."

Janos opened his bag and pulled out a buffalo robe. He spread it on the ground.

"Not there, here," Bubbling Water demanded. Rojo brushed the rocks away and spread the robe at her feet while Janos dug for the receiving blanket the mother-to-be had made. In almost one motion, Bubbling stepped barefooted onto the robe, pulled her skirt up, and squatted. Sleepy Eye stooped behind her and held her steady with his hands under her arms. Rojo stared, pale and fascinated. A dark-haired head appeared, then tiny shoulders. Janos handed the spread blanket to Rojo.

"Take the baby, Rojo," Bubbling Water whispered hoarsely.

Rojo fell to his knees and cradled the child in his hands as it emerged from the womb. It only took a few moments, but it seemed like forever, there in that deep cañon, no sound but the crickets nearby and distant shooting echoing off the walls.

"It is a boy!" Rojo whispered. He wiped the child's face clean and made sure his nose was clear.

"Janos, give Rojo the cord so he can tie off the tube," Bubbling Water instructed, and Rojo fumbled through tying off and cutting the umbilical cord near the baby's stomach.

"Turn him over and rub his back," Bubbling Water instructed.

Rojo felt weak and shaky and fumbled the wet child over on his stomach and rubbed the tiny back — how small and delicate he looked. He rubbed, but there was no reaction from the child. Sleepy Eye reached over Rojo's shoulder and gave the baby a smart smack on the buttocks. The reaction was immediate, infant taking a deep breath — his first — and giving loud objection to his mistreatment. Rojo glared at Sleepy Eye who shrugged, "It is how grandmother does it."

A dove called from the brush and Sleepy Eye replied. In a moment, Otter cautiously peeked through the button willows, then stepped into the small clearing. A middle-aged woman followed, and taking in the scene, took the infant and shooed the men away.

"Where is Red Dog?" Sleepy Eye asked.

Otter's face betrayed his emotions and he whispered, "Red Dog has taken the Long Trail . . ." emotion choking off any further words.

Rojo felt dizzy; it seemed the world brightened for a moment, and then went very dark. It seemed to spin slowly around him. Red Dog gone? How could it be? "Otter is mistaken," he heard himself say.

"No, Rojo, he has gone," Otter replied. "I have hidden his body so the Man-Eaters cannot find him."

"This cannot be, surely, Otter, you . . . He is just hurt. We will bring him here to heal," Sleepy Eye declared.

"You shall see," was all Otter said and turned away. "We must get to the cave."

The cañon had turned as they ascended and now ran north. The east wall was sheer, seeming to be solid rock.

The men moved as if in a dream, gathering weapons and what little gear they had and moving on through the head-high brush to that east wall of the cañon. At a spot determined by landmarks Rojo could not detect, Sleepy Eye dug in the sand and a foot down uncovered the end of a stout log. It took the three men an hour to uncover and lift the fifteen-foot-long notched log.

"Now, we wait until dark, then we will climb the ladder to our hiding," Otter explained.

Bubbling Water and the woman, Bad Foot, worked with the baby, cleaning him and dressing him in the gown Bubbling Water had made. They cleaned Bubbling Water's bottom parts while the men found things to do elsewhere.

Soon she was nursing a hungry baby. "What have you determined to name my son, Sleepy Eye?" Bubbling Water asked. Sleepy Eye, as a friend and reluctant witness to the birth, had the priviledge of naming the child.

The young warrior thought a moment, then lifted the blanket from the suckling infant's head and said to him, "Tiny one, I name you Little Red Dog." And so he was.

When it was so dark they could not see the opposite wall of the cañon, they retraced their tracks to a small scree where rocks had washed off the top of the cliff into the valley. They leaned the ladder against the wall and Sleepy Eye scrambled up to a short ledge where he crawled behind a large flat rock leaning against the cliff. In a moment, he reappeared and tossed down one end of a rope. Otter tied on one of the bundles to be hauled up. When it had disappeared behind the rock, the rope again descended, and in only a few minutes their meager supplies were stowed. Otter looped the rope under Janos's arms and Rojo boosted the boy on his way up the ladder. In like manner, the two women were lifted, Little Red Dog snuggly tucked into the cradleboard on his mother's back.

The last two men scrambled up the ladder after Otter had tied the rope around the bottom notch. The three men laboriously pulled the ladder up and laid it on the ledge out of sight from below, the notches hidden so that it resembled an old log from the top of the opposite bluff.

Behind the big rock was a hole that led into a large room. It was pleasantly cool after the heat of the day. The cave had obviously been used as a shelter for some time, for there were stored there the things to make its occupants comfortable. The Indians called the place the Stone Tipi. It was to be home to the seven refugees for the next six months.

■ ■ ■ ■

Thompson and his scouts met stiff resistance in getting to the bottom of the cañon, but as soon as they were down, he led a charge that broke up the Indian defenses, and Captain Beaumont's Second Battalion with Mackenzie had room to form up. Mackenzie ordered the scouts and two companies to sweep the encampments and the remaining two companies to guard their flanks.

The soldiers swept through the camps and chased the retreating Indians up the cañon. Mackenzie sent messangers to warn Beaumont of a possible ambush, and the pursuers returned to the villages with a large horse herd.

The latter end of the descending army had watched helplessly as the Indian women, followed by the warriors, climbed the west wall on a narrow trail to the plains above. There were few horses in the retreat and the people were burdened with few provisions. It would be a long hungry winter.

Most of the Indians escaped, but the real damage to them was the loss of their horses and homes and winter supplies, which the soldiers looted and destroyed. There was much anger when the soldiers found that most of the food, clothes, and blankets were newly issued from the agencies. It had always been suspected that the "wild" Indians had been sustained by the reservation Indians and their government-issued supplies. The proof was here.

The destruction of the three camps was thorough and the little army rode south out of the Palo Duro, driving a herd of one thousand to fifteen hundred Indian ponies while the angry warriors watched from the rim of the cañon. "Tonight, we will have our horses back," they told each other.

Mackenzie led the way up Tule Cañon toward their camp on the plains. Near the top, he called a halt and allowed the Tonkawas to choose horses from the captured herd. Then he gave the order that sealed the fate of the plains Indians, "Kill the horses; all of them."

It was an action and sight that haunted the memories of both races for a lifetime, and the bluecoats wasted no time removing from the site.

The Indians wandered the killing field, shocked and saddened at the destruction there. This was the culmination of a disastrous year of defeats and omens for the Kiowa/Comanche and Cheyenne. Harassed by six pursuing armies and with no food, no shelter, and no horses, the tribes surrendered to the white man's authority and reservations. Only the Kotsoteka and Quahadi clans would remain on the plains.

The scavengers of the plains had a great gorging, and when they were through, the whitening bones remained for years as a reminder of the end of the era of the plains horsemen. Rojo Pelo would have been heartened to know that King was still living, the proud posession of a Tonkawa Man-Eater at Fort Griffin.

General Mackenzie kept his six divisions of the army pursuing the renegade Indians until January, '75, and when spring approached, the Kotsoteka found themselves high on the Llano Estacado with no food or shelter and no chance to acquire any.

CHAPTER 23
THE QUAHADI SURRENDER

The Stone Tipi proved to be a secure refuge for the six survivors of the Mackenzie raid. Fearful that the lack of game would betray their presence, they did not hunt in the close vicinity of the cave. This meant hauling the game they killed a long way back to the cave. As a result, they hunted in pairs.

Scavenging through the burned village provided them with other needed items, including blankets to wrap Red Dog's body when they buried him. When they left the Stone Tipi, it was well stocked with equipment and weapons found in the village.

A sizable herd of buffalo wintering in the lower cañons provided meat and fresh hides the whole winter. The unusual number of wolves and coyotes in the lower cañon made the hunters curious and they searched down toward the mouth of Tule Cañon.

"Look at the buzzards, Rojo," Sleepy Eye pointed.

"I've been watching them. There must be a thousand of them circling from low to as high as you can see."

"Maybe more," Sleepy Eye said. "If there are that many up there, how many are on the ground?" A most foul odor wafted down the cañon.

"I do not want to know what is up there," Rojo said.

"It could be dead bluecoats," the ever-optimistic Sleepy Eye offered.

"Not likely. I suppose we must find out." Rojo led the way up the right hill to the flat above Tule and they walked toward the head of the cañon, keeping back from the edge to avoid being seen from below. The stench grew as they neared the top. Clouds of millions of flies darkened the sky. Above their buzz, they heard a continuous growl and snarl.

Sleepy Eye grabbed Rojo's arm and stopped. "We should not go closer, I fear some monster has done an awful thing."

"Very well, Sleepy Eye, we go no further. I will crawl to the edge and peek over. You do not have to come." Rojo crouched and moved toward the brink of the cañon; closer, he lay down and crawled, pushing his rifle ahead. He peeked through the grasses into the cañon and lay still a long time.

"What is it, Rojo?"

"You may come and see for yourself, Sleepy Eye, it is safe." Rojo sat up and stared at the cañon floor.

Sleepy Eye, standing behind him, ventured a glimpse and stiffened, "What is that?" He saw a large area filled with dark bodies and hundreds of creatures swarming around them.

"Horses, Sleepy Eye, our horses and vermin."

There was so much movement in the valley with scavenger birds and wolves and coyotes that at first glimpse the whole valley seemed alive. Even the bodies of the horses seemed alive with movement.

"They walk," Rojo muttered, "they don't have horses." The three had smiled at the bluecoats taking the herd, knowing that the warriors would recover them as surely as they breathed. No army had been able to keep the captured Indian ponies, and more times than not, had lost their own horses in the bargain. The enormity of the villages being on the Llano without horses numbed their minds. Even if they had a few horses there would not be enough to hunt food for the whole tribe.

"The bluecoats have done this thing and many of our people will die because of it," Sleepy Eye said. His face was pale and his hands shook with anger and shock. A tear coursed down his cheek — for the thousand dead horses and the helpless comrades and kin on the Llano without them. He turned and walked back toward the Palo Duro. At the brink, he shot a skulking wolf.

Returning from a hunt late one afternoon, Otter and Sleepy Eye startled three Indian ponies grazing along the creek near the village. It was good to know they were there, though they did nothing to contain them. They would be needed if the little group had to travel any distance to find their village in the spring.

Little Red Dog was the joy of the camp. He gave the others hours of entertainment as he grew. Sunny afternoons were spent in the cañon below the cave while someone kept watch from the ledge above. March was windy and stormy but the longer days and milder temperatures made the little group restless for a change.

"Where do you suppose the Quahadi are?" Rojo asked one evening as they sat around the fire.

"They are probably one or two steps

ahead of the army that chases them," Sleepy Eye replied.

"Maybe the army has gone to the forts to resupply and our friends are not harassed," Bubbling Water said. In the close confines of their life, the traditional divide between the genders had relaxed and the two women entered into the conversations of the men.

"We must begin watching for them," Otter said. "We have those three horses and one of us could ride out and scout for signs of the villages or the army."

"And we should begin tomorrow," Rojo said.

"I shall go," two voices answered almost in unison.

"Bad Foot, we need three straws of three lengths." Rojo laughed. "Shortest straw first, longest straw last."

Otter won the draw, but he didn't go out to scout the next day, for it took all day to capture the three ponies. They had grown quite independent of human interference in their lives. Late in the afternoon, they managed to turn the ponies into North Cita Cañon.

"Now, we have them, they can't go as fast in this brush," Sleepy Eye called. But though they were slowed, the weary men were just as much hindered by the brush and they slowed also.

Bad Foot was sitting on the ledge weaving a reed basket while Bubbling Water wove a mat on the ground below and watched Little Red Dog as he played with a feather on his robe.

"Horses come," Bad Foot called. She stood and watched a moment, "Men behind them."

Bubbling Water gathered the protesting baby, put the cradleboard on her back, gathered up the robe, and stood by the ladder, ready to climb if necessary. She heard the horses pushing through the brush as they approached. "Hie, you horses," she called, and a curious horse pushed his head between button willows to see where this familiar female voice came from. "Hie, you horse, where are you going?" Bubbling Water stood very still, holding out her hand with a wild turnip resting in her open palm.

Horse eyed turnip, then eyed woman. She held no restraining rope, and the turnip was irresistible. It was only a few steps away and the crackling of brush heralded the approach of the other horses that might beat him to the fruit. Five steps away, three steps away. The horse stretched his neck, but could only smell the aroma of the turnip. One step away, and he took the proferred tuber. While he savored the morsal, the woman rubbed his face and scratched between his ears. He came to the sudden realization that there was a rope around his neck and jerked away, only to find that the rope was anchored to the notched ladder, which toppled to the ground at his pull. He was trapped and he knew there was no use fighting, though he stood with feet braced against the pull.

"I have one," a triumphant Otter called as he approached the anchored horse.

"No, you don't 'have one,' *I* have one," Bubbling Water corrected. "But you may borrow him to catch the other two."

Otter snorted his disgust and pulled a hackamore over the horse's ears. Forgetting the noose in his hurry, he leaped on the horse's back. Horse objected. Trying to buck with a log around your neck and a man on your back was quite a challenge, but he managed to unseat the man. The log rolled down the slope, the noose tightened, cutting off his air, and the horse followed the pull of the log, trying to relieve the constriction of his neck. He was wobbling, about to sink to his knees, when the calming voice and touch of the woman quieted him some. She led him forward and loosened the noose as the rope slackened.

Sleepy Eye and Rojo appeared and took over the handling of the horse. Bubbling Water moved out of the way and watched Otter pulling prickly pear spines out of his legs.

"Would you replace the ladder before you leave so I can go start your evening meal?" she asked sweetly. Otter grimaced. Women were as prickly as cactus.

The other two horses were caught in short order and all three tethered to stout trees for the evening while three exhausted vaqueros climbed the ladder to a fine meal and sleep. Nothing was said about a woman's ability to catch horses, but somehow the smiles and solicitude of the two women were irritating.

THE QUAHADI RETURN

It's hard to grasp the enormity of the Palo Duro Cañon. From the edge of the caprock to the head of the great gulch is over fifty miles. Added to that are the side cañons such as Tule and the two Cita Blancas. The cañon has a milder climate than the plains above and is a good shelter — as it has been for eons on end — for man and beast.

The Quahadi noticed the foul smell and taste of the Prairie Dog Town stream. As they ascended the cañon that early spring, it became more and more polluted until it was unusable for man and the few horses they had. They were at the point of turning around when the scouts came in and reported the water was still sweet above Tule Cañon. No one mentioned the source of the polution; it was still too painful to think about.

The spirit of their lost homes was pulling them back to the site of the old village at the Cita Blancas. It was where they left their possessions, and deep within them was the hope that they might somehow be there when they returned. They hurried past the mouth of the Tule, faces covered against the smell, and drank deeply of the pure running stream.

Rojo Pelo, long thought dead, met them as they broke camp the next morning. Family and friends rejoiced at the news of the other five survivors and the new child. It quickened their pace and they arrived at the old camp late in the afternoon to find the lone tipi of Rojo and Bubbling Water. Their dismay at the destruction soon faded as they again set up their camps in their favored spots and searched through the ruins for such usables as they could find.

Otter, Sleepy Eye, and Bad Foot found their families, who enjoyed an unexpected reunion with those thought lost.

The next day, the hunters found the buffalo herd, and the celebration of the clan's return lasted until the stars faded before the rising sun. The bluecoats had not pursued them that long miserable winter and the hope that the ordeal was over pervaded their thoughts. This was to be the last peaceful stay of the free Quahadi in their beloved Palo Duro.

The Kotsoteka band had suffered greatly the winter of 1875 and on April 18th, 1875, Mow-way, and a hundred and seventy-five ragged and starved villagers with him, surrendered at their reservation. White Crow, the warrior who bought Castaño Rojizo (our Eve) from the Apache, kept his white wife hidden from the anglos. White Crow and his first wife, Meadowlark, mistreated and abused Rojizo.

Mackenzie sent Jacob Sturm and three others to negotiate a truce with Quanah. It resulted in Quanah agreeing to surrender if there would be no punishment of the tribe for their resistance. The date was set as June 2, 1875. The clan began a leisurely trek to Fort Sill, stopping several times to hunt and rest.

As they approached the fort, anxiety rose among the people and several families slipped away, returning to the west Texas plains. Strum had insisted that the white captives would be returned to their white families upon surrendering, something Rojo strongly opposed. It would mean separation from Bubbling Water, Janos, Little Red Dog, and his Comanche companions. Two nights before the band crossed Salt Creek, Rojo Pelo and his family turned back west. Sleepy Eye followed behind dragging a cedar bush to wipe out the travois tracks. It would have been easy to track them down, but nobody did. The conviction that their way of life was dying with the death of the buffalo restrained the whole tribe from bolting. They rode toward the rising sun, blurred by their tears, buffeted by anxiety and trepidation of the unknown to come.

CHAPTER 24
FOUNDING THE JA

In the spring of 1875, Charles Goodnight sent his foreman and brother-in-law, Leigh Dyer, to Twin Butte Creek, southeast of Las Animas, Colorado, with a large herd of cattle. That fall, Goodnight drove his herd south to the Canadian River to winter in northeast New Mexico Territory, something they could not have done the year before because of the Comanches.

The spring of 1876 found Goodnight drifting his herd down the Canadian to summer on Alamocita Creek. While there, passing Mexican ciboleros on their way to the buffalo herds told of a vast cañon that cut deep into the Llano Estacado. Goodnight hired one of the Mexicans to take him to the cañon. His guide had almost despaired finding the cañon when they suddenly rode upon the brink of the Palo Duro near Tule Cañon. "At last, at last," the Mexican cried. That fall, Goodnight drove his herd down a narrow trail near the head of the cañon and established his JA ranch in the

411

great Palo Duro.

Eventually, there gathered some fifty Comanches who refused to surrender with Quanah. Rojo was pleased to find that Otter, Sleepy Eye, Rattle, Black Knife, and Rock were in the band. As usual in a band, the women outnumbered the men. The few children with them were older, only five had not yet seen four summers.

The band lived on the mostly empty plain avoiding contact with all men except for the occasional encounter with isolated buffalo hunters, whose total disappearance was known among the hunters but disbelieved by Indian agents and the military. By the winter of 1876, the band had gathered enough buffalo hides to make shelters for all the families. They avoided the tall tipis, which could be seen from afar, and reverted to the low wikiups that blended more with their surroundings. Their horse herd was small, but adequate for their needs. In times past a visitor would have counted horses and clucked at the poverty of the band. "Poor, but free," Sleepy Eye would declare.

Otter and Rattle had been gone several days from our Palo Duro camp just north of Tule Cañon. When they returned from the Llano, they rode directly to headman

Black Duck's hut. They emerged a few minutes later and Black Duck called, "We will have a council at sunset after all have eaten."

A low fire signaled the council meeting and all gathered to hear Black Duck and the scouts. "Rattle and Otter have returned from the upper Prairie Dog Creek where they found that a great herd of cattle has been driven down into the cañon." There was a murmur among the people.

Rattle stood, "They are driving the buffalo down the cañon and we cannot make our winter camp here."

"How far up are they?" a warrior asked.

"Where the cañon runs east, before it turns toward the south," Otter answered.

"There should still be room for us down here below the Citas Cañons," another said.

"There are many buffalo in the cañon and as they drive them down, they will fill the whole cañon. It would be dangerous to live anywhere in the bottom near water," Rattle replied.

"The water is already being fouled by the cattle and it will be bad even to here," Otter said. Living among the buffalo herds was easy, for they took care not to foul the water, while cattle would wade into streams and stomp the banks into mud, leaving mud, urine, and offal to spoil the streams.

There was a long silence, then Black Duck spoke, "We will stay here while the warriors scout the cañon. When they return, we will decide where to make the winter camp." With that, the council broke up and the people returned to their huts and sleeping robes.

The need for constant vigilance was necessary now and made life more complicated. Scouts were out all the time and Black Knife complained, "I've spent more time among the cactus and rocks than in my robes. It would be good if one never had to sleep."

"One sleeps well on the reservation," Rock replied.

"Sleeps well so long as they have full bellies, which seems to be a rare thing there," Black Knife replied.

"They come to us for a little while, then return to the agent in time for the distribution. Isatai'i was right, White Man's way will be our downfall." Rojo pulled his robe closer.

"Spoken like a true Comanche." Sleepy Eye smiled at the irony of a redheaded Indian condemning the way of the white man.

They all had noticed the transformation

of self-sufficient men and women to dependence on those government handouts. Even when free on the plains, they felt the pull of unearned and mostly insufficient provender and returned to it.

Rock yawned and rose. "Talk on, you old women, I go to my robes. Perhaps you will talk of nothing all night and sleep while I ride out to see the whites and their cattle."

"We could sleep 'til the sun casts no shadow and still catch up with you on that nag you call your warhorse," Otter retorted. Even so, he rolled in his robe and turned his feet to the fire.

Much to his disgust, Rock was chosen to stay with the village when they "cast lots" the next morning. Sleepy Eye and Rojo Pelo were cast with the scouts. Rattle was appointed to be the guide to the group. No one showed any emotions that would antagonize the ones left behind. Left Hand, the oldest warrior, was appointed leader of the scouts, and they followed him up Tule Cañon to a point they could climb out the north side and bypass the killing field where the spirits of the great horse herd lived. Soon, they stopped and Left Hand drew the path of Prairie Dog Creek in the sand.

"They came into the cañon on the west trail," Rattle pointed to the single file trail the tribe had used to escape Mackenzie, "and they are moving down the stream. They were about here," he said, pointing to the bends where the cañon turns southeast, "when we left them."

Left Hand considered the map for a moment. "Where were they driving the buffalo?"

"They were well ahead of the cattle. Four men drove them."

"We will go toward this bend until we find the herd and the buffalo," Left Hand said, pointing to the easternmost bend. He stood and rubbed out the map with his foot.

They rode, each man making his own path to keep dust to a minimum. There was water in the upper end of the South Cita Blanca Creek and when they climbed out of the arroyo, they turned north toward the bends of the cañon. Soon, they saw a thin column of dust rising from the depths of the Palo Duro and as they rode further north, a second dust appeared that had been hidden by the first.

Left Hand called the scouts together, "The first dust must be the buffalo being driven and the second dust comes from the cattle. They are still moving and we need to know how far down the creek they go. Kingfisher, take Rojo and Rattle and scout the buffalo. Silvertip, Sleepy Eye, and I will watch the cattle."

We rode together until Kingfisher signaled and turned toward the leading dust cloud. Before we reached the brink of the cliffs, we bound our hair and painted our faces.

One cannot get used to the suddenness of the appearance of the cañon. Even the horses were nervous approaching the edge, and we tied them to bushes well back from the rim. There was no need for the branches we held before our faces, for the herders were two or more miles away in the bottom of the cañon, riding through dust too thick to enable them to see very far. I tossed my limb out into the cañon and the wind picked it up and blew it back up the cliff and over our heads to fall well out in the flats behind us.

"The Palo Duro does not like your offering, Rojo," Rattle muttered.

It seemed an omen. Lying there on our bellies, we could feel in the earth the rumble of the hooves of hundreds of buffalo as they thundered down the valley. The vision of the buffalo being driven away by the white man and his hoards of cattle filling the land behind was a picture of what was happening in all our land. It was as if we were watching our way of life driven away with

417

the buffalo and the void filled by the surging blackness of strange men and strange animals. There was no longer room for the red man.

"There," Rattle pointed across the valley, "they dig Mother Earth."

It took me a moment to find what Rattle saw. "They are digging a dugout in the bank. It is where they will live," I explained.

"It must mean that they stop the cattle near here," Kingfisher said.

"I count four or five men running the buffalo and more than that will be with the cattle," I said. "They won't dig a hole big enough for ten or twelve men. Some of them will be living elsewhere."

As I spoke, Kingfisher pointed to a group of maybe fifteen men who rode down the valley together. "They have stopped driving the cattle. We should watch to see if they continue driving them in the morning."

I realized with a start that the shadows of the west wall had reached the bottoms of the eastern cliffs and begun their climb toward the top and sunset. We had spent several hours watching the action below us. Now it was our time to seek a place to rest.

Charlie Goodnight poured another cup of coffee and sat on his bedroll to sip and think. "Leigh, leave enough men here to finish the dugout and build a small corral. When it's finished leave one man here to keep th' buffalo and cattle from mixin'. The rest of us will go back to that flat we saw and see if it is suitable for our headquarters."

Leigh Dyer nodded, "Shore nice not to have to worry about that herd scatterin' an' mixin' with other herds. We'll have enough spare time to build corrals an' headquarters an' such."

"After we've found a place, I'll go back to Las Animas and send back supplies for th' winter. I want you to drag up enough timber for a house an' bunkhouse. When I get back, we'll frame 'em up."

"You gonna lay out th' buildings so we'll know how much timber t'drag?"

Goodnight nodded, tossed the dregs from his cup, and crawled into his roll. *Sometimes Leigh could ask the simplest questions — things he should know without asking. He does a lot better when I'm not around and he has t' think for himself — and I do a lot better when I don't have t' talk so much.* He fell asleep sorting out the hundreds of things that he needed to do to get established on this new range. Not far from the top of his list was the hope that Molly would come to the ranch with him. She was in California visiting family and it would sure be good to see her.

The flat on the southwest side of the cañon proved to be a good site for the headquarters. There was a spring trickling from under the caprock that would supply plenty of water. They spent the next couple days laying out the buildings and corrals. Two days later, Charlie and Nicolas Martinez rode out of the cañon on their three-hundred-mile ride to Las Animas. Out here, a man could think and not have to talk so much.

Dave McCormick won the right to sleep in the new dugout and ride line. He didn't count on it being so lonely, only seeing someone every week or two when they rode over to bring supplies and see how he was getting along. He was busy enough catching flies for his horned toad friend, but the feller didn't talk.

The Indians watched the activities in the cañon for several days. It became obvious these were not the everyday run of white men, for they were always alert and heavily armed.

"We can kill the lone man in the hole easy enough," Rattle said one afternoon.

"Yes, but then the other whites will know we are here, and the army will come for us," Silvertip answered. "These are careful men, and strong. It would be folly to think we could kill them all without bringing harm to ourselves."

"We should let them have the Palo Duro?" Rojo asked.

"The cañon is very big and there may still be room for us lower down the river," Left Hand said. Studying the three young men, he thought, *Their blood runs hot; they do not see that the life we have lived is gone.*

"We must stay unseen if we wish to stay free," Kingfisher, who seldom spoke, said.

Rattle persisted, "We should kill them all and their cattle with them."

"You would turn our refuge into a battle-ground?" Left Hand asked. "We cannot afford to lose one warrior and it would be sure more than one of us would take the Long Ride if we fought these men. No, it would be best if they did not know of us."

"Think on this as you lay in your blanket," said Kingfisher.

"We return tomorrow," Left Hand said.

A night's sleep and thought sobered the three young warriors and it was a quiet group that rode down the Llano to the Tule camp.

The council heard the reports of the scouts and after much thought it was decided that the village would move west to the Place of the Ruins at Horse Creek on the Canadian. It was a good camp, but game was scarce and hard to find.

In the late summer, the little band traveled back to the Palo Duro and camped again at their Tule Cañon camp.

CHAPTER 25
THE GOODNIGHT-PARKER TREATY

1877

Quanah Parker and his Quahadi were full of reservation life. The people were hungry on the meager food afforded them. A particularly bad distribution angered Quanah so that he demanded a pass to leave the reservation for a hunt. The agent, seeing the ugly mood of the people, wrote a pass for them. As they traveled west that summer and fall, a band of Kiowa, away from their reservation without leave, joined them. They traveled and hunted together but, as was their custom, camped separately.

They rode through a country dotted with rotting carcasses of their beloved buffalo. The boom of the Sharps was no longer heard; the buffalo were gone. "We go to the Palo Duro," Quanah announced. "Perhaps the hunters missed the herd there."

The people watched as the escarpment of the caprock rose slowly far to the west. It seemed they would never get there. The mouth of the Palo Duro beckoned, and they rode until darkness hid it and they were forced to camp.

"Tomorrow," they told each other.

The Prairie Dog Town stream was murky but usable, and they greeted it with joy, the women bathing themselves and their children in the cold waters.

"Tomorrow."

Scrubbed children slept in their warm blankets while the men sat around fires and spoke of their hopes and times passed in the cañon. Conversation died with the flames and the camp slept.

Meantime, Black Duck and his band waited among the rocks and boulders of lower Tule Cañon. Just at dark, the scouts had come in to report the sighting of a dust approaching the cañon from the east.

"Such a large dust could only mean soldiers," Sleepy Eye opined. "There would not be that many Comanche leaving the reservation at one time."

There was no time for a council; Black Duck thought a moment. "Drive the horses up the cañon and break camp. We will hide in the rocks tonight and send out scouts in the morning. If need be, we can escape up the Tule."

Driving the horses through the jumble of the lower Tule was slow and laborious. "We will at least be between the soldiers and the horses," Rattle said.

"If they don't come around behind us and down the cañon," Rojo returned. "Whatever happens, we are going to spend an uncomfortable night among the rocks."

They scattered, drawing warmth from the rocks until the cold wind of dawn chilled both rock and man.

Two Comanche camps arose early that morning, one full of excitement and anticipation, the other sleepless and anxious.

Quanah Parker, dressed in his finest and riding his battle horse, led his clan.

The Black Duck warriors stretched their cramped limbs and renewed their war paint. This could be the day of their Long Ride. They moved down to the mouth of Tule and hid in the rocks. Black Duck sent Rojo and Rattle to scout the advancing host.

We rode down the stream until the tiny dots of horses and riders came into view under that rising column of dust.

"Rojo, climb up there to that rock. There is a place behind it where you can picket your horse out of sight. You can see far down the valley from there. I will hide behind the willows across the creek where I can watch and escape unseen to warn the others. You can ride along the bluff until you get to a place you can descend to the bottom."

I led my horse up a slope, too steep to ride, to the cliff. There was ample space to tether him behind that big rock and a trail along the face of the bluff I could ride to escape.

Rattle rode across the creek and into the willows and lay atop a high dune where he could see me and the trail. We waited, watching the dots draw nearer and more distinct. Soon, it became clear that this was not an army, but a tribe on the move. The task now was to determine who they were and if they would be hostile to our presence.

Scouts rode ahead on either side of the travelers. It soon became clear that the scouts on the far side would be behind the willows and ride right into the place where Rattle hid. I was still secure on the hillside.

The chief was a tall man, and his horse, easier to see than the man's features, was familiar. It was Quanah's warhorse, and no one but Quanah could ride that straight and tall. Still, I waited to be sure. I could see that Rattle also had ideas of whom we were watching. It had to be. We both stood at the same moment and voiced the Comanche call of welcome.

It took the travelers a moment to comprehend what had happened, then many voices were raised in response. Quanah rode on as if our greeting were expected and Rattle raced to his horse to report to our people. I rode Amigo straight down that slope and out on the valley and waited for Quanah to approach.

He didn't waver or alter his path, "Ride with me, Rojo Pelo, and tell me what news you have."

"We have buffalo in the cañon, Quanah Parker — and cattle in the upper end."

"Ahah, they have found our cañon."

"Yes, they burrow in the hillsides and build with logs."

"Still, there is room for us?" Quanah watched the dust of the approaching fugitive band.

"We will find out soon enough," I replied.

All progress up the cañon ceased when the two groups joined and there was much visiting and finding of kin. Quanah and the elders of both groups pulled aside and conferred.

Soon, Crier moved through the tribe announcing that they would camp at Tule Cañon with Black Duck's clan. The march resumed with quickened pace, pushed by the advancing sun and by the prospect of a settled camp.

They began to see scattered buffalo that turned and ran back up the valley at the scent of their hated enemy, the Indian.

"They are here, Quanah, but there are so few," I said.

"I can see that — too few to kill," the chief replied. "Perhaps the white man's buffalo will be plentiful enough to provide us meat." He smiled and I couldn't help but grin. Cattle in the valley might be fortunate for us after all.

Quanah's band set up camp not far from our camp and the Kiowa chose a place across the stream in the willows opposite the Quahadi. Even before all the tipis were up, warriors were killing cattle. Fires burned brightly all night as the women prepared the meat for a homecoming feast. It was a quiet celebration, the tired travelers content to rest around the fires and enjoy their first abundant meal in weeks.

The weather turned cold, with rain and snow, and the people were content to stay in camp and inside warm tipis, rest, and enjoy Charlie Goodnight's JA beef.

Dave McCormick was curious and just a

little worried. For the past three days, he had heard gunfire down the valley, and it was far more than any of the boys would do. Occasionally he would glimpse a rider in the brush along the creek — and they didn't resemble any vaquero he knew. No one came a-visitin', and he was glad, for they wore feather headgear. Betsy, his twelve-gauge, was constantly at his side, and neither strayed far from the dugout. The buffalo came up the cañon in a hurry and the unrestrained cattle drifted downstream, seeking greener pastures.

"Betsy, it's time to visit headquarters," he said as he saddled his horse. "Surprised you're still around here ol' boy. You could be standing in front of some tipi waiting for your new owner." When the shooting stopped and dusk settled into the valley, Dave rode for the ranch. He found Leigh Dyer on the front step of the bunkhouse, picking his teeth after his beans-n-beef supper.

"Unload yer saddle, Dave, beans 'er still hot an' Cookie has a spare steak."

"Sounds good, Leigh, gittin' tired o' my own cookin'."

"Yore beans-n-steak not good enough for you?" Frank Mitchell asked.

" 'Nother man's cookin' always tastes

better'n mine." Dave grinned at the young man and hustled to the kitchen for a plate and cup of coffee.

Several of the other hands drifted back to the stoop to listen. Dave wouldn't leave his post and ride in after dark unless something was up. He emerged from the bunkhouse and elbowed his way to the stoop.

"Make room, boys, and let me get around this banquet." He sat and ate off his lap table while the men talked among themselves and waited for Dave to explain his visit. "That was plumb good cookin'. Lost my starter an' ain't had a biscuit fer a week."

"Is that all th' reason you come skulkin' in here after dark for?" Cape Willingham asked. "To git bread starter?"

"It's th' main one, an' thought I'd mention Injuns killin' off cattle."

"Injuns?" Leigh asked.

"Well, they ain't Republicans," Dave replied. "Republicans don't go naked an' wear feathers in their hair. Leastways they don't wear feathers. They's lots o' shootin' down th' creek an' all th' buffalos is headin' this way. They must like Injuns es much es we does."

John Mann nudged Frank with his elbow. "It's natural that a man that lives alone and yearns to hear another human voice will talk

430

too much when he gets the chance."

"Guess th' rumor's true 'bout a bunch of bronco Comanches not goin' in," Cape said.

"Lots of 'em, Dave?" John asked.

"Ain't counted many heads from th' dugout door, John, but if they's killin' fer meat, they's killin' fer a bunch."

"Guess we ought t' go up an' tell Charlie your story," Leigh said. "He keeps th' sourdough starter in th' safe, anyway."

"Charlie's back a'ready?" Dave asked.

Cape chuckled. "Yeah, couldn't stand thinkin' o' us out here havin' all this fun without him."

The men listened to Dave explaining how he lost his starter as he and Leigh crossed the yard to the ranch house.

"Got th' livin' alone chatters," someone observed.

"Ain't he got that horned toad t' talk to?" Frank asked.

"Yeah, an' what about his horse?" John asked.

"That horse's too smart fer him, won't listen t' mor'n ten words from Dave." Frank laughed.

"Huh," Cape snorted, "if he's so smart, why ain't *he* ridin' Dave?"

Leigh hung back as the two clumped across the ranch house porch and the door swung open just as Dave raised his fist to knock. There, in a ruffled dress, stood Mrs. Goodnight. Dave stared a second, then jerked his hat from his head. "G-Good evenin', Mrs. Goodnight, I-I-I didn't know you was here," he stammered. "W-we was comin' t' talk to Ch— Mr. Goodnight."

Mrs. Goodnight opened the door wide and motioned the two into the house. "I wouldn't let Mr. Goodnight leave without me, Dave McCormick. Come on in, he's in the parlor." They entered the great room, which was what Mrs. Goodnight called the parlor, to find Charlie standing by his chair in his stocking feet, silhouetted by the blaze in the fireplace.

"Come in, Dave, what brings you out on a cold night like this?"

"He's been tellin' us about visitors in th' lower cañon," Leigh said.

"Visitors?"

"Injun's been killin' our cattle at a fierce rate, Ch— Mr. Goodnight," Dave explained.

"How many Injuns?"

"Don' know, they stay away from th' dug-out."

"We'll go see about it in th' morning, Leigh. Have the boys ready early. Leave Frank and John here to watch the place and make sure everyone has plenty of shells."

Leigh, as well as Mrs. Goodnight, knew Charlie's order to "watch the place" meant to "guard Leigh's sister, Mary Ann Dyer Goodnight."

"We'll be ready when you are," Leigh pledged. The two said their good nights and left.

Dave poked Leigh's ribs and whispered, "Why didn't you tell me Mrs. Goodnight was here?"

"Would'a missed that look on yer face if I had." A snicker, ill concealed, from the stoop told the hapless hand everyone was in on the joke. Soon, the lights of the bunkhouse were out, but not before the lights at the ranch house.

Cookie was grumpy when he started breakfast at three o'clock and it took two cups of black coffee to settle his temperament. Coffee didn't improve Frank Mitchell's attitude after standing last watch in the cold — that and the fact he had to stay at the ranch while the rest rode away to adventure.

It was still dark below the rim of the cañon when the Goodnight band rode past numerous cattle carcasses into the sleeping Kiowa village; the band stopped in a semicircle before the headman's tipi, rifles across their laps.

The headman showed his contempt for his visitors by making them wait. The camp's warriors gathered around the group while women and children were herded into the brush by the old men. The following discussion with the sullen Indians was contentious, and the cattlemen left without any solution to the situation.

Whether by design or accident, the two Comanche villages moved unseen past the vaqueros at the Kiowa camp and up the valley undetected. They settled on the old campgrounds at the Cita Blanca Cañons, five or six miles below the ranch house.

The ranch hands rode into the Comanche camp at sundown and Goodnight sought out the headman, Quanah Parker. He ordered the Indian to come to his house the next day to treaty.

At the meeting the Indians questioned Charlie closely, trying to determine if he were a hated *Tejano.*

"What were you doing on the Pecos?" one of the Indians asked. "We used to handle cattle there."

"Yes," Goodnight replied, "you damned pups licked me once and stole my cattle."

The Indians laughed and decided that the

rancher was not a *Tejano.*

"What do you propose, Charles Goodnight?" Quanah asked.

Goodnight motioned to the men standing around him. "I have good men well armed, but I do not want to fight unless you force me." He charged Quanah to keep the peace and leave his property alone and pledged to give the Indians two beeves every other day until they found the buffalo. The Indians agreed and the two groups settled down and lived together peacefully.

The Kiowa stayed in an ugly mood and Goodnight sent young Frank Mitchell to report the breakout at Fort Elliott despite his wife urging him to send an older man. Mitchell came back with Lieutenant A. M. Patch and a detachment of Tenth Cavalry. The lieutenant reported to his commander that he counted fifty Apaches, sixty-four Quahadi Comanches under Quanah, sixty-seven Kiowas, and seventeen Pawnees living peacefully with the ranchers in and around Palo Duro Cañon. In addition, six Comanches and two women were living up North Blanca Cita Cañon. Asked how he accomplished the peace, Goodnight replied that he gave his word, the Indians pledged peace, and the rancher said he never heard of an Indian breaking his word.

It took Captain Nicholas Nolan nearly two weeks to convince the various Indians to return peacefuly to their reservations, including Quanah and his Quahadis with their hunting permit, who were enjoying the rancher's hospitality — and his beef.

"I will not go to Fort Sill with the Buffalo Soldiers," Rojo Pelo swore to Black Duck. He was tired of hiding from the soldiers like a prisoner in his own tipi, though playing with the Little Red Dog and being with Bubbling Water, who was heavy with child again, was not without its pleasures.

"I do not wish to go there either, Rojo. There are still buffalo on the plains and we can live well when we find them." There were "hous" of agreement from the other warriors gathered, so while the Quahadis were preparing to return to their reservation, Black Duck and his band quietly left the cañon and lost themselves on the Llano Estacado.

"We will camp in the Yellow House Cañon and let the buffalo come to us," Black Duck said a few days later. They camped under the yellow bluffs that gave the cañon its name.

"This day, I will be the first to see the return of the buffalo," Otto said as he and Rojo rode south to see if the migrating herd was nearing.

Rojo stopped and listened a moment. Far away and faint came the boom of a Sharps, the sound softened by distance.

"You may be the first to *see* the buffalo, but I am the first to *hear* their return, Otto."

It was chilling to both men that the presence of the animals was announced by the sound of that buffalo gun. Otto shaded his eyes and studied the dust rising from the march of the herd. "They will be here this time tomorrow."

"And opposite Yellow House this time the next day," Rojo said. He was staring at dust rising not too far southeast of where they sat. "Here come the hide men."

Farther northeast, they could see a large dust cloud rising where an even larger group of hunters was riding to intercept the path of the buffalo. They turned and rode back to camp, each lost in his thoughts.

"Tomorrow, we hunt the hunters," Sleepy Eye said, as Rojo stooped to enter his tipi.

"Tomorrow I will show you how to count coups on stinking hide hunters. It will be a good lesson for you," Rojo returned.

CHAPTER 26
HUNTING THE HUNTERS

Though they both feigned enthusiasm for the prospects of a strike, there was a weariness behind their eyes. Stopping the white man's incursion was like stopping a flash flood or turning the wind. All their victories were small and insignificant. Rojo knew more than the others how futile the fight was. Still, he would fight on with his companions — most likely until they all were no more.

Juanita, the Mexican-Indian midwife for the clan, brushed past him as he entered. "She is ready," she murmored in passing. Rojo tied the flap closed and turned to his wife.

"Now would be the best time," she sighed. This child had been especially active and Bubbling Water was very tired. Rojo and Janos had taken over most of the household chores out of sight of the disapproving eyes of the neighbors. A woman of the tribe was expected to carry on her many duties regardless of her condition, whether sick or heavy with child — and the women that did aged early, most becoming crippled or dying before reaching their fortieth winter.

In the privacy of their home, Rojo slept with his wife in the white man's manner. It was a practice Bubbling Water enjoyed, for he kept her warm in the high plains nights. A night or two before, while snuggled against her husband's back, the baby had kicked so hard that Rojo had felt it. He awoke with a grunt and Bubbling Water had laughed at him. "Now you know how I feel ten times a day."

"That child must be half mule," he muttered, then laughed with her. Now, the child was upside down in the womb, a good sign that the time was near. In the night, Bubbling Water's water broke, and by sunrise, she presented Rojo with a robust girl child she named Dancing Bird after the baby's grandmothers, Little Bird and Dancing Water.

"You should have named her Kicking Bird," Rojo said as he held the sleeping bundle. Little Red Dog was puzzled about the sudden appearance of this baby and jealous of the attention she was getting. "She is your sister, Red Dog, and you must take care of her," Rojo explained.

Midwife Juanita bustled in and shooed the men out. "Stay near, Janos, and watch Red Dog. Keep the fire going and help Bubbling Water when she needs you," Rojo instructed. "I go to collect hide man hair." He saddled and rode to the edge of the camp and waited for his companions there. On the plain above the arroyo, they could see the advancing cloud of dust raised by the buffalo. It seemed that Rojo could hear the booming guns, but it could have been a disturbing memory.

They gathered around Black Duck, who said, "No Hair, take Rojo, Silvertip, and Black Knife and ride to the herd. The rest of us will ride to the big camp up north and send them on the Long Ride before they kill a single buffalo."

No Hair nodded and the four trotted off south toward the advancing animals. Soon enough, they could hear the real sound of the booming gun and followed it to the stand the hunter had made. He had methodically shot animal after animal until all his ammunition was gone.

Marshal Sewell sat up and searched for more shells. *Dammit, why didn't I bring more?* he wondered, even though he had killed more than Wild Skillet and Moccasin Jim, his skinners, could handle in a day. He rose and started walking back toward camp.

"Now, I will count coup." No Hair grinned and the four raced for the honor of counting first coup. Their sudden appearance sent a jolt of fear through Sewell and he raced for camp, yelling for his skinners. Glancing back, he saw that one rider had pulled slightly ahead of his companions, and his heart jumped a second time when he recognized that the long mane of hair the rider wore was red. Again, he turned and ran, stumbled, and fell. The thundering hooves were upon him as he rose, and a shout of triumph rang in his ears as Rojo Pelo's quirt struck first coup across the hunter's shoulders. The blow turned him around to be immediately run down by three riders straining to count second coup. The rifle spun away and a hoof stepped on his leg, snapping the bone. Desperation pushed as he crawled for his rifle, but he couldn't rise to swing it at his attackers. The Indians toyed with him until he died, then raced for the camp in search of more coups.

"Hustle up, Skillet, he's quit shooting," Moccasin Jim called as he finished honing his knife. Wild Skillet hurried over with the mules and they were harnessed and hitched to the wagon in a wink. "Come on, Jim.

He's gonna be yellin' at us agin." He clucked the mules into a trot as Jim dove over the tailgate and scrambled to the seat.

"Listen t' that. Ain't been stopped shootin' a whole minute an' he's already yellin' for us," Skillet growled.

"We shoulda a'ready been there if you'd got them mules up like you should of."

"You tell that to th' mu— whoah." Skillet pulled the mules into a tight turn back toward camp and whipped them into a run. "How many are they?" he asked, his voice rising as his throat constricted.

"Must be eight or nine of 'em," Jim called from the wagon bed. "Head for Rath City."

"Gotta git my rifle."

"You stop t' dig out that rifle an' you'll be tryin' t' outrun those Injuns afoot, for I'm gonna keep on running these mules 'til they drop," Jim vowed.

"How're we gonna pertect ourselves 'thout guns?"

"They's eight er ten o' them savages, Skillet, how many o' them you propose t' git afore yo're dead? Th' best thing we got is a head start, an' that won't last long."

Wild Skillet turned the wagon a little northeast until they intercepted their tracks from Rath City. The pursuers gained steadily and in the bottom of a gully, Skillet turned the mules sharply and they crashed into the heavy brush.

"C'mon, Skillet, we gotta hide." Moccasin Jim led the two through the thick brush, a place no horse could go.

Two of the Indians followed on foot until the skinners' pistol shots clipped twigs close to their heads and the cost of counting coup became too expensive. With a yell of defiance, the Indians returned to take the mules, burn the wagon, and plunder the camp of anything they desired. The rest they threw on the fire and piled the slashed hides on top. Returning to Sewell's body, they took two scalps, slashed his temples, and drove a sharpened stick into his stomach.

Eventually, as they rode homeward, their dark anger cooled and there was much good-natured discussion about who had counted second coup — good-natured because while once it might have caused blood to be shed among friends, it now no longer mattered.

Charles Rath had gone into partnership with the Lee & Reynolds Company to establish a trading and hunting camp on the Double Mountain Fork of the Brazos River. Rath led the expedition from Fort Supply, between fifty and sixty wagons following with everything a trading camp would need, including a saloon and brothel.

It was into this saloon tent our two intrepid skinners stumbled, their bare feet wrapped in their ripped-up shirts, their bare heads sunburned and blistered. "Well, if it ain't Wild Skillet an' Moccasin Jim back from th' killlin' fields so soon. Must have had good hunting," Joe, the barkeeper, said as he saluted the men.

"Ain't got time fer talkin', Joe, pour us —"

"Naw," Skillet interrupted, "*give* us th' whole bottle. We don' need no cork er glasses." He turned and plopped into the nearest chair, raised the bottle, and took a long pull before handing it to Moccasin Jim. The scent of a story drew the half dozen other patrons to the two skinners. Life in town was a welcome change, but soon paled to the adventures available on the open plains.

"Where ya been, Jim?" someone asked. "Huntin' good?"

"Huntin' buffler's good fer us, huntin' hide men's better fer Injuns," Jim replied.

"Got to yuh, did they?" another asked.

"Got t' Sewell real good, an' chased us inter th' bresh. Had t' walk all th' way from south of Yellow House, an' ain't got nothin' t' show fer hit," Wild Skillet said.

Barkeep eyed the half empty bottle. "We'll carry you on th' cuff 'til yuh git on yer feet, boys."

" 'Preciate that, Joe," Jim replied, eyeing the free lunch bar, "shore could use a couple o' them sandwiches."

Soon two heaping platters of food were being eagerly devoured by the two guests and their story eked out between bites.

"We found th' herd 'bout twelve-fourteen mile south of Yellow House Cañon an' set up camp. Marshal, rest his soul, was out early on a stand an' accordin' t' his shots killed at least a dozen animals —"

"Ef I tole him a fifty times, I tole him a hunnert, 'Save a few bullits fer th' Injuns,' but no, he got greedy an' shot his whole wad," Skillet interrupted.

Moccasin Jim glared at his partner and continued. "He was headin' back to camp hollerin' fer us when th' Injuns hit him."

Skillet swallowed a bite, "Musta been twenty of 'em."

"More like thirty."

"Yore ma ever teach you not t' talk with yer mouth full?"

Jim swallowed and continued, "We was holdin' our distance good 'til Skillet wrecked th' wagon in a ditch."

"Didn't wreck hit, I hid us in th' bresh . . . woulda worked, too, ef you hadn't stood up in th' wagon an' popped off at 'em like 'at."

"Skillet was supposed to unhitch th' mules while I held them savages off with my pistol, but he was so nervous an' slow we had t' leave 'em an' save areselves."

"They woulda 'ventually had us if th' prospects o' mule steaks an' plunder in th' camp hadn't been callin' so loud." Skillet waved the empty bottle at Barkeep and Joe set up another bottle.

"We hid out and walked that hunnert miles at night without a single thing t' eat, an' only a sip o' muddy water," Moccasin Jim added.

"Where'd you boys go? It's only 'bout forty mile to Yellow House," one of the listeners asked.

"Dam-well seemed like a hunnert," Skillet muttered.

News of the attack spread quickly and before morning an army of hide hunters was formed up, well fortified with John Barleycorn and armed to the teeth. They rode to Yellow House Cañon and surprised the Indians in their camp. The women were the first to react to the attack, scrambling to the top of the bank and firing arrows and guns down on the befogged and confused hide men.

Seeing a dozen heads peering down on them and shooting, one hide man panicked, "Run, fellers, they's a hundred of 'em shootin' down on us." He led half the army in a galloping retreat down the valley.

The van of the army had ridden through the camp and now dismounted and were walking back through the deserted village, firing at every imagined movement. At the other end of the camp, some ten or twelve men had not retreated and, still mounted, mistook the walkers for Indians. "They're commin' at us from the tipis, men, git 'em."

By some miracle, the ensuing battle between hide men and hide men garnered no victims, but gave the Indians time to rally and shelter under a nearby hill. There, they made good use of their captured buffalo rifles and held off the army of hide hunters.

"I tell yuh, Pete, one o' those Injuns is redheaded," his companion argued.

"You been listenin' t' Wild Skillet's yarns, an' it's clouded your mind," the doubter rejoined. "He's a Injun wearin' some kind of headdress."

Pete eased up on his elbows and aimed his rifle, "Just keep thinkin' that an' I'll have me a red scalp t' show you."

"You wouldn't take a white man's scalp, would you?"

"If he's shootin' at me an' wearin a breech-clout, he's a Injun, red hair or no." He squeezed the trigger and saw his shot shatter rock behind the hidden Indians. "Dad-blast-it."

No Hair looked at Rojo and grinned, "I'm tired of this sitting around, Rojo. If I charge them, will you bring me a rope?"

"Surely, I will — again — No Hair."

"Then I go," the warrior replied and painted his face and his horse. With a shout, he rode circles in front of the army, defying the many bullets seeking him. Rojo sat on his horse waiting his time to ride. Instead of completing his last circle, No Hair raced straight into the fire of the army. "His horse is down, Rojo," Otter called. "Ride!"

Rojo galloped toward the fallen horse and watched as No Hair emerged from the cloud of dust, running straight into the fire of the hide men. Rojo yelled and almost simultaneously, No Hair and Rojo's horse were shot. Rojo was able to jump clear of the horse and crawl behind him even as the horse breathed its last. From there, he hurled insults and lead at the white men, who began to methodically snipe away at him.

Rattle stood and called, "They are going to get you, Rojo, run for the cañon."

It was a good fifty yards to the brink of the valley and Rojo lay his heavy Sharps beside the horse, gathered his unspent shells, and ran.

"There he goes, boys, git him," a hunter yelled. A volley of fire from the Indians kept heads ducking and the few shots gotten off were ineffective.

"Tole yuh he was redheaded," Pete's companion crowed.

"Hold still, I got a shot."

Rojo reached the brink of the cañon and paused a second. Pete fired, and the warrior jumped.

"Got him," the shooter said.

"Well, go get yer red scalp, you scallawag," someone said.

The vertical fall was only about ten feet, then the bluff tapered off in a steep gravel bank strewn with rocks. Rojo landed on his feet, but his right leg buckled, and he rolled almost to the bottom, ending up wrapped around an errant willow bush. Carefully, he gathered himself and slid around until the bush was between him and the top of the bluff. Only then did he examine himself, looking first to his right thigh. There was a ragged hole in the front with gravels and dirt caught in it. The immediate need was to stop the profuse bleeding. He tied his headband around his leg above the wound, and with a stick from the bush inserted into the band twisted it until the bleeding was almost stopped. Carefully, he picked the trash out of the wound and found pieces of bone. The entry hole in the back of his leg was just a neat hole, relatively clean. Pain and shock washed over him and he fainted — a fortunate thing, for the, tourniquet relaxed some and allowed blood to circulate back through his leg.

Rojo wandered back through a cloud of pain and noise of battle to consciousness and retightened the band. He didn't know if he slept or passed out again, but late in the afternoon, he awoke in the shade of the walls and was cold. It was so quiet he tapped a rock to hear a noise. *Battle must be over. Now, someone, friend or foe, searches for me.* The thought troubled his mind as he drifted back into the blackness.

Midafternoon was telling on the hide men. They had consumed the last of their whiskey; the heat and the process of sobering were taking their toll. It was thirst more than anything else that drove them from the field of battle. They rode out pursued cautiously by the warriors that were able to follow. The women gathered up, loaded the wounded men on horses, and started down the cañon to their camp.

Bubbling Water had seen Rojo's charge and watched him jump over the bluff and was anxious to find him. It seemed he was hurt when he jumped. She and Janos watched for him as they descended the arroyo, Little Red Dog trotting along asking a hundred questions. A half dozen women passed the willow bush in the gloom. Perhaps Rojo Pelo's stillness resembled a log lying under its limbs. No doubt, the worries of their situation filled their minds: they would have to move; they needed meat; were the horses safe or had they gone with the hide men?

"Look, Bubbling Water, what is that?" Janos peered at the object under the tree.

Without an ounce of fear or caution, Little Red Dog approached the tree before anyone could stop him, "It just Papa. He sleep. Dirty." And he turned and trudged on.

Rojo was vaguely aware of some great disturbance of his rest, of being laid by a warm fire and washed in cold water. Gradually, the disturbance subsided; he was

covered by a warm robe, and welcome dark-
enss descended again.

He could tell before he opened his eyes
that daylight had returned. Small grunts
and mutters came to his ears and he became
aware someone was near — very near. When
at last his eyes obeyed his command to
open, he beheld the face of a cherub, not a
hand's breadth away from his nose.

"He awake, Bub, Papa open he eye, he in
there," the cherub called, not moving.
"Bub" was as close as the boy could pro-
nounce his mother's cumbersome name. It
became the name she was known by. The
child's close examination continued. "You
got holes in you leg, Papa, why you do that?"

"The "booms" got me, Red Dog. They are
very dangerous." He could anticipate the
next question.

"What dangerous?"

"Like the fire," Rojo replied. It had taken
only one burned finger to teach the toddler
to avoid the fire.

"Boom burn you?"

"Boom shot small arrow through my leg."

Next subject: "Papa, we find you ver'
dirty." The little face wrinkled in disgust,
"Phooo."

"Sit back, Red Dog, and let me feed
Papa." Bubbling Water knelt beside the bed.

She felt his forehead and detected fever there and gave her husband a dipper of water. He drank eagerly and had two more dippers before he was satisfied. She would have fed him the meat, but he took it himself and winced. His shoulder was very sore.

"You got bruised rolling down the bluff," Bubbling Water said.

Rojo took inventory of his body and grinned. "All over me, Bub, all over."

CHAPTER 27
A TONKAWA SCOURGING

"Why de cap'in take so many o' dem liva eatin' Tonkaways wid us, Bandy?" Ike Casey asked his friend, Bandy Huein, as they rode from the parade ground of Fort Griffin.

"Dat's *Corporal* Huein to you, *Private* Casey. An' as to yo dumb private question, de cap'in want t' git dose bronc Comanches, dat why."

"Don' yo go pullin' rank on me, Corporal Bandy, I been in dis army long afore you."

"Yeah, a hull year, an' yo still be de corporal ef'n yo didn' git cotched wid de widow Jones on suds row whin yuse sposed t' be patterollin' de per-*rim*-ater guards. Think I'll fine yu somp'in t' do lak keepin' up de drag. Lil' bit o' dust do yu good," the corporal said.

"Druther eat dus' than fill my ears wid yo prattle, *Corporal.*" Private Ike Casey moved back in the line, but didn't go to the drag. *Smart aleck dam darky.*

General Mackenzie had ordered Captain Philip Lee into the field with ten Tonkawa scouts and forty Buffalo Soldiers from the Ninth Cavalry. They attacked our camp on Tierra Blanca Creek when we were away hunting buffalo and hide men. The only ones in camp were women and children and those warriors who had not recovered from the Yellow House fight. We rode into camp midafternoon the day after the attack and found a terrible sight. Bodies of the people had been mutilated in horrible ways and left where they had fallen.

"Here, Rojo, I have found Otter," Sleepy Eye called from a buffalo wallow.

He was hardly recognizable except for the tattoos on his chest. There was a woman lying close beside him.

"He must have put up a good fight," Sleepy Eye said, "by the number of shells he fired." We found a number of patches of blood within Otter's range of fire, some as near as ten yards of him.

"They sneaked up and shot him in the back," Rock said. "Did you see the woman's arm?"

She lay on top of a broken bow. There were no arrows, but her left forearm and wrist were scraped and bloody where the bowstring had struck when she fired without the protection of an arm guard.

Rattle pointed to the tracks of shod horses and an army glove in the dust. "They were cavalry, Buffalo Soldiers, I believe."

"Soldiers don't mutilate or take scalps," I said.

"Or eat their victims," Black Duck said. "Tonkawa scouts." He was standing over a body that had its legs cut off and gone. They had also taken his organs.

I turned away, and threw up. "We owe the Tonkawa a great debt."

"I will not rest until I have taken vengeance tenfold on the Tonkawa," Left Hand swore.

"I, too, will take your oath, Left Hand," Rattle said, to the affirmation of a half dozen men who had heard.

Many of the bodies were not recognizable and I searched in vain for my family. We trailed one of the victims through the brush.

"Here is the midwife, Juanita," came the call. She was lying facedown under a cedar bush with two arrows in her back. By her right hand, she had laid an arrow pointing to an arroyo that drained into Tierra Blanca Creek.

We split into three groups, two riding the ridges either side of the arroyo to its head and the third starting up the gully from below, and found the survivors of the massacre huddled under a rock shelter in the end of the gully. Much to my relief, there was Bubbling Water with all three children. They had been off picking up walnuts left over from last fall and heard the firing from the camp. Hurrying down the arroyo, they had been met by a group of refugees and had taken them back to the shelter. The people had busied themselves building a rock wall around the entrance, but the army had not found them. For the better part of three days, these suvivors had lived on walnuts and what water they could carry in their nighttime trips to the creek.

"We do not have to worry about the army," Black Duck said. "They hurry to the fort to brag of their victory. This is a good place to stay while we take care of our fallen."

We found a place to bring our horses down into the arroyo and unload the buffalo meat we had taken from the hide hunter's camps. There was little sleep among the witnesses of the massacre and when they slept, visions of mutilated friends and children tortured them.

The best we could do for our dead was to wrap them in wickiup hides and lay them in the buffalo wallow. We piled the brush from the houses on top of them and rode away in great sorrow three days later.

"Sergeant, I need a detail to take a message to Fort Griffin," Captain Lee called from his tent.

"Yas, suh, they'll be up right away, suh." The old sergeant smiled to himself, *Now, I'll be rid of them two jays an' we'll hev some peace an' quiet in th' ranks.* All he had to do to find his two candidates was follow the sound of augering to Ike Casey and Bandy Huein sitting on their bedrolls mending harnesses.

"Corporal, you and Casey report to the captain. He has a job for you." *Now, one more man would make the detail.* But try as he might, he couldn't find a man who would volunteer to accompany Corporal Huein and Private Casey. "I'm of a mind t' *order* one of you darkies t' go with those two," he threatened.

"Ain't none o' us been bad 'nough t' deserve that kinda punishment, Sergeant," an old ex-sergeant private asserted.

It was a fact, the present sergeant knew, and was the reason he asked for volunteers instead of ordering someone to go. He feigned anger and glared at the men, "Shoulda knowed you goldbrickers was too lazy t' volunteer fer a detail."

"We ain't lazy, Sergeant, why we three —" the speaker motioned to two companions standing beside him — "will volunteer if you leave those two here."

A storm of protest and threat blew through the group and it seemed for a moment that there would be trouble in the ranks. *They ain't even in sight an' cause a fuss.* He held up his hands in surrender. "Calm down, men, it occurs to me that two men will be adequate for this job. I'll send Casey with the corporal." Relief in the crowd was visual.

Now, it's fair to explain that Casey and Huein were good soldiers who acted above and beyond their assigned duties. No two men could be more welcome in a tight spot. It was just . . . well . . . it was too much to listen to their constant conversation without relief. As to the fact that the two could do the work of three men, there was no doubt. So it was that only two men reported to the captain. It caused his eyebrows to rise, then he too thought of the tranquility about to descend on the outfit and nodded agreement to himself. *Have to compliment the sergeant on his choice.*

Sleepy Eye and I had been watching the

soldier camp for two days when two soldiers rode out to the east with two Tonkawa driving a small herd of our horses.

"Our first chance to get some horses back, Rojo," Sleepy Eye said as we mounted to follow.

On that flat plain, it was impossible to hide, so the three of us, Rattle, Sleepy Eye, and I, followed the soldiers out of rifle range. When the soldiers camped for the night, we gathered and made our own camp. We could see their fire and we made sure they could see ours. Rattle chewed his jerky and suggested a plan, "We sleep the first two nights, while the white-eyes watch for us, then the third night while they sleep, we attack."

"That sounds good to me," I said. I had found it hard to sleep since the massacre because horrible visions came with my dreams. Now that there was some diversion, I hoped tonight would be sleep without dreams.

When our fire died, we moved away and slept.

The soldiers descended from the caprock to more broken ground and growth late the second day, and we could get closer to them without being seen. They camped at sunset.

"What do those two Buffalo Soldiers talk

so much about, Rojo?" Sleepy Eye asked. "They have made my ears tired with their prattle."

"I do not know what they talk about; the language is strange to me."

Rattle chuckled. "Now we know why the Tonkawa stay so far ahead of them."

"They had rather face the danger of being separated in an attack than to listen to their talk," I laughed — and realized it was for the first time since we found the massacre. It was strange, but I felt grateful to those two black men.

"They have given us an advantage we did not have before," Rattle said. "Instead of attacking them tonight, we should ride ahead and find a good place to ambush them tomorrow. We can get between the two groups and they will be easier to take."

We found that good place at the second gully the track crossed. It had been dug out on both sides so a wagon could drive across, and it was the only place to cross for some distance in both directions. The Tonkawa crossed with the horses, and when the two soldiers were in the bottom of the gully, we attacked. Rattle and Sleepy Eye raced after the Indians. I rode to the lip of the gulley — and a bullet screamed past my ear. I dove for the ground and my horse trotted off a ways.

The soldiers had approached the gully in silence, their rifles across their laps, and must have heard our horses running. I could tell by the drifting gunsmoke that the one who had shot at me was down below the crossing. The other man could be anywhere.

The fading sounds of fighting with the Tonkawas let us know that it was a running fight, and the two soldiers would guess that a lone man held them at the crossing. I grinned at the irony that hearing no sound meant that those two must have separated. It was likely one had dashed down the gully and the other had gone upstream, leaving me in the middle. No horse could climb out of the arroyo for a long distance both ways, but a man could scramble up that bank easily enough. I could become the hunted.

"Does yuh sees 'im?"

"Hush."

"All I asks is does yuh sees 'im?" Ike hissed.

Corporal Huein gave his partner a long baleful stare. "Listen here, darky, we ain't gonna talk our way out'n this, now shut up an' let me think."

"Ain't callin' me that agin," the private muttered. He moved back toward the crossing to watch for movement on the bank.

Some moments later, Bandy approached, "T'ink I got us a out."

Ike waited a moment, then asked, "You gonna tell me er keep it all to yoself?"

"See dat mesquite on de bank down dere? It got roots washed out'n de bank an' a private could climb up mighty easy. Ef he's good er'nough, he could fine dat Injun an' give 'im a little lead. Whilst dat's goin' on, de odder sold'er rides out b'twixt dese two hosses, fights dat Injun, an' picks up de private on da way t' ol' Fort Griffin."

"Whyfor de private climb dat tree?"

"Book say corporal don' climb trees ef private a-*vail*-a-ble."

"Don' nuther," ex-corporal Casey replied.

It should be noted here that neither of our friends could read the *Manual of Duties and Customs for Noncommissioned Officers.* The occasion did not permit extended debate and Private Casey departed for the tree. "Jes you know Ise not shootin' my rifle up dere. Ef you 'accidental forgets' t' pick me up, one o' dem horses is gonna hafta drag t'other an' you t' git away."

"Huh!" exclaimed the corporal as he tied the inside reins of the two horses together.

When Casey disappeared over the bank, Bandy mounted between the horses, a boot in the inside stirrup of each saddle. As soon as he heard the first shot, he drove for the track and scrambled up the bank. He turned sharply right and galloped for the Indian. As Rojo rose to fire at Bandy, the right-hand horse hit him with his shoulder and knocked the warrior over the bank into the ravine.

Private Casey ran for the horses and mounted as the corporal untied the reins. They raced down the ridge toward the Double Mountain Fork of the Brazos and safety. Where the Double Mountain turned north, they climbed back up to the Llano and followed the Clear Fork of the Brazos down off the caprock to Fort Griffin.

Rojo Pelo came to under the bank of the ravine, spitting dirt and blood. He was lying on his rifle and it gouged into his lower back. Sitting up without further jostling of the cocked gun was a chore. Just as his weight relieved pressure on the gun, the hammer fell and the gun fired.

(The author will not here record the sentiments expressed in several languages by our redheaded friend.)

Someone called from above and Rojo saw the face of Rattle looking down on him from the top of the bluff. "Come help me with

Sleepy Eye, he is hurt."

It seemed his voice was far away and he had to repeat three times before Rojo understood. He stumbled a few steps toward the track and Rattle called, "Get your gun."

Rojo returned and picked up the gun, fighting the impulse to sling it into the brush. His head hurt, his ears rang, and his vision dimmed. It seemed he was seeing through that familiar long tunnel that got narrower and narrower as he stumbled toward the track.

Rattle met him leading Rojo's horse. "Are you hurt, Rojo?" The man's slurred reply was not understandable. They rode in silence to the scene of the fight with the Tonkawas where they found Sleepy Eye lying under a bush on a robe. Rojo didn't notice the two bloody Tonkawa corpses.

Sleepy Eye had his hand raised in salute and when Rojo grasped it, the hand was stiff and cold. Sleepy Eye was dead.

CHAPTER 28
"I DO NOT KNOW THIS PLACE"

1877

"Yes, Mackenzie, there is still a band of Quahadi on the Llano." Colonel Ranald Mackenzie was visiting his friend Quanah Parker at the Fort Sill distribution center. "I do not think your whole army could catch them, they are very good at hiding," Quanah continued.

Mackenzie nodded. "I agree with that, Quanah, but the longer they stay out, the more likely it is that they will come to grief, either from the army or settlers. With the buffalo gone and cattle coming into the area, they will have a hard time finding game. Killing beef will only anger the cattlemen, and no good would come from that."

"Perhaps one could convince them to come in peacefully," Quanah said.

"It would not be possible by the army, would it?" Mackenzie replied.

"No, but it may be that I could convince

them," the Quahadi chief said. The prospect of riding again the plains and cañons of his beloved land was no small incentive for the chief.

There was a long silence; the only noises were the soft sounds of one of Quanah's wives moving around the tipi. "I think that what you propose has merit, Quanah, and I will advise my superiors of our desires."

Quanah nodded and hid his displeasure that a warrior such as Mackenzie had to ask permission for so small a thing. After all, was not this man in charge of an army and large fort such as this? Why should he have to ask?

As if in answer to his thoughts, Mackenzie smiled and said, "Sometimes it is a good thing to ask your superiors about a plan. They will think this over until it becomes their idea and they instruct us to carry it out."

Quanah laughed. "Perhaps you are right. I have often suspected I have been victim of the same trick."

The conversation drifted to other subjects and the two men enjoyed the evening while Mackenzie's aide watched their horses and worried about returning to the fort on a dark night among these wild people.

The fruit of their idea ripened slowly, and

it wasn't until the middle of July, 1878, that Quanah, with three of his warriors and three women, began their journey west. They traveled under a white flag with a letter from Colonel Mackenzie warning that no one interfere with their mission. Several pack mules with U.S. branded shoulders carried their supplies, their hooved commissaries having been destroyed by the hide men.

"Those mules are for carrying your provisions," Mackenzie teased, "*not* for your meat." Even so, the quartermaster did not give the Indians their best animals.

"We shall see, my friend, we shall see," Quanah called as they rode out of the parade ground.

The little band traveled early morning and late evening, resting in the heat of the day. Even before they got to Palo Duro Cañon, the little river was turbid where it had once been clear. The lower Palo Duro did not show any sign that the clan had been there recently.

"We will visit Goodnight," Quanah said the night they camped at Tule Cañon. "It may be that he will know where we might find our friends."

They rode through close-cropped grass and noted with dismay that the trees had been shorn of leaves as high as a cow could reach. Cottonwood saplings stood dead and dying, stripped of leaves and bark. The creek banks where the cattle drank were torn and muddy and the little stream flowed red. Cattle as wild as deer ran in every direction at their approach. The willow bushes along the stream were shattered and broken by their passing.

The Cita Blanca campsites had not been used since the Quahadi had left for Indian Territory, and the Comanches rode into the ranch yard late afternoon to Charlie Goodnight's warm greeting.

The three warriors stayed mounted and one after the other watered their horses at the spring-fed water trough. The women watered Quanah's horse and the other animals.

"Have you come to stay a while with us?" Goodnight asked.

"No, Goodnight, we are searching for Black Duck and his clan."

Charlie noted Quanah's reserve as he took the proferred letter and read it. "You look for the bronco clan," he said as he handed the paper back to the Comanche chief.

"Yes, Goodnight. We hope you have some idea where they are."

"I do not, but maybe Leigh Dyer or some

of the boys know something that will help you."

The hands had gathered from their various chores and stood on the bunkhouse porch or in the shade of the barn door. They all wore sidearms and it was sure that rifles waited, handy and out of sight. It paid to be cautious and prepared. Leigh approached the group at Goodnight's call.

"Leigh, Quanah wants to find the bronco clan, know anything about them?"

Dyer nodded to the chief, who did not offer his hand. "Last we knew of them, they had left the cañon headed southwest across the Llano."

"About all there is for them in that direction is th' Pecos," Charlie said.

"We will go there to look for them," Quanah said as he mounted his horse.

"It's late," Goodnight said, "Stay and we will eat and talk."

"We must go, Charlie Goodnight, I do not know this place." The Indian turned and they rode out of the yard, turning left to leave the cañon by way of the west trail. At the top of the trail, they gazed back into the cañon, now shrouded in shadow. After long silent minutes, Quanah said, "I do not know this place." He turned and rode away. It is said among the people that he never returned to the beloved Palo Duro.

The second day after they left the ranch house Leigh and Cape Willingham rode up the valley following the trail of the Indians. That night, Goodnight asked, "Where did they camp, Leigh?"

"Not in the cañon. We followed them to the west trail before we turned back. They took a cow with them."

Goodnight nodded; it had been expected.

"Wonder what he meant when he said he didn't know this place?" Leigh asked.

They found a tank that still held some water and camped. Quanah poked at his food and pushed it away. He was sitting near the little fire when the others lay down and he was sitting there, wrapped in his blanket, by the dead fire when they arose. From there, they angled northwest to the old pueblo ruins on the Canadian River. Finding no sign of the Black Duck clan there, they rode up the river to north of Tucumcari Mountain and left the dry Canadian, traveling a little west of south in order to hit the Pecos south of Fort Sumner.

The little group stayed east of the river, where settlers were scarce and grass was plentiful. Two days later, they found sign of a large herd of horses passing down the

471

river. They found Black Duck camped up Cibolo Draw with over three hundred horses in the clan's herd. The wikiups of six Apache families were nearby.

Quanah Parker was headman of the Quahadi clan for good reasons. He was smart, a good debater and speaker, and a charismatic leader. It was significant to the Black Duck clan that their leader, the last headman to accept life on the reservation, would seek to convince them to join him. They had seen signs of the incursions of the white man and his cattle into their last refuge. Their time of free life on the plains was drawing to a close. Sometimes they were hungry.

Even so, it took Quanah several days of debate to convince the broncos to turn themselves in to the reservation. Rojo watched the debates with sinking heart. The sacrifice he would have to make would be greater than any of his Indian friends. In addition to giving up the free life he enjoyed, the whites would take Janos away from them. Rojo would be forced to return to his white family; and Bubbling Water, Dancing Bird, and Little Red Dog would not be allowed to go with him.

Black Duck called the people together and they fixed the day they would begin their journey to the white man's way. All was bustle and hurry, for they had to gather and prepare food for the trip, which meant the men would first have to hunt. They left early the next morning, and the women were not much amused when they returned that afternoon driving two cows.

"You could have brought the cows early this morning and saved us a day of waiting," Bubbling Water fussed.

"Are you that anxious to get to the white man's camp?" Rojo asked. He had not told her all that would happen to them when they got there. She only knew that he would have to return to his white parents. Somewhere along the way, she learned that Janos would be returned to his kin in Mexico. Rojo was surprised at her anguish and had to take her knife so she wouldn't slash her arms. "He is not gone yet, Bub, perhaps he never will, and your scars would be for nothing." Rojo gave her knife back when she was calmer.

"Do not worry, Bub, I will return to you as soon as I can," Janos had promised. But Bubbling Water knew that was not likely to happen. She had seen other children and wives taken in the same manner with the same promises, never to be seen again.

"She could not bear it if she knew you could not take her with you when you go to

473

the white parents," Kingfisher said as they rode along the now well-defined road to Fort Griffin.

"This is true, Rojo," Silvertip agreed. "What will she do when she learns that?"

The question bothered Rojo a lot. As far as he could tell, there was nothing good for him and his family about entering the white man's world. As they approached Fort Sill the last day of their journey, he and his family suddenly bolted away and fled back toward the Llano Estacado. Quanah raced after them for several miles before he caught up, but he was not able to convince Rojo to return. "Go to the mountains, then." He pointed northeast to the mountains on the horizon. "I will find you there."

"I do not know those —"

"There are no white men there, Rojo, they cannot plow the hillsides, and cattle don't prosper there," Quanah interrupted. He was a man of great patience, but today that well was almost empty.

"I . . . do not know . . ."

"Very well, go where you may." The headman got on his horse and turned for the fort. He had to catch himself before he took his frustrations out on his horse. "Sometimes that redheaded Indian can try the patience of an owl, my friend." The horse nodded as if he understood — and agreed.

Rojo Pelo stood and watched Quanah ride away. Turning to Bubbling Water he said, "We need to move on."

Bubbling Water glared at her husband, "Where do we go, Rojo, back to the Llano where the cattle and white men are gathering? Where there are none of our people? Are we to be as the Diggers and live on locusts and worms? Would you not go to those mountains where there is game and water and we are near our people?"

"We have mountains —"

"Yes. Where the Apache bury their dead and hunt. Or the other mountains where there is no water and grass for our horses. Or the mountains far to the south where the white man is running his cattle and the soldier lives. Which do you choose, Rojo Pelo?"

Rojo wrapped his arm around his wife's shoulders and suddenly grinned, "I choose . . ." He raised his free arm westward and then swung around to point to the mountains of the northeast, ". . . those! We will continue west until we find a place where we can hide our trail, then turn to the Bubbling Water Mountains."

"You have mountains, Bub?" Little Red Dog asked, wide-eyed.

"It would seem so," came her sharp reply, but the fire had gone from her eyes and the corners of her mouth wished to turn upward.

They rode west until they came to a draw with a solid rock bottom that ran north. This was East Otter Creek, mostly dry in this late season. Here, he turned Bubbling Water and the packhorses up the creek, "Go with the draw and camp when the sun is one hand high. Janos and I will drive the horses farther along, then find you."

"Here me go, Bub," Red Dog called as he turned and led his mother up the creek.

Rojo helped Janos drive the horses on westward a few miles, then turned them north toward the Glen Mountains. Halfway there, Rojo pointed out the eastern end of the mountains where the East Otter flowed, and sent Janos to find Bubbling Water. At the base of the mountains, he allowed the herd to scatter and graze and let his horse graze also, gently guiding him eastward. After a couple of miles, he took up the reins and rode for the creek. It was fully dark when he found camp.

They watched a broken horizon brighten behind the Wichita Mountains looming over them. "Where do we go, Rojo?" Bubbling Water asked.

"I do not know, Bub, I suppose we will find a place where there is water and grass. Some place hard to find."

"Do you want to stay here a while?"

"No, this is too open. Storms and men will find us too easily here. We will find a place that will hide us in the mountains."

They rode up Sandy Creek and found a well-hidden arroyo just east of the mountain the white man calls Big Four. The east side of the arroyo got the afternoon sun and would be a warm place for a winter camp, and they would be close enough to the grass of the plains to keep the horses fed.

The mountains were well stocked with game and it was no trouble filling the houshold needs for meat. The spring sun began to make the campsite too warm, and one morning they moved to the west side of the arroyo under some big cottonwoods. It was a good site except for the three days of the March blizzard that swept down on them, as if Mother Nature was reminding them that winter could return any time she pleased.

Rojo and Janos were hunting deep in the heart of the mountains when Janos found evidence that other hunters were about. "Who do you think they are, Rojo?" he asked as they studied the signs.

"There were three of them . . . one was carrying a heavy load, a woman . . . two hunters. I believe they are Apache, Janos."

Goose bumps traveled up his arms and neck, "That is not good, Rojo. I do not wish to see any Apache hunters."

"Neither do I. Let's go elsewhere to hunt," Rojo answered. He led them up the hillside away from the trail of the Indians.

The Apache One Antler cursed. "They go up the mountain," he said to his wife Liduvina. Their hope of ambush lost, he signaled to Two Bears, who was hidden on the other side of the trail. Liduvina stifled a sigh of relief.

Two Bears had harbored a hatred for the white warrior ever since he had taken the water bottles and more so when he shot him and took away his wife, Rosita. When he saw him coming up the trail, he grasped the opportunity for revenge. It was one of the things that he held in common with One Antler, for the man was first cousin to Yellow Spots, and he watched for the opportunity to exact blood revenge for his death. Though their ambush had failed, they were encouraged that Rojo Pelo was in the mountains. There would be other opportunities.

The two Indians watched Rojo and Janos until they disappeared over the shoulder of the mountain. "We go now," One Antler growled to Liduvina and the two warriors strode up the trail, leaving the woman to shoulder her heavy burden and trudge after.

"What have we done to have so many enemies?" Bubbling Water asked when Rojo told of the day's happenings.

"It seems we have no friends." he replied. "The soldiers pursue us, the Apache would kill us, even our Comanche people would lure us to the white man's road. When the buffalo are gone, there will be no other road to take."

"Many of my people have gone far to the north to join with the Sioux." She spoke of the Southern Cheyenne who had gone north to join their cousins, the Northern Cheyenne.

"Do you want to live in a land where summer lasts only two moons?" He asked with a grin.

"It would not be so bad if I had someone to warm my feet at night." She smiled as she handed him his supper.

Rojo ate in silence and when Bubbling Water came to get his bowl, he whispered, "We must be very watchful, Bub. Keep your knife close and watch the children."

"I do not wish to live this way long, Rojo."

"Neither do I. An answer will come," he whispered, but he was not so sure the solution would be what either of them wanted. The immediate solution would be to eliminate the danger from his Apache enemies, and he began working on it immediately. He followed the trail of the three and found their wickiups well on the east side of the Wichitas. Though he watched for several days, he only saw Liduvina. Two Bears was not at home.

There followed a game of what his German family had called "cat and mouse." Sometimes Rojo was the mouse and sometimes Two Bears or One Antler were when Rojo stalked one or both of them. Neither side could gain the advantage on the other.

CHAPTER 29
FINDING EVE

It was an irony that Rojo and his family were living on the reservation. Agent Lawrie Tatum and the army were well aware that there was one last free Comanche warrior. Though there were rumors of his locations and accusations of thievery and destruction laid to his credit, the searches sent out by Mackenzie were desultory at best. No sign of the Last Warrior, as he had become known, was ever found. No one ever thought to search *within* the reservation, and as long as he stayed, no search was ever conducted there.

The family moved around a lot and in so doing came in contact and sometimes camped with old friends and other Comanches. It became well known that the Apaches Two Bears and One Antler hunted Rojo, and the Comanches took great pleasure in misdirecting and misleading the two frustrated Indians. More than once they came to a camp inquiring about Rojo and were directed and sometimes led to some remote part of the mountains while Rojo watched them from one of the tipis.

The once visible clan divisions began to blur on the reservation and the different clans intermingled, though clan affiliation remained important. Rojo became acquainted with several Kotsoteka Comanches and always inquired about his sister, Castaño Rojizo. He learned that White Crow was the warrior that had bought and married Rojizo, and he eventually found her in a Kotsoteka village.

Rojo was shocked and dismayed at his sister's condition. She was with child the third time and worn down by the strenuous life of an Indian wife. She could have been cleaner and if she were, her bruises would have been much more apparent. Her ragged clothes barely covered her. White Crow kept her a prisoner so the agent or army would not find her.

When Rojo entered the tipi, he said, "Hello, Eve," and his sister only stared at him. She didn't recognize her Christian name. "Rojizo, it is me, Rojo," he said.

"I do not know this Hello Eve," she stammered. "But . . . I do know . . . my brother Rojo." Realization seemed to come to her slowly and she allowed Rojo to hug her. Two tykes watched them quietly, and Rojo took note that they were cleaner and better dressed than their mother. Rojo's anger burned in the pit of his stomach.

I turned to the door to go find this White Crow when the man stepped into the tipi. "Who is this dog that enters another man's tipi when he is gone?" he yelled, striding toward me and pulling his knife from his belt. As he raised his knife to strike, I rushed him and drove my fist into his face. Indians do not fight with their fists and the attack shocked White Crow. His slash with the knife only drew air and taking advantage of the swing, I propelled him on around and pushed him hard into the side of the tipi and kicked his feet from under him. The man slid down the side of the tipi face first. The two children ran from the tipi.

I stomped the hand still holding the knife and kicked the man hard in the ribs. I didn't know if the crack I heard was the sound of toes or ribs breaking, but White Crow was gasping for breath. The impulse to stick that knife between his ribs was almost too strong to overcome. Instead, I grabbed the man by his hair and jerked him upright. Before White Crow knew what was going on, I had stripped his beaded shirt from him. "Put this on, Rojizo."

Comprehension spread over her face and she stripped the rags from her with a scream and flung them into the fire. I stared at the beaten and bruised body and an anger that had been dying rose again. I slammed my fist into the simpering face again and jerked his hair so hard my hand came away with a fistful. The man laid back, blood running from smashed nose and lips.

I snatched the man's moccasins and tossed them to Rojizo. "Tie them on your feet, Rojizo. We go now."

Rojizo ran through the door and I limped after her. That crack I heard was not White Crow's ribs breaking. I had broken my big toe and the one next to it. They hurt still when the weather changes.

My sister stopped suddenly, and I bumped into her and was surprised to behold a circle of people watching. Rojizo's two children were hiding behind the skirt of a well-dressed woman and realization struck me like a slap. White Crow had two wives — one who couldn't bear him children and one who bore them for her. I ducked back into the tipi and returned dragging the warrior by the hair.

There was an angry murmer among the people and I scanned the crowd, picking the warriors for special attention. "Is this how the Kotsoteka live, taking a woman and treating her like she is no more than a brood mare or bitch dog, to bear their children yet live like a slave? This is my sister, my *gemelo* sister. I claim the right to be her protector and remove her from this dog's mistreatments. Does anyone challenge me?"

Two or three warriors would have stepped forward if not for a solid line of women who had pushed themselves forward and now barred the way for any man to pass. "It is his right, it is his right," they began to chant the canon of the tribe. The men hesitated, glanced at one another and stood still. There was wisdom in not provoking the women, they who sang of the bravery of a warrior — or much louder and longer of his cowardice.

After pausing a moment, I motioned to a boy nearby, "Bring me White Crow's horse."

When the horse had pushed through the crowd, I sat Rojizo on him and mounted my own horse. The women, still chanting, opened a pathway for us and escorted us to the edge of the village.

A few days later, Quanah visited Kotsoteka Headman Moh-way and the word went out through the village that no man was to interfere with Rojo or White Crow.

White Crow stayed secluded in his tipi and when he finally appeared, the women changed his name to Crooked Nose, a name he carried to his grave.

I took my sister home where Bubbling Water took over the care of her. A few days later, Bad Foot appeared in the camp. "I have come to help Bubbling Water and your sister, Rojo."

"You will always be welcome in my camp," Rojo replied.

Rojizo's time came without warning one night and the women were surprised that there had been no water. "White Crow beat me," was her only explanation. The child was stillborn.

Rojizo wrapped him in a blanket and Janos and I took him up a mountain on the north end of the reservation. Near the top, we found a cleft the baby fit into.

Rojizo improved from that time on, her bruises faded, and there were only a few scars left to remind her of what she had endured. It seemed she could not bathe enough, and I laughed at her. "Do not rub through your skin, sister," I warned.

"I have been dirty so long that I am darker than I should be, Rojo. You should be so clean," she sniffed. Her dark moods were coming less and less, but there would always be a reserve that no one could penetrate. "Adam, I wish to go home and see Mother and Father, Noah, Mary, and Martha. Do you ever think of them?"

"Sometimes, Rojizo."

"Please call me Eve when we talk alone. You were born Adam Bain, don't you remember?"

"That was long ago and those people are all dead. You can't go back to them."

"They live, Adam, between Bain Creek and Panther Creek on the Llano River, don't you remember? Remember when you and Noah jumped off the bluff and the Indian fell with you?"

"The Apaches told me they were dead."

"No, they are not. The Apaches told you that to keep you from going back. White Crow was there and I heard him tell of the people who lived between the bluffs on the Llano, two men, a woman, and two girls who have a bitch wolf-dog guarding them. Don't you remember Dap?"

"I do remember Dap, but they told me . . ."

"*They lied,* Adam. It is how they convince the captives that they can't go back, you have to see that."

"I have killed white people, Rojizo — Eve."

Eve was quiet for a moment, "Haven't you also killed redskins? Wasn't it because they were trying to kill you? You killed Indians to preserve your white kin. You fought for the people you lived with. Can that be so wrong?"

"The white man will say it is so. I won't go back, but we will go to Quanah Parker and he will tell us how to get you back to your people."

"Oh, Adam, they are your people too."

But I didn't feel that way. My white father had been too invloved in working the ranch to spend time teaching me things I should have learned. He was not like Elkhorn, my Apache father, or even like Raven when I joined the Comanche. They took the time to teach me things.

Several days later, we moved camp to near where Quanah camped. After a day of getting reacquainted and catching up on the news of the people, Rojizo and I talked to Quanah about her returning to her people.

"I will take you to the agency and Tatum will send soldiers with you to protect you," he said.

Eve became upset, "No, I will not go with the soldiers, they are mean to women."

"They will not harm you," Quanah said.

"Yes, they will, you do not know them like

the women do."

Rojizo became more and more upset as they talked until finally I said, "Rojizo, I will go with you and see that the soldiers do not harm you." Just like that, I was compelled to return to my first family. I had to remove Rojizo from this society where a woman's life was short and filled with difficulties and pain. At least with the whites, her lot would be better.

A few nights before we were to leave for the agency, Black Duck visited our tipi. He wore pants above his moccasins and a long shirt, his belt buckled over the shirt. Already he was taking on the white man's dress. It was good to see him and talk of our friends. Near time for him to leave, he said to me, "Rojo, if you go to the agency, they will take away your clothes and dress you in white man clothing. They will cut your hair and forbid you to speak Comanche. They will take away your guns and knife. I have come to warn you of these things."

"I have promised to go with my sister to protect her from the soldiers. It is better for her to live among her people. When she is safe there, I will return here to my family and friends."

Black Duck nodded, "It is good. We wish you to be one with us." When he left, he shook my hand in the white man's fashion.

We left two days later, Rojizo's clothes packed away so she would be able to keep the beaded shirt and moccasins. Eve wore a calico dress. We made a leisurely ride of two days to the agency. Half a day before our arrival, we met a squad of soldiers riding toward us. "They will escort us to the agency," Quanah said. "Rojo, they will take your weapons, so do not be alarmed."

"They will not take my weapons or my horses," I vowed. "Eve, I will meet you on the trail to the Llano and go with you." The soldiers were still half a mile away when I turned and loped away. Quanah called a time or two, but I didn't look back. The soldiers didn't follow me, and I circled around the agency to the trail they would take to the Texas hill country and waited.

AFTERWORD

We leave Rojo Pelo and his sister Eve Bain here, for we have completed the tale of the Last Comanche Warrior. Rojo Pelo is a fictional compilation of the experiences of several captive children among the various Indian tribes. It is a historical fact that the last Comanche warrior to surrender to the agency or army was a redheaded German immigrant boy, just as Rojo is in this story. The difference here is that our fictional warrior never surrendered. His adventures as an army scout in the Apache wars is another story.

Problems arose when a captive was returned to his original culture. The former captives found that they did not fit in the new world they found themselves in, and many of them returned to the Indian culture they had grown up in. Some, tortured by conflicting memories, could never fit in either world and lived isolated from both.

As we previously stated, the Indians stole children and women primarily to supplement losses of children and women in their tribe. The captives fulfilled several roles within the tribe. The more fortunate ones were adopted into the families and became accepted members of the tribe. It is true, then, what Louis L'Amour's Barnabas Sackett said, "Man is not far from the wilderness and it takes him but a short time to go back living with it."

— James D. Crownover

LIST OF HISTORICAL FIGURES

Nicolás de Lafora.

Marqués de Rubi.

Big Bow, Little Robe, Comanche.

Captain Phillip Lee, 10th Cavalry officer.

Charles Goodnight, Leigh Dyer, Frank Mitchell, Cape Willingham, John Mann, Dave McCormick, Nicolas Martinez, JA owner and vaqueros.

Mrs. Charles Goodnight.

Cynthia Ann Parker, Quanah's mother.

Dr. Rufus Choate.

General Ranald Mackenzie.

Lieutenant Baldwin, 9th Cavalry.

Lieutenants Boehm, William Thompson, Captain E.B. Beaumont, 4th Cavalry officers.

Jacob Strum, scout.

Lawrie Tatum, Comanche Agent.

Lean Elk, Quanah's grandfather.

Lone Wolf, Kiowa.

Marshal Sewell, Wild Skillet, Moccasin

Jim, hide men.

Kit Carson.

John and J. Wright Mooar, hidemen.

R.M. Wright, merchant .

Moh-way, Kotsoteka Headman.

Pecos, Quanah's brother.

Peta Nocona, meaning Lone Wanderer, Quanah's father.

Pohibits-quasho, Iron Jacket, Quanah's grandfather.

Quanah Parker, last hereditary Comanche Chief.

Quenosavit (White Eagle), Comanche seer, later named Isatai'i (Wolf bitch's vulva).

Terheryaquahip, witness to Quenosavit's miracles.

Satanta, Lone Wolf, Dohasan, Kiowa chiefs.

Stone Calf, White Shield, Cheyenne.

Tahkuh, son of Peta's brother.

Topsana, Quanah's sister.

Whirlwind, Cheyenne chief.

Otter Belt.

*Hide Hunters and Merchants
at Adobe Walls*

Blue Billy.

Carlisle.

Chatman, Amos, half-breed Cheyenne.
Dixon, Billy.
Dudley, Dave.
Hanrahan, James.
Hunt, James W.
John (Cheyenne Jack) Jones.
Johnson, Andy.
Langton, James.
Lee & Reynolds, Camp Supply sutlers.
Masterson, Bat.
McKinley.
Mooar, John, & J. Wright.
Myers & Leonard.
O'Keefe, Thomas.
Ogg, Billy.
Plummer, Joe.
Rath, Charles.
Shadler brothers.
Shepherd.
Tyler, Billy.
Wallace, Tommy.
Watson, Hiram.

ABOUT THE AUTHOR

James D. Crownover had two careers: first as an Air Force pilot, then as a structural engineer. On retirement, he decided to attempt a third career writing historical fiction novels. Having spent most of his life reading and studying life in frontier America, James decided to wipe the dust away from some of these events and times and present them to readers, young and old, to remind them of the men and women who brought us to our present world. His first novel, *Wild Ran the Rivers,* won two Western Writers of America Spurs and encouraged him to continue writing.

The fictitious characters in his historical novels experience many real incidents and interact with real historical characters of the times. In this, his ninth novel, the fictional characters encounter or interact with more than sixty historic figures. A list of them can be found in the back of the book.

The employees of Thorndike Press hope you have enjoyed this Large Print book. All our Thorndike, Wheeler, and Kennebec Large Print titles are designed for easy reading, and all our books are made to last. Other Thorndike Press Large Print books are available at your library, through selected bookstores, or directly from us.

For information about titles, please call:
(800) 223-1244

or visit our Web site at:
http://gale.com/thorndike

To share your comments, please write:
Publisher
Thorndike Press
10 Water St., Suite 310
Waterville, ME 04901